THE WIFE'S SECRET

Barbara Hannay writes women's fiction, with over twelve million books sold worldwide. Her novels set in Australia have been translated into twenty-six languages, and she has won the Romance Writers of America's RITA award and been shortlisted five times. Two of Barbara's novels have also won the Romance Writers of Australia's Romantic Book of the Year award.

Barbara lives in Townsville with her writer husband and enjoys being close to the Coral Sea, the stunning tropical scenery and colourful characters, all of which find their way into her popular stories.

barbarahannay.com

ALSO BY BARBARA HANNAY

BARBARA HANNAY

THE WIFE'S SECRET

MICHAEL JOSEPH
an imprint of
PENGUIN BOOKS

MICHAEL JOSEPH

UK | USA | Canada | Ireland | Australia
India | New Zealand | South Africa | China

Michael Joseph is part of the Penguin Random House group of companies
whose addresses can be found at global.penguinrandomhouse.com

First published by Michael Joseph in 2024

Cover image © Sandra Cunningham/Trevillion Images
Cover design by Nikki Townsend Design © Penguin Random House
Australia Pty Ltd
Typeset in 11/17 pt Sabon by Midland Typesetters, Australia

Printed and bound in Australia by Griffin Press, an accredited
ISO AS/NZS 14001 Environmental Management Systems printer

A catalogue record for this
book is available from the
National Library of Australia

NATIONAL
LIBRARY
OF AUSTRALIA

ISBN 978 1 76134 410 7

penguin.com.au

MIX
Paper | Supporting
responsible forestry
FSC® C018684

We at Penguin Random House Australia acknowledge that Aboriginal and
Torres Strait Islander peoples are the Traditional Custodians and the first
storytellers of the lands on which we live and work. We honour Aboriginal and
Torres Strait Islander peoples' continuous connection to Country, waters, skies
and communities. We celebrate Aboriginal and Torres Strait Islander stories,
traditions and living cultures; and we pay our respects to Elders past and present.

For Anne and Trish,
who asked the right questions . . .

CHAPTER ONE

On most days of the year, Beacon Bay was a postcard-worthy little town. Nestled in a cove where the rainforest meets the sea, it boasted a palm-fringed beach of pristine white sand curving around a half-moon bay of sparkling turquoise.

On this March morning, however, a leaden sky smouldered, heavy with thick, low clouds. The air was ominously still, the sea murky and dark, a brooding reflection of the unfriendly sky. No sound of birds. Not a breath of wind. Not a single glint of light on the water.

Lisa Anders knew what these signs meant. All her life she'd lived in Queensland's far north, so she understood the patterns of tropical cyclones. This morning's oppressive stillness was the classic calm before the storm. And Lisa was ready and waiting.

In the five years since her divorce, she'd learned to be self-reliant. Along with many new activities, she'd joined Beacon Bay's Cyclone Preparedness Committee, and she was also a devoted follower of a storm chasers website.

For the past week, ever since an unnamed low-pressure system had first appeared as a blip on the distant edge of the Coral Sea, Lisa had been tracking its progress. The storm chasers were always a little overexcited, making bolder predictions than the official weather bureau, and they'd forecast the system's transition into a cyclone long before the bureau moved from a Watch to a Warning.

While many of the locals were complacent after almost a decade of cyclone-free summers – convinced that the newly named Pixie would stay well out to sea – Lisa had kept up to the minute with the chasers' reports. She understood about pressure systems, core circulation, ridges and windshear, and she hadn't been at all surprised when, in the early hours of the morning, Pixie made a sudden turn west towards the coast.

Fortunately, Lisa's house was strong and safe. Rolf, her ex, had been a professional builder. He'd made sure their home was cyclone-proof, and she would always be grateful for that. As well, she'd already spent the past few days conscientiously cleaning up her yard, storing all the pots and barbecue furniture in the back of the garage.

Lisa had actually startled a venomous black snake when she'd picked up pieces of timber abandoned from a long-ago project. She'd frightened herself, but the snake had been even more frightened and had slithered away, so the scary moment hadn't stopped her from getting on with the job. Her final task had been to fix the storm shutters over the windows.

Of course, she'd also added her own advisory post to Beacon Bay's Community Facebook page. And, today, as an extra precaution, she'd texted all her phone contacts in the town, actually phoning the more elderly residents who were somewhat confused by text messages, instructing them to make sure they were prepared. Yes, the ABC radio was very good at sending out similar advice, but it didn't hurt to double up.

Don't forget to pack a bag with medical supplies, a change of clothes, a radio with batteries, insurance documents and USBs with anything else important . . .

Midmorning, Lisa re-checked her to-do list. She'd already rung her son, Dave, a chef with a café on the Bay's waterfront. She'd given him the latest report from the storm chasers and had been relieved to hear that he'd managed to secure at least one generator in case the town lost power. Nevertheless, he'd sounded somewhat strained and frustrated.

'Thanks for the heads-up, Mum, but I'm dealing with it.'

Dave was always edgy if he felt Lisa was getting too 'motherly'. She'd wished him all the best and hung up.

Now, she really should check on the Blunts, who owned the garden nursery on the far side of town. The large yard surrounding their nursery's store was always filled with rows and rows of potted plants, and these palms and shrubs, herbs and fruit trees wouldn't merely be destroyed by a cyclone, they could become dangerous missiles if they weren't moved someplace secure.

Melody Blunt sounded tired when she answered the phone. 'Jim and I have been up since dawn trying to shift the pots.' She gave a small attempt to laugh. 'Only the reckless would set up a plant nursery in a cyclone-prone area.'

'Don't you have any extra help?'

'Not so far. Unfortunately, our two part-timers are both caught up with their own worries. Doug's shifting his fishing trawler as far south as he can. And Sarah's still trying to finish nailing battens over her windows. Her cottage is shaky at the best of times.'

'Okay,' said Lisa. 'I'll see if I can round up some of the revegetation group to help.'

'That'd be great, thanks, Lisa. Only problem, we're running out of shed space.'

Lisa could well understand this might be the case. The nursery's sheds weren't especially big, and they'd already been piled high with bags of potting mix and manure.

'Jim tried to get old Charlie Short to lend us a couple of his shipping containers, but he reckons his crane needs repairing and he can't shift them.'

'Damn.' Lisa was instantly racking her brains. 'Surely we can find a farmer in the area with a winch and a truck that could do the job?'

'I guess,' said Melody doubtfully.

'Don't you worry about it, Mel. You keep helping Jim and I'll see what I can find out.'

Dave Anders felt his heart drop to his toes as he viewed the trays of mini quiches his conscientious kitchenhand had just lifted from the oven. Janet had done a great job. The quiches smelled great and looked as good as any he'd seen anywhere – and he'd worked in top restaurants all over the world.

But after the latest warning from the weather bureau, Dave was pretty damn sure this party food wouldn't be needed after all. He couldn't hold back a heavy sigh.

Janet, plump, late fifties and momentarily flushed with her success, now frowned. 'I wasn't game to listen to the radio, but have you heard the latest about that cyclone?'

'I have, yeah.' Dave had also received a somewhat alarming phone call from his mother. Nevertheless, he now kept his tone as calm as he could. 'Pixie's a category three. She could get to a four and she's definitely heading this way.'

Janet's face fell.

There was little need for further comment. They both knew what this meant. They'd gone to a huge amount of trouble that would now almost certainly be wasted.

But first Dave needed to confirm this was the case. It was time to make a phone call.

The answer came in a smug baritone. 'How can I help you?'

'Dave Anders here, ringing from the Frangipani Café in Beacon Bay. About the party food you ordered for Renata?'

Renata Ramsay was an operatic superstar based in Sydney, who also happened to own a very attractive holiday house in the Bay. This weekend, to celebrate her fiftieth birthday, she'd been planning to bring a tribe of her celebrity friends north for a massive party. Motels had been booked, cars hired and Dave Anders was the official caterer.

'Ahhh, yes.' The voice on the other end of the phone managed to sound excessively apologetic. 'Sorry, Dave, you were next on my list of the folk I needed to call. Given the way your weather's shaping up, I'm afraid we're going to have to cancel Renata's party.'

Dave had been braced for this news, but it still sent a sickening shudder through him. It wasn't just the pile of food going to waste, or the money he was bound to lose. He'd lined up several of the local high-school kids to be waiters, and they'd been looking forward to earning good pocket money. 'Right,' he said tightly.

'Sorry, mate. I should have called earlier, but I've been flat out cancelling all the flights and motel accommodation for the guests.'

'Yeah,' Dave responded wearily, while wondering what the hell he was going to do with all these handmade quiches Janet had laboured over, along with the herb and vegan cheese wafers he'd made, as well as the mountain of meatballs, both vegan and genuine pork, that he'd prepared, ready to barbecue. And the fridge filled with scallops and prawns.

Even if Beacon Bay managed to hang on to its power supply and Dave didn't lose the lot, he'd be hard-pressed to make good use of so much food.

One of Lisa's many phone calls for the morning was to her good friend Heidi. 'You should come here and stay with me tonight, Heidi.'

'Are you sure?'

'Yes, most definitely. That cottage of yours —' Lisa stopped before she said anything too uncomplimentary. 'Well, it's quite old, isn't it? And you never did get around to having your roof inspected.'

'I know, I know.' Heidi sounded suitably regretful. 'I'd been thinking that I should probably go to the Community Hall. The council's setting it up as an evacuation centre.'

'Well, I'm sure that would be safe, but you don't really want to be sleeping on the floor with a horde of people, do you?'

'I wasn't looking forward to it, especially if I couldn't keep Juno near me. I'd hate to have to put her in a cage.'

Juno was Heidi's extremely fluffy, silvery grey and somewhat ancient cat. Lisa wasn't a huge fan. In fact, many people in the Bay were actively against cats, given their tendency to go feral in the forests and hunt the wildlife, but she knew this was unlikely to happen with Heidi's feline companion.

'Juno could come here,' she said. 'I'm not allergic. And the house should be safe. Rolf went overboard with cyclone bolts when he built this place.'

'Yes, I know your house will be fine.'

'I guess the only problem might be parking.' Lisa was thinking of all the gear she'd crammed into her garage. 'Actually, I'll pick you up and then you can leave your car in your carport.'

'Thanks. I guess the carport is safer than out in the street.'

'Definitely.'

'It's a lovely offer, Lisa. Thank you. I'll bring dinner. I'm making a beef casserole, is that okay? And wine, of course.'

'Wonderful. Sounds perfect.'

'I've put the casserole on early, so at least it'll be ready if we lose power.'

'Good thinking. And we can always reheat it on my gas stovetop.' For Lisa, the thought of sharing a delicious dinner and wine with her friend while cyclonic rain and wind howled and raged outside her strong, safe house was, somehow, ridiculously appealing.

She'd been making these phone calls from her kitchen and now she looked around her, once again grateful that she'd been able to keep this house after the divorce.

Of course, after Rolf had left, she'd had to learn all sorts of new skills – changing light bulbs, rehanging a towel rack, cleaning the aircon filters – and she was proud of the independence she'd achieved.

Now, though, Lisa was distracted by a memory of the excitement she and Rolf had shared when they'd first moved into this house. She was remembering them here, eating picnic-style – French onion dip and corn chips, as she recalled – sitting cross-legged on the shiny new timber floor, as they hadn't yet bought their dining furniture.

But she mustn't let herself dwell on that now. After Rolf left, she'd found it important to put her own stamp on her home.

Originally, they'd gone for the natural timber look that had been so popular at the time, but after their breakup, Lisa had painted all the interior timber walls white, including the ceilings. Yes, even the exposed beams and rafters. Quite an exhausting time she'd had up there with trestles and planks and ladders, but the transformation was very satisfying.

And she'd given the kitchen cupboards a total makeover with sage green chalk paint. Determined to prove just how brilliantly she could manage on her own, she'd also paved the outdoor barbecue and then re-lined the breakfast nook off the kitchen with a mosaic of colourful tiles.

Lisa had always been proud of this house. But in recent years it had become a personal statement and somehow important to her sense of self. She'd also made a determined effort to share it with her friends, so it was very reassuring to know that tonight she and Heidi would be cosy and safe.

*

Midafternoon, she'd pretty much ticked off everything on her check-list. She'd managed to twist the arms of several of the reveg team to help the Blunts to shift pots. By a minor miracle, she'd actually tracked down a farmer on the edge of town who'd been able to transport two much-needed shipping containers. Last she'd heard, the pots were safely stowed and the containers tied down.

Now, with cyclone shutters over the windows, Lisa made herself a mug of tea and took it out onto the balcony to get a better feel for the weather situation. The wind had definitely picked up. Clouds were racing across the dark sky and the wind lifted her hair and her shirt tails, but she felt unexpectedly jubilant.

She was always happiest when she felt useful and in control. Her parents and grandparents had been hardworking sugarcane farmers, and they'd raised her to be handy and self-reliant.

Today was not the first time she'd felt a kinship with the cartoon character Lisa Simpson, the most 'on-the-ball' person in town.

CHAPTER TWO

Beacon Bay lost power at around 4.30pm. By then the wind had really ramped up its intensity and the heavy rain was almost horizontal.

'Cyclones with cutesy girls' names are always the wildest,' someone who'd rung in to the ABC remarked dourly.

The announcer, who'd been doing a good job of balancing important, serious information with comforting banter, chuckled. 'I wonder if we could get the bureau to reduce this storm's intensity by renaming it Agatha. Actually, no, there's a rule about alphabetical order for cyclones. It would need to be another name starting with P. Maybe Priscilla? Or Phyllis?'

Smiling as she turned down the radio, Lisa made one more call to check in with her son and was relieved to hear that Dave had the generator firing, and had also bought in as much ice as he could find.

'Take care, love.'

'Yeah, you too, Mum.'

'I'm sure I'll be fine here. But, Dave, if there's any sign of a storm surge —'

'God, Mum, don't talk about storm surges.'

'Sorry.' She knew he was picturing his café being swamped. 'Actually, they seem to think Pixie will cross at low tide, so a surge might not be a problem. The council hasn't ordered any evacuations, but keep listening to the radio, won't you? And if there's any threat – you must come here.' Her house was not only highset, it was on a more elevated block at the back of the town.

'Yes, yes, I'll come.'

'And that new girlfriend of yours is welcome too.' Lisa tried to sound warm as she said this, but it irked that she didn't even know the girl's name.

'She's gone home to her family in Tully.'

'Right, that's sensible, I guess.'

'And she's not really a girlfriend.'

'Okay.' Lisa worried that Dave never seemed to stay in a relationship for longer than five minutes. She feared his parents' divorce might have affected him, possibly made him commitment shy. But then, she also knew that mothers had a talent for feeling guilty or somehow responsible for their kids' problems. Not that Dave had ever mentioned a problem.

Stop fussing, Lisa. Dave might be her youngest and quite a bit younger than her other boys – an afterthought, they'd joked at the time – but he was also a grown man who'd worked all over the world. She'd been thrilled when he'd decided to come back to Beacon Bay, but he needed space to live his own life.

It was time for a shower, and Lisa indulged in a luxuriously hot one, wondering how long the heat in her system might last and whether she might soon have a week or more of cold showers to look forward to.

Outside it was almost night, and the house was very dark behind the closed and bolted shutters. Refreshed after the shower, Lisa turned on her battery-operated lamps, lit candles and turned up the radio to hear the determinedly cheerful local ABC. She rang Heidi again, suggesting she come over to collect her before the storm got any wilder.

Then she looked around her. She had a gas stovetop and plenty of light, and she had a radio, plus a portable charger for her phone, so she'd be able to stay in contact throughout the storm if needed. Everything was ready.

The drive to Heidi's wasn't far, but given the force of the wind and the pelting rain, it was dramatic. No point in even trying to use an umbrella. With every button on her raincoat firmly fastened, Lisa hurried up her friend's front path.

Heidi was packed and ready. With a grateful smile, she handed Lisa a warm casserole dish in a padded carrier. 'Here, can you take this and the wine? I'll bring Juno and my overnight bag.'

Lisa hurried back to the street with the casserole in one arm, two bottles of wine in the other and her head bowed against the buffeting wind. Despite raincoats, they were both drenched by the time they were safely in the car.

'Phew,' said Heidi. 'My back door was rattling like crazy. I jammed the kitchen table up against it.'

'Good thinking. I'm going to back this car against the inside of my garage door when we get home. I know those roller doors can sometimes blow in.'

Peering through the driving rain, Lisa could see that the footpath and street were already littered with fallen branches and leaves. Halfway down the street, a garbage bin was lying on its side, its contents strewn across the road. Someone hadn't bothered to make it secure.

She was about to get out and hurry into the rain to fix this, when a figure in a billowing raincoat suddenly appeared and dragged the bin off the road. 'I hope he ties that down,' she muttered.

'That's Ted. I'm sure he will.'

*

'Do we have an escape plan?'

Heidi's question, posed as she stroked the fat cat curled sleepily in her lap, caught Lisa by surprise. By now, they were safely in her house, with the car securely backed against the garage door and an old swag wedged in as a buffer against the rattling.

Outside, rain lashed at the shutters and the wind bellowed and howled, but they were towelled off and dry and comfortable on lounge-room sofas, sipping glasses of a fine shiraz, while enjoying flickering candlelight and the enticing aroma of their dinner gently simmering in the kitchen.

On hearing Heidi's question, however, Lisa gave an almost embarrassed little laugh. 'I'm not expecting that we'll need to escape from here.'

'No, I know it's highly unlikely, but I guess I'm thinking worst-case scenario. You know – just in case.' Heidi's smiling shrug was almost apologetic. 'You're such a planner, Lisa, I thought you'd have it all worked out.'

Indeed, Lisa *had* got it all worked out and that was why she'd invited Heidi here. She was confident this house was as safe as anywhere in town.

But clearly, Heidi wanted an extra level of reassurance.

To keep her friend happy, she said, 'Well, if things get really hairy, I suppose we could hide under a bed.' She hoped that wouldn't be necessary. It had been quite a while since she'd properly vacuumed under any of the beds.

'Or in the bath with a mattress over us,' suggested Heidi.

Lisa couldn't help pulling a face. 'Sounds squishy. But yes, if it was a matter of life and death.'

As these words left her mouth, she realised that Heidi was genuinely worried and perhaps she should have been more considerate.

After all, Heidi's husband had been killed in a freak skiing accident when they'd been holidaying in Switzerland. Real life had taught her friend that cruel accidents could happen out of nowhere. Perhaps Heidi was thinking about Ben right now?

'I suppose,' Lisa said more gently. 'In the very worst-case scenario, we could run down the internal stairs to the garage and get into the car.'

Heidi nodded. 'That should work.' She stroked Juno's silvery ears and took another sip of her wine. 'And there's always the evacuation centre as a last resort.'

'Yes.' *If we could make it there safely.*

The music on the radio stopped just then and the announcer gave a weather update. Pixie's centre was 100 kilometres offshore and moving fast. The station was inviting callers to ask questions, or to share their stories as they waited for the worst.

A woman came on, telling the announcer how she'd tied plastic tags with her phone number around her horses' necks, but then she broke down before she could finish her story.

Oh, dear.

Lisa got up to fetch the wine, surreptitiously turning the radio's volume down as she did so. Then, as she topped up Heidi's glass, she somewhat clumsily changed the subject. 'You never did tell me how that last date of yours went.'

Heidi had been a widow for six years, and she'd moved to Beacon Bay three years ago to start over. She'd been doing quite well as a freelance photographer and recently, she'd also started using a new online dating site for over-fifties. Just last week she'd gone out to dinner with a vet from Mission Beach.

'Oh, it was fun,' she said. 'Phil's very nice, actually. A cut above.'

'That's great. Nice looking?'

'Nice enough. And he doesn't talk about himself the whole time.'

'That has to be a bonus. So you'll probably see him again?'

'Yep. Maybe. But today I couldn't help thinking he must be flat out trying to keep all the animals in his hospital calm.'

'I daresay. The poor things are probably terrified. I've been thinking about the cassowaries. They often turn up in people's backyards after a cyclone.'

'Do they? Goodness.' Heidi had moved north from New South Wales and hadn't yet been through a cyclone.

'That's the thing about a weather event, isn't it? It's not just something dramatic that happens to one or two people. Everyone in a wide area is affected, as well as all the animals and wildlife.'

'Yes,' Heidi agreed thoughtfully. But then, after taking another sip of her drink, she arched a cheeky eyebrow. 'Getting back to the subject of dating, when are you going to test those waters?'

Lisa couldn't help gritting her teeth. 'You must be tired of asking that question. You already know the answer.'

Her friend smiled coyly. 'But I have to keep trying. You need a little fun.'

'Not that kind of fun.'

Lisa always bristled when anyone tried to discuss her private life. The divorce had been bad enough, especially with so many people, including her elderly mother and her adult sons, all shaking their heads as if they couldn't understand how the marriage had fallen apart.

Lisa knew that if she tried dating again, there'd be another round of scrutiny and comment, along with all manner of advice, and that was the last thing she needed. She was doing very nicely on her own, thank you.

And yes, she knew her former husband was seeing other women. The rumour mill had made sure she'd heard all about Rolf's close encounters with the owner of a newspaper up on the Atherton Table-lands, as well as his friendship with an actress of some renown. And then there'd been a reported affair with a woman in the Diplomatic

Corps in Washington, DC. All of these women were well-o̶
and accomplished, so thoroughly suitable for the new version of
ex, who was no longer just another tradie, but an internationally
successful author.

Lisa had accepted the news of these women as uncomfortably
clear confirmation that she and Rolf had never been a suitable
match in the first place. But that didn't mean she wanted to start
looking for anyone else. She really was far better on her own.

Anyway, this wasn't the first time she and Heidi had discussed
this dating business, and she knew her friend didn't understand.
Heidi had suggested that bouncing back after a divorce should be
easier than getting over a husband's death.

'Although I can't really imagine how you turn off the love,'
Heidi had said at the time.

Lisa had been shocked. 'It's not a matter of deliberately turning
it off.'

'So, it just fades, like the tide going out?'

'I – I guess . . .' It wasn't a concept Lisa had wanted to dwell on,
but now, as her thoughts once again spiralled down a well-trodden
path, she could feel herself sinking. Trapped back in those terrible
final months with Rolf, experiencing an inner rage towards him
that had consumed her.

And she was hearing her dying mother's words of reproach.
'You let a good man slip away.'

This had hurt so deeply at the time. But the sad truth was that
Rolf hadn't slipped away. Lisa had sent him packing.

She'd been so mad with him. Just at the point when all three of
their boys had finished their education and were off their hands,
and it was time to start saving sensibly for their retirement, Rolf
had got a bee in his bonnet about wanting to become a writer. An
author of spy novels, of all things.

To Lisa this had seemed out-of-this-world absurd.

ilder, well-established with an excellent
ıing up. But instead of working to expand
ıe'd spent hours every night and all of his
y in a back bedroom, tap-tap-tapping on

d finally been offered a publishing contract
with a miniscule ⸰ vance, he'd been so elated, he'd abandoned his
building business altogether to devote his entire time to his writing.
Lisa had been devastated.

Anyone with half a brain knew that a career in any of the
creative fields was a precarious enterprise. All those stories about
starving artists were based on real-life evidence.

And Rolf's subsequent success had been a total fluke.

But damn it, this was the very worst night to be wading through
those dark memories again.

Lisa jumped to her feet. 'I think it's time for dinner, don't you?'
To her relief, Heidi stood too, letting Juno take an elegant leap from
her lap to the carpet. And there was no further mention of dating.
Or former husbands.

In the kitchen, Lisa checked the radio. An elderly man, alone in his
house in Babinda, was talking to the announcer. It seemed he was
pacing up and down his hallway, clearly terrified, but gaining a
little strength by just having someone to connect with.

The announcer was doing a brilliant job, but Lisa switched to
a different radio station. Soothing music would be a much more
pleasant backdrop for their dinner.

Outside, the roaring wind was beginning to sound like an angry
monster circling the house. Every so often there was a bang or a
crash, and Lisa imagined tree branches and torn metal flying about,
but her house didn't budge or vibrate, or show the slightest sign

of weakness. The women sat down to their candlelit dinner and clinked wine glasses.

Heidi giggled. 'I won't say bottoms up.'

'No,' Lisa agreed. The middle of a cyclone was probably not the right time to get pissed, even though a sense of reckless abandon almost felt like an appropriate response to this wildness. Nevertheless, with a careful smile, she said, 'Let's stick with *cheers*.'

CHAPTER THREE

When Rolf Anders's phone buzzed in his breast pocket, he did his best to ignore it. He was in Dymocks in Melbourne, seated at a table, pen in hand. In front of him stretched a long line of readers, all of them clutching copies of his latest release, *A Telling Silence*, and clearly impatient to have their books signed.

The phone's vibration against Rolf's chest felt more frantic. It might have been his imagination at play, but he knew the call could be news, quite possibly bad, from North Queensland.

A woman with pink and silver curls was waiting next in line. Rolf flashed her an apologetic smile as he reached for his phone.

'Er – excuse me, Rolf. Sorry.' Aiden, the young publicist who was accompanying Rolf on this tour, suddenly stepped forward, his hand extended. 'Best to leave the calls till later.'

'But —' Rolf wanted to protest, to explain about the concerning news he'd heard just this morning, when he was travelling to the store. A tropical cyclone had taken an unexpected turn towards the North Queensland coast. Late yesterday, it had sped up and had already made landfall south of Cairns.

But Rolf's phone had already stopped buzzing, and Aiden was

actually holding out his hand for it. 'Maybe I should take that, Rolf. So it doesn't bother you.'

The cheek of the kid.

Rolf, who was well into his sixties, saw most of the younger generations as kids these days. But now, the usually amiable twenty-something Aiden was looking quite stern, almost masterful. Reluctantly, Rolf handed over his phone.

Aiden switched to a sympathetic smile. 'Thanks, mate.'

Rolf's smile, on the other hand, was warm but resolute, as the silver-haired woman stepped forward and set her book down. 'I'd like this copy signed for myself, please. My name's Beth. And this one's for my friend Lesley.'

As Rolf set to work with another flourishing message and signature, he was, of course, grateful for the enthusiastic response to his new spy thriller. While it might be true that he was happiest when locked away tapping on his laptop and lost in a make-believe world, he did enjoy meeting his readers. After all, these were the very people he worked so hard to connect with through his stories.

This morning's gig was the third bookstore engagement Rolf had undertaken this week. All of them had been similar, involving pre-signing author talks, a reading from his new release, followed by questions from the audience about his writing process, as well as hints about this particular story and what might be in the pipeline. This week, between the bookstore events, there had also been radio interviews and library talks.

Being 'on show' was somewhat tiring. Most writers were introverts by nature, and today, as Rolf's reward, his publisher was taking him out to lunch. To Florentino's, no less. Curious, Rolf had already taken a squiz at the restaurant's website and he'd been impressed to discover photos of a grand Renaissance-style dining room, with dark wood tables and tall upholstered chairs. Not to mention a menu that was gourmet heaven. Venison carpaccio, roasted partridge, hand-cut fettuccini with rock lobster, plus outrageously high-quality wines.

Unfortunately, the gloss of this idyllic plan had been somewhat dimmed by the news of the cyclone. As a North Queenslander born and bred, Rolf knew the havoc such a weather event could cause.

His own home on the far north's Atherton Tablelands near Lake Tinaroo was strong and built to the latest cyclone standards, so he was fairly confident it should be fine, especially as it was somewhat inland and up a mountain range. But he couldn't stop his thoughts from straying to his family, to his friends and their coastal community.

This morning, as he nodded and smiled and signed his books, his mind kept replaying memories of other cyclones he'd experienced, recalling that unnerving calm before the storm, when the air was still and the sky was heavy with clouds pressing low. And then the onslaught.

And he kept thinking of everyone he knew up there. Yesterday, they would have been rushing about in frantic preparation and then, last night, while he'd been chatting in a library and enjoying wine and cheese, his family and friends in the north would have been buckling down for the scary and wild reality of Mother Nature at her most furious.

By now, quite possibly, they were dealing with the aftermath, involving all kinds of damage and hardship, while he loitered here in the south, lunching in ultimate luxury.

As Rolf flashed a smile to greet yet another of his readers, he was fighting visions of houses unroofed, of rainforests smashed and electricity poles toppled.

The really strange thing – and a fact that none of these southerners could possibly guess or even understand – was that Rolf almost wished he'd been there in the midst of that drama. He was fighting a deep longing to be home, feeling those destructive forces and experiencing that intense, violent wind, that skin-searing rain.

He'd always been conscious of a kind of pride in being a North Queenslander, a sense of belonging to a community that carried an extra layer of resilience. Yes, life could be tougher up there – the storms fiercer, the summers hotter and the wildlife more dangerous, but this morning, Rolf could empathise with soldiers who wanted to rejoin their comrades in the front line.

Life elsewhere seemed somehow less important. *Tame*.

But now, in front of Rolf, an elderly chap, stooped and grey-bearded, stepped forward and placed his book on the table with a flourish. 'Love your work, Rolf.' The fellow had a broad Scots accent. 'Our entire book club has turned up here this morning. We're all enormous fans.'

With that, a long string of people who were next in the line all grinned and waved enthusiastically. Rolf was sure his phone was probably ringing again, but Aiden had disappeared. He smiled at his fans and asked the fellow his name.

'Alistair,' he was told.

'Great to meet you, Alistair.' Rolf turned to the book's title page and began his inscription.

Whatever news his phone had so urgently wanted to share, it would have to wait.

Almost an hour later, the last book was signed.

Rolf stood and stretched his stiff shoulders. On the other side of the store, his young publicist dragged himself away from the raven-haired girl he'd been chatting up at the cash register. Sending Rolf a beaming grin, he crossed the store to shake hands.

'Another amazing event, mate. You totally smashed it.'

Rolf winced at the boy's choice of words. For the past few hours, he'd been trying not to think about *anything* getting smashed. But he gave a polite nod. 'Thanks, Aiden.'

'We can head off now.'

Rolf held out his hand. 'Hang on. I need to check my phone.'

'Oh, yeah, sure, of course.' Aiden extracted it from deep in a trouser pocket. 'Sorry about banning it, but I had all sorts of trouble last month with an author. Won't mention any names – but she kept taking calls from her ex. Totally wrecked the signing. There were fans who gave up and left.'

'I get it,' Rolf grunted as he tapped his phone, where a quick glance showed at least three missed calls – all from Dave, the youngest of his three sons.

Dave lived in Beacon Bay, which Rolf feared may have lain right in the cyclone's path. He'd left voice messages, but Rolf rang straight through without bothering to listen to them.

'Dad.' A tight note in his son's tone suggested frustration.

'Dave, sorry I missed your calls. I've been caught up in a signing in Dymocks. How are things up there?'

A sharp little laugh. 'Pretty shit.'

'I'm so sorry. I haven't been able to keep up with all the news. Did you cop that cyclone?'

'Sure did. Came right through here.'

Rolf swore. 'Are you okay? Was your café hit?'

'I'm okay, but yeah, we were hit. The big window facing onto the street was smashed. But I managed to nail an old tarp over it, so the inside wasn't too knocked around. Nothing too drastic, I guess, in the scheme of things.'

'Well done, son.'

'And at least the cyclone crossed at low tide, so there wasn't a huge tidal surge.'

'Thank God for that.' Dave's café was right on the waterfront.

But before Rolf could comment further, or ask more questions, Dave said, 'Listen, Dad, I can't talk for long as I'll run out of battery. At the moment we don't have any power, but one of the towers had backup, luckily.'

'Jeez, mate. Sorry. You'll need a generator.'

'Yeah. I have one. But it's only small and flat out keeping the fridges and freezer cold. I could do with more. I have three fridges chockers full of food.'

Rolf bit back a comment, but with a café to run, his son should have been better prepared.

'Actually, I'm mainly ringing to let you know that Mum's house is in a bad way.'

This news slugged Rolf so hard he sank back onto the chair he'd recently vacated.

He'd built that house twenty-five years ago. Back in the days when he'd still been happily married to Lisa, still a contented family man, running his business as a professional builder – before he'd followed his writing dream.

But damn it, he'd most definitely built his family's home to the highest cyclone standards.

'What's the damage?' His voice was raspy with dismay. Had the windows blown in despite the shutters he'd made? The roof couldn't have come off, surely?

'That huge tree fell on it and smashed the roof.'

Rolf swore again. 'That great, tall milky pine?'

'Yeah.'

Of course. How many times had he told Lisa that tree was too big to be left so close to the house? Naturally, the stubborn woman had refused to listen. Rolf's jaw tightened as he remembered the last time they'd argued about that.

'Is your mother okay?'

'She wasn't hurt. Luckily, she and her friend Heidi were in the bedrooms at the other end of the house when it happened.'

'So where's the damage? The kitchen? Dining room?'

'Yeah. Dining room, mainly. Mum's pretty upset.'

'I daresay.' Lisa's reaction was all too easy for Rolf to imagine.

So many mixed emotions pummelled him now. Recollections from a happier past mixed with more recent memories of the toxic months leading to their divorce. But those flame-throwing days of yelling and fighting were behind him. Rolf had worked hard to move past them.

He'd forged a new life. A ridiculously successful life when it came to his books' sales figures. Even his private life had been more highs than lows.

'You'll make time to fix the roof for Mum, won't you, Dad?'

Dave, Dave.

How could he go possibly back to work for his ex on that house? This was way too much to ask.

Closing his eyes, Rolf ran a hand over his face to cover his grimace. He knew Aiden was watching on, somewhat puzzled, and no doubt other people in the store were observing him as well.

Swivelling to turn to the tall bookshelf behind him and lowering his voice, Rolf said, 'That's a big ask, son. And anyway, even if the insurance company approved, I'm not sure your mother would want me.'

'I know, I know.' Dave sounded weary and Rolf could sympathise. Last thing his son needed at a time like this was worrying about his problematic parents. Then Dave said, 'But unless she's prepared to wait for ages, I honestly don't think she'll have much choice.'

Rolf sighed. He knew that builders in the north were already in short supply, and the damage from this cyclone would only compound that problem. Just the same – asking him to work for Lisa? Surely that was a bridge too far.

'Anyway,' Dave went on, 'I thought I should at least give you a heads up. It's your decision, of course, but I know that house used to mean a lot to you. And surely the two of you could try to be civilised for a bit?'

CHAPTER FOUR

'No way.'

By the time Dave found his mother late in the day, she was on her friend Heidi's front porch, hands wrapped around a large mug of tea and eyeing off an opened packet of chocolate-coated biscuits.

The weather almost seemed to mock them now. The storm clouds of the past twenty-four hours had already swept inland and in their wake, Beacon Bay had been left with a clear sky and a setting sun that highlighted the litter and destruction everywhere.

Irony of ironies, Heidi's little cottage had weathered the storm quite well, except that her laundry door had been blown open, knocking her washing machine askew and sending the clothes trolley flying to the bottom of the garden with pegs scattered hither and yon.

Her cottage's exterior walls and windows were splattered with mud and plastered with leaves, but that was also the state of every other house in the Bay. And now, from the porch, the women were tiredly surveying their battered little village and the backdrop of denuded rainforest that surrounded it.

The magnificent trees had been totally stripped of leaves and the understory was littered with a massive tangle of uprooted trunks, fallen vines and broken branches. Like everywhere else in the Bay, Heidi's street was a sorry mess of smashed fences and twisted and dangling guttering. Fallen powerlines snaked along the footpath, their poles leaning at odd angles, and a couple of houses had lost huge sheets of roofing iron that now lay mangled in the yards.

At the bottom of the street, the soccer fields, where Lisa's sons had spent hundreds of happy hours, were a flooded sea of sludgy brown water. And as well as all of this, Lisa and Heidi were still recovering from the dreadful disaster they'd endured during the night.

It had been close to midnight when they'd retired to their bedrooms. Outside it had been calm, but they'd known this was the cyclone's eye passing over them. Soon the winds would pick up again, coming from the opposite direction, fiercer than ever.

They hadn't really been expecting to sleep, but were hoping for a little rest, when suddenly the winds had erupted to an even higher intensity and then, with absolutely no warning, there'd been an explosive, deafening crash on the roof.

It had scared the bejesus out of them, but Lisa had guessed straight away what had happened. Rolf had warned her about leaving that huge milky pine standing so close to the house. It was the one and only pre-cyclone gamble she'd taken.

The sickening crash was the possibility she'd both feared and prayed to be spared. Her punishment for being stubborn. Mother Nature had the last laugh.

The tree had come down, crashing onto her roof, its massive trunk and heavy branches cracking the metal sheeting and timber trusses and creating a huge, gaping hole that instantly filled the house with pelting rain and a roaring wind as loud as an express train in a tunnel.

The two women had spent the rest of the night in Lisa's bedroom, huddled in terror, together with Juno. Keeping the door tightly closed, with a chest of drawers wedged against it, and only torchlight for comfort, they'd listened in horror as the insides of Lisa's beautiful home had been trashed.

It was, without question, the worst night of Lisa's life. When daylight had arrived at around the same time as the storm eased, she'd opened the bedroom door and had broken down completely when she'd discovered the full extent of the damage.

Eventually, when she'd run out of tears, she'd wanted to start straight away on the clean-up, but she'd barely begun when a council building inspector had arrived and declared the house uninhabitable. She'd been ordered to evacuate.

Lisa had been quite sure her heart was literally breaking as she'd grabbed clothes from her wardrobe and toiletries from the ensuite, along with the evacuation kit she'd advised so many others to pack, but had never dreamed she would actually need for herself.

Despite her devastation, however, in the humbling hours since the storm had abated, Lisa had been schooling herself to be grateful for small mercies. Beacon Bay was a shattered town with many damaged homes and no electricity, and this situation might last for some time. But the pump station had generators, so the town at least had a water supply, and Heidi had offered her a spare bedroom.

Heidi also had candles and a battery-powered lamp, and she was still able to boil water and heat up soup on her gas cooktop. And Lisa, knowing that she had to conserve her phone's battery, had sent a blanket text message to the townsfolk she was most concerned about, asking them to let her know if they needed help.

It was the best she could manage for now and she hadn't expected immediate answers, but quite a few people had responded to tell her they were okay and were looking out for their neighbours.

At least, according to official reports, the only person with a serious injury was a Danish backpacker who'd foolishly gone out in the middle of the cyclone to film herself for an Instagram reel.

She'd scored a broken leg and a knock to the head, so the local ABC had reported.

Around noon today, they'd all heard the clatter-clatter-chop of a helicopter whirring overhead and then landing on the beach. It had flown the woman to hospital in Townsville, and the good news was that she should be fine.

Then, just half an hour ago, the SES had managed to clear enough debris from the road leading into town to allow them to bring through their trucks laden with tarpaulins to cover damaged roofs. In fact, they'd already started on this task.

So now, Lisa and Heidi were coming to terms with this new, smashed and imperfect world. They'd been through a harrowing night and a miserable day, but at sunset, Lisa was finally starting to feel calmer. Soon, the hole in her roof would be covered and she'd assured herself that she and the good people of Beacon Bay would all work through this ordeal together.

But now, here was Dave, arriving on Heidi's doorstep and delivering his gobsmacking announcement.

'No way!' Lisa cried for the second time. 'Tell me you're joking.'

Her son's glare in response to this was mutinous. 'Yeah, Mum, sure. I've had nothing better to do today than make up sick jokes.'

'Sorry, Dave, but I don't want —' Lisa stopped, tried again. 'I don't need your father here. It's stopped raining and first thing tomorrow morning I'll have a tarp over the roof. After that, I can wait till my insurance company sends me a suitable builder.'

'Mum, that's ridiculous. Dad's a highly suitable builder.'

'No, Dave. Dragging your father back into my life is what's ridiculous.'

He gave a tired shake of his head. His hair was thick and rust-coloured, so like his father's, although much longer, reaching his shoulders, so he had to tie it back when he was working. 'Look, I've already spoken to Northcover.'

Lisa choked back a gasp.

'You're still insured with them, aren't you?'

'Y – yes.'

'Yeah, well, I also have them for the café, and I was a bit cheeky and asked if Dad was still on their books. I knew he's done plenty of work for them in the past, mostly after cyclones.'

'But – but—' This new assertiveness was a side to Dave that Lisa had never seen. She felt bulldozed. She wondered if Rolf felt the same way.

'The Northcover guy I spoke to couldn't see a problem,' Dave said next. 'Dad's still registered, he has a reputation as a top-class builder, and with so much damage everywhere, they won't knock him back. They're going to be hard-pressed to find enough tradies to cover all the jobs.'

With a touch of drama now, he threw up his hands. 'Think about it, Mum. You've got one of the best builders in the district to mend your roof. You'd be silly not to use him.'

Lisa knew that on one level, Dave's proposal made good sense. But she and Rolf were finished. Over. Their parting had been neither smooth nor painless, and they'd said their goodbyes. End of story. Lisa had been managing so well on her own.

Okay, so she'd neglected to hire a tree lopper and she might not be able to mend a shattered rooftop, but she was by no means a helpless woman. Perhaps more importantly, while her ex might have kept up his registration and was still on Northcover's books, he could well be finished with the building trade.

Except, Lisa did know that he'd built himself a beautiful house up in the mountains near Lake Tinaroo. She hadn't been able to avoid seeing the article about that house in *Country Life*. Half of Beacon Bay's population had waved the magazine under her nose, and that had been a bitter enough pill to swallow without everyone also rubbing in all the other news about Rolf's roaring success as an author.

Rolf.

For some inexplicable reason, it upset her to say his name out loud, but even contemplating it in silence hurt. Hurt in complicated ways Lisa had no wish to explore.

How on earth could she cope if he was actually here in the Bay? Staying here for weeks on end and working on her house?

More importantly, where would he stay? Accommodation was bound to be scarce. Lisa wasn't even sure where she might stay until her home was liveable. It was a bit much to expect Heidi to put her up for weeks on end.

And how often would she have to see Rolf? How much would they need to discuss?

Surely it was all too hard?

Meanwhile, of course, Dave was still waiting on Heidi's front steps.

Lisa tried to be reasonable. 'You should have spoken to me before you rang your father.'

'Yeah, right. And we both know how that would have gone.'

Dave had a point. She would have pleaded with him not to make the call. 'I would have at least asked you to wait until we had a better idea of the situation here.'

'Well, the situation is pretty clear. You have a huge hole in your roof that invited a cyclone to do its worst inside your home.'

'Yes.' Thinking of her sodden lounge suite, the ruined paintings and shattered, mud-splattered dining area, Lisa drew a deep breath, sat straighter. 'Look, I know you're trying to help, Dave – and thanks. It was thoughtful of you to try to support me you when you have your café to worry about.' With a wincing smile, she couldn't help adding, 'But I still wish you'd checked with me first.'

Her son shrugged. 'If it's any comfort, Dad predicted that you wouldn't want him.'

Lisa could almost hear what Rolf might have said.

'Should I tell him not to bother?' Dave asked.

Yes, of course. She swallowed the tight lump in her throat.
'I – I guess not.'

Heidi had been discreetly silent during this conversation, but as
they watched Dave head back down the street, carefully dodging
fallen powerlines, she spoke. 'Lisa, honey, I know this is none of
my business, and I know the whole Rolf thing is like a landmine for
you. But at a time like this, most people would give their eye teeth
to have their very own builder on hand.'

Lisa pulled a face. 'I'm not most people.'

Heidi's smile wavered and Lisa could almost hear her unasked
question – *Who are you then?*

In that moment, Lisa wasn't sure she knew the answer.

CHAPTER FIVE

How can I go back?

Rolf's thoughts were whirling as he paced Melbourne's city streets, paying absolutely no attention to the shops and office blocks, arcades and interesting little side alleys that he usually loved to explore.

His internal battles were fierce. His son was asking too much.

Dave couldn't expect him to go back to Beacon Bay to repair Lisa's house – a house that had once been Rolf's home too and, at one point, his pride and joy.

For starters, Rolf was contracted by his publishers to produce another book, and the deadline was looming. A building project like this could take weeks, possibly months if there were holdups with supplies.

Given the circumstances, of course, Rolf's editor would probably agree to an extension of the deadline, but then, if Rolf went to Beacon Bay, he would have a much bigger problem – the whole proximity thing.

Arrgh. His divorce from Lisa had been a huge enough ordeal. There'd been times in the dizzying aftermath when he'd found it hard to fathom how a once happy marriage had imploded with such force.

Admittedly, his stubbornness had been as fierce as Lisa's fury. They'd both been out of control. And once the bomb had detonated, there'd been no retract button.

In the months that followed the breakup, Rolf's adjustment to single life had not been smooth. But now, with five years of separation under his belt, he'd come to appreciate his new independence.

He was damn sure this was also the case for Lisa. Actually, she'd been so keen to be rid of him, he knew she'd be desperate to hang on to her precious freedom.

So, while there might be a certain moral obligation to help his former wife in such a difficult and upsetting situation, Rolf was also pretty certain his ex would be even less happy than he was about his possible return.

Ever since Dave's phone call, Rolf had been wrestling with alternatives, including a call yesterday evening to his good mate Liam Flint, an electrician who lived near Rolf on the Tablelands.

After the usual greetings and a chat about the cyclone, which, luckily, had weakened by the time it reached either of their homes in the mountains, Rolf had enquired whether Liam knew of any builders up there who were on Northcover's books and might be available to help with repairs on the coast.

'Don't really like your chances,' Liam had warned him. 'But I'm happy to ask around.'

However, Liam had called back quite early this morning and, as Rolf had feared, all the builders on the Tablelands were already flat out. In fact, tradies all over the far north had been inundated with requests to help down on the Cassowary Coast.

This news wasn't really surprising. Rolf had suspected he was nursing a false hope. In desperation, he'd actually played with the foolish idea of trying to persuade Lisa to move away for a bit, do a little travelling, until another builder was available.

When he'd suggested this to Dave, his son had roared. 'Now I know why you pair are divorced. You don't understand Mum at all, do you?'

Rolf had refrained from responding to this. Inevitably, he'd been left with the sense that he had no choice but to agree to repair Lisa's roof and any other damage the house had copped. He'd rung Dave back.

'I'll do it. I'll ring the insurers and let them know.'

But no way was he looking forward to the job.

Hence the pacing.

Despite the steady rhythm of his step, however, Rolf found it hard to keep his thoughts on track. As soon as he contemplated going back to the Bay, unhelpful memories jumped into his thoughts. Happy family times in the past with their boys – on birthdays, picnics and fishing expeditions. Memories of campfires on the beach, watching the moon rise while the boys kept a lookout for shooting stars. He even found himself remembering the day he'd met Lisa on a sultry afternoon in November, when a sudden tropical thunderstorm had erupted over Cairns.

They'd both been caught without umbrellas, and while the thunder crashed and rain pelted down, they'd sheltered under an awning outside a florist shop.

Rolf could still see the scene so clearly. The sheeting rain and flashes of lightning, as well as the buckets of bright sunflowers and white lilies arranged in a display around the shop's entrance. Then, the attractive young woman in her mid-twenties, with shoulder-length dark curly hair and chocolate-brown eyes.

They'd exchanged smiles.

Wham!

Such a life-changing moment.

Her smile was so beautiful. Not over-the-top dazzling, but glowing and genuine.

Heart-piercing. Straight from Cupid's arrow.

He'd been as nervous as a schoolboy as he'd tried to start a conversation, but something had worked, and as soon as the rain eased they'd headed to a coffee shop. They'd spent the rest of the afternoon talking as if nothing else mattered but getting to know each other.

And what the bloody hell was the point of remembering this now?

Annoyed with himself, Rolf charged on down the footpath. He needed to stay focused on the present and he had to start planning. Luckily, he'd almost finished his book tour commitments, but while he'd been down this way, he'd been hoping to fit in a private road trip along the Great Ocean Road.

He'd have to cancel that and change his flights. He also needed to speak to his publishers about the deadline for his next book.

Of course, he also needed to talk to the insurers and investigate the availability of building supplies, as well as searching for available accommodation in Beacon Bay. The list was endless.

When Dave's phone rang from an unknown Sydney number, he was removing broken glass from his café's front window frame. As he worked, he was reliving the astonishing force of the cyclone, the thundering wall of rain, the angry, monstrous, roaring wind. It was a miracle the whole town hadn't blown away.

While he carefully picked at the shards of glass and threw them into a wheelie bin, he couldn't help remembering the view from across the street that the café's window normally reflected. Most days the scene showed an idyllic tropical beach, a haven for tourists, framed by palm trees, with calm, sparkling aquamarine water and an emerald island offshore.

Today, although the sea was already losing the sludgy brown that had come with the storm, the view was marred by shattered trees and rubbish blown from who knew where.

With so much mess and damage all over the town, tourists were unlikely to visit Beacon Bay any time soon. Which was damned depressing for a young man who'd just started a new business here.

Now Dave hesitated before answering the phone. He didn't have time for scammers. He'd already heard there were plenty of them out to make the most of other people's misfortune. But there was always a chance the call might be from Renata Ramsay's agent, so he tapped quickly before it rang out. 'Good afternoon. Frangipani Café.'

'Oh, good afternoon.' The caller's voice was feminine, mature and mellow, and extremely cultured. 'It's Renata Ramsay calling.'

Dave needed a moment to swallow his surprise. He'd only ever spoken to her agent. 'Hi,' he said. 'I mean, good afternoon. Dave Anders speaking.'

'Wonderful. You're the chef and the new owner of the café, is that right?'

'Ahh . . . yes, that's me.'

'I'm so sorry about the ghastly cyclone. Such a shame. The footage on television has been very grim. How are you faring up there?'

'Must admit we're all pretty shaken. Plenty of mess to clean up.'

'Oh, I can imagine. It must be awful.' Renata managed to sound genuinely sympathetic. 'I'm calling about my cancelled party, of course.'

'I see. Okay.'

'I don't believe you've sent an invoice for the food you prepared.'

'No.' Dave swallowed another gulp of surprise. 'I – I haven't yet.'

'Well, you must, of course.'

Now he punched the air with his free fist. This very issue had been worrying him. He knew he should have made sure there was a cancellation policy in place, but Renata's party had been his first big booking after he'd bought the café three months ago. Before that, he'd always worked in other people's kitchens, so when it came to running a business, he was still learning the ropes.

His mum had offered advice, as she'd had experience running his dad's office, but Dave had been pig-headed and hadn't wanted to listen. He'd been mentally gearing himself up to ring Renata's agent and brace himself for some awkward wrangling.

'I'm sure you will have ordered in all the food and ingredients, and no doubt you've also done quite a deal of the preparation,' Renata said.

'Well, yes. There was a fair bit of advance prep.'

'I was a little cross with Brian, my agent, when I realised he'd cancelled without discussing what we might owe you. But anyway, you may as well send your invoice directly to me now.'

'Thanks.' Dave was breathless with relief. 'Th–that's very good of you.'

He'd met women with posh accents like Renata's when he'd worked in restaurants in London. They'd tended to talk down to him, while calling him sweetheart or darling. Now, as he found pen and paper and wrote down her email address, he was grateful that she was straightforward and businesslike.

'As for the food —' Renata began and then paused, giving Dave time to recall the mountains of meatballs and seafood he'd been trying to keep cold and safe. 'I was wondering if you couldn't just give it away?'

'Excuse me?' Had he heard her correctly?

'A kind of charity event?' she said. 'To cheer people up?'

'Oh, right. I – I—' *Wow*. He needed a moment to take this in.

Perhaps sensing his hesitation, Renata said quickly, 'I'm getting carried away, aren't I? Totally jumping the gun. I'm sure it's probably too soon for you to start thinking about anything like that when you're probably still cleaning up. And it's very presumptuous of me to throw this request at you from long-distance. I don't even know if you have the power you need for cooking.'

'Well, I have a generator that's running the fridges.' Dave's mind was racing now. He'd be hard-pressed to use his electric ovens, but he had a gas barbecue, gas cooktops. 'And it's certainly an interesting idea. I'm pretty sure it'd be doable.'

'I'd pay you extra for your effort.'

'Right . . . thanks.' Fuck the mess. Dave would find a way to do this. 'Actually, a charity event is a really great idea.'

'Good. I'm glad you like it, Dave. But I know I've taken you by surprise. You need a chance to think it through before you commit.'

'Yeah, I guess.' But he was already beginning to feel excited. 'I do know there were definitely people whose homes were damaged and they needed to evacuate. They're sleeping in the Community Hall at the moment.'

'Oh, the poor things. They'd be the perfect recipients then. I'd love to think we might give them an emotional lift with that food.'

'Absolutely.' How awesome was this woman? 'Can I check a few details and get back to you?'

'Of course, Dave. I'd love that.'

Dave was swirling with emotions as he disconnected. He was super relieved that this cancellation would not mean a huge loss, but he was also elated by the do-good potential of Renata Ramsay's proposal.

It was her idea, of course, her generosity, but Dave certainly wouldn't object to playing the role of the good guy in town. He could do with a few brownie points. He'd come back to his hometown for several reasons, one being a need to prove that he wasn't a failure after all.

*

Lisa supposed she shouldn't have been surprised when she answered her phone and heard Rolf's voice. Momentarily, she closed her eyes and drew a quick breath as she felt her heartrate pick up.

Don't be silly. Treat him like any other tradesman.

Ever since the divorce that she'd pushed so hard for, she'd dealt with wobbly moments by reminding herself that Rolf wasn't suffering any regrets. He was living his dream life now, being a famous author, travelling the world, getting involved with other women.

'Hi, Rolf,' she said extra brightly.

'Lisa, how are you?'

His voice was still so incredibly familiar, she felt her skin heat. 'Oh, I'm bearing up.'

'I thought I should ring you directly instead of using Dave as a go-between.'

'Yes, of course.' They were grownups after all, and Dave had enough to worry about with getting his café back on track.

'I'm really sorry to hear about the damage to the house.'

'Yes.' And then, remembering how much the house had once meant to them both, Lisa was fighting tears.

'At least you weren't hurt.'

'No.' It took quite an effort to speak calmly. 'But I'm not allowed back in the house, so I've been working in the yard, trying to clear up the mess.'

She half-expected Rolf to make a comment about the fallen milky pine, suggesting that this whole problem was her own silly fault – which it pretty much was. If she'd had it cut down, as he'd suggested . . .

'So,' Rolf went on. 'That roof damage must have been a shock for you.'

'It certainly was.' Lisa knew she sounded extra nervous. Having Heidi within earshot didn't help. Her friend was working at her computer, editing photographs, but Lisa decided to step outside, to take a little walk to the back fence. She would feel better talking to her ex in private.

Once safely out the back door, however, and much to her own surprise, Lisa found herself saying, 'I know I should have had that milky pine removed.'

A pause followed and she braced herself for a cutting retort.

'I've spoken to Northcover and made enquiries about other builders.' So, Rolf was deliberately avoiding the tree topic, which somehow made Lisa feel worse. 'But it seems there's not much chance of getting anyone else to do the repairs for you. Not for some time, at least.'

Lisa had already phoned every builder listed in the district, so she was sadly aware of this fact.

'I guess you'll have to put up with me,' he said.

'It's very good of you, Rolf. I – I know you're busy and this won't be easy for you, so I do appreciate the offer.' She still sounded stiff, but at least she was being civil.

'I'm flying back to Cairns first thing tomorrow morning.'

Already? This was unexpected. 'Do – do you have somewhere to stay?'

'Not sure yet. There'll be an insurance assessor in the Bay by then, and I guess my first trip might just be to check out the damage. See what I need to order. I might not be there for long.'

'I see.'

'Don't worry about accommodation, I'll sort something out.' He sounded almost amused now, as if he sensed how tense she was, while feeling quite at ease himself.

Lisa bristled. Would Rolf's return signal the start of a new kind of battle? A competition to see who had emerged from their divorce in the best emotional state?

'If necessary,' Rolf added, 'I can always throw down a swag on Dave's floor.'

Oh, Lord. 'I'm sure Dave can offer you something better than his floor.' Dave's flat above his café might be small, but it had two bedrooms. 'I'm pretty certain he at least has a stretcher and a mattress.'

'Don't worry, Lisa, I'll be fine.'

Of course Rolf would be fine. He was the white knight coming to her rescue and she was the undeserving damsel in distress. Or rather, she was the undeserving, ageing divorcee in distress.

'Safe travels,' she said quietly, before disconnecting.

CHAPTER SIX

Pixie had passed to the south of Cairns, so when Rolf's plane landed in the far-northern city, there was no sign of a severe weather event. The sun was shining, the sky cloudless, the air balmy and the sea millpond still.

Rolf had been expecting to be away in Victoria for some time and hadn't left his vehicle parked at the airport. He'd been dropped off by a Tablelands neighbour who regularly commuted to Cairns, and today, for the drive to Beacon Bay, he'd ordered a hire car.

He wasn't looking forward to the journey and all that would follow. No point in wasting time, though. As soon as he disembarked, he headed straight for the appropriate desk where there was a bit of a queue, but he didn't have too long to wait.

An earlier check on his phone had already shown that the highway to the south was clear, but Rolf double-checked with the chap at the counter. 'I'm assuming I can get right through to Beacon Bay?'

The fellow frowned. 'You can get through, but they don't have power down there and I hear the accommodation's very tight.'

Rolf nodded. 'That's okay. It's what I expected.'

'Excuse me?' A rather cultured and commanding female voice sounded close behind Rolf.

Turning, he discovered the woman next to him in the queue. She was almost as tall as he was and had a rippling fall of shiny auburn hair. Probably somewhere around her late forties, she was dressed in silky black – city clothes that stood out against the more casual whites, corals and aquas of the locals.

She smiled. 'Sorry for interrupting you, but I couldn't help over-hearing that you're going to Beacon Bay.'

'That's right.'

'I'm heading there too.'

Rolf might have nodded politely and left it at that, but there was something about the woman, an air of confidence, almost of expectation, that held his attention.

She extended a well-manicured hand to him. 'Renata Ramsay.'

The name rang a faint bell and she exuded the kind of self-assurance that often accompanied success, but Rolf couldn't place her. He shot a quick look to the fellow who'd been serving him and who was still waiting somewhat impatiently for his credit card. Quickly slipping this from his wallet and tapping it to the card reader, Rolf turned back to the stranger.

'Rolf Anders,' he said, shaking her proffered hand.

'Anders?' she repeated with surprising excitement.

For a moment Rolf thought she must be one of his fans. Was she about to rave about his latest book?

'You're not related to Dave Anders, are you?'

Touché. Rolf couldn't help a small smile. Served him right for making up-himself assumptions. 'Yes,' he said. 'Dave's my son.'

'What a fortunate coincidence.' She was positively beaming at him now. 'I'm going to the Bay to meet Dave. He's organising a wonderful charity event for me.'

Really? Rolf hoped he didn't look as surprised as he felt.

The guy at the counter was clearing his throat. He'd printed out the paperwork and was waiting for Rolf's signature.

About to attend to this, Rolf turned back to the woman. 'I could give you a lift if you like.'

Hands clasped to her chest, she heaved an overly dramatic, happy sigh. 'That would be absolutely perfect.'

Lisa was feeling a good deal better this morning. The SES had covered her roof with a tarpaulin and Dave had actually asked her to help him at the café. Despite the boarded-up front window, he was trying to get the place looking decent again.

The locals, struggling with no electricity, would no doubt be grateful to have somewhere to come to for a decent coffee, or perhaps a meal they hadn't had to cook on a camp stove. At least, that was what Dave was hoping might happen, and Lisa had been happily sweeping, mopping, dusting and polishing. Dave was also catering for an unexpected charity event this evening, and Lisa would be helping with this as well.

She was secretly delighted that he'd asked for her assistance. And what better cause than a party for the unfortunate people who'd been evacuated out of their damaged homes and forced to sleep in the Community Hall?

Foldable trestle tables, cooking equipment and eskies full of food all needed to be transported to the hall. As soon as Lisa had finished with the cleaning, she would make several trips back and forth, carting gear in her Subaru Forester.

The glow of satisfaction that warmed her now was so welcome. She'd copped a bitter blow from the damn cyclone, but with this chance to keep busy and help others, Lisa was finding her happy place again.

Unfortunately, her buoyant mood took a nosedive while she was setting small wrought-iron tables and chairs back on the footpath outside the café and giving them a final wipe down. Usually, each table also had a little coloured-glass bottle filled with frangipani flowers, but thanks to Pixie there was next to no hope of finding fresh, unblemished blossoms of any description.

However, it wasn't the lack of frangipani that sent Lisa's spirits plummeting. It was the sight of Rolf pulling up opposite the café in a mud-splattered new Mazda, with a glamorous redhead in the passenger seat beside him.

A flash of panic zapped through Lisa, startling her. For a moment she was frozen, and she could feel her heartbeats continuing to thump even after she realised that Rolf's passenger was Renata Ramsay.

Lisa hadn't actually met Renata, but she'd seen her around town and in the supermarket. In recent years, more and more southerners had been wintering in North Queensland and Renata owned the most beautiful holiday house in the Bay.

Of course, Renata was also sponsoring Dave's charity event, but somehow, in this moment, that knowledge didn't seem to help Lisa. Clearly, Renata and Rolf had travelled down from Cairns together, and judging by the dazzling smiles and happy glances they shared, they were quite taken with each other.

She was gripped by an urgent need to escape from this spectacle. Hastily, she backed into the café.

'Your father's here,' she snapped to Dave who was busy filling an esky with food from one of his fridges. 'You'll have to speak to him.'

Dave frowned. 'Where are you going?'

Waving a desperate hand, Lisa pointed in the direction of the front door and out to the street. 'Just go out there, will you? He's with Renata Ramsay.' And leaving a puzzled Dave to attend to the greetings, she scurried to the back of the café and slipped out through the doorway into a small brick-paved yard that housed rubbish bins for the café and several other shops.

Once there, she took deep and hopefully calming breaths. But it was almost impossible to keep her thoughts from racing.

She wasn't sure what she'd been expecting when she saw Rolf again. It wasn't as if they'd had absolutely no contact in the past five years. Rolf had come to her mother's funeral in Tully, to their middle son Nate's wedding in Sydney and to their eldest Chris's thirty-fifth birthday party in Brisbane, but he'd mostly remained at a distance. When they'd been required for photographs, she and Rolf hadn't stood together, and they'd only spoken briefly at any of these events. Nevertheless, they'd always been pleasant and polite, if somewhat strained.

This time felt different, though. Rolf looked different. He'd spent most of their married years in the typical overalls of a tradie, or in casual beach gear. It was a shock to see him back in the Bay today, not looking a day older, and as big-shouldered and macho as ever, dressed in smart-casual chinos and an open-necked, long-sleeved white shirt with the sleeves rolled up just so, especially when he had a female companion who was at least fifteen years younger and all kinds of glamorous.

When had Renata Ramsay and Rolf become such great buddies? And wasn't that woman a perfect match for him?

An opera singer and an author. Of course!

Rolf was climbing the social ladder with every new woman he acquired.

So what?

As Lisa stood there, hugging herself in the scungy little backyard that smelled of rotting rubbish, while an ibis poked its long curved beak into one of the bins, she told herself she had no real interest in what Rolf did, or who he spent his time with. And she didn't. Not really.

Why should she?

Except . . . here she was in frayed denim shorts and a shabby old T-shirt, with her hair streaked by grey and pulled up in a messy knot. No makeup. Her feet in thongs. And Renata Ramsay looked like she'd just stepped out of a photoshoot for *Vogue* magazine.

Even though Lisa had fled from the footpath, she'd seen enough to know that Renata's black top and slacks might look simple enough, but they had the deceptive elegance that always came with a hefty price tag. And her black patent sandals had higher heels than any Lisa had worn in a decade, plus they'd shown off her sunset-gold toenail polish to perfection.

And why should any of that matter?

Lisa was exceedingly annoyed with herself.

Until five minutes ago, her heart had been light. She'd been busy and cheerful. Feeling good about herself.

She had to hang on to that feeling now. She wasn't normally a jealous type, and it wouldn't help anyone to be upset with Rolf from the very moment he arrived back in the Bay. She wasn't upset. Not really. It was just that this was the first time she'd actually seen him with another woman, instead of merely hearing about it.

She needed to absorb this new reality, to accept, to adjust.

'Mum?' Dave appeared at the café's back door. He was frowning, but it was hard to tell if he was worried or fed up. 'Are you okay?'

Lisa nodded. 'I'm fine. Sorry, love. I just needed a moment.' She tried to peer past him into the café. 'Is your father still here?'

Dave shook his head. 'He's taking Renata up to her place.'

'Right.' And then, Lisa couldn't help herself. 'I suppose he's staying at Renata's place too?'

'Stop it, Mum, don't do this to yourself.' Dave slapped a hand against the door frame, making no attempt to hide his frustration.

Feeling guilty now, Lisa tried to ease the tense mood with a shrug. Of course, she'd overreacted.

Unfolding her tightly locked arms, she let her hands drop to her sides. 'I'll handle things better next time I see him.'

'I should bloody well hope so.' But the wariness in Dave's eyes made his doubts about this possibility depressingly clear.

CHAPTER SEVEN

Rolf had been surprised to remember that he still had a key to the house. During the turmoil of his marriage breakup, he'd somehow missed handing over the backup key he'd kept under the driver's seat in his truck. Later, perhaps out of exhaustion or spite, or a mix of both, he hadn't bothered to post it back to Lisa.

Handily, it was still part of the mix dangling from his keyring, which meant he could get straight on with checking the damage to the house without bothering his ex. Probably just as well, given that she was going out of her way to avoid him.

Dave hadn't actually admitted it, but Rolf could read between the lines. Lisa had been at the café when he'd arrived this morning, but she'd refused to greet him.

It wasn't the most helpful start to an already difficult situation. Then again, perhaps limited communication was the easiest way to get through these next few weeks.

Now, Rolf was tense as he set the key in the lock, and his uneasiness was followed by a heavy, sinking feeling. Returning to the house was every bit as hard as he had feared it might be.

He'd been prepared for the physical damage to the building, but was hoping madly that it wasn't even worse than he'd imagined. But now that he was here and about to open the so-very-familiar front door, the slug to his emotions was hellishly fierce.

Over the past twenty-four hours, he'd been reminding himself that this was *not* a homecoming. This was merely a damaged building and no longer his home. He would treat the job like any other building assignment.

Yeah, right. Ha bloody ha.

From the moment Rolf began to climb the internal stairs, he was bombarded by memories. Damn it, he'd planned every square inch of this house. His dream home. He'd poured his heart and soul into it.

The memories were so painfully clear. Rolf had taken such care when he'd selected the Tasmanian oak for these stairs, as well as the spotted gum for the floorboards and the specially treated roof trusses. And when he'd fitted every window and door, hammered every nail and secured every bloody cyclone bolt, he'd known he was doing it for his family.

Now, as he reached the living area, made dark and stuffy by the tarpaulin over the roof and storm shutters left on the windows, he was hit by the stench of sodden carpets and muddied sofas.

A gaping hole in the roof was filled by a tree trunk and a smashed rafter had hit the dining table, breaking it in two. Leaves and branches were strewn everywhere. Smashed ornaments littered the floor. Precious photographs had fallen from walls. And the humidity in the closed-up house was unbearable.

Rolf's first task was to open the windows and shutters, and it was only then, as light and fresh air flowed in, that he realised Lisa must have painted the walls and ceilings white. But her efforts were now spoiled by streaks of mud and dirty water. Everywhere.

Even though the house's interior was like a scene from a war zone, other memories unfortunately chose that moment to arrive, and a very different kind of storm flooded Rolf. The shattered dining table in front of him was where he, Lisa and their boys had gathered for so many years.

An involuntary honking sob broke from him. How many birthday cakes with candles and sparklers had they lit at this table? How many Christmas dinners with bonbons and turkeys and that sparkling red wine Lisa loved?

Over how many simple evening meals had the boys shared news of their days – complaints about teachers, giggling reports of antics in the playground, triumphs after sporting wins and commiseration after losses?

Here in this house, he and Lisa had raised their boys. They'd cared for them together. *Together*, damn it.

He was remembering the year the three boys all had chicken pox, one after the other, and the seemingly endless itching spots he and Lisa had dabbed with cottonwool dipped in calamine lotion. Then there'd been the time Chris had come off his bike and the little beggar hadn't been wearing his helmet. He'd fractured his skull and been rushed to Cairns hospital.

There'd been no lasting damage, thank heavens, but Rolf would never forget the terrifying phone call from his wife. He'd rushed home from a job at Wongaling Beach just as she and Chris were taken into the ambulance, and then raced up the highways after them.

There'd also been the many times they'd helped Nate with his asthma. And what about that scary afternoon when they'd had to rush Dave to the doctor after he'd eaten the poisonous flower from a Captain Cook bush?

Okay, okay.

Enough with useless memories. He ought to know by now that there was nothing to be gained from living in the past. He was here to do a job of work.

But when he turned, he saw the doorway just off the living area. This room had originally been Chris's bedroom, but it was also the place where Rolf had first sat down to try to write a novel. After Chris had left for uni and his room was free to use as an office, Rolf had started on his first manuscript, chasing a deeply cherished dream that he'd put on hold for so long.

And a few years later, he'd been right here in this kitchen when he'd received that unforgettably exciting phone call from the publisher in Melbourne. Lisa had not shared that excitement.

On the very same day that Rolf had achieved one dream, he'd lost another.

'Ellie, what's this about Renata Ramsay making a big splash in Far North Queensland?'

Ellie spun around from her computer to find her boss, Daphne, with her hands set firmly on her hips, and looking as put out as she'd sounded.

'Sorry?' Ellie said. 'I'm not sure what you mean.'

'What I *mean*, my dear, is that Renata Ramsay is in Beacon Bay, where they've just had a massive cyclone, and it's all over the internet.'

'It is?' Ellie had been focused on writing a news release for the opening of a new Hunter Valley winery and doing her best to ignore the distracting social media prompts that kept popping up in the corner of her screen.

But she was also Renata Ramsay's designated publicist, which meant she was supposed to keep on top of the singer's movements.

'Last I heard, Renata cancelled her birthday party up in the Bay. I was sure she said she was staying in Sydney.'

Her boss shrugged. 'Seems she's changed her mind and gone up there anyway. And instead of a birthday party, she now has some charity event planned.'

'Gosh. And Renata's been tweeting about it?' This seemed totally out of character. Renata Ramsay was one of her most circumspect clients.

'No, not Renata,' admitted Daphne. 'The news isn't coming from her account. It's some PR guy working for the Cassowary Coast Council.'

'Oh? Okay.' Ellie was already reaching for her phone. A charity event would be news they could certainly use. Quickly she scrolled and then tapped the opera star's number.

Renata was on the point of turning fifty, but it was a milestone that she'd begged Ellie not to publicise. Apparently, reaching this age could mean the kiss of death for an operatic soloist's career, especially for a soprano.

So, although Renata had wanted to celebrate with her friends, she hadn't wanted to broadcast her age far and wide. It was one of the reasons she'd planned to host her party in the far north, rather than in Sydney. She was still hoping to stay on stage in starring roles for as long as possible.

Ellie could sympathise. There must be nothing worse than reaching the pinnacle of your career and then being told you had no choice but to gracefully dive from those giddy heights.

Mind you, Ellie was nowhere near the top of her own career. She felt like she was still stumbling over the rocks at the very bottom of the cliff, still searching for the right path. And this charity event in Beacon Bay definitely ticked plenty of boxes.

A feel-good story about a star's generosity in a setting that was currently in the news spotlight would be wonderful PR, an opportunity that shouldn't be missed.

Renata, however, was not answering her phone.

'I don't seem to be able to get through to her,' Ellie reported to her boss.

Daphne's eyes narrowed. 'There could be problems with power up there. Possibly no network.'

'Mmmm ... perhaps.' Ellie hoped Renata wasn't deliberately avoiding her.

'You'd better get up there then.'

Ellie gulped. 'To Beacon Bay?'

'Yes, to Beacon Bay,' Daphne responded glibly. 'Why not?'

So many reasons ... Ellie felt somewhat frantic as she ran through a mental list of the costs and impossible logistics this task might entail. A three-hour flight. Another hour's drive south in a hire car, arriving, if she was lucky, by the end of the day. Then the distinct possibility there'd be no accommodation in a town that had just been flattened by a cyclone.

'The event could be all over by the time I get there,' she said. 'And – and there's bound to be a television news crew up there. They'd be all over a story like that.'

And it's running into the weekend, Ellie almost added, except that this wasn't exactly relevant anymore, now that her boyfriend had delivered his devastating bombshell – although Ellie still couldn't think about Anton without feeling sick.

Being dumped after six naïvely happy months had been devastating, especially as this wasn't the first time it had happened. It seemed Ellie had a hopeless habit of falling for fabulously good-looking men who had major problems with commitment. But although she was still nursing raw and painful wounds, her new freedom actually appeared to be convenient.

Daphne, who'd been looking thoughtful, as if she might back-pedal, said, 'I think it could still be worth your while. You know Renata's at a point in her career when she needs all the boost she can get.' After a tiny pause, she added, 'And by some lucky coincidence, it seems Rolf Anders is there as well.'

This news made Ellie sit straighter. 'Rolf Anders, the spy thriller author? In Beacon Bay?'

'Yep and yep.'

'How amazing.' Anders wasn't on their firm's books, but that wouldn't bother Daphne.

This new info sent a fizz of excitement through Ellie. Instantly she was typing the author's name into her search engine, and her screen was filled with images of dark and dramatic book covers, along with photos of a rather distinctive-looking man. Probably somewhere around the mid-sixty mark, he had an impressive mane of thick rust- and grey-streaked hair, big shoulders and a strong face, almost a Viking vibe.

'Are Rolf Anders and Renata together? A couple?'

Daphne shrugged. 'I have no idea. But it's a tiny town and they're both celebrities and they're both there.'

'Wow.' The chance to get both those big names together in a touching story about a natural disaster was seriously tempting. Even if they weren't actually together as a couple, surely it would be interesting to find out about their common connection to an out-of-the-way little tropical town that was currently hitting the news?

'You might be able to organise an interview with them, or even a podcast,' suggested Daphne.

'Yes.' Ellie was actually grinning now. 'I guess I'd better see if I can book a flight to Cairns.'

'Definitely.' Daphne was still in the doorway, her expression thoughtful. 'And you'll need accommodation. Cairns will probably be your best option. Oh, and cyclones usually mean power outages, so don't forget to take a portable travel charger for your phone, will you?'

Ellie nodded. 'Good idea, thanks.' She had better start making a list.

CHAPTER EIGHT

When Lisa got back to Heidi's place, she had a cold shower and shampoo, then wrapped herself in a towelling bathrobe and found her friend in the kitchen peeling potatoes.

'I had leftover cream that's about to hit its use-by date,' Heidi said. 'So I thought I'd make potato soup. Luckily, I remembered to bring my pot of chives inside, so it didn't blow away.'

'Great idea,' Lisa told her. 'I'm sure it'll be yum.'

'I guess you'll be eating at the Community Hall tonight, though.'

'I guess.' Lisa would be helping Dave to serve up Renata's party food. This afternoon there'd been quite an excited buzz in the hall when the evacuees saw the event being prepared for them. 'Actually,' she began and then paused. She was a little embarrassed about the request she was about to put to her friend. 'I was wondering if there's any chance . . .'

Heidi looked up from her peeling, her expression curious.

'I was wondering if you might be able to lend me something to wear?'

'Oh?' Heidi seemed momentarily surprised, but then she smiled. 'Of course. All your decent gear's still up at the house.'

'Yes. I wasn't really thinking when I grabbed those few things from my wardrobe.'

'But I don't suppose the people sleeping on stretchers in the hall will be in their glad rags either.'

'No,' Lisa admitted. 'That's true. I guess I . . .'

She paused again, feeling uncomfortable about her foolish request. For heaven's sake, what was wrong with her? Some of those poor people in the hall had lost everything.

But then Heidi suddenly grinned, her eyes flashing bright and knowing, as if a penny had dropped. 'This is about your ex, isn't it?'

Lisa winced. 'Sort of – but actually, no, not really.' She couldn't bring herself to admit it wasn't so much about her ex, as his glamorous new female companion.

Luckily, her explanation no longer mattered. Heidi was already won over. With a tinkling laugh, she abandoned her potatoes and wiped her hands on a kitchen towel. 'Come on. Let's have a look. Luckily, we're about the same size.'

In her bedroom she opened her wardrobe doors. 'What were you thinking? Slacks and a top? Or a dress?'

'I don't mind, really. But I'm a bit shorter than you, so maybe a dress?'

'I don't suppose you'd want anything too fancy. You don't want to look like you're trying too hard.'

'Not at all, and I'll probably need to wear an apron anyway. I'd hate to spill anything on your clothes.'

Heidi nodded. 'Actually . . . how about this?' She lifted out a sunflower-yellow cotton dress. It had cap sleeves and a pintucked bodice, and was cinched at the waist, with a slightly flared skirt that allowed enough room for easy movement.

'Oh, it's lovely,' Lisa said, but then she frowned. 'But I don't think I've ever seen you wearing it. You're not saving it for a special occasion, are you?'

'No, no. This was an impulse buy. I actually found it in a second-hand shop in Mission Beach.'

'Really? It looks quite new.'

'I know. That's why I grabbed it. Ten bucks. A bargain. And it seemed like a good idea at the time.' Heidi pulled a face now as she held the dress out and looked it over. 'But I don't really think yellow's my colour. I'm too pale. It makes me look washed out.' She held it up against Lisa. 'I reckon it'll look great on you with your dark hair and eyes. You have exactly the right skin tone.'

'You think?'

'I do. And I also think it should impress this Rolf of yours.'

Lisa held up a silencing hand. 'He's not mine and I'm not trying to impress him.'

'Of course you're not.' The cynical edge to Heidi's tone was unmissable.

Lisa felt compelled to explain. 'I wasn't worrying about what to wear because I wanted to impress Rolf. It's just that Renata Ramsay will be there as well. She's sharing her party food with the evacuees.'

'The opera singer with that beautiful holiday house in Neptune Avenue? The house with all the natural timber and the massive deck?'

'Yes. And she also has a glamorous wardrobe to match.'

Heidi shrugged. 'But we'd expect her to dress up, wouldn't we? She's our local celebrity. And it's her charity event, after all.'

'You're right.' Lisa winced. 'And I'm being a total dickhead.' She handed the dress back. 'Thanks, Heidi, this is lovely, but you've made a very good point. I don't need it. Not tonight. Not when there'll be people in that hall who've lost their entire homes. I don't know what got into me.'

Indeed. What on earth was wrong with her? How could her thinking have become so warped?

This evening she was going to be busy in the background helping

Dave. A kitchenhand flipping meatballs on a barbecue, or setting out trays of mini quiches and bowls of seafood and salad on the trestles, while Renata swanned around, smiling and greeting people and being thanked for her generosity.

'My jeans and a T-shirt will be fine,' Lisa said.

But Heidi dismissed this with a wave of her hand. 'No, hon, you're welcome to this dress. As I said, I never wear it.' She gave another wave, shooing Lisa towards the doorway. 'At least try it on.'

With an apologetic smile, Lisa accepted the offering. 'Well, all right, if you insist. Thanks.' But as she retreated to the spare bedroom, she was momentarily whisked back in time to her school-days when she'd been choosing a dress for the high-school formal. *Shudder.*

Blanking out that regrettable and totally irrelevant memory, Lisa slipped Heidi's dress on, and when she saw her reflection in the dressing table mirror, her jaw dropped with surprise. The dress not only fitted her well, but it really did suit her.

The cap sleeves covered her upper arms that were unfortunately on the flabby side these days, and somehow the colour gave her a lift. It might even make her look a bit younger. Or was that wishful thinking?

Lisa couldn't stop a flutter of excitement as she returned to show Heidi.

'Oh, wow!' Her friend gave a happy clap of her hands. 'I knew it would be perfect for you.'

Yes, even when it was mostly covered by an apron, the yellow dress would look good on her. Different. Distinctive. The boost she shouldn't need – yet needed all too badly.

'It'll give your ex something to think about.'

'I told you that's not why I'm wearing it.'

Heidi was smart enough to make no further comment.

*

Dave was already at the Community Hall when Lisa arrived. He'd set up two gas barbecues just outside the building's entrance, and his assistant Janet was there as well, taking seafood and meatballs from eskies, ready for cooking.

They were both dressed alike in jeans and grey T-shirts, as well as the café's special denim aprons, with a simple white frangipani appliqued on the bib. Dave lifted an eyebrow when he saw his mum in her new yellow dress. 'You're looking very swish.'

It was not the greeting Lisa wanted. 'I've got an apron, of course.' Already she was pulling the blue gingham cover-up out of her shoulder bag and slipping the looped strap over her head. 'So, tell me where you want me,' she said as she reached behind to tie the strings.

'I'm thinking that Janet and I can look after the barbecues. So, can you take care of the inside trestles with the cold food?'

'Of course.'

'Renata will help you when she arrives.'

'Renata?' Lisa blinked in surprise. 'Don't tell me you're expecting the star of the show to help with serving the food?'

'Why not? She wants to, and anyway, it'll mainly be self-serve. I've made sure there are plenty of tongs and salad servers, so you two will mostly just have to keep an eye on things. The eskies are there behind the trestles, so if you could top up the salad bowls, or the platters with the little quiches or cheese wafers?' Dave grinned. 'Until we run out?'

'Of course.' Lisa swallowed uncomfortably. 'Okay.'

Dave frowned. 'What's the matter, Mum?'

'Nothing.' She was blinking again. She forced a smile. 'Sounds great.'

Except that here she was, yet again having to adjust her expectations. She'd been picturing Renata arriving with Rolf, being greeted with all the ceremony you'd expect for a prima donna. Renata would be looking glamorous and smiling serenely as she sailed around the hall, greeting the grateful recipients of her generosity, almost like a member of the royal family.

The last thing Lisa had expected was that the opera star would be standing behind a trestle and helping her with the serving.

Good grief. Deep breath.

Okay. So perhaps Renata wasn't up herself after all, but normal and likeable and genuinely wanting to help. This was a good thing, surely? Especially for Rolf.

Given the tragedy that had befallen the people gathered in the hall, the atmosphere inside was surprisingly upbeat. All the stretchers where people had been sleeping were now neatly lined up along one wall, and folk were milling about, or seated on chairs in small circles and chatting. Some of them did look woebegone and lost, which was understandable, but most were smiling, many of them with drinks in hand.

The council had set up a generator, so fluorescent lights had been turned on and there was even enough power for a rock band up on the stage. Boys from Tully High's Year Eleven, Lisa was informed, and they were happily strumming or plucking at their electric guitars, while their drummer hammered his heart out and an angelic-looking young fellow with a mass of blonde curls clutched a mic and belted out some modern rock song that Lisa hadn't a hope of recognising.

No one seemed to mind the racket. People were somehow managing to talk over it, but Lisa wondered what Renata would think. Surely she would be more used to a discreetly classical string quartet as a backdrop to her soirees? Would she charge up there onto the stage, grab the mic from the boys and blast them with an operatic aria?

When Renata arrived five minutes later, however, she didn't seem at all worried by the kids' music. She came into the hall, *minus* Rolf, and dressed – *of all things* – in jeans and a plain navy T-shirt, with her auburn hair pulled back in a simple braid.

Not a sniff of swanning about. She looked just like one of the locals, and after greeting Dave and Janet, she headed straight inside, sent Lisa a bright-eyed smile and a wave, and then stepped behind the next table to help with serving the food.

For Lisa, more deep breaths were needed.

At least things were quite busy for a while, with people coming in from the barbecue, plates in hand, chatting and smiling and excessively grateful as they added salad or little quiches to their plates. Lisa recognised quite a few of the families and commiserated with them about the damage to their homes, and she was conscious that Renata was having similar conversations at the next table.

By the time the plates were filled and everyone was sitting around in groups and enjoying their food, the band had stopped playing, which certainly made the conversations much easier.

Almost immediately, a local councillor called Marj Porter took advantage of the sudden quiet to grab the microphone and make a speech – a somewhat gushing welcome for Renata and sincere commiseration for the evacuees. Being a politician, Marj quickly followed this with lavish promises of a rapid recovery for the region. The state government had declared Beacon Bay a disaster area, and the local council would do everything they could to have the town up and running as quickly as possible.

'Our counter-disaster group includes police, fire brigade and SES, and they're working around the clock.'

This was met by polite applause, and then it was Renata's turn. She had excellent diction, as you'd expect from someone who'd spent so many years on stage, and she was totally at ease as she responded with gracious thanks for the welcome, mentioning that she was especially grateful to the people who'd been working out in the dark, hoping to soon restore power.

'I wasn't here to share the dreadful cyclone experience with you all,' she said. 'But I wanted to be part of the recovery. And I certainly couldn't let all the delicious food Dave Anders had prepared go to waste.'

Amid the applause and cheers that followed, Marj Porter suddenly appeared at Lisa's side and gave her a nudge. 'You should speak now.'

'Me?' Lisa asked in a shocked gasp.

'You're on so many of the relevant committees and one of the most active members of our community. The perfect person to give Renata a vote of thanks.'

Oh, Lordy. Lisa tried for a smile and missed. She swallowed.

'Better get going.'

'Yes, all right.' Hurrying forward, Lisa tried to compose a speech in her head, but she was still too stunned to think straight, and in no time, she was in front of the crowd in her sunshine yellow dress and apron. A glance down showed a bright red smear of tomato sauce on her yellow sleeve. Served her right, didn't it?

Renata was smiling warmly as she handed over the mic, and just in time, Lisa remembered that she should smile too.

'This is great, isn't it?' she said to the crowd. 'So many of us here together?' *Help. What next?* 'How – how many towns manage to have a party in the middle of a tragic disaster?'

Someone cheered and clapped at this, and then everyone else joined in. It was only as the applause faded that Lisa remembered her actual task was to deliver a vote of thanks. 'And of course this amazing event wouldn't have happened without the wonderful generosity from Renata Ramsay.'

With a sea of grinning faces in front of her, it was easy to grin back. Lisa decided to keep this simple. 'So let's give Renata another huge thank you.'

As the exuberant clapping and cheering died, she nodded a final thanks to the crowd. 'And now we all need to work together for the rebuild.'

She was feeling pretty good as she returned to her work station – until she thought about Rolf and realised that the whole 'working together' idea was her own major stumbling block.

About five minutes later, Dave popped inside. 'Hey, Mum, don't forget to help yourself to the food too. Come and grab some of the seafood and meatballs, won't you?' Then he flashed a grin to the next table. 'You too, Renata.'

'Wonderful,' called Renata. 'It all smells so good and I'm starving.' She shared a conspiratorial smile with Lisa. 'Okay, we're not needed. Let's eat.'

They ended up walking out to the barbecues together. By now the air outside was tinted with the purple magic of dusk. Palms – the only trees that had managed to hang on to their leaves, although their coconuts were scattered everywhere – were silhouetted against a rose and gold sunset.

'How beautiful.' Renata stood for a moment, drinking in the scene. 'Such a gorgeous skyline, but a bloody shame about all the damage.'

'Yes,' Lisa answered quietly. She was still coming to terms with the fact that this woman was so much nicer and humbler than the smug celebrity she'd expected.

Renata turned to her, smiling warmly. 'We haven't met properly, have we?'

'No, I'm Lisa. Lisa Anders.'

'And you're Dave's mother?'

'That's right.'

Now Renata's smile took on a slightly puzzled tilt. 'So that must mean that you and Rolf Anders . . .'

Lisa frowned at her. Surely she must know? 'Rolf and I are Dave's parents.'

'Right. Yes.' Renata continued to look puzzled.

'But we're divorced, of course.'

After a beat, Renata nodded. 'Of course.'

By now, they had reached the barbecues, where Janet was waiting and grinning a greeting. 'Dave made sure we saved a little of everything for you,' she said as she loaded their plates.

Together, Lisa and Renata thanked her.

'This smells amazing,' said Renata.

Janet, whose round face was nearly always flushed, looked extra pink as she beamed back at their special guest. 'But it's such a pity you couldn't have your party,' she said. 'Many happy returns, by the way.'

'Thank you.' This time Renata gave a gracious dip of her head.

'Oh, gosh, yes. Happy birthday, Renata.' Lisa felt bad that she'd forgotten to mention this during her speech.

Again, there was no fuss from the woman, just a simple, 'Thanks.'

As they went back inside to add salad to their plates and find spare seats, Renata said, 'So is it your house that Rolf's come to repair?'

'It is, yes.' Lisa wondered what Rolf had actually told her. 'I thought he might be here this evening.'

Renata gave a small shrug. 'I guess he could still be at the house. He was going there straight after he dropped me off this morning. I imagine it's a huge job – all the inspections and measuring and taking of notes, gathering info for the insurers and making sure he orders everything he needs.'

'Yes, you're right,' came Lisa's faint response and she wondered if she could feel any smaller. She was certainly ashamed of the energy she'd wasted this afternoon, getting stirred up over the possibility that this woman was Rolf's newest acquisition.

After all, even if Renata and Rolf *were* a couple, they were being very discreet about it, and Lisa knew she should be adult enough to accept this. In retrospect, she couldn't quite believe she'd been stewing over what to wear tonight, while Rolf had been getting on with the seriously challenging job of restoring her home.

CHAPTER NINE

You'd better hurry up or there'll be no food left.

Rolf hadn't heard the ping of the text message from Dave. He'd been up on a ladder, measuring rafters and cross beams by the light of a head torch and also using the torch to make notes. Almost half an hour had passed before he checked his phone.

By then it was almost dark. He'd been taking his time with his checks and measurements, having learned as far back as his apprenticeship that an accurate 'assessment of quantities' was important. In a disaster situation, it was more crucial than ever. There would be a rush for everything – scaffolding, nails, insulation, roofing iron, plaster – you name it, builders would be wanting it.

But it was time to stop work, or else he'd have some kind of accident, just to add to the already existing drama. At least, after several hours of steady work, he was feeling calmer.

The repairs weren't going to be easy, but they were all achievable, and Rolf had sketched out a plan that he'd share with the insurance assessor in the morning. He consoled himself that while it was hard to tell how long this job might take, it wouldn't last forever. The end date might be hazy at this point, but it would arrive and then he could get on with his own plans, his own life.

His goal was to get this job done as efficiently and quickly as possible without reopening old wounds. Tomorrow, he would start placing orders with suppliers, and he'd also start clearing out everything that could be safely extracted from the house and needed to be replaced.

The only foreseeable stumbling block was his need to discuss his plans with Lisa. He knew she would leave any structural decisions to him, but she would certainly want to make decorating choices. The interior would need repainting and she would also need a new lounge suite and carpet squares for the living area, and possibly new electrical appliances. Another decision would be whether she wanted the dining table repaired or replaced.

The lack of any discussion about this bothered Rolf, but as he locked the house and returned to his vehicle, he decided that it was probably up to his ex to make the first contact. After all, she couldn't stay in hiding forever.

Dave seemed to be packing up by the time Rolf arrived at the Community Hall.

'Sorry I'm late.'

His son sent him a rueful grin. 'No worries. I'm afraid I couldn't keep the food hot. It should be still edible, though.'

'Of course. It'll be fine. Thanks, Dave.'

His son lifted alfoil from a disposable cardboard plate laden with seafood and salad and handed it to Rolf, along with bamboo cutlery. 'How's the house?'

Rolf shrugged. 'Much as I'd expected. A gaping hole in the roof, broken trusses, quite a bit of wind and water damage inside.' He speared a barbecued prawn with his fork. 'This looks great.'

A moment later, he flashed a smile. 'And it tastes even better.' He sampled a meatball next, realising how hungry he was.

'Is Renata still here?' he asked.

'Yep, she's inside. Everyone's wanting to pose with her for selfies.'

'No doubt.' As Rolf tucked into potato salad, Dave said, 'You know your mate's turned up?'

'Which mate is that?' Curious, Rolf looked around. Most people were inside the hall by now, but it was well lit and the doorway was wide open, so he could see several locals that he recognised, but none he'd count as a close mate.

Still wondering, he brought his gaze back to the street, and it was then he saw the cute van parked halfway down the block – a renovated tradie's van. 'Don't tell me Liam Flint's here?'

'Yep.' Dave's grin widened. 'He's the best, Dad. His girlfriend, Kate, brought that van down. But Liam drove your ute, as well, so you'd have transport. You must have left keys with him?'

'Yes, I did. Wow, that's fantastic.' Rolf knew his sparkie mate and Kate would be comfortable if they stayed the night in the van. Kate had renovated it pretty much single-handedly and had done an amazing job.

'And Liam's also organised some other contact to bring a trailer load of generators down from the Tablelands. One's a 9kVA that's good for my café. And there's another bigger one for the supermarket.'

'That's fantastic.' Rolf's grin was now as wide as his son's. He was totally chuffed by his mate's thoughtfulness. 'That's exactly what you need.'

'It is. I'm stoked. The guy's a hero.'

'He is.' Seeing lights in the van, Rolf said, 'I'd better have a quick word with your mum and then pop over to Liam and say g'day.'

*

'Oh, am I too late?'

Dave had just finished loading the last of the trestle tables onto the back of his ute. He'd already sent Janet home and his dad had headed off too. Dave was looking forward to getting back to his flat, putting his feet up and knocking back a beer.

The voice spoke again. 'Excuse me?'

He turned to find a young woman on the footpath.

'I understood there was to be a charity event here tonight,' she said. 'Am I too late?'

'I'm afraid so. I just gave away the last of the food.' *A pity.* With no streetlights, the footpath was very dark, but there was just enough light spilling from the hall to show Dave that this girl was classy. Long legs just the way he fancied. Lovely shiny honey-gold hair and sparkly bright blue eyes.

Not a local, though, he decided, also noting her businesslike straight skirt, blouse and high heels, and a leather handbag with long straps hitched over her shoulder.

'Oh, I wasn't looking for the food,' she said. 'It was more the generous celebrities who were providing it.'

Dave frowned. 'You mean Renata Ramsay?'

'Yes. She's one of them. I look after Renata's publicity, but I've had trouble making contact with her today.'

'I'm pretty sure Renata's already gone home.'

This news was met by a heavy sigh. 'What about Rolf Anders?' the girl asked.

Dave almost chuckled, but he managed to curb his reaction just in time. With everything that had happened in the past twenty-four hours, it was easy to forget that his dad was some kind of international celebrity – at least as far as his readers were concerned. 'I'm afraid you just missed him too.'

'Damn.' The girl sounded totally fed up.

'I know it's not actually all that late,' Dave admitted. 'But for us it's been a long day.'

'Tell me about it.'

Now there was no missing the frustration in her voice. He asked, 'How far have you come?'

'From Sydney.'

'Today?'

'This afternoon, actually.'

'Not just to report on this barbecue?'

She offered him a sad little smile. 'Does that sound crazy?'

'Yeah, kind of.' But Dave softened this response with a smile of sympathy.

'It seemed like a good idea at the time,' she said. 'Or at least my boss thought so.'

'Well, yeah, I guess a big cyclone always attracts publicity. There was a TV crew here for a while. A journo from Cairns and a cameraman. They spent time with Renata.'

'Of course they did.' She gave defeated sigh, as if she'd given up any hope of completing her mission.

Dave had experienced his own share of times he'd felt like a loser. Wanting to offer her at least a glimmer of hope, he said, 'I'm pretty sure the journo was reporting on the town rather than this evening's event. And Renata and Dad will still be here tomorrow.'

'That's something, at least.' She frowned at him, clearly puzzled. 'Did you say *Dad*?' After a beat she asked, 'You don't mean Rolf Anders is your father?'

''Fraid so.' Dave gave a shrugging smile to make light of it. 'Small world and all that.'

But already she'd brightened considerably. 'What a lucky coincidence.' And she was holding out her hand. 'It's great to meet you . . .'

'Dave,' he said. 'Dave Anders.'

'And I'm Ellie Bright.'

'Hi, Ellie Bright, good to meet you.' Her hand was soft and delicate in his and he couldn't help thinking that her name suited

her perfectly – pretty and feminine and straightforward. Under
different circumstances, Dave might have contemplated the chances
of a hook-up. Unfortunately, this was neither the time nor the place.
'Did you drive down here from Cairns?'

'I did, yes.'

'And were you able to find accommodation?'

'Um – I booked a room in a hotel in Cairns.' She screwed her
face in a grimace. 'But I really don't fancy driving back there tonight.
I kept my carry-on bag with me. Do you think I'd have any chance
of finding somewhere here in Beacon Bay?'

Nil. Dave couldn't bring himself to be so blunt. He said, 'Reckon
I'd better show you where Renata lives. She has a big house.' Already
he was stepping forward to open his ute's door. 'Grab your vehicle
and follow me carefully. Some of the roads are still blocked off with
fallen trees and powerlines.'

What an absolutely bizarre day. Arriving up here in the north was
like finding herself in another world, like something from *The
Wizard of Oz*. As Ellie followed the rear lights of Dave Anders's
ute back through the pitch-dark little town, she was still recovering
from her scary drive south from Cairns.

She'd been gobsmacked to discover entire mountains covered in
bare sticks that had once been leafy trees. In one little town she'd
passed through, there'd even been huge trees, with root systems as
large as their canopies, just lying on the side of the highway, as if
some giant had ruthlessly ripped them out and tossed them away
like weeds.

The vegetation had seemed even more damaged once she'd
turned off the highway onto the narrower road that led into Beacon
Bay. She'd had to stop and wait while several trucks barred her way
and men in helmets and reflective vests worked busily to shift fallen
power poles.

Now, as she passed house after house with just a candle or lamp-light blinking from an occasional window, Ellie was imagining all the people in this little coastal village trying to carry on as normally as possible in the hot, humid darkness.

Dave had almost reached the edge of town when he pulled up. Parking behind him, Ellie peered through the faint moonlight and saw a tall double-storeyed house set back on a large block. It seemed to be built of natural timber with lots of glass, and as far as she could tell, it was surprisingly unscathed.

Lights flickered from behind the ground-floor windows, and she felt suddenly nervous. What on earth would Renata Ramsay think when she found her publicist on her doorstep? It bothered Ellie that Renata hadn't answered any of the text messages she'd sent, but that may have been because of power issues.

Oh, well, there was only one way to find out. Ellie got out of her car and went to thank Dave.

'I'll wait here while you make sure Renata's home and every-thing's okay,' he said.

'That's very good of you, thanks.' She knew she was lucky to have come across someone so helpful. 'And thanks for guiding me over here.'

'No worries.' His smile, framed by his shoulder-length slightly wavy hair, was friendly and warm and a little too easy to like. 'Good luck,' he said.

Ellie nodded and set off, using the torch on her phone to guide her way. The yard was strewn with fallen branches, and her high heels sank into the ground that had been made soft and muddy by all the recent rain. Halfway across, she pulled off her shoes and continued in bare feet.

As she reached the front door and knocked, she wished she didn't feel quite so foolish. What would Renata say when she heard how naïve Ellie had been, booking accommodation in Cairns and assuming she could slip down to the Bay, take care of the interviews and be back in her hotel within a couple of hours?

The door opened and Renata appeared. She was wearing a comfortable-looking kaftan in a tropical print. Her eyes narrowed as she looked out cautiously into the dark.

'Ellie Bright?' she said, with a start. 'What are you doing here?

'Sorry,' said Ellie. 'I know this is out of the blue, but I couldn't seem to reach you on your phone. I was hoping to cover your lovely event tonight. It was so good of you to share your party food with those evacuees.'

'Really? You came all the way from Sydney for that?' Renata dropped her gaze to Ellie's muddy bare feet.

'It's really good PR for you, Renata. Such a positive story.'

But Renata was shaking her head. 'But surely you don't honestly think I'd want to take advantage of a natural disaster to boost my PR image?'

Eek. When she put it like that . . .

'That's not the way we would present it,' Ellie protested. 'I – I'd be very careful with the wording.'

'I should hope so.' Renata looked back over her shoulder into the living room where her guests were chatting.

Following her gaze, Ellie saw several people inside, relaxed on sofas. A trio of candles flickered on a coffee table and the guests had glasses of red wine. Laughter rippled. It all seemed very convivial.

'Look, I won't send you back to Sydney without at least having a chat,' Renata said. 'But I don't think this is quite the right time.'

'No, I won't bother you now.' And then, with a guilty shock, she remembered, 'Oh, my God, it's your birthday, isn't it?'

'It is,' Renata said with a smile.

'I certainly couldn't hold you up now.'

'Perhaps in the morning then?'

Phew. A reprieve. 'That would be great. Thanks.' And then, because she could hear her boss's voice nagging in her head, Ellie said, 'I'm hoping to speak to Rolf Anders in the morning as well.'

Renata's eyebrows rose. 'Two birds, one stone?'

Ellie could feel herself blushing. 'Something like that.'

At least Renata was still smiling as she took a step back, clearly about to bid Ellie good evening and close the door.

Left now with an unhappy vision of the somewhat precarious drive back to Cairns in the dark, Ellie grimaced. 'Actually, Renata, there's one last thing. I know it's a huge imposition, but Dave Anders suggested that you might have a spare bed?'

'Did he now?' The flash of amused surprise was momentary. 'Under other circumstances that would have been fine, Ellie. But I'm afraid I have my neighbours staying here. Their house was damaged, you see. And Dave Anders's father, Rolf, is actually here as well. I offered him a bed, as there was only a stretcher at his son's place.' She looked back into the room again. 'I guess you could sleep on the sofa.'

Ellie sent another glance through to the guests inside, so comfortably chatting on the sofa where she might eventually sleep. She felt, all at once, exhausted.

'That's very kind of you.' She nodded back to the ute parked out in the street. 'Dave's waiting. I should put him in the picture.'

Leaving Renata looking somewhat confused, Ellie hurried away again, her bare feet squelching across the muddied yard.

'All good?' Dave asked when she reached him. Clearly, he was keen to be on his way.

'Renata's house is full,' Ellie told him. 'She offered me the sofa, but she has neighbours staying there, and at the moment they're all happily sitting around, drinking wine. It's her birthday, of course, and I – I felt like an intruder.' She didn't like to admit to Dave that she hadn't really felt welcome. 'Your dad's there too.'

'Yeah, I knew that.' Dave tapped at his steering wheel for a beat or two. 'Listen, you'd better come to my place for tonight. I only have a stretcher in the spare room, but I can sleep on that.'

'No,' Ellie protested. 'I'm not kicking you out of your bed.'

'I know Dad grabbed a chance to avoid the stretcher, but it's actually quite comfortable. And you can have my bed.'

'No way. I'll go back to Cairns.' But Ellie regretted this almost as soon as it was out. Perhaps a little too quickly she added, 'But honestly, I'd be fine on the stretcher. Thank you.'

Dave grinned. 'Go tell Renata you're sorted and we can fight about where we'll sleep when we get back to mine.'

CHAPTER TEN

Heidi already had the kettle humming on her single gas burner when Lisa arrived back. 'I heard the car pull up outside and I thought you might be in need of a cuppa.'

'Aren't you wonderful? A cuppa's *exactly* what I need.' Slipping an arm around her friend's shoulders, Lisa gave her a hug.

'You've been on the go all day. You must be tired.'

'Yeah, I am rather.'

Heidi was making tea the old-fashioned way, warming the pot and adding loose leaf spoonfuls, before pouring in the boiling water. As she set the lid on the pot, she sent Lisa a quick searching glance. 'You okay?'

'Sure.' Lisa's response was just a shade too quick, but she was hoping Heidi couldn't tell how shaken she was. She was still very annoyed about her silly reaction to seeing Rolf at the hall.

Her ex had arrived quite late and she'd been busy stacking Dave's containers back into eskies. But she'd been on edge all evening, knowing Rolf would probably turn up at some point, even though she'd been schooling herself to be totally calm and together.

Unfortunately, her lectures hadn't helped. One glance at her former husband's familiar broad-shouldered figure, at his intelligent grey eyes beneath bushy grey brows, and Lisa had been rendered utterly nervous and shy. She'd wanted to hide. Again. How ridiculous was that?

Rolf, on the other hand, had been completely at ease. He'd greeted her politely and with a very comfortable and pleasant smile, and he was totally calm as he gave her an update on the house's damage.

'I'm not sure how long it's all going to take, but I'm having a meeting with the Northcover chap in the morning and I'll keep in touch,' he assured her.

Lisa's thanks may have been a little stiffer than she'd intended, and Rolf hadn't hung around to make conversation. He'd moved on to greet Renata Ramsay, who'd been kept busy by grateful locals lining up to take selfies with her. And when they'd seen Rolf, people had wanted photos with him as well.

During this process, Rolf and Renata had laughed and chatted like old friends, and then Rolf had taken off to spend the night at Renata's place and not on Dave's stretcher after all.

Lisa had learned this particular detail as Renata and Rolf wished her goodnight, and she'd had to squeeze her cheek muscles extra tightly to hold her smile in place. But she was extremely disappointed with herself for finding the situation so difficult.

She was determined to be better company now, as she settled in one of Heidi's armchairs with a mug of blessedly strong tea, which she knew had been poured with exactly the right amount of milk and sugar.

'So, the evening went well?' Heidi asked as she lowered herself into an opposite chair.

'Yes, the food was great. Everyone was very appreciative, and that was nice for Renata. And Dave got lots of praise, which he totally deserved. I think the event will be a good advertisement for his café, actually, and that can't hurt.'

But having summed up the evening so quickly, Lisa already found herself hunting for further details that didn't involve Rolf. 'What about your evening?' she asked.

'Actually, I was invited to a barbecue too.'

'How nice.'

'Yes. It was such a lovely surprise. The Joneses who live across the road have barely waved to me in the past, but this afternoon they came over to see if I was okay and told me they had a generator they'd be happy to share, if I wanted to charge anything. And then they also invited me to a barbecue. Most of the people in this street were there. It was amazing, really. Everyone was so friendly and caring. I mean it wasn't all good news. Pamela and Bert's dog went missing in the middle of the cyclone, so we all need to keep an eye out for a little black Staffie.'

'Right. Let's hope someone finds him. It's amazing how a disaster can bring people together, isn't it?'

The two women were sitting in a small circle of lamplight, and Heidi was watching Lisa with a gentle smile.

Don't ask me about your yellow dress, or about what Renata was wearing.

Heidi didn't ask these questions, but Lisa found her friend's silence almost as bad. What was wrong with her? She should be able to relax now, to be grateful that this evening had gone so well. It was ridiculous to still be tense when she'd witnessed so much goodwill this evening.

'Lisa, what is it? You're looking so upset.'

'It's nothing really. I'm just being a bit of an idiot.'

'About your husband? I mean your ex?'

Lisa let out her breath in a slow sigh, followed by an unhappy nod.

'I'm so sorry.'

'But it doesn't make sense, Heidi. I'm over him. Totally.'

For a moment or two, they sipped at their tea in silence, but it wasn't a comfortable silence.

As Heidi set her mug down on a little side table, she asked, 'You can tell me to shut up, but I can't help wondering what caused the divorce. Did he cheat on you? He wasn't violent, was he?'

'No, no, it was nothing like that.' But Lisa wasn't sure she should try to explain. It had been a long day and she was tired, and the story was complicated. Then again, she and Heidi had known each other for several years now and she'd always avoided this topic, but she owed her generous friend a degree of honesty.

Sitting straighter, she said, 'It all started with Rolf becoming obsessed with wanting to write a novel and get it published. He used to lock himself away for hours on end. And then, the rest of the time – even when he wasn't off on his own, tapping on his laptop, when he was actually in the same room as me – he still had his head in the clouds, still thinking about his story.'

'It's very unsettling to feel ignored.'

'Exactly. I certainly wasn't happy, but —' Lisa began to gnaw at her thumbnail. 'But it wasn't only that. I – I thought it was all such a waste of time.'

Of course, this needed explanation, so Lisa hurried on. 'Rolf already had a successful business. He was a builder, a tradesman, good with his hands. People loved the houses he built and I enjoyed looking after the office side of things. We were a team. Not only that, but we were also, finally, in a position to start seriously saving for our retirement. And Rolf wanted to give up that security to write his damn novels.'

As she said this, adding a disparaging note to the last word, Lisa was remembering the afternoon an editor from Melbourne had phoned Rolf to tell him they wanted to publish his book. Lisa had been in the kitchen, standing at the stove stirring mince and onions for a cottage pie, and Rolf had been there too, in the middle of the room, clutching the phone and listening so very intently to his caller.

She could remember his jubilant shout of triumph when he'd finished the call, punching the air with his fist and then dancing a happy jig. Even now, the memory sent a shiver slicing through her.

Back then, in his moment of victory, she had turned the heat off under the mince and gone outside to cry.

But Lisa certainly couldn't tell Heidi that. She couldn't expect her friend to understand such a selfish reaction, and she also couldn't mention what else had happened at around that time, adding unhelpful fuel to her fire. Heidi was already frowning and obviously puzzled.

'Don't worry,' Lisa told her tiredly. 'You're not the only one who doesn't get it.' Plenty of their mutual friends, as well as their three sons, had made their mystification over the breakup patently clear. 'I suspect my problem is somehow connected to my background.' She shrugged. 'I come from a family of hardworking Italian migrants. My father and grandfather were cane farmers and they worked *so* damn hard. Back in the early years, they had to cut their sugar cane by hand and it was so hot out there in the fields. Back-breaking work.' Even now she could hear her father voicing one of his favourite sayings.

Laziness is a disease, Lisa.

And it was thanks to her hardworking parents' bequest that she'd been able to manage financially, without having to find another late-in-life job. She gave the arm of her chair a little thump to emphasise her next point. 'But it was honest toil.'

'And you think writing, or being an artist, isn't honest?' Heidi asked. 'Or toil?'

Ouch. Lisa knew she was on shaky ground here, especially as Heidi was a professional photographer.

But she was remembering how proud she'd been of Rolf when she'd first started dating him. He'd just finished his apprenticeship and she'd loved being able to tell her parents that she was going out with a highly skilled, hardworking tradesman.

'I thought Rolf was throwing away his really useful and practical skills, *plus* all our security – the same security my family had worked so hard to achieve.' With a rueful smile, she admitted, 'But I suppose, in retrospect, that doesn't make much sense, given how successful he's been with his writing. But I wasn't to know he'd be a bestseller. And at the time, he didn't know it either. He reckoned he'd been good at writing back when he was a kid. But you can't assume that an A+ on a school essay means you can write an entire novel that people will want to spend their hard-earned money to read. He was taking a huge gamble. And I was scared.' Another shrug. 'Scared and angry.'

Heidi, perhaps wisely, made no comment. Even so, Lisa suspected her friend still didn't really understand. 'It probably doesn't make any sense to you.'

'Well, I do know that anger can be quite irrational. I went through a time when I was really angry with my husband for dying and leaving me. I only learned later that it's a normal part of grieving.'

'Oh, God. I'm sorry, Heidi.' Her friend's loss had been real and devastating. 'I must sound so self-absorbed and insensitive.'

'No, not at all. I was trying to suggest there's possibly a similar kind of grieving that comes with divorce.'

This was actually true, although Lisa wasn't prepared to admit it. 'I'd say that in our case, Rolf's writing obsession shone a light on how truly incompatible we were.' She picked up her mug and downed the last of her tea. 'I've never been very interested in reading fiction.'

She couldn't remember ever having any fairy stories read to her during her childhood, and she'd decided at an early age that any kind of fantasy was rather nonsensical.

Now, she held up a hand, suggesting it was time to end this particular conversation. Heidi seemed to agree, which was fortunate. The last thing Lisa wanted was to find herself confessing the whole truth.

CHAPTER ELEVEN

Dave would have preferred to check that his place was more or less tidy before inviting a girl like Ellie to stay for the night. But since the cyclone, he'd been too busy managing all the food and cleaning up his café to pay much attention to the small flat above it.

Now, after he'd backed the trailer into the shed next to the café, Ellie asked, 'Would you like me to help you unpack that gear?'

'No, thanks, it'll keep till morning.' He'd had enough for one day and already he was fishing for door keys. 'The accommodation's pretty basic,' he warned Ellie, as she followed him up the stairs, bringing her carry-on bag.

'That's fine. It's very good of you to put me up.'

They arrived in his small living area, just big enough for two armchairs, a coffee table and a TV stand. Adjacent was the tiny kitchen, which Dave hardly used, given his full commercial kitchen below.

Thanks to the newly arrived generator, he was able to turn on a light, although that quickly revealed the empty beer cans and used coffee mugs he'd left on the table.

'Guess we'll have to manage without aircon,' he said as he

pushed windows open as wide as they'd go. At least there was a faint sea breeze. 'So,' he said, 'this bed probably needs changing.'

'Not for me, Dave. I'm sleeping on the stretcher. No argument, okay?' Ellie accompanied this statement with a surprisingly squared jaw and stern frown.

Dave matched this with a grin. 'Maybe we can toss for it later. But I promise the stretcher *is* quite good quality and it *does* have a mattress.' He gave a wave of his hand, 'Take a look.'

She went to the doorway of the spare bedroom, then turned back to him with a smile he found hard to read. 'I'm sure it will be very comfortable.'

As she set her bag down just inside the room, Dave said, 'I don't suppose you've eaten?'

'Don't worry. I'm fine.'

'What have you had since you left Sydney all those hours ago? A coffee? A little pack of cheese and crackers?'

Her response was a shrug. 'You've just cooked for practically half this town. You don't want to have to worry about feeding me as well.'

'Ellie, stop it. I actually like cooking. It's my chosen career. I have an entire commercial kitchen downstairs and thanks to a newly donated generator, I also have plenty of power. I can knock up something very simple. How about pasta carbonara?'

A pretty dimple formed in her cheek now as she smiled. 'That sounds amazing, actually. Carbonara's one of my favourites. How did you guess?'

'It's a hit with most folk.' And with that settled, Dave led her back down the narrow staircase to the kitchen.

'I'm going to have a beer,' he said. 'Would you like one?' Glancing back to Ellie, he caught a slight hesitation in her eyes. He grinned. 'Or there's wine, if you'd prefer? Can't do cocktails, though.'

'I – uh – do you have any white wine open?'

'Can do. How about a pinot grigio, seeing as you'll be eating Italian?'

'Sounds perfect. Gosh, Dave, I really am incredibly grateful.' She looked around at the kitchen's stainless steel benches, the efficient-looking industrial stoves. 'Now tell me how I can help.'

'All good. Take a seat.'

Slipping an elastic from his wrist, Dave tied back his hair. Ellie pulled up a stool to the bar where she still had a view into the kitchen. Dave plugged his phone into the power. 'Wi-fi's still dodgy, but luckily I have music downloaded.' Next minute Ed Sheeran was singing 'Eyes Closed'.

Dave poured Ellie a glass of chilled wine, snapped the top off a beer and took a swig, then went to work, setting a pot of water on the stove to boil, dicing pork speck and grating pecorino, then whisking eggs and pepper in a small bowl and putting it aside.

Luckily, Ellie seemed happy just sipping her wine and watching in silence. He supposed she was pretty tired after her travel. At least she seemed relaxed and happy. He felt unexpectedly happy too, with just the two of them and the music and the gentle hum of the generator in the background.

Once the water was bubbling, he added spaghetti to the pot. He'd begun to sauté the fatty strips of pork when Ellie asked, 'That's not ordinary bacon, is it?'

'No, it's a bit of a specialty. We call it speck, but the Italians call it guanciale.'

'It looks and smells amazing.'

'You can buy it from most delis. I reckon you'd have no trouble finding it in Sydney.'

'No, I guess not.' After a small pause, she said, 'So how long have you lived in Beacon Bay?'

Somehow, Dave hadn't expected this question, but he supposed it was as good a conversation starter as any. 'I grew up here in the Bay,' he said.

'Really? And was Rolf Anders here during those years as well?'

Dave nodded, but he didn't really want to start discussing his messed-up parents. 'Mind you, I moved away in my late teens. Itching to see the world and all that. I've travelled quite a bit, actually, and I've worked in plenty of places overseas.'

'But you came back.'

'I did, yeah.' He flashed her a rueful grin. 'Still don't know if it was a good idea.'

'Was it a spontaneous decision? A whim?'

This time, her question caught Dave totally off guard. He stopped stirring the speck pieces. 'What are you? A journalist or something?'

He'd meant the question as a joke, but Ellie seemed to take it seriously.

'I trained as a journalist,' she said. 'And I did quite a bit of travelling overseas too. I tried freelancing.' She gave a small shrug. 'And then I came home.'

'To stay?'

'I'm still working that one out.'

Across the kitchen they shared smiles – cautious yet warm smiles, almost like comrades in a moment of mutual understanding that felt potentially more significant than the situation warranted.

Dave turned back to his cooking. It was time to reserve some of the water for the sauce and drain the pasta. With this achieved, he tumbled the spaghetti into the frying pan and tossed it with the crispy pork strips, making sure the strands of spaghetti were coated with the tasty fat.

As he worked, he was still thinking over Ellie's question. Had his return to the Bay been an impetuous whim?

He'd told himself that he'd chosen to come back here because he'd wanted the relaxed, non-urban feel of the tropics. He really liked the idea of catering to unpretentious locals and tourists in holiday mode, rather than busy city types with their unmissable competitive edge.

But he suspected that his true motives for choosing Beacon Bay had been a little more complicated than that. His older brothers, Chris and Nate, had both excelled at high school. They'd been born just a year apart, while Dave had arrived five years later. He'd spent his early years chasing after his brothers.

According to his mum, *Wait for me . . .* had been practically the first words he'd uttered.

Chris and Nate had both gone on to do well at university. Chris now lived in Brisbane and was a successful civil engineer with a rapidly rising career in Main Roads. Nate was in Sydney enjoying a ridiculously well-paid job doing something fancypants in energy trading.

For the record, neither of them had rung Dave to see how he was coping after the cyclone, but he knew better than to expect a rush of brotherly concern. He could only hope they'd rung their mum.

Back at school, Dave's best subject had been English. He'd loved all kinds of writing, and he realised now that he must have inherited this skill from his dad.

In Year Twelve he'd written a one-act play that had actually won a competition and been published in a collection of scripts by bright young things. His dad had been ecstatic, and Dave had gone to uni to do an Arts degree. But he'd failed English 1. Twice.

Of course, he might have scored better results if he'd actually gone to the lectures, but he had quickly realised that he and uni were not a good match. After two years of stuffing around and failing spectacularly, he'd been anxious to find a career where he could be a success.

In desperation, he'd turned to cheffing, and luckily the gamble had paid off. Dave loved cooking. He'd aced his years at TAFE and since then he'd worked in kitchens around the world – in London, in French ski resorts, on a millionaire's yacht sailing the Greek islands, for a Canadian mining company in Mongolia.

You name it, Dave had tried it. Until the Covid pandemic, when he'd stuck to working in hotels.

Coming back to Beacon Bay, he'd been conscious that locals knew how successful his brothers and father were, and he didn't want to be the family loser. But he wasn't sure if he was trying to prove something to himself or to the town.

And now, thanks to Cyclone Pixie, he'd just had his first decent event in the town aborted. Needless to say, he hadn't minded turning that event into a charity affair. He'd been able to help out folk who needed it, and, as many long-time locals knew his history, he wouldn't complain if the barbecue had also gained him a small tick of approval.

'You're going to have some of this too, aren't you?' Ellie asked, as Dave handed her a bowl of pasta sprinkled with grated pecorino.

'Sure will. I was too busy to eat much at the barbecue.'

As he filled another bowl, she felt better knowing he hadn't gone to all this trouble just for her. He topped up her wine glass and grabbed his beer, then suggested they take their meals outside to the footpath where it was cooler.

The tables out there were small and round, just right for two diners. Dave lit a candle in a glass jar and it smelled of citrus and roses. Ellie twirled her fork in the pasta and lifted shimmering strands with pieces of crunchy bacon attached. She slipped them into her mouth.

Oh, wow. What bliss. For Ellie it had been a long and weird day, and this salty, smooth deliciousness was not only the perfect comfort food, but sitting here and eating it with this thoughtful, friendly guy, outside his strangely empty café, felt almost other-worldly, like something in a dream. A very pleasant dream.

Ellie thought about Anton and then quickly deleted that thought. For the first time since he'd dumped her, she was feeling as if she might have turned a corner. Not happy, exactly, but her spirits had definitely taken a shift.

From here, she could see across the street to the beach, where an almost full moon shone high, lighting a silvery path across the calm surface of the sea and onto the sand, and then making silhouettes of the palm trees.

The air was warm, but there was a whisper of a breeze bringing a faint salty scent from the ocean. A solitary figure came into view down at the water's edge – a man walking his dog. A trio of young teens on bicycles whizzed down the road. There was no sign of anyone else.

Ellie found it hard to believe she'd been in Sydney this morning, surrounded by skyscrapers and busy traffic and footpaths crowded with hurrying pedestrians. She could understand why Dave might have wanted to come back to this place.

Despite the damage and problems the cyclone had caused, it really was a slice of paradise. Why wouldn't he want to make his life here?

As she ate more pasta and drank a little more wine, she decided it was probably just as well she'd already booked her return flight to Sydney for the following afternoon. The temptation to linger would be strong. But this wasn't a vacation, and her focus was securing the interviews with Renata and Rolf, uploading them as soon as she had internet access and then getting on with the next job.

It was probably time to raise this issue. 'I'm hoping to speak to your father tomorrow morning.'

Dave didn't look surprised. 'Might not be easy. He's pretty busy.'

Ellie wondered why an author would be busy in a little town recently ravaged by a cyclone. 'Is he doing research for a new book?'

Dave chuckled. 'I doubt it. He's repairing my mum's house. A tree fell on it.'

'Yikes.' She frowned as she digested this. 'So your mother's here too?'

'Sure is. She still lives here. And Dad used to be a builder before he took up writing.' With an eye-roll he added, 'Yes, it's a bit of an unusual situation.'

'Are you telling me that Rolf Anders used to be a tradesman?'

'Sure. He built houses all over the north. Built the house I grew up in too. But now it's damaged and —' Dave gave a wave of his fork, almost like a conductor brandishing a baton. 'Tradies are scarce, so Dad's fixing the house for Mum.'

Wow. What a story! Ellie couldn't help being excited by the news that the famous author was also a skilled house builder. It was possibly a whole side to this highly popular writer that most of his fans didn't know about.

'And are you telling me that the famous Rolf Anders actually lives here too?'

'No. Not anymore. He and Mum are divorced.'

Dave looked so suddenly fed up as he said this that Ellie found herself telling him, 'Mine are dead.'

'Your parents? Both of them?'

'Yes.'

His expression was instantly sympathetic. 'Hell, Ellie, I'm so sorry.'

'It's okay. I was very young at the time.'

'Can – can I ask – how?'

She nodded. 'It was a plane crash. A light plane. Dad worked in mining in Western Australia, and I was only four when it happened. I lived with my grandmother after that.'

'In Sydney?'

'Yes, but she died three years ago.'

'That's tough, Ellie.' Dave looked like he wanted to hug her.

Quickly, before she became maudlin, she added, 'That's when I headed overseas.'

'In the middle of Covid?'

Her response was a rueful smile. 'Silly, I know. I was planning to stay with an aunt and uncle in England, but I had to quarantine first, and by the time I'd finished with that, they'd both got sick. They weren't too ill, thank heavens, but I ended up staying with their daughter, my cousin, instead. In a tiny stone cottage on the west coast of Scotland.'

'Sounds interesting.'

'Oh, it was. It was actually quite magical.' She looked again to the palm-framed view of the bay across the street. 'I imagine this place would have been a nice little haven for city folk wanting to get away.'

'Yes, I believe quite a few Covid escapees came here.'

By now she'd finished eating and there was only a thimbleful of wine in her glass.

'I'm grabbing another beer,' Dave said. 'You'll have more wine?'

She'd been enjoying the wine very much, but she said, 'I'd better not.'

He smiled. 'I think I'll take that as a yes.'

Ellie was definitely feeling much more relaxed by the time she went back upstairs. There was only one bathroom, and Dave told her to use it while he threw a few things in the dishwasher and closed up the café.

She'd brought a totally boring and respectable nightie with her. It was pretty much an elongated T-shirt in a leopard print and almost reached her knees, so she saw no need for coyness as she came out of the bathroom. She thanked Dave for dinner and wished him goodnight.

Even so, there was an unmistakable flash in his dark eyes. 'You really don't have to sleep on that stretcher, you know.'

She was sure this was a subtle invitation to share his bed. A tempting invitation, as he stood there now, tall and good looking, with his warm brown eyes, his defined cheekbones and strong jawline and his long rusty hair flowing free. It would be a casual hook-up. No strings. And tomorrow she would be gone.

A little bit of fun. An oasis in the middle of her current drought.

Except . . . this man wasn't merely good looking. He was kind and thoughtful and generous. And there was a certain shimmer in his eyes that caused a catch in Ellie's breathing and sent a feathery whisper over her skin.

It was time for her to remember she was no good at casual hook-ups. She'd been hurt too many times by good-looking guys who'd only wanted a few weeks of fun. Case in point, her wounds from Anton were still stinging. And with someone as comprehensively attractive as Dave, she would inevitably end up feeling emotionally involved and then stupidly disappointed.

'I'm all finished in the bathroom, thank you,' she told him now, flashing a bright smile as she fast-tracked to the spare room and the stretcher. 'Goodnight, Dave.'

CHAPTER TWELVE

Somewhere around midnight, another band of heavy rain arrived in Beacon Bay. Lisa was tossing restlessly in the spare room at Heidi's place when she heard the sudden downpour thundering up the bitumen road and then onto the roof. A moment later it was splattering through the bedroom window and she had to get up to close the casements.

The force of this rain surprised her, lashing at the glass almost as hard as it had during Pixie. She decided she'd better check the other rooms in the house, and sure enough, the living room windows also needed closing. As she attended to this, she felt somewhat put out that she hadn't known the rain was on its way. But with the day's distractions and the limited power, she hadn't really had a chance to check weather reports.

Back in bed, she was wider awake than ever and, to her annoyance, she found herself wondering how things were going over at Renata's place. Almost immediately, an unbidden image of Renata and Rolf arrived, their limbs entwined. But were they actually sleeping together?

The chances were pretty high, Lisa figured. She didn't actually know Renata's marital status, but she suspected that attitudes might be somewhat flexible in the esoteric world of opera stars. Then again, the fact that Renata's neighbours were also staying there might have slowed them down.

Give it a miss, Lisa. It's no longer any of your business and you don't care.

Rolling over again, she gave her pillow a savage thump. Then, very deliberately, she closed her eyes and tried to hypnotise herself by visualising an innocent grey blob, a cloud perhaps . . . holding it in her vision, concentrating, concentrating.

The technique had often worked in the past, but this evening it was useless. Lisa rolled the other way, gave the pillow another thump and tried counting sheep. And it was then she found her thoughts drifting backwards . . .

She was fourteen again and it was late afternoon in summer. She was with her best friend, Bianca, on a rocky bank beside the Tully River. The rapids were too strong for swimming at this point, but the girls had a favourite rockpool where they liked to cool off.

Lisa had worn the new pink gingham two-piece bathers that her mum had made for her, while Bianca had a similar set in navy with white polka dots.

Their pool was just big enough to comfortably fit the two girls, and if they bent their knees, they were pretty much underwater. It was a welcome chance to cool off.

With her head resting back on a smooth slab of sandy stone, Lisa closed her eyes. The world was quiet and still, and the only sound was the nearby river rushing over rocks, until she heard Bianca's voice.

'You want a smoke?'

Lisa's eyes flashed open. Bianca was smirking at her and sat poised with a cigarette that she'd already lit.

At first, Lisa was too surprised to speak. Bianca waved her cigarette and a curl of smoke hung in the afternoon light. When the smell of it reached Lisa, it made her nose twitch.

'Want one?' Bianca asked again.

Smoking wasn't an activity Lisa had ever considered. Her grandfather had been a heavy smoker and he'd died too young of a heart attack. She knew guys from school who liked to hang outside the movie theatre with cigarettes dangling from their lips, trying to look cool.

She supposed Bianca's older brother, Gerry, had supplied these. He was part of the cool brigade.

But now, as Lisa watched Bianca take a drag and expel a thin stream of smoke like an expert, she did feel rather curious. She supposed she might as well give it a go. At least, out here by the river, she was safe from her parents' prying eyes.

'Okay,' she said, and Bianca grinned before reaching into a drawstring beach bag on the rock beside her to retrieve a packet of Benson & Hedges and a lighter.

Lisa felt surprisingly calm as she selected the slimly rolled paper and tobacco. There was a filter, so she knew which end to set between her lips.

'Suck in a little when I light it,' Bianca instructed.

Flame flared from the silver lighter and Lisa sucked. Smoke hit the back of her throat and she was instantly coughing. '*Yuck.*'

Bianca laughed. 'It's always like that the first time. Don't suck in *quite* so hard.'

Lisa nodded. She didn't want to be totally uncool. She drew more gently, but felt a little giddy and huffed the smoke out quickly. This smoking caper was trickier than it looked.

She took in a few breaths of fresh air before she tried again, and this time there was no coughing or giddiness. She was taking another draw when Bianca's brother suddenly arrived from around a bend in the river, carrying a fishing rod and a small canvas backpack and leaping easily from rock to rock.

Gerry was only fifteen months older than Bianca. Tall and athletic, with thick dark hair, he had the movie-star looks that made the girls at their school swoon. Lisa was no exception, although she'd always felt shy if she visited Bianca when Gerry was home.

He grinned and waved at them now, and Lisa's immediate instinct was to throw away her cigarette. But Bianca made no attempt to hide hers as she waved back to her brother, so Lisa kept her smoke as well.

Next minute Gerry was coming quickly and easily over the rocks to them.

'G'day.' Now he was standing on a rock above them, still grinning as he looked down at the girls in their little pool.

Lisa was sure he had a view straight down the top of her bathers, and she could feel herself blushing. Then, with another careless leap, he was level with them.

'Nice spot you've got here.' This time, he was looking directly at Lisa, letting his gaze linger on her bathers, on the cigarette and her bent bare knees poking above the water. He smiled – a smile that was clearly just for her, and his blue-grey eyes seemed to shimmer with an emotion that reached deep inside her.

She had never experienced a moment like this. Ever. A moment of skin-tingling, breath-robbing connection. And in that moment, she knew she was falling head over heels into a whole new world.

Many more years passed before Lisa realised that this romantic teenage moment had also marked the very beginning of a painful journey. And on restless, sleepless nights like this, she was racked by a fear that this journey had not yet reached its final destination.

*

Lisa was still awake by the time a dull grey dawn arrived, and it was still raining. Water now covered the road leading past Heidi's house and the already soaked yard was a lake. Of course, Lisa had spent much of the past hours worrying that the rain had also forced its way past the tarpaulins covering the hole in her roof.

Damn it, this downpour was the last thing the Bay needed on top of a cyclone. Rolf had a meeting with the insurance assessor this morning and he wanted the repairs done as quickly as possible. They both needed to get back to their normal, *separate* lives.

But if Lisa had learned anything in recent years, it was that feeling sorry for herself never helped. Now, desperate to be grateful for at least one small thing, even a decent cup of tea, she went to the kitchen to put the kettle on.

At Renata's house, Rolf was standing at the kitchen window, staring bleakly out at the sheeting rain. He was alone, the grateful neighbours having already left. They had a newsagency business in town and needed to check how the shop was coping with this extra rain.

From experience over previous summers, Rolf knew there was every chance that creeks would now be flooded and roads cut, so he was glad his electrician mate, Liam Flint, had decided to head straight back to the Tablelands last night. Once power was restored, Liam would probably come back and he'd be a real help, but in the meantime he was better off out of here.

Hearing footsteps behind him now, Rolf turned and saw his hostess coming into the kitchen. She was dressed in a long blue kimono-style robe, tied at the waist. Her auburn hair trailed softly past her shoulders and she wore no makeup, and yet her entrance seemed to demand attention. The woman had an arresting aura.

Rolf wondered if this was the result of the many stage entrances she'd made during her operatic career. This very moment could perhaps be a scene from *Madama Butterfly*.

But of course, he was being fanciful.

Renata squinted briefly at the gloomy world outside and then sent him a questioning smile. 'So this is what a proper wet season in the tropics looks like?'

''Fraid so.'

'Not exactly good weather for a house builder.'

'No, not at all.' Rolf wasn't looking forward to heading out in the rain to check how Lisa's house was coping with this latest weather event. Hopefully, the insurance assessor had made it safely into town yesterday and the meeting wouldn't take too long. He gave a small shrug. 'At least it's good writing weather.'

Renata grinned at this. 'Of course it is. Have you brought your laptop with you?'

'Actually, I have.' And overnight Rolf had also been struck by a couple of bright ideas for his current work in progress. He really should jot them down before he lost them.

'Well, that back bedroom's all yours,' said Renata. 'Feel free to lock yourself away.' As she reached for matches to light the single camping gas burner that was currently all she had for cooking, she added, 'It's good to know someone can actually benefit from such a torrential downpour.'

'What about you, though? Were you hoping to get back to Sydney?'

'Not today.' Having placed a full kettle on the burner, Renata was smiling again as she shrugged. 'It's okay. I don't have a show lined up right now, so there's no rush for me to be anywhere, which makes a nice change.' With a nod to the window, 'This is also great weather for readers.'

'Well, yes, that's true.'

'And I have the perfect distraction.'

'What are you reading?'

'Your book *First Snow*.'

'Really?'

'Of course. As soon as I realised we still had wi-fi, I checked out Amazon, and when I saw all those five-star ratings, I had to buy it. It's wonderful, Rolf. I love the setting in Otaru in Japan. Your descriptions of the canal lined with glowing snow lanterns are just so beautiful.'

'Thanks. I enjoy describing scenery.'

'It's so vivid, Rolf. I wanted to be there. And now I'm just up to the part where the body's been found.' With a cheeky smile, Renata gestured to her kimono. 'I'm wearing this to stay in the mood and I'm desperate to find out what happens next.'

Rolf grinned. 'Looks like we both have our day sorted then.'

But now Renata was frowning. 'Oh, but I've just remembered Ellie, that PR girl. She wants to interview us.'

Damn.

CHAPTER THIRTEEN

Dave had slept late and was woken by his phone buzzing beside him. He yawned noisily as he groped for it on the bedside table. 'Morning.'

'Dave, it's Janet.'

Another yawn. 'Hi. What time is it?' He hadn't bothered to check when he'd sleepily grabbed the phone. Was Janet already downstairs wondering why he wasn't in the kitchen?

'Don't panic. It's not quite eight,' she said. 'But listen, I'm sorry, I'm afraid I'm not going to be able to get into work today.'

'Really?' Dave was blinking awake now. 'What's happened?'

'Well, I came in to Tully to visit my daughter, Jess, last night. You know, just to see how she and the kids were coping after Pixie. But we had a few drinks, and Jess talked me into staying over, which was sensible, I guess. But now, I'm stuck here, 'cause the creek's up.'

Dave frowned. 'Venus Creek?'

'Yep. Both Venus and Neptune creeks are totally flooded. I've been listening to the ABC reports. Apparently, it's been raining up on the Tablelands ever since Pixie came through and all that water's been making its way back down here to the coast. So, on top of the rain that we've had overnight, Venus Creek is now right up over its banks and you can't even see the bridge.'

Shit. Dave was a sound sleeper. Until Janet's call, he hadn't even realised it was raining outside. Now he shuffled over to his bedroom window and pulled the cord to open the timber blind. Luckily there was an awning over the window that had prevented the rain from coming in, but the usual view of the beach and the sea was almost entirely obscured by a grey wall of rain.

Far out.

'Sorry, Dave. I know you wanted to get the café up and running again as soon as possible.'

Yeah, that had certainly been his plan. So many of the locals were going to be fed up with trying to manage meals without electricity, and Dave had been looking forward to providing delicious and heartening lunches and dinners they could enjoy in his café. He'd had so many visions, especially for the evening meals: a variety of pastas, baked chickens, slow-cooked lamb . . . rich fried onions and crunchy, golden potatoes . . .

But this plan would be a massive, or more correctly, an *impossible* challenge without his assistant. Worse, with the main access out of the Bay cut by two flooded creeks, Dave had almost certainly lost his best chance of restocking his dwindling supplies.

Just in time, he resisted the urge to swear into the phone. Instead, he managed to force brightness into his voice. 'No worries, Janet. You weren't to know about this weather. And you stay there till it's totally safe. I don't want you taking any risks. If it's flooded, forget it.'

'Yes, boss. I feel bad though.'

'Then stop it. Enjoy your grandkids instead.'

Her chuckle was somewhat rueful and Dave remembered that one of her grandchildren, a boy of about six, was pretty wild and almost always seemed to wear her out after only a short visit.

She'd actually claimed that working in the café was relaxing by comparison.

Oh, well . . .

It was only as Dave ended the call that he thought about Ellie. No doubt she'd also be miffed by this news of flooded creeks, as it meant she'd have no chance of getting back to Cairns airport any time soon.

Then he couldn't hold back a small grin. Having Ellie Bright stuck here for another night or two wasn't entirely bad news, was it?

Ellie had taken a while to get to sleep on the stretcher. It hadn't been uncomfortable, exactly – just *different*. It didn't help that she'd found herself overthinking Dave Anders's offer to share his comfy bed with her. But luckily, she'd eventually managed to squash those outlandish fantasies, and once she'd nodded off, she'd slept surprisingly well.

She'd woken a little later than her usual time of six-thirty and jumped up quickly, realising that she hadn't thought to ask Dave what time he needed to start work.

Dave's door was still closed, however, and the café was silent. Meanwhile, outside it was raining. Hard.

Ellie might have been tempted to snuggle back under the sheets and have a lazy lie-in, just listening to the steady drumming. But she needed to show Daphne, her boss, that she hadn't wasted her time by making this trip north. Which meant she'd better get on with her own prep for her interviews.

Thank heavens Renata had already agreed to a meeting, and if this rain kept up, Dave's dad might be free and cooperative as well.

As Ellie's gran had been fond of saying, *No time like the present* . . .

Promptly, Ellie dressed, settled herself in one of the lounge chairs in Dave's little sitting area and began to plan her potential interview questions. Like most lesser mortals, she'd always been in awe of highly esteemed professionals in rare and exalted fields. She loved that her job involved discovering and sharing their secrets to success.

Tapping into Notes on her phone, she began to write questions as they came to her. She would organise them later.

She would ask what a typical day was like for an opera singer. Or for an author. Were there tricks to keeping a singer's voice in top condition? And how did an author keep coming up with exciting new story ideas?

Ellie knew that being an opera singer wasn't quite as glamorous as it looked, but it would be fun to delve into that question. Fans would be interested to know about all the travel and costumes, wigs and makeup, but it would also be good to learn how long it took to prepare for a show. Or how long it took Rolf Anders to write a novel.

Once she started, the questions kept flowing. When had Renata known she wanted to be an opera singer? And when had Rolf changed his career from builder to author?

She would also love to ask Renata why she'd chosen to buy a house so far away from the bright lights of southern cities. Dare she ask that? Was it being too nosy?

Pity she wouldn't also have time to interview Dave about how he became a chef and what it was like to open his own café.

'Hey, Ellie.'

She hadn't heard Dave's door open, and she gave a little start as she looked up to find him standing there in a rumpled T-shirt and boxer shorts, with his long hair tousled and his jaw rough with overnight stubble.

'Good morning,' she said with annoying primness. *Yikes*. Anyone would think this was the first time she'd seen a guy who'd just got out of bed.

'Morning,' Dave said, smiling in an easy-going, doesn't-know-how-good-he-looks kind of way. 'You sleep okay?'

'Yes, thanks.' Ellie was trying to come up with a relaxed opening remark when he jumped in with a question.

'Have you seen the weather reports?'

'Actually, no.' Despite the obviously heavy rain, Ellie hadn't thought to check for any news on her phone. She'd gone straight into conscientious mode, making her notes. Now she wondered what she'd missed. 'What's the story?'

'The creeks are flooded and the road to the highway's cut off,' Dave said gloomily. But then his expression switched to a cheeky smile. 'I'm afraid you're going to be stuck here for a while.'

She knew this should have been bad news. Daphne certainly wouldn't be happy. But although it made no sense, Ellie felt strangely elated.

CHAPTER FOURTEEN

'Yoohoo!' Lisa called as she closed her dripping umbrella and set it just outside the open doorway of Frangipani Café.

It was midmorning and the rain still hadn't let up, so she'd walked to the café in rubber Crocs, which she now slipped off, before wiping her wet feet on the mat.

Just inside the café's doorway, a blackboard had been set on an easel. Menu items were written with white and pink chalk in a surprisingly attractive, curling script, and a pretty bunch of frangipani flowers had also been drawn in one corner.

Who had done this? Lisa wondered. She was quite sure neither Dave nor Janet had ever produced anything so artistic.

Curious, Lisa continued inside and was greeted by the enticing smell of frying onions and the sight of tables set ready for patrons, with red place mats and red-and-white striped paper napkins.

'Hello,' she called again, having heard no response to her initial greeting.

'Hey,' answered Dave's voice. 'In here.'

Lisa crossed to the kitchen. 'I thought I'd pop in and see if you needed a —' She stopped, her mouth gaping open in surprise.

She had expected to find Janet at the stainless-steel bench helping Dave.

Instead, there was a complete stranger – a young woman – a very pretty, twenty-something woman with glossy copper-toned hair and sparkling blue eyes. She was dressed in jeans and a T-shirt and wrapped in a Frangipani Café apron, and she was concentrating rather ferociously on slicing a tomato with one of Dave's massive knives.

Could this be the blackboard artist? Yet another casual girlfriend?

Still in bare feet, Lisa felt less composed than she would have liked, but it was too late to go back and dry her feet properly and put on the spare shoes she'd brought in a shoulder bag.

Dave had stopped stirring a mountain of golden-brown onions and bent to quickly check an oven. 'Hey, Mum,' he called over his shoulder.

'Hi, Dave. Where's Janet?' Lisa was bursting to know.

'She's stuck at her daughter's place in Tully. All the creeks are up.'

'Oh, dear.' Lisa had heard about the flooded creeks, of course, and knew they were causing fresh havoc for so many people. 'You should have called me, Dave. I would have come sooner.'

He adjusted the setting beneath a large pot of soup that stood beside the onions, then turned to her, but now he was grinning. 'I've been lucky enough to have Ellie's help.' He nodded to the pretty girl. 'This is Ellie from Sydney. Ellie Bright.'

'Hello, Ellie.'

'Ellie, this is my mum, Lisa.'

The girl smiled shyly. 'Hello, Mrs Anders.'

'Ellie flew up here yesterday,' Dave explained. 'She came to interview Renata Ramsay, but thanks to this rain, she's stuck here now too.'

'And you're assisting Dave.' Lisa had never been good at handling surprises, but at least she'd stopped blinking and she remembered to smile. 'That's very good of you, Ellie.'

'Oh, I'm happy to help. I can't get back to Sydney and Dave kindly offered me a bed, so this is the least I can do.'

The girl managed to look both innocent and delighted as she shared this information, and Lisa chose not to speculate on the details of her son's accommodation offer.

'And have you managed to interview Renata?' she couldn't help asking.

'Not today,' Ellie responded cheerfully. 'But it's all teed up for tomorrow morning. I felt it was more important to help Dave today.'

Which was Lisa's cue to tell Dave. 'And that's why I'm here too. I came to see if you needed a hand with waiting tables or washing dishes or whatever.'

'That'd be brilliant, Mum.' With an apologetic smile, Dave said, 'I was about to ring you, actually. I added a couple of specials to the regular dinner menu, and the Mission Beach radio station has spread the word. Seems most people have battery-powered radios, and the bookings from folks on the coast have been pouring in. We're pretty much fully booked already.'

'Gosh.' Lisa swallowed a sudden ripple of nervousness. It was all very well to make these offers, but she had very little experience at waiting tables. If there was a crowd, would she cope? 'That's – that's wonderful.'

'I decided I might as well make the most of what's in the fridges while I can,' said Dave. 'But I don't like my chances of restocking any time soon.'

'No, I guess that's going to be a challenge.'

'I'll be keeping lunch simple – just soup, sandwiches or burgers.'

'Sounds very sensible.'

'And even though there's wi-fi, the EFTPOS is a problem, so I'll be running a tab. Ellie's going to help with keeping the list in order.'

Lisa sent a smile to Ellie, who by now had produced quite a pile of sliced tomatoes. 'Do you have much experience in commercial kitchens?'

'Only a little,' she admitted. 'I worked in cafés back in my uni days. But I'm afraid coffees and toasted sandwiches are pretty much my limit.'

'Well, they're always very popular, and it looks like you know how to handle a chef's knife, so that's a pretty good start.'

The girl seemed to appreciate the compliment, as did Dave. But then Dave spoiled the moment by saying, 'Dad and Renata have made a booking for tonight.'

'Ah.' Why hadn't she guessed this would happen?

'Don't worry, Mum,' her son added with a surprisingly sensitive smile. 'You won't have to wait on them. I have two of my regular high-schoolers coming in as well.'

Relieved, Lisa nodded. Then she drew a deep breath. Okay. Waiting tables would be rather different from serving at a buffet, but it would be lunchtime soon, so it was time to make herself useful.

And time to stop fretting about you-know-who.

Thanks to the rain, it had been a somewhat lost day for Rolf. Once he and the Northcover fellow had finished the inspection of Lisa's house, which had, thankfully, suffered no extra damage under the tarp, he'd rung building suppliers in Cairns. They weren't at all optimistic about being able to transport the materials he needed, given the current weather. But his mood had lifted after he'd spent a few hours happily tapping away on his laptop.

Meanwhile, Renata had read more of *First Snow*, but she'd also spent time in her small soundproof studio at the back of her house, doing yoga, apparently, and practising scales – or whatever it was that singers did to keep their voice in top form.

By evening, the rain had finally stopped, but the ground was still waterlogged, the air heavy and humid. The neighbours who were staying with Renata were barbecuing hamburgers and planning an early night.

Rolf was looking forward to taking Renata to dine at the Frangipani Café. He needed to thank her for her hospitality, and he wanted to support Dave, of course.

Rolf knew how keen, maybe even desperate, his son was to make a success of this café, so the least he could do was buy the most expensive wine on offer and add a generous tip.

Fortunately, there was a breeze down on the seafront and Dave's café felt refreshingly cool. The venue wasn't flash, especially with the big front window still boarded up, but this evening, with candles flickering and happily chatting diners, the atmosphere was very pleasant and welcoming.

A slim teenage girl with carefully darkened eyebrows showed Rolf and Renata to a discreet corner table. Their progress across the café caught the attention of several diners, but it was Renata who was quite clearly the attraction, and she rewarded them with gracious smiles.

The girl who was serving handed them menus and asked if they'd like sparkling or tap water. It was only as she left that Rolf saw Lisa, wrapped in an apron and delivering plates to a nearby table.

So unexpected! His comfort level took an instant deep dive. And his dismay wasn't helped by the very tense glance – or was that a glare? – that Lisa had fired in Renata's direction.

Damn it. Lisa's reaction wasn't warranted.

'Are you all right, Rolf?' Renata asked.

He couldn't help a small sigh. 'I'm beginning to wonder if coming here mightn't have been such a bright idea.'

'Oh?'

'My ex is here too, serving tables, and I know that shouldn't be a problem, but . . .'

Already, Renata was turning and looking around the room. 'Oh, yes,' she said brightly. 'I met Dave's mother, Lisa, last night.' And now she was smiling and waving to Lisa, as if they were old friends.

Lisa sent a shy, somewhat embarrassed smile back to Renata, but she avoided looking at Rolf before hurrying back into the kitchen.

Returning her attention to Rolf, Renata asked kindly, 'Are you really uncomfortable?'

'It is a bit weird, with two members of my family – or what used to be my family – working here. I almost feel like I should be out there helping in the kitchen, rather than sitting here being waited on.'

Renata gave a gentle nod. 'I can see that might be awkward. Maybe . . . if you go and speak to them?'

She was right, of course. It was the only sensible thing to do.

'Yes, I'll have a word.' Rolf offered her an apologetic smile. 'If you'll excuse me?'

'Of course.'

He could only hope that Lisa was in a reasonable mood. 'But perhaps I could order some wine for you first?'

'No, no.' Renata waved this offer away and tapped her glass of sparkling water. 'I'm fine. You go and clear the air and then you can relax.'

Right. Rolf stood. He wasn't totally comfortable about deserting his guest, but he knew Renata had plenty of experience at dealing with a curious public.

Just the same, he chose not to make eye contact with other diners as he re-crossed the café. There were bound to be folk he knew and they would be wondering, but too bad. This wasn't the time for complicated explanations.

In the kitchen, everyone was busy. Dave seemed to be managing several stoves at once, flipping mushrooms in a frying pan, adjusting the heat under a saucepan, lifting a lid to inspect a simmering sauce, then bending to check an oven. Next to Dave, a young woman Rolf didn't recognise was carefully grating cheese over linguine.

A teenager was waiting to take the laden plates out to diners, while another girl was pinning an order onto a corkboard. Lisa, who was nearest to Rolf, was collecting wine glasses from a rack, along with a bottle of red.

When she turned and saw Rolf so close, she gave such a start, the bottle slipped from her hand.

Whoosh.

By a miracle, Rolf caught it.

He felt ridiculously shaken. It didn't help that their fingers brushed as he handed the bottle back to her, but she looked even more upset, and she certainly didn't thank him for the rescue.

'What on earth are you doing here in the kitchen?'

'I was hoping for a quick word.'

'Now?'

From the stoves, Dave looked over and frowned at Rolf, but he didn't stop working.

And Lisa was most definitely frowning as she held up the wine and glasses. 'I need to deliver these.'

'Yes, I understand. I'll be quick.'

Her dark eyes remained wary and nervous.

'I checked the house with Northcover this morning,' Rolf told her. 'I thought you might like to know that despite all the rain, the house is okay. Or at least, it's no worse. The tarpaulins seem to have kept the water out.'

'Well, that's very good news. I – I did wonder.'

You could have called.

Or perhaps I should have called you.

Quickly, Rolf said, 'I have the go-ahead to do the work, but the main problem now will be getting the timber supplies. There'll probably be a holdup with the roads cut.'

'Yes.' Lisa's mouth twisted in what might have been a poor attempt at a sympathetic smile. 'I think Dave said something about a ship coming down from Cairns with food supplies. He's placed quite a few orders.'

'That's good to know.' Rolf wondered if this ship might also bring building materials. 'I'll look into that.'

'Actually . . .' To his surprise, Lisa's eyes brightened now, as if a great idea had struck. 'I know a fellow who took his trawler down to Townsville to escape Pixie. I could check to see if he's still down there. He might be able to bring you building supplies.'

'That would be brilliant.' Rolf chanced a smile. 'I'd really appreciate that.'

Lisa's cheeks had turned quite pink and he felt a strange breathlessness, as if he'd been caught in a time warp and was experiencing a moment from their past.

But she was quickly quite businesslike again. 'If I find a spare moment tonight, I'll see what I can find out.'

'That'd be great. Thanks, Lis. Let me know and I'll have a list ready.' Looking around at the busy kitchen again, Rolf said, 'I feel I should be offering to help out here.'

Clearly surprised, Lisa studied him now. 'It's a small kitchen,' she said and for a longish moment, and with a faintly cynical smile, she made a point of looking at his broad shoulders. 'You'd take up too much room.'

Rolf huffed a soft laugh. 'Point taken. I'll leave you to it.'

She turned then to head for the doorway, clearly keen to attend to the guests who were waiting for their wine.

'I'll keep in touch about the house,' he called after her.

Her response was a nod, but she didn't look back.

CHAPTER FIFTEEN

Renata greeted Rolf with a warm, hopeful smile as he returned to his seat. 'All good?'

'As good as I can hope for.'

His companion's expression became thoughtful, and Rolf suspected she would have liked to ask more questions. But she made no further comment, especially as the young girl with the distinctive eyebrows returned to take their orders.

They made their choices, including the most expensive bottle of shiraz on the wine list, and, when the wine arrived, it was as rich and full of depth as Rolf had hoped. He and Renata shared very satisfied smiles.

As Renata set her glass down again, she said, 'I used to avoid alcohol, back when I was younger and more conscientious. To protect my voice.'

'Sorry, I didn't even think of that. I should have asked.'

'No, it's fine, Rolf. I love a good red. And I could have spoken up. But I don't worry so much, these days. Now that I'm fifty, I'm pretty much over the hill – as far as a singer's concerned, especially a soprano.'

'Really?' To Rolf this seemed incredibly unfair. Renata was surely far too young to be facing the end of her career. He'd passed fifty before he'd even started his writing. But then, he supposed singing was a very physical activity, so singers might have a shelf life, like dancers and athletes.

'Don't worry,' she said, as if she'd noticed his concern. 'In my industry, it's been ever thus. The voice is a precarious instrument, and producers are eternally on the lookout for anyone younger, more beautiful and marketable.'

'So does this mean you're looking to retire?'

'Not retire, exactly. But I know my roles in the future will probably be ones designed for more mature voices.' She put finger quotes around the word mature and her tone was disparaging. 'And those roles are rarely the major ones.'

He could understand how this might happen, but he was sure it couldn't be easy to wind down such a public and illustrious career. What came next? Teaching? A change to something entirely different? An unhappy sense of displacement?

Grateful for the relative privacy of their corner table, he asked carefully, trying to find the right words, 'You've never mentioned a partner.'

'Possibly because I don't have one.' Then, with an ambiguous smile, 'Not currently, at least.'

Rolf nodded and reached for his wine. Despite the relative privacy of their table, he should have known better than to initiate this conversation in his son's café and with his ex hovering in the wings.

'I've never been married,' Renata said next. 'And I don't have children. My career has always come first.'

He didn't like to ask if she had regrets about these life choices.

And then, she added, 'But there *was* a man who was very important to me. He was German and his name was Gerhard. Fo' more than ten years we were incredibly happy together. But he died. Of cancer.'

Her face tightened and she dropped her gaze as she told him this.

'I'm so sorry,' he said softly, and a small silence fell, while they both took more sips of their wine.

Then their young waitress returned with their meals – slow-cooked lamb for Rolf and seafood pasta for Renata.

With her cheerfulness restored, Renata said, 'After last night's event, I already knew that your son's an excellent chef, but this looks amazing.' She sampled her first mouthful and her face broke into a rapturous grin. 'Oh, my God, Rolf, it's superb.'

Rolf had also tasted his lamb and found it rich and flavourful and tender. *Good one, Davo.* He sent a mental high five to his son, and he couldn't help being pleased that Renata was also impressed.

She was still smiling and shaking her head in amazement. 'You don't expect gourmet food like this in such an out-of-the-way little town – especially so soon after a cyclone.'

'I guess not,' Rolf agreed. 'But Dave's worked in top restaurants all over the world.'

'And yet he chose to come back to Beacon Bay?'

'Indeed.' Rolf was glad she hadn't asked why his son had made this decision. It was a question he'd also wondered about and he hadn't yet arrived at a convincing answer.

He supposed he could have asked Dave straight out, but his son was sensitive and still lacking in confidence, despite his many successes. Rolf hadn't wanted to rattle him. But with that thought, he was caught by an unexpected slug of regret.

Here was Dave, his youngest and sometimes troubled boy, bravely starting up a restaurant on home soil, and his family should all have been here to celebrate with him. His mother, his brothers, his sisters-in-law should have all been sitting here, enjoying this delicious food and singing Dave's praises to the skies.

'*You* chose to leave, though.'

Rolf blinked and took a moment to process Renata's comment. 'Well, yes,' he said. 'After the divorce it made sense to leave and start somewhere fresh.'

'Pity,' Renata said, but then she quickly countered this. 'Sorry, that's me being selfish. It's just that I've so enjoyed meeting you, Rolf.'

'This is a small town,' he replied. 'Lisa and I needed space.' But this wasn't the first time he'd worried that the divorce had also deepened cracks in their family.

It seemed appropriate to slow their conversation now as they gave their food the attention it deserved. But eventually Rolf felt compelled to ask, 'I'm a little curious as to why you bought a house in the Bay. I know it's not your full-time residence, but I've always imagined that opera singers would prefer to stay in major cities – close to concert halls and other musicians.'

She smiled. 'You're right. That's our usual scene, although in reality, our only true home is the stage, and we live out of suitcases. Mind you, when I was with Gerhard, we made our home base in Vienna and I loved living there.'

'I can imagine why. I think I read once that Vienna is the world's most liveable city?'

'I wouldn't be surprised. It's full of history, art and culture, and the amenities are first class.'

Her plate was almost empty now. She set down her fork, sat back and looked across to the other diners, seeming to consider what she wanted to say next. 'But I have to admit, more recently, city life has been losing its appeal.'

'I can understand that,' said Rolf. 'But then, while I'm happy to visit cities for brief periods, I've never wanted to live in one.'

Renata nodded. 'I suppose knowing that my career will change in the future has been part of why I've felt this way. In my world, city life is all about egos and celebrity status, about getting noticed and networking, socialising with all the right people. Always being on show. I've had enough of that. I woke up one morning and realised I wanted something else. Something more.' She gave a small shrug. 'Or maybe something less. Whatever – I had an urge to find something quite different.'

'You've certainly found that here.'

The serious expression that had accompanied her explanation softened. 'My secret love has always been the seaside. I adore the sea in all its moods – pounding with rough surf or serene and tropical – and I love going for long walks on sandy beaches.'

'Do you sing on those walks?' Rolf couldn't help asking.

Renata chuckled. 'Sometimes. Not loudly, of course, but I might sing if there's not too many people around.'

He thought how amazing it would be to come across a woman like Renata singing on a beach. He could picture her pouring her heart into her song, lifting her voice and her graceful hands to the heavens.

Perhaps it was a scene he could use in a novel? Could the singer's body be found washed up later in the shallows?

Somewhat guiltily he realised Renata was still speaking.

'I wasn't expecting to come so far north, but I looked around in northern New South Wales. I checked out Byron Bay, of course, and then over the border to the Gold and Sunshine coasts. But none of those places felt quite the right fit. They're beautiful, but they were all so bustling and busy. I wanted something quieter. A true retreat.'

Giving her wine glass a thoughtful twist, she said, 'Then I remembered a holiday from my childhood, when I'd come here to Beacon Bay with my parents. I mustn't have been more than six or seven, but it has always been such a happy memory. There was something rather magical about that time and place. I think it was because my parents were so happy here.'

Her eyes were shining as she shared this memory, but the light quickly died and she gave a shrug. 'Not long after they went back to Sydney, their marriage fell apart.'

Rolf, having experienced a marriage that had shattered like falling crockery into countless pieces, could find no ready response for this.

'Anyway,' Renata went on as if she hadn't expected him to comment. 'The feeling began to grow in me that this could be my happy place.'

'And I'm sure it will be,' he said quietly. 'Although this cyclone won't have helped. It's a pity it ruined your party plans.'

Smiling again and leaning closer, so her voice was little more than a whisper, Renata said, 'This is going to sound terrible, but I didn't really mind that my city friends couldn't come to my party. Half of them were waiting to grab my role in the next production.'

At this Rolf chuckled, then he lifted the wine bottle and shared what was left between their glasses.

CHAPTER SIXTEEN

The rush was over. Only one table of diners had lingered – Ellie supposed there would always be at least one. Tonight, it was a group of eight who'd ordered desserts along with a further two bottles of wine, with the result that their voices and laughter had become progressively louder.

By the time they'd eventually called it a night, the teenage girls who'd been waiting tables had already left and the kitchen clean-up had begun. Ellie was weary, but her tiredness was counterbalanced by a surprising sense of achievement.

The day had been a huge success for Dave. Customers had made a point of popping over to the kitchen to let him know how much they'd enjoyed their meals. In fact, they'd raved, and although Ellie's role had been minor and very much a case of strictly follow-ing Dave's sharply barked orders, she'd loved every minute of their busy teamwork.

She was stacking glassware into a dishwasher when she saw Lisa, Dave's mother, reach for a huge soup pot that needed to be washed separately in the sink.

'No, Mum,' Dave called. 'There's no need for you to do that.'

He went to her and gave her shoulder a gentle pat. 'Thanks for your help. You've been amazing, but I'm sure you should go home now. You've worked two nights in a row and you look dead on your feet.'

'Yes,' Ellie couldn't help chiming in. 'Please, Mrs Anders, don't feel you have to stay. I can help Dave with finishing up here.'

As she said this, Dave flashed her a grateful grin that sent a highly unnecessary river of warmth rushing through her.

His mother stood for a moment, as if she was making up her mind. Then she smiled tiredly and nodded. 'Okay,' she said. 'I'll call it a night.' Turning back to her son, she kissed his cheek. 'Congrats, Davo, you were brilliant tonight.'

Her use of his nickname touched Ellie unexpectedly. Without warning, she was missing her own parents and wondering if they might have used a pet name for her in moments of fondness. It wasn't often that Ellie wished she was part of a close-knit family, but when the longing arrived, it hit hard.

'We've just gotta hope those supplies come through soon,' Dave was saying. 'I need to keep the momentum going.'

His mother nodded. 'At least it's stopped raining and there's no talk of more rain in the near future.'

'Yeah, and it was great you were able to give Dad good news about that shipment from Townsville.'

'It was, wasn't it? The last thing Rolf wants is to have to hang around here any longer than he has to.' On this somewhat gruffly delivered note, Dave's mother gathered up her things and departed.

Dave went back to cleaning the stoves and benchtops, while Ellie switched the dishwasher on and then moved to tackle the pot in the sink.

'We could leave that pot to soak till morning,' Dave told her.

'I don't mind doing it now. Wouldn't it be good to have everything finished?'

He sent her another of his skin-heating smiles. 'Don't be too perfect, Ellie, or I might not be able to let you go.'

And I might not want to leave.

Wtf? Where had that thought come from? How could she find herself in that headspace after just one day?

Ellie concentrated hard on the simple task of filling the sink with hot water, adding detergent and then scrubbing at the bottom of the soup pot where pieces of potato had stuck. It was an easy task, soon finished, and when she set the pot on a rack to drain and turned around, she found that Dave was lifting two laden plates from a warmer. Pan-fried barramundi and sweet potato chips.

Oh, my. Her tummy rumbled.

'Leftovers,' he said. 'I'm guessing you're hungry?'

'I sure am. I'll get the lemon and aioli.' Adding such extras to the required dishes had been among Ellie's many tasks this evening.

Now, having set the plates on one of the steel benches, Dave quickly fetched a beer and a glass of chilled wine. They ate sitting on high stools, too tired and hungry to bother with much conversation. Ellie was yawning before she finished.

'You're going to sleep in the bed tonight,' Dave told her.

Before her lips could form 'no', he was shaking his head.

'No argument, Ellie. I know you're not used to being on your feet for so many hours. You *have* to be tired.'

She *was* tired. Her back and feet were aching too. And tomorrow she would have to be up bright and early and on the ball to interview Renata – and perhaps Rolf Anders, if he was available. She would also have to attend to all the text messages that had been rolling in from Daphne.

She certainly didn't have the strength for an argument, so she nodded. 'Thanks, Dave. Would you like to go first in the shower?'

As she asked this, she made the mistake of looking up and catching a look in his coffee-brown eyes that didn't merely warm her skin, but set it aflame. For too long, the look lingered between them and simmered, leaving Ellie trapped by a breathless tension, while she totally forgot about being tired and battled fizzing thoughts of getting naked with this gorgeous guy.

But then Dave was shaking his head. 'You shower first and I'll find clean sheets.'

'Dave, you really shouldn't have to —'

He held up a hand. 'It's okay. I really appreciate all the help you've given me today and the very least I owe you is a comfortable night's sleep.'

She almost said something reckless like – *it's a double bed, isn't it?* Luckily, she stopped herself just in time.

But the sudden intensity in Dave's eyes suggested he'd been thinking something very similar, and when their gazes connected again and held, Ellie's heart beat like thudding horse hooves.

No, Ellie, don't be foolish.

Leaving Beacon Bay was going to be difficult enough. Fooling around with Dave would only bring her emotions deeper into the mix, and she needed to remember that her heart was not available for target practice.

One of these days, she was going to meet a guy who was nice and ordinary and safe, and she'd have the long and happy marriage her parents had been denied. Unfortunately, while Dave Anders was *nice* to the nth degree, he wasn't any version of ordinary, so for Ellie, he also wasn't safe.

Pity about that.

All was quiet when Rolf drove Renata back to her house. Her other guests had already retired, leaving a single lamp glowing on the front doorstep, although Renata still needed the torch from Rolf's phone to help her get the door key into the lock.

'Coffee or a nightcap? Or both?' she asked as she moved quickly to light candles on the coffee table in her lounge room.

'Can I be boring and ask for a cup of tea?'

'Of course.' Renata lit more candles on a sideboard. 'And just for the record, Rolf Anders, you could never be boring.'

His reaction was a dry chuckle. 'You might change your mind, if you saw me locked away for days on end, hunting words.'

She'd been heading for the kitchen and now, in the doorway, she paused and turned back to him. 'That sounds as if you're speaking from experience.'

'I am. It's a big part of the reason I'm divorced.'

Her eyes widened. 'Good heavens.'

'Lisa hated it,' he said tiredly. 'All those hours I spent shut away in my study made her furious.'

'And that finished your marriage? How – how amazing.'

'You're surprised?'

'Well, yes. Very.' Renata moved into the kitchen, turned on another lamp, found matches and lit the burner. 'Perhaps I've spent too much time in the world of opera,' she said as she filled the kettle and set it to heat. 'There's always so much over-the-top drama, including endless infidelity, both on and off the stage. I tend to automatically assume that some kind of cheating is involved in most relationship breakups.'

'I guess the whole concept of cheating is open to interpretation,' suggested Rolf.

'Perhaps . . .'

Hearing the question mark in her tone, he decided to explain. 'Lisa could never understand why I'd want to give up my safe, stable business to take a gamble on a writing career. She'd married a builder, not a writer. I was pulling the rug from under her and she most definitely felt cheated.'

'So she obviously couldn't understand how very strong that yearning for artistic expression can be.'

'No, and I was damn stubborn about it.' He gave a shrug. 'We both were.'

Renata's expression was solemn as she considered this, before turning to the cupboard to find mugs and teabags. 'I guess real-life stories are always more complicated than the ones in a novel, or a stage drama.'

'Yes, I'm sure they are.'

'And it sounds as if it can't have been an easy divorce, if there ever is such a thing. But you're okay now, Rolf? Have you been able to – to move on? Is that the right term for it?'

'Yes, it took a while, but I believe I have moved on. Or perhaps I should say that I thought I had – but having to attend to this cyclone damage adds another layer of complication.'

'I can imagine,' she said quietly.

'Lisa doesn't want me here. I don't want to be here. But her roof needs fixing and builders are scarce.'

'And you have a chance to get back in her good books.'

He stared at her for a moment, wondering if she was making a joke, but no, she looked quite serious. He shook his head. 'That's not going to happen.'

By now the tea was ready. Renata handed him a mug and they returned to the lounge room. As she sat opposite him, she set her mug down, kicked off her shoes and stretched, rather luxuriously. Then, reaching for the hairclip that must have secured the neat updo she'd worn to the restaurant, she gave her hair one brief flick and silken auburn tresses were rippling over her shoulders.

Rolf drew a sharp breath.

CHAPTER SEVENTEEN

'Ellie, where the bloody hell are you?'

'Sorry, Daphne, I'm still in Beacon Bay.'

'What's going on?'

After a surprisingly sound night's sleep, Ellie was sitting on the edge of the bed, still in her nightie. Her phone on the nightstand had been set to silent, but the furious buzzing after two missed calls had finally woken her.

'It's been pretty wild up here,' she told her boss. 'But I was planning to answer all your texts this morning. Did you get my message yesterday about the roads being cut?'

'Yeah, yeah, but are you going to do those interviews?'

'Yes, I have a session booked with Renata Ramsay for this morning.'

'Thank God for small mercies. And lock in Rolf Anders as well.'

'I'll try.'

'Don't just try, Ellie, make sure of it. There's a good story there, with the cyclone and both of those celebrities trapped in Beacon Bay.'

'Yes, I know. Rolf Anders is pretty busy, though. He's mending a damaged roof, but I'll definitely speak to him.'

'Rolf Anders is what?'

'Mending a roof?'

'How on earth?'

'It's his ex-wife's house. It was damaged by a falling tree during the cyclone.'

'Good grief. That's gold, Ellie. Grab the story, for God's sake.'

'Okay, I'll certainly do my best. Actually, I was wondering . . . Rolf's son is here as well, and he's a fantastic chef.' She wouldn't tell Daphne that she was planning to help Dave out with today's lunchtime rush at his café, but she did add, 'I actually worked in his kitchen last night 'cause —'

'Really? You're not being sidetracked by that son, are you?'

'Sidetracked?'

'That's polite speak, Ellie. I'm in the office. Not alone.'

'Oh. Well, no.' Ellie smiled as she thought of Dave with his man bun and his sexy grin. 'No sidetracking.' *More's the pity.*

'Anyway,' said Daphne. 'It sounds like you've got stories coming out your ears. Use your journo's nose and make sure you don't waste a single crumb.'

'Okay, Daphne, but I'll also —'

Her boss had already hung up.

The interview with Renata went really well. Ellie was thrilled. The singer seemed to know exactly what Ellie was interested in, quite possibly because she'd been asked similar questions umpteen times before. Nevertheless, Renata was very patient and cooperative and also happy to add little titbits to give the story extra colour.

She talked about her childhood and how her mother had signed her up for singing lessons when she was only nine, and then she told Ellie about the wonderful tutor she'd been lucky to discover later on, after she went to London. He'd more or less made her start all over again, teaching her to use her voice in a whole new way.

Renata described her busy and sometimes exhausting lifestyle, flying all over the world to so many concert halls, but she added funny stories about wigs and costumes, and other inspiring stories about special mentors and friends, balancing these with the realities of constant practice and rigorous rehearsals.

She even told Ellie a hilarious 'in house' tale about a cheeky soprano who'd sung with a very famous tenor – no names, of course. Apparently, just as the tenor had been poised to fill the concert hall with the opening notes of a hugely famous aria, the soprano had whispered in his ear, 'I'm not wearing any undies.'

'Oh, my,' Ellie laughed. 'That's priceless.' Then, almost in disbelief, 'I can't use it, though, can I?'

Renata shrugged. 'If you like. As long as you keep it all anonymous.'

'Of course.'

'And you might like to explain there was no malice in the joke,' Renata added. 'The soprano didn't do that to undermine him, or anything nasty. In a stressful career, we sometimes let off steam in weird ways.'

Ellie nodded. 'I get it.'

But the conversation also left Ellie with questions about her own life. She'd just spent a second night sleeping alone, and not being sidetracked, to use Daphne's terminology, while the delicious Dave Anders had remained next door on the stretcher. But she couldn't help seeing herself as terribly straitlaced, compared to the circus Renata had described.

There was a whole world out there, full of folks having fun without hang-ups, and Ellie found herself wondering if her caution was unwarranted. Perhaps her strict Scottish grandmother's upbringing had left a deeper impact than she'd realised.

Then again, perhaps she'd been too easily impressed by Renata's over-the-top stories? Surely she should be grateful that her common sense had saved her from what could only be a casual hook-up with Dave? Which, given her history, would almost certainly be followed by another round of heartache.

By midafternoon, Rolf had managed to clear most of the ripped metal and broken timber that had fallen inside the house. The easiest way to remove this rubble had been to toss it from the balcony onto the lawn below, where some of the falling pieces had damaged Lisa's shrubbery. She would no doubt think he'd been too careless, but the alternative would have meant carting everything down the internal staircase, and that was far too time consuming.

At least the SES had been able to remove the massive fallen milky pine before the roads were cut, and now, with the first stage of the clear-up pretty much completed, he was taking a moment to sit on a back step and enjoy a cup of tea from a thermos, when he heard a car pull up.

Lisa?

Rolf instantly tensed and sent another quick glance to the rubble littering her yard. Was he in for a lecture?

But it wasn't his ex who appeared around the corner of the house. It was the eye-catching young woman who'd been helping Dave in the café.

Rolf might have relaxed if the girl's smile hadn't looked so nervous. He hoped she wasn't bringing bad news.

'Hi, Mr Anders,' she said. 'I know you're very busy, but I was hoping to have a quick word.'

'Sure,' he replied, puzzled.

'My name's Ellie Bright and I work for the PR agency that helps promote Renata Ramsay.' She held out her hand and Rolf quickly got to his feet.

'Hello, Ellie. Good to meet you. You're also working in my son's café, aren't you?'

'Yes.' This time when she smiled, a very attractive dimple formed in her cheek. 'I flew up from Sydney to see Renata, but now, with the roads cut, I'm stuck here. Dave kindly offered me a bed at his place and so I'm helping him as fair exchange.'

Dave had offered her a bed, eh? Rolf wasn't at all surprised.

'I interviewed Renata this morning,' Ellie went on. 'And I understand that your publishers usually use a different PR company, but this is such a unique situation – to have two celebrities like you and Renata both here in Beacon Bay because of a cyclone – I was hoping to speak to you as well.'

'I see,' Rolf said cautiously. 'I presume you also know I'm staying at Renata's house?'

'Yes. That's part of the reason I ended up at Dave's place.'

'I see,' Rolf said again and then realised he sounded like a second-rate TV detective who didn't really have a clue. 'So, this story you'd like to write – it doesn't need to focus on where I'm staying, does it? I mean I —' He couldn't believe he was making a dog's breakfast of this very simple conversation.

'No, no, nothing like that,' Ellie assured him. 'The story that has my boss excited is this one!' She gestured to the house with its blue tarpaulin roof, to the rubble strewn over the lawn. 'The fact that a writer of your international standing is also able to mend a broken roof.'

'Ah.' Rolf nodded. 'You know this is my ex-wife's house.'

'Yes, and I think it's fantastic that you're prepared to —'

'Good heavens.'

Rolf swivelled as a new figure charged around the corner of the house. This time it was definitely Lisa, and she was marching towards him in her usual businesslike manner. But she came to an abrupt halt and then remained perfectly still, with her mouth open, as she took in the scene.

Rolf knew it was ungallant, but he couldn't help hoping that Ellie Bright might provide sufficient distraction from the damage he'd done to Lisa's garden.

Then, as if in answer to his silent prayer, it was Ellie who broke the awkward silence. 'Hello, Mrs Anders.'

Lisa stared at her. 'You're Dave's kitchenhand. Weren't you working at the café just a few minutes ago?'

'That's right.' Ellie's smile was a bright contrast to Lisa's scowl. 'But I'm juggling two jobs today.'

'Ellie's also a journalist,' said Rolf, now conscious of a need to rescue Ellie from his ex at her frowning best. 'We're teeing up a time for her to interview me.'

Lisa gave a puzzled shake of her head, as if this news was somehow incomprehensible.

'Actually, Ellie,' Rolf said now. 'I'll be busy here for the rest of the afternoon, but I'll call in at the café when I'm finished. Perhaps we can talk about a time for the interview then?'

'Absolutely, Mr Anders. That'd be awesome. Thank you.' Ellie's pretty blue eyes were shining, as if Rolf had made her day. 'Actually, while I'm here, would you mind if I took a photo? Of the damage?'

Rolf sent a questioning glance to Lisa, who rolled her eyes to the heavens, as if this was the dizzy limit, but then she also gave a shrug and said, 'Sure, why not?'

'Great!' enthused Ellie, who ignored any tension and snapped away happily. When she was done, she sent another bright smile and a jaunty wave to Lisa. 'I'll be off then. Bye, Mrs Anders.'

'Bye,' Lisa responded faintly. 'Oh, and you'd better call me Lisa.'

'Bye, Lisa,' Ellie corrected politely.

Lisa fell silent while the girl departed, but she made a point of returning her gaze to the litter on her lawn. The broken rafters, the pieces of roofing iron and clumps of plaster were not a pretty sight. She frowned and pursed her lips when she saw the smashed stems of her ginger and heliconia plants.

Don't start, Rolf warned her silently. The last thing he needed was a revving.

Perhaps she sensed this. Instead of delivering the expected complaint, she said simply and quietly, 'I'll help you with cleaning this up.'

Rolf swallowed his surprise. 'Thanks. I'd appreciate that, although there's not a lot we can do right now. As soon as the roads are clear I'll hire a handy skip.'

She nodded, her mouth suddenly twisting in a sceptical smile. 'You might need to order two skips.'

'Quite possibly,' he agreed.

She was wearing jeans and now she retrieved her phone from her back pocket. 'I should probably take plenty of photos of all this, as well. For insurance.'

'Yes. I'm sure that's a good idea. They already have photos inside of the hole in the roof and damaged furniture upstairs. I've left that upstairs for now, so you'll want to check it. But I rolled up the carpet from the dining room. It's at the back of the garage at the moment.'

'You don't think it's salvageable?'

'I'm not sure.'

'It could be a while before I can get to a carpet cleaner.'

'Yes. I was wondering if it might be worth giving it a good clean here – maybe even with the hose to start with. And then you could try drying it in the sun. You never know . . .'

As Rolf said this, his thoughts inadvertently flashed back to the day they'd bought the vibrant, tropical carpet. He and Lisa had been so excited when they'd driven back from Cairns and spread it on the newly varnished dining room floor, before setting the table and chairs carefully in place.

At the time, Lisa had been in raptures. 'It's like something you'd expect to see in one of those flash magazines!'

'I just hope the wet carpet doesn't smell like a wet dog,' she said now.

Rolf blinked, coming back to the present. 'Well, I'm afraid it's certainly on the nose at the moment.'

A beat later, he felt compelled to ask a question he'd been wanting to ask her since he'd arrived back in the Bay. 'On the subject of dogs, I was wondering how Tucker is these days. I haven't seen him around at all.'

He'd been incredibly fond of the beautiful border collie that he and Lisa had bought as a pup about thirteen or so years ago. Even before that, when Dave, their youngest, had still been quite small, they'd had a labrador called Bailey. Dave had been heartbroken when Bailey died. But six months later, Tucker had won everyone's heart.

Such a beautiful, intelligent, faithful companion he'd been. 'Tucker's okay, isn't he, Lis?'

'Oh, dear.' Her face had gone quite pale and she looked away quickly, but not before Rolf caught a suspicious silver sheen in her eyes.

Anger flared. Surely, she would have let him know if Tucker had passed away. The dog was like a member of the family.

But then, he had to admit there'd been years of silence between them, with not so much as a Christmas card exchanged, and he was as much to blame for that as Lisa.

'I – I'm sorry,' she said now, softly.

'You mean Tucker's gone? He – he died?'

Lisa nodded and her mouth pulled out of shape, as if she was fighting an urge to cry. She drew a noisy breath and her throat rippled as she swallowed. 'I should have let you know, shouldn't I?'

As she asked this, she looked up and there was a painful mix of regret and uncertainty in her dark brown eyes.

What could he say?

They both knew perfectly well that Lisa should have told him about this. Of course, she understood how fond he'd been of Tucker. Rolf had always been the family member who religiously took their dog for walks on the beach. Tucker had loved digging up treasures – pieces of driftwood, strings of dried seaweed, a bird skeleton or a plastic water bottle.

During the unhappy weeks of divorce wrangling, Lisa had been only too conscious that Rolf had come close to contesting the custody of their pet. If he hadn't planned to travel overseas as part of the research for his novels, he might have argued harder.

'What happened?' he asked now.

'He died of old age, Rolf. The vet assured me that he wasn't suffering, but everything was failing – his hearing, his joints, his heart. He – he died in his sleep.'

'Wow.'

She shot him an emotion-filled glance. 'You know how he always slept on that mat near the kitchen door? One morning he just didn't get up.'

Rolf kept his lips tightly compressed as his vivid imagination pictured Lisa's heartbreaking discovery. It was a moment or two before he could speak. 'That's the best way to go, I guess. And he had a fair innings.'

'Yes.'

'Where did you . . .?' He couldn't quite finish this question.

'He's buried down there.' Lisa pointed past all the rubble and mess to the very back of the yard. 'Under one of the lilly pillies along the fence.'

'Ah, yes, of course.' Tucker had also been a huge fan of chasing and fetching tennis balls, and he'd been particularly fond of diving in under that dense bushy hedge to find them.

'He never got tired of chasing those balls, although he was much slower towards the end.' With a wistfully sad smile, Lisa said,

'I – I buried a ball with him and made a little cairn of stones and shells. You know how he loved to sniff at them on the beach. They should still be there. I doubt the cyclone would have shifted them.'

Rolf nodded, his eyes stinging, his throat tight. 'Nice touch. I'll definitely check that out sometime.'

'I may as well show you now.'

Surprised, Rolf took a beat or two to respond. 'Sure, thanks.'

Sidestepping the cyclone debris, they crossed the length of the lawn where the boys had once kicked soccer balls. The yard was still edged by the stone-rimmed gardens that he and Lisa had once planned and built together with so much enthusiasm.

At the midpoint along the back hedge, Lisa stopped and pointed. 'Yes, it's held up okay.'

The cairn was made from carefully stacked smooth sea-washed stones and shells, as well as little pieces of driftwood and coral.

Rolf pictured her carefully building this, making sure it was strong and sturdy. He managed a nod and a gruff 'Thanks', but he didn't trust himself to make eye contact, and standing around in silence was unhelpful. It left way too much room for memories.

Abruptly, he said, 'I guess I should show you what I've managed so far with the roof.'

Lisa nodded and together they headed for the stairs.

CHAPTER EIGHTEEN

Renata had just finished her daily yoga routine in her little backyard studio, and she was about to move on to her vocal exercises, when she found a strange creature staring at her through the window.

She jumped and gave a little scream. But almost immediately, she came to her senses. Those peering eyes belonged to a cassowary.

Renata had seen cassowaries a few times since she'd bought her house in Beacon Bay, but only in the wild and at a distance, never in her backyard. This bird was standing perfectly still, close to the glass, and staring in at her with startling amber eyes.

At least it was on the other side of the glass, and now that she'd calmed down, she couldn't help admiring her visitor, even though it was enormous, and she knew how very dangerous it could be, with its massive size, its huge clawed feet and scarily strong, sharp beak.

Most of its plumage was an especially glossy black, although its neck was vivid blue and purple. But its impact was made all the more splendid by a tall brown helmet on the top of its head, as well as interesting long red wattles, trailing like a scarf or a priest's stole.

It looked as striking and majestic as any opera star on stage, and Renata could well understand why the locals treasured and respected these unique flightless birds. No wonder there were so many signs on roadsides throughout this stretch of the coast, warning visiting motorists to slow down to avoid a collision with cassowaries.

At least *this* bird showed no immediate signs of having been injured by the cyclone, but Renata was very aware that its rainforest habitat must have been badly smashed and defoliated. She supposed it would be feeling extremely disoriented and quite possibly lost.

'I'm sorry,' she told it. 'But I'm not sure that I can help you.' She wasn't in the habit of talking to wildlife, and her window was soundproof, so there was no real point. But this bird's continued intense stare felt like an attempt to communicate. 'Are you hungry?'

She was sure she'd read that cassowaries mostly ate berries, a fact she'd found quite astonishing given how enormous they were. And she supposed there was a very good chance that the berries they depended on had been stripped by the fierce cyclonic winds and flattened by falling branches.

But although she felt sorry for this visitor, she wasn't inclined to cut up fruit to feed it. She fancied she'd heard that feeding cassowaries was illegal, but even if it was allowed, fetching the fruit would entail a risky journey across the yard to her kitchen and she wasn't prepared to render herself vulnerable to this fellow's beak and claws.

She supposed the only sensible option was to continue with her singing practice and hope it wandered away.

By the end of the afternoon, Lisa was feeling somewhat better about working with Rolf, but the process had by no means been a piece of cake.

Their conversation about Tucker had left her feeling both guilty and vulnerable, and, at first, as she and Rolf went upstairs to check out the house, an unnerving tension lingered. Every glance they shared seemed charged with discomfort, every question or answer felt stilted.

As they examined the sodden carpet and the damaged furniture, Lisa was conscious of an unavoidable familiarity. This man's grey-green eyes beneath bushy brows, his squarish hands, his wide-shouldered stance, even his mellow voice had been an intimate part of her life for so long.

While they discussed cleaning down walls and potential areas that needed repainting, Lisa was taunted by unhelpful memories. Rolf was explaining the repairs he had planned, but she was remembering the giddy happiness of those exciting days when they'd first moved into this house.

It didn't help that she'd sensed this conversation was almost as difficult for Rolf as if was for her. She'd been in danger of completely losing it, until she'd reminded herself of the many reasons their breakup had been necessary. After all, this was also the man who'd shattered her dreams.

When Rolf had turned his focus to writing, he and Lisa had no longer felt like a team. He'd locked himself away, leaving her to feel alienated and unnecessary. *And* he'd been bloody stubborn about it.

This afternoon, as she'd indulged in these anger-sparking recollections, common sense eventually prevailed. She concentrated on current practicalities – which had always been her forte. With the discussions about the roof more or less settled, Rolf elected to take the carpet outside for a hose down, while Lisa filled a bucket with hot water and detergent and threw herself into the task of cleaning up her kitchen.

Fortunately, there wasn't much water damage inside the cupboards and drawers. She left the doors open to air, but all the contents – pantry items, cookware and crockery – seemed surprisingly fine. While she was at it, she retrieved items from her pantry that she could stow in large storage containers to take to the Community Hall. The council had set up barbecues and cooktops, and townsfolk were leaving food donations – a lovely idea – and she would set aside a few things to take to share with Heidi as well.

Then she turned her attention to the walls and tiles, doors, benchtops and flooring, all of which were splattered with mud, leaves and other debris. One of the tiles on the backsplash behind the stove had been cracked by a flying piece of metal and, while Lisa was scrubbing, she played with the idea of replacing it with something more decorative.

Perhaps she could scatter a few extra coloured tiles around for a new effect? A change would be quite uplifting.

She was polishing the stove cooktop when Rolf came up the stairs, holding out his phone.

'It's Renata,' he said. 'I thought it would be best if you spoke to her.'

'Me?' Lisa couldn't imagine why she should speak to this woman. *His* woman.

Rolf smiled, as if he understood her surprise and, for a moment, Lisa wondered if he might reassure her that he and Renata weren't 'a thing'.

'It's about a cassowary,' he said. 'And I know you've had experience helping the wildlife rangers. You were very busy after Cyclone Larry.'

Still recovering from the surprise, Lisa took the phone quickly, aware that most people's batteries were running low, although she'd been lucky enough to recharge her own phone using the power provided by Dave's generator.

She spoke in her most businesslike voice. 'Hello, Renata, Lisa here. How can I help you?'

'Lisa, Rolf tells me you're the person to speak to about cassowaries.'

'I might be. Do you have one in your yard?'

'Yes, good guess. It's been here on and off for most of the day, and I'm pretty sure it's hungry.'

'Okay. That's not surprising, actually. Your place backs onto the forest and cassowaries often wander into people's yards after a cyclone.'

'This fellow seems a bit lost. But I wanted to check. There are rules about feeding them, aren't there?'

'Well, yes, normally it's illegal. The authorities don't want cassowaries associating our towns and backyards with food. It's not safe for the birds or the people.'

'No, I can imagine.'

'But everything's a bit different after a cyclone. The people who live near the forests often cut up fruit and take it out into the scrub at night and scatter it around. That way the cassowaries can find the food without associating it with people and settlements.'

'I see. That sounds sensible.' Renata gave a nervous little laugh. 'Except that I've been eyeing off this chap's beak and claws, so I'm wondering if I'm brave enough to go into the forest at night.'

'You should be fine.' Rolf was still standing near Lisa and she sent him a defiant smile. 'After all, you'll have Rolf. I'm sure he'd be more than happy to go with you.'

There was an extra beat in the pause before Renata replied. 'Of course, good idea.'

'But I'll also find out what the wildlife rangers have planned,' Lisa offered. 'A group of us got together after Larry and Yasi, and we cut up bucketloads of fruit in the Community Hall. Then the rangers took it all away and distributed it as they saw fit.'

'Oh, how wonderful. I really like the sound of that.'

'I'll keep you posted.' Lisa was about to hang up, but Renata was talking again.

'Yes, please do let me know. If I'm still here, I'd love to help. I'd like to be more involved in the community.'

'Right.' Lisa wasn't too fussed about the prospect of Rolf's latest 'lady friend' elbowing her way into their close-knit little community, but she knew this was mean-spirited. 'All the best, Renata.'

Promptly disconnecting, she tried to keep her face noncommittal as she handed the phone back to Rolf. She read slight puzzlement in his eyes, but he didn't question her – and she wasn't sure what to make of that.

CHAPTER NINETEEN

Dave was on a high after another successful night in his café with a regular flow of very happy diners.

Several locals, including a few he'd gone to school with, had ducked around the kitchen doorway to give him the thumbs up.

'Ace evening, Dave.'

'We had no idea you were such a talented chef.'

Behind these compliments, Dave had heard unspoken hints to his former 'loser' status, but he could wear that. These were the sorts of messages he'd been secretly hoping for.

Tonight he'd also been really pleased with his team. The high schoolers had put in another terrific effort as waiters, and his mum had shown up again, mainly to look after serving the alcohol, which she didn't believe should be left to teenagers. But Dave knew she'd also been working on the house and she had looked worn out, so he'd made sure she left early.

Ellie, meanwhile, had been amazing. Not only had she chopped a gazillion onions and tomatoes and capsicums, but she'd also attended to stirring any sauces that needed attention, as well as any cheese grating and garnishing Dave had required. On top of that, as the EFTPOS was still unreliable and Dave was keeping orders on a tab, Ellie had taken care of recording the necessary names and phone numbers of the customers.

Now, with the last plate stacked in the dishwasher, she looked across to him and saw that he'd saved leftover mushroom risotto for their meals.

She sent him an ecstatic grin. 'Wow, Dave! That risotto was such a popular choice tonight, I didn't expect there'd be any left.'

He gave a deliberately casual shrug. 'The supply boat arrived this afternoon with a stack of fresh mushrooms, and I couldn't resist making extra.' He didn't add that he'd seen Ellie eyeing off the risotto so hungrily that he'd purposely made more than necessary.

Truth to tell, Dave had done his own share of eyeing off this evening. He'd been way too distracted by Ellie's sparkling eyes and enchanting smile, perfectly framed by her honey-gold hair. It was a wonder he hadn't burned half the night's meals.

Now, as she did a little happy dance in anticipation of the risotto, he grinned at her. 'For a moment there, I thought I was going to score a hug.'

To his surprise, Ellie returned his grin and then held out her arms.

Oh, man. It was only a quick, friendly hug, but the contact with her was enough to set his blood pounding. Perhaps it was just as well that she released him quite promptly and stepped away. He might have been tempted to take things further.

Time to remind himself that Ellie would be out of this town just as soon as the creek waters went down and the roads were open. Any day now she'd be off, flying back to Sydney, and she hadn't seemed keen on a casual fling. Dave might have wished otherwise, but he would respect her choice.

Actually, he had a host of reasons to respect Ellie Bright. She'd fitted into this place so easily – not just in the kitchen, where she seemed surprisingly at home, but she'd been getting on well with the locals too. There'd been quite a deal of good-natured banter when she'd taken down customers' details for the tab. And plenty of cheery calls of goodbye to her, from both men and women, as they'd left.

Even Dave's dad had been all happy smiles when he'd called in earlier to make arrangements for an interview with Ellie.

Now, as Dave set a glass of wine and another of beer beside the bowls of risotto on the bench that had become their eating spot, he asked, 'So you're going to interview my father, as well as Renata?'

'Yes.' Ellie settled quickly onto the stool and picked up her fork, as if she couldn't wait to get started. 'But my focus won't be so much on his books. I'll acknowledge his amazing writing achievements, of course, but that's already been covered by so many journalists. My boss is really excited that he's come back here to fix your mother's house. That makes for a really good story.'

Somewhat uneasily, Dave asked, 'And Dad knows? He's okay with that?'

'He seems to be. Why? You don't think it's a good idea?'

'I guess it all depends on how you write it.'

Ellie's expression was more cautious now.

Dave said, 'I suppose I'm just conscious that *I* was the one who phoned Dad and dragged him away from his book tour in Melbourne. I more or less insisted he come back here to do those repairs for Mum.'

Her expressive eyes widened. 'And Rolf didn't want to come?'

'No way. Not at first. And Mum didn't want him here.'

Her expression morphed from surprise to thoughtful reflection as she took this in.

'I mean, they haven't had one of those civilised divorces where they continued on like old mates.'

'Okay, I can see it could be tricky.' After a bit, she gave a slow nod. 'I'll be careful, Dave. My story was always going to be positive. It seems quite amazing to me that your parents have been through a divorce, but are still able to work on this project together. And if the divorce was difficult, it shows how mature and evolved they must be. Total heroes.'

Dave gave a smiling shrug. 'That sounds like a fair angle.' But now he found himself wondering why he'd started this conversation. Did he really want to waste valuable time with Ellie discussing his parents? 'Anyway,' he said. 'Don't let your risotto get cold.'

'No, that would be a crime.' Tucking in with her fork, she took her first mouthful, closed her eyes and gave an appreciative moan. 'Oh, my, Dave, this is even better than I imagined.'

'Glad you like it.'

'Like it? It's practically orgasmic.'

Wham. Ellie should have been more careful with her word choice. Clearly she had no idea of the direction of his thoughts this evening.

Now, battling his testosterone-fuelled reaction to her praise, Dave also turned his attention to the food. Apart from the distant hum of generators, everything was quiet, with just the chink of cutlery against china. Outside the café, the night was calm, still and warm, with no hint of the autumn chill that most of Australia enjoyed on March evenings.

The silence might have become awkward if a black Staffordshire terrier hadn't suddenly appeared in the doorway, sniffing at the doorpost and then at the mat. No owner followed, so it was quite possibly a stray.

'That little fellow looks hungry,' said Ellie.

'Could well be,' Dave agreed. 'Plenty of fences are knocked down during cyclones and dogs take off and then get themselves lost.'

'That's sad. Should we feed this fellow?'

'I should probably check the collar first.' Dave stood, but before he could reach the doorway, the dog scampered off again, disappearing into the night.

Dave went out onto the footpath, but with no light shining from lampposts, he couldn't see very far. It didn't help that the dog was jet black, and the street seemed quite empty.

He gave a helpless shrug as he came back inside. 'I guess we can only hope he's reunited with his owner soon.'

Ellie's face was full of sympathy. 'It's easy to forget that cyclones affect pets and wildlife, as well as people. I think your father said something about helping Renata feed a cassowary tonight.'

'He did?'

Ellie nodded. 'I got the impression they're going to spread fruit out in the scrub at the back of Renata's place.' After a small pause, her eyebrows lifted and her mouth tilted in a wily smile. 'Do you think Rolf and Renata might be . . .?'

She didn't finish the question. She didn't need to. Dave knew exactly what she was implying.

'Dunno,' he said gruffly. 'They only met a couple of days ago.' Then he quickly added, 'I know that ah – doesn't necessarily mean —' Damn it, he was making this worse. 'To be honest, it's not something I want to speculate about. I mean, no one wants to think about their parents' sex life.'

'I guess not, although I wouldn't know from experience.'

How could he have forgotten that Ellie was an orphan? 'Sorry, Ellie.'

'No need to apologise.' By now there was scarcely a morsel left on her plate.

Dave seized on one of the many questions he'd been pondering. 'Is Ellie short for anything?'

'Elinor,' she said. 'But that's boring.'

He grinned. 'Hardly boring, but I agree, Ellie suits you better.'

She set down her fork and reached for her wine glass. After taking a sip, she said, 'Do you mind, if I ask you about the divorce?'

'It's not my favourite subject.'

'Fair enough.'

But after a moment or two, Dave relented. He didn't want to disappoint Ellie when she'd been so helpful and it made sense that she'd like to have a little background before the interview with his dad.

After downing a deep swig of his beer, he said, 'I don't have the blow-by-blow details, but I know they had a massive row about Dad's writing. Right from when he first started, Mum was totally against the idea. She thought he was wasting his time. Wanted him to concentrate on his construction business.'

'Writing must have been quite a big change. I guess it felt like a risky gamble to her.'

'That was it exactly. Mind you, I was away when most of that happened. And my brothers had already moved south, so they were also out of the scene.'

'So maybe there was an empty nest element for your mum, as well?'

'Maybe. But I'm kinda glad I was out of it.'

Dave drank a little more of his beer. 'Of course, I was always aware that Mum and Dad had quite different personalities. Mum was super practical. You know – kept the house spotless, cooked meals exactly to the recipe.' He chuckled. 'I remember once, I caught her in the kitchen with an actual ruler, measuring diced pumpkin to make sure it matched the exact centimetres listed in the ingredients.'

'Oh, my goodness,' laughed Ellie. 'That's mega conscientious.'

'Or shows she wasn't prepared to trust her instincts.'

'That too, I guess.'

'And of course she was always trying to keep three grubby boys clean. That was probably a full-time job, but Mum didn't just do endless washing. She ironed everything too. I mean, literally *every-thing*. Pillowslips, tea towels, Dad's overalls, our school uniforms.'

He gave a wincing grin as he remembered the ribbing he'd once copped from a schoolmate about his perfectly ironed shorts with neat, sharp creases down the centre.

Ellie was smiling and nodding as if she was imagining it all.

'Dad was the one who read us bedtime stories, while Mum was out in the kitchen ironing. And he taught us to play cards, to swim and to play soccer.'

'Sounds fun.' Ellie's wistful smile reminded Dave, yet again, that she'd lost her own parents.

'We were lucky,' he said. 'Dad also took us boys camping, and snorkelling on the reef, but Mum hardly ever came with us, unless it was for Easter up at Lake Tinaroo. She reckoned she didn't have time. But even though they were so different, I always thought they both seemed happy. The "opposites attract" thing seemed to work well for them.'

'I can imagine how hard the breakup must have been for you,' Ellie said gently.

'Yeah, and that's why I'm glad I was overseas. I would have hated to have to take sides.' Dave drained his glass, then set it down. 'In the end, I'm not really sure who left who.'

Ellie looked thoughtful as she finished the last of her wine. 'Thanks for telling me about them.'

'But the subject's now closed.'

'Yes, of course.'

'Would you like more wine?' Dave asked.

She shook her head. 'No, thanks. This meal has been perfect.'

Standing now, she picked up her plate, as if she was about to take it with her glass to the sink. But instead of moving, she turned back and looked at him, her blue eyes wide and lit by a new, shining tension that punched him square in the chest.

What? He wanted to ask her, but he couldn't speak. Which was bizarre. Dave had never been shy or awkward with girls.

Ellie was smiling now. Cautiously. Beautifully. 'I guess this is where we have that debate about who has the stretcher and who has the bed.'

'No.' Out of sudden necessity, Dave found his voice. 'No, let's not, Ellie.' And then, bravely, or perhaps recklessly, 'I have a way better idea.'

'You do?'

'I do, yeah.' Emboldened by the special warmth in her eyes, Dave also stood and he took the plate from her and set it back on the bench. Then he reached for her hands. And she didn't pull away.

The temptation to kiss her was overwhelming. But by some kind of miracle, he held back. He'd promised himself he wouldn't stuff things up with this girl. 'Why don't we take a walk on the beach?' he suggested instead.

A huff that sounded both breathless and happy broke from Ellie. 'Oh, I'd love that, Dave. The beach is always so beautiful at night.'

Outside, the air was finally beginning to cool down. Ellie drank in the night and let her head fall back as she stared up at the sky. Pitch black, but cloud-free and sprinkled with glittering stars.

The street was empty, the town perfectly quiet. They crossed the road to the narrow strip of parkland that bordered the sand, where a concrete path to the beach had been cleared, leaving piles of broken branches and fallen coconuts on either side.

After a day of bright sunlight, the white sand here was soft and dry. A gentle breeze drifted towards them, bringing a faint, salty freshness from the sea. Ellie could see the moon lighting a silver path across the still waters of the bay.

Again, she looked up at the sky and the spectacular spread of stars. 'That's the upside of having no power,' she said. 'We get to see all those stunning stars.'

'Yeah,' Dave agreed, and for a moment or two they stood there, breathing in the beauty. Then they kicked off their sneakers, tucked their socks into them and walked barefoot to the water's edge. And now, Ellie was tingling from head to toe.

Here she was, alone with a guy she'd been eyeing off for days, in the moonlight on a tropical beach.

What could be more romantic?

Pity these serene waters were also home to crocodiles, sharks and marine stingers, or she might have been tempted to strip off completely and dive in. Instead, she was fighting all kinds of other temptations.

From the moment she'd met Dave Anders, she'd been schooling herself to stay sensible. But tonight that rule had begun to feel a bit silly. And nigh on impossible.

During the simple process of working beside Dave, something had happened. While Ellie had been following his instructions and jumping to respond whenever she saw anything he might need – butter from the fridge, a hand to stir a pot or to plate a sizzling steak – she'd also felt an uncanny, totally unexpected connection with him.

It almost felt as if they'd known each other for ages. An impossibility, of course, and yet finally, at the end of their dinner, when she'd been preparing to leave the kitchen and retreat back upstairs, there'd been a magical, sparkling moment, when she'd looked into his brown eyes and . . .

Everything had changed. Her previous rules had no longer made sense.

And now, as they stood at the edge of the Coral Sea, Dave was drawing in a long, deep breath and letting it out slowly, almost as if he was deliberately calming himself.

'It's astonishingly beautiful here,' she said.

'Yeah. When you look in this direction, out to sea, it's hard to believe there was a cyclone raging here just a few days ago.'

'I know. The water is so calm again now. It's almost like a promise from the gods.'

He gave a soft chuckle. 'And what might that promise be?'

'Oh, ahh . . .' For a moment, Ellie felt caught out and foolish. She'd been getting carried away. But then she dived in anyway. 'Maybe – that after the brutality, there's a chance for healing and restoration?' But almost immediately she was apologising. 'Sorry. I'm looking for meaning where there probably is none.'

'But why not?' said Dave.

'Well, yes, I guess. Some places do seem to send messages, don't they? I mean, when I was in Scotland, I visited Culloden in the Highlands and there seemed to be this overwhelming sadness. The battles had happened centuries ago, but you could feel this sorrow, still hanging in the air there, over the fields.'

In the moonlight, she saw Dave's slow smile. 'Showing your sensitive side, aren't you?'

Right now she did feel super sensitive, but she was pretty sure she was reacting to the man rather than the land or the seascape.

'But I do like your suggestion that nature can be trusted to heal and restore,' he said.

'Given time,' Ellie added.

'Yeah, time is the issue, of course. It can't happen overnight.'

'And we humans have never been patient.'

'No.'

Ellie was fast losing the very last shreds of her own patience. Here she was at the water's edge with this gorgeous man and all she wanted was to have his arms around her, his warm, masculine body pressing close, his lips searching hers.

A kiss in the moonlight. Such a perfect memory to take back with her to Sydney.

Problem was, for two nights now, she'd made it quite clear that she wanted to sleep alone, which meant that Dave could also rightly assume that she wouldn't be looking for moonlight smooches.

Until this moment, Ellie had been grateful that he'd respected this wish.

But now . . .

Now they were bathed in silvery magic, with a gentle breeze whispering over their skin and little waves lapping at their feet.

And while Ellie was trying to will Dave to sweep her into his arms and kiss her senseless, he remained the gentleman, making no move to come closer.

Instead, he stood, still and straight, with his hands sunk deep in his jeans pockets. Then he drew in another deep breath. And let it out.

'Okay,' he said. 'Best we head back.'

They used a tap in the park to rinse the sand off their feet and didn't bother to put their shoes back on. But as they crossed the road to the café, Dave was wondering why the hell he'd thought it was such a great idea to take Ellie for a moonlight stroll on the beach.

Unless he was deliberately trying to sabotage his commendable restraint, it was the worst idea he'd ever had.

It hadn't helped that he'd been sure she was waiting for him to kiss her. But he'd known damn well that stopping at a kiss would be close to impossible. And where would that leave them when they arrived back at the flat?

His chest was tight as they dumped their shoes inside the door of the café, and a pulse drummed hard as he set about the straightforward business of stacking their dinner crockery into the dishwasher and turning it on.

Complicating everything, Ellie was waiting at the bottom of the stairs, all slim and pale and lovely, and her eyes seemed to hold a new intensity.

With another of her shy smiles, she said, 'So, this brings us back to the same old conversation – about the bed and the stretcher.'

Now, Dave tried to swallow the constriction in his throat. 'I – I guess so.' But as he saw pretty pink creeping into Ellie's cheeks he added, 'Although I do have a suggestion about that.'

'You do?' Her voice was little more than a breathy whisper, her gaze locked with his. 'I'm listening.'

Damn it, if this wasn't a come-on message, he was totally losing his touch. 'Well, the thing is – on the first night when you arrived here and even the second night, I felt kind of gallant about —'

'About leaving me to sleep on my own?'

'Yeah.' His heart was picking up speed and he was actually nervous, ridiculously so. 'But now it's the third night and —'

'And *I've* been a fool.'

He needed a moment to take this in. 'You think so?'

'I do.'

'But you —' He almost said something clumsy and unhelpful about her leaving soon. Just in time, he stopped.

Ellie was speaking. 'I realise now that I would just be torturing myself to spend another night on my own.'

As he stepped forward, they shared cautious, wondering smiles and then, her silky hair rippled against his fingers, as he raised his hands to cup her face. Her perfect, pretty, utterly kissable face.

'Tonight, just having you close by in the kitchen, I've already been torturing myself, Ellie.'

'It's been the same for me.'

'Then I guess we'd better do something about it.'

She was still smiling shyly as she lifted her soft pink lips to meet his, and when he kissed her, she gave a small moan and melted into him, slipping her arms around his neck, pressing close and then deliciously closer.

At last. Oh, Ellie.

CHAPTER TWENTY

From the first brush of Dave's lips against hers, Ellie was already quivering with need for him. Then he pulled her closer and she felt his arms around her, felt the warm roughness of his unshaven jaw, and any lingering caution evaporated.

His kiss was gentle, seeking and sexy – so, so right in every way. But as their fever built, a kiss was not enough. Soon, they were running and laughing as they hurried up the stairs, holding hands, almost tripping in their eagerness to reach the bedroom.

Of course they chose the bedroom with the actual bed, the lovely, comfortable double bed with the pillow-topper mattress and the clean sheets that Dave had found for her yesterday.

Now the pace slowed and Dave stopped just inside the doorway. Drawing her close again, he kissed her slowly, but with delicious thoroughness, letting the reality sink in. This was actually going to happen.

Ellie was shivering with excitement as she slipped her fingers beneath the band that tied back his hair. And as his thick hair fell free, she could feel his lips curve in a smile, and he took the kiss deeper.

Seemed they weren't quite bold enough to rip each other's clothes off, but they did a good job of undressing speedily.

As they joined each other on the bed, any further questions were asked in silence – in a bold caress here, in a tender kiss there.

And in every case, the answer was *Yes, please!*

'Lisa!' Bianca's eyes were shining with excitement. 'I've been talking to Gerry and he's on the brink of asking you to go with him to the senior formal.'

'You're joking.'

'Not at all. He was talking about it last night.'

'You mean he definitely said he was going to ask me?'

'Well, he was talking about who he would take and your name definitely came up. He said it was a good idea and he looked really interested.'

Lisa was more than ready to believe this. Recently, she'd been catching quite a share of those super-exciting interested looks from her best friend's brother, the hot and handsome Gerry Maffucci.

Oh, my God. She was still in Year Eleven. How amazing to go to the Senior Formal with a guy like Gerry.

Her schoolmates would be gobsmacked. And Lisa would be floating with delirious excitement.

Okay, she would probably be a tad nervous too, but it was beyond thrilling to know that Gerry liked her enough to drop her name as his potential partner.

'I reckon we need to go shopping to look for a formal dress,' Bianca suggested.

'Oh, yes.' Lisa would much rather go shopping with Bianca than with her mum, who had the most boring taste in clothes. 'Will you come too and help me choose? Oh, wow! What colour do you think suits me best? Actually, what's Gerry's favourite colour?'

'Red, no question about that. Most definitely red.'

*

Lisa woke with a start to find herself in darkness and once again in the spare room in Heidi's cottage. Good grief, she'd been dreaming. But she couldn't believe she'd been dreaming about her schooldays. All that was ancient history. Decades ago. What on earth was the matter with her?

But she knew, of course – it was the Maffucci factor. She managed to forget about Gerry for weeks, months, even years. And yet, back in high school, she'd been obsessed with him, and every so often during her adulthood, he'd popped up to annoy her subconscious.

Now, lying in the dark, she was once again remembering that fateful day when she and Bianca had gone shopping for a formal dress. Cairns was quite a distance from Tully, and Bianca's mother had driven them. Mrs Maffucci had a dental appointment, and so she'd gone off to have her teeth seen to, leaving the girls to explore the dress shops in the city centre.

Such fun they'd had trying on glamorous gowns, although neither Lisa nor Bianca had planned to actually buy a dress on that day. And even if Gerry did invite Lisa to this year's event, she knew her mother would never agree to these expensive options.

But Mrs Maffucci had finished with the dentist sooner than expected and found the girls in a main-street boutique, with Lisa posed in front of a long mirror and draped in an amazing red-sequined mermaid gown.

'Oh, my word, Lisa, you look stunning. With your dark hair and eyes, that dress suits you perfectly.'

'Gerry will love it,' Bianca had also enthused.

'Gerry?' This was the first Mrs Maffucci had heard of her son's plans.

'But he hasn't actually invited me,' Lisa had tried to explain. 'Bianca and I were just trying on these dresses for fun. Getting in practice for next year, when we're in Year Twelve.'

Bianca's mother, however, had insisted that Lisa must have

this dress now. The colour and style suited her so amazingly well. She would never find anything better, and if Gerry was planning to invite her, there wouldn't be time to make another trip back to Cairns before the formal.

'I'll pay for it today and sort things out with your mother later.'

Oh, yeah.

Ha ha. What a mess.

Now, rolling over restlessly in the bed in Heidi's spare room, Lisa relived the rest of that day. Mrs Maffucci had driven them back to Tully, only to discover that Gerry had just, that very afternoon, asked Annie Blaine, the sexiest blonde in his class, to be his partner at the formal.

And if that hadn't been devastating enough for Lisa, her own mother had been absolutely furious about the unnecessary waste of money on a very expensive gown that wouldn't be needed for at least another twelve months.

Not only had Lisa been heartbroken over Gerry's desertion, so much so that she'd cried herself to sleep every night for the next fortnight, but her mother had also demanded that Lisa hand over the stash of pocket money she'd been saving to buy her own record player. *And* Lisa hadn't been allowed to have any more pocket money until the dress was paid for, a process that had taken an entire term.

While most teenage girls might expect a motherly hug if their high-school crush had disappointed them, for Lisa there'd been punishment and a lecture.

'Lessons learned the hard way will stick with you forever,' her mother had told her.

And wasn't that damn right?

Lisa had learned never to trust a promise or a fantasy that seemed too good to be true.

*

Ellie lay with Dave in a breathless tangle, marvelling at what had just happened.

Wow!

She was so ecstatically happy to lie there, with her head nestled in the crook of his shoulder, listening as their breathing calmed down, while she let her mind replay everything they'd just shared. She'd never experienced anything quite like that amazing symphony of tenderness and pleasure, culminating in the most fabulous, skyrocketing finale.

Wow, and double wow!

She was so glad she'd taken this reckless gamble.

But tonight, Ellie had also promised herself that if she took this risk, she would make sure she kept her emotions in check. And now that the fun was over, it was time to get back to reality. Fast.

Deep breath. This wasn't going to be a repeat of her sad experiences with Finlay or Anton. She'd had her heart well and truly broken in both Scotland and Sydney, but it wasn't going to happen a third time here in Beacon Bay.

Determined to keep the 'after' conversation necessarily light, she said, 'That was fun.'

'Fun, Ellie? It was amazing.' Dave's voice sounded rather rough around the edges, as he gently lifted a strand of her hair and tucked it behind her ear. 'Have you any idea how sexy you are?'

She smiled and rubbed her nose into his strong, tanned and tattooed shoulder.

His response was a soft chuckle, as he traced a shiver-sweet line with his fingertips, along her thigh from her hip to her knee. 'I'm going to miss you like hell when those damn roads clear.'

Uh oh. He wasn't supposed to talk about missing her. Almost immediately, Ellie felt wobbly and her vision blurred. But surely she wasn't going to get all dramatic and weepy? Not this time. She mustn't cry. She absolutely mustn't.

Her imminent return to Sydney was an inescapable truth that she couldn't avoid. She'd known from the start this could only ever be for one night, or possibly two if she was lucky.

Keeping her eyes extra wide, she stared hard at the ceiling. But it was impossible to lie here without thinking of the man in bed beside her, without remembering all the sweet ways he'd made love to her, as well as reliving the long hours she'd spent with him in his kitchen downstairs, where she'd felt so at home.

It made no sense that after such a short stay in a tiny flat above a café in Far North Queensland, she might feel as if she belonged here. It made even less sense that the guy who lived here, who wasn't just good looking, but also talented and sexy, had also somehow managed to eclipse the previous guys who'd broken her heart.

'I need the bathroom,' she said, sitting up quickly and hurrying from the room, not wanting him to notice how close she was to tears.

Sitting on the loo, she used toilet paper to blow her nose and scrub at her eyes.

Pull yourself together, Ellie.

It was time to get everything into perspective. She knew she couldn't possibly be in love with this guy. That simply wasn't believable after a couple of days in his town and one bonk session. Okay, so maybe the bonk had been out-of-this-world amazing and an experience she might long to repeat. But as for her other yearning – to stay on here in Beacon Bay – *Get real, girl.*

Janet, Dave's sous-chef, would soon be back. And where was a Sydneysider going to find a job in journalism or PR in a tiny Far North Queensland town that was struggling to get back on its feet after a natural disaster?

Of course, Ellie knew what her problem was. It was the same problem she'd been dealing with for the past three years, ever since her granny died. With no family of her own, she was looking for an anchor.

But she couldn't expect to find that here.

'You okay in there, Ellie?'

'Yes, sure.' Guiltily, she rattled the toilet paper roll.

'Okay. Take your time.'

To her relief, Dave's voice was retreating. But she couldn't stay here all night.

At the basin, she splashed her face, patted it dry with a towel, and when she checked in the mirror, she was pleased to see that her eyes weren't too puffy and red. With any luck Dave wouldn't guess she'd been crying.

When she got back to the bedroom, he was lying on his side with his eyes closed. Quietly, Ellie slipped in beside him.

'All good?' he murmured sleepily.

She kissed the back of his neck. 'Everything's perfect.'

Lazily, he rolled back to her and gave her a gentle kiss. 'Another big day tomorrow.'

'Yeah,' she whispered. 'Go to sleep.'

A click sounded as he switched off the bedside lamp, leaving the room in darkness. 'Night, Ellie.'

'Night, Dave.' She rolled away and pressed her face into the pillow, determined to put an end to her tears.

CHAPTER TWENTY-ONE

Dave looked different.

The change in his son was the first thing Rolf noticed when he arrived at the café for the early morning interview with Ellie Bright. As soon as Dave greeted him, Rolf was aware of a happier glow in the young man's eyes. Then, he sensed a new lightness in Dave's step as he brought their coffees out to a table on the footpath.

'I should have asked if you've had breakfast,' Dave said, as he set Rolf's coffee down.

'Yes, I have, thanks.' Renata had already filled Rolf with granola, yoghurt and defrosted berries – not his favourite morning repast, but acceptable given the current scarcity of cooking facilities.

'Okay. I'll leave you to it.'

It was now, as Dave was about to return to the kitchen, that Rolf caught the flashing smile his son shot to Ellie, and the equally glowing grin she sent back to him.

Whoa.

Seemed the café's recent popularity might not be the only success lifting his son's spirits. Pity the girl was about to leave the

Bay – although Rolf supposed he might change his mind about that after he'd faced her inquisition.

She certainly looked ready for business, dressed in a white linen shirt tucked into navy trousers, and with a notepad and pen ready on the table in front of her, as well as her phone set to record.

Rolf took a sip of his coffee, pleased to find it was hot and strong, just the way he liked it. He looked across the street to the view through the smashed vegetation to the sea. This morning, the waters were a quiet oyster grey under a blanket of clouds, but Rolf had checked the radio for a weather forecast and there'd been no suggestion of rain.

'I suppose you've heard, the floodwaters are going down at last,' he told Ellie. 'The roads will probably be open by the end of the day.'

'Today?' Ellie looked instantly stricken, as if this was terrible news.

Interesting. Seemed she wasn't keen to leave? 'Probably by late today,' he said more gently. 'According to the ABC.'

'And they don't usually get it wrong.' Ellie definitely sounded downbeat and when she gave him a smile, it looked rather forced.

Rolf found himself stirred by unexpected sympathy.

'Right, Mr Anders, I guess we should —'

He stopped her with a raised hand. 'Please, call me Rolf.'

She gave a polite nod. 'I'm really grateful that you're giving me this time, Rolf. I know you're busy replacing that badly damaged roof, so I'm sure you'd like to get started.' Her finger hovered over the record button.

'Sure,' he said. 'Fire away.'

'If we could begin with a little background – about your child-hood, perhaps?'

Rolf nodded. He'd been asked questions about his writing journey many times, and as she pressed record, he was ready with his answers.

'From as far back as I can remember, I've always loved books,' he said. 'And I started making up stories when I was quite young. I was the eldest of three kids. I had a brother and a sister and my parents were always quite busy, so I often entertained the younger kids with stories I'd invented.'

Ellie smiled. 'As an only child, that sounds quite magical to me.'

Rolf wasn't sure why this information about Ellie's own childhood touched him. It wasn't as if she would be part of Dave's future. She was a publicist heading back to Sydney.

Nevertheless, he found himself picturing her as a lonely little girl. The image bothered him momentarily, but then he tucked it away. Perhaps it was merely a new thread he could include for one of the characters in the piece he was working on.

'I imagine you enjoyed school?' Ellie asked next.

'I did, yes. Like all kids, I loved the playground – mucking around with my mates and playing sport. But I showed up quite early as being good at writing, and in high school I scored top marks in English.'

A slight frown puckered her forehead now. 'But you didn't move into a career that used your writing skills.'

'No.' Rolf gave Ellie a silent high five. Not all interviewers picked up on this contradiction, but for him it was a pivotal point in his life story. He decided she deserved the full picture.

'Halfway through my final year of high school, my father died.'

'Oh, no, I'm so sorry.'

Her interjection surprised him, especially as she seemed unnecessarily upset. Rolf paused, half-expecting her to explain.

'Sorry,' she said again, giving an apologetic flap of her hand, as if she wanted him to ignore her. 'Please, continue.'

'Well, Dad's death was totally unexpected, of course. He was only in his late forties, and as you can imagine, it was a massive blow for my mother. Suddenly, she wasn't just a grieving widow, she had three children to raise on her own.'

Ellie's expressive blue eyes signalled genuine sympathy. 'Am I right in guessing that, as the eldest child, your mum needed you to go out and earn a living?'

'Exactly. I'd been planning to go to uni. I'd hoped to study English and the Classics, History, Philosophy, that sort of thing. And I finished Year Twelve with good grades and the offer of a place at the University of Queensland.' He shrugged. 'But the obvious problem with those kinds of courses is that there's no clear path to employment at the end. We lived in Cairns, the uni was in Brisbane. And my mum had four mouths to feed.'

'She needed you to get a *real* job,' Ellie said.

'Exactly.' Even now, Rolf could feel the weight of that time – his mum's sorrow, plus his own grief and the whole family feeling lost and bewildered and, at times, angry with the cruel hand they'd been dealt.

He could also remember the pain of watching his friends' excitement as they planned to head off to uni. The sky was their limit, while the lowering of his own limits had been unavoidable.

'I got lucky when the school holidays arrived,' he told Ellie. 'A friend's dad was looking for labouring help. I wasn't sure if I'd enjoy work as a builder, but I liked the sound of the pay he was offering. So I turned up, and he handed me a hammer – and I wasn't exactly hooked from that moment, but I was certainly interested.'

'And did you eventually enjoy being a builder?'

'I enjoyed the physicality. I was much younger and fitter back then, of course. But I also got satisfaction from watching things take shape. That first summer we built a gazebo in this wealthy woman's garden and it was really quite special. Then there was an extension for a lawyer in Edge Hill – a sunroom, overlooking the sea. It was a whole new world for me, and by the end of the summer, when I was offered an apprenticeship, it was too good an opportunity to refuse.'

'They do sound like interesting projects,' said Ellie. 'And it must have been a big relief for your mum.'

'Absolutely. And by then she'd also managed to score a job in the local library, so along with my dad's modest insurance payout, we managed okay.'

Ellie looked at her notes now, but then set them aside. 'Might I ask if any of your younger siblings ended up going to university?'

Damn it, she knew how to ask searching questions, but Rolf had no wish to revisit these particular memories. 'Sore point,' he said. 'Best we don't go there.'

Again, her smile was sympathetic. 'Gotcha.' Then, after a brief pause, she said, 'Rolf, I can only guess you're extremely happy to have a professional writing career at last. Was it a difficult decision to switch careers in midlife?'

'Hell, yeah.' *It wrecked my marriage and my family.* No way did he want to revisit that right now. 'The thing was,' he said, thinking carefully, 'I'd reached a point where I realised that too many of us spend our lives doing what we think we ought to do and not what we really want to do. I needed to question myself about that. And when I did, the answer was so blazingly clear, I couldn't ignore it.'

'That's – that's . . .' For a moment Ellie sat there, silent and staring into space. Lost in her own dreams, perhaps? Then she blinked and came back to the task at hand. 'And it must be amazing that your novels have been so well received.'

'To be honest, it's taken me a while to get used to all the excited fuss from fans.' He gave a small chuckle. 'As a builder, I would spend six months pouring all my heart and my skill into a job and more often than not, the only response would be questions like why was this job taking so long? Or why did it cost so much?'

'Ouch.'

Ellie went on to ask questions about restoring Lisa's house and the general difficulties for builders in post-cyclone situations, which

Rolf was happy enough to answer. He half-expected she'd also quiz him about the divorce, but apart from acknowledging it as a *fait accompli*, she didn't go there.

Nice one, Ellie. She wasn't just a pretty face, but intelligent and sensitive.

Now he was thinking again about the change he'd noted in his son this morning – the new confidence and lightness of heart – and he was sure the reason had to be Ellie. Was there a chance here?

'I might add,' he said as she finished up her questions, 'I can't help thinking Dave's been very lucky to have you turn up like this. I know you've been very helpful in the café's kitchen, but I suspect you've —' He paused, realising he should have given the wording of this compliment more thought. 'I'm sure you've been good for him – the sort of company he needs.'

To his dismay, Ellie blushed bright red and then her lower lip trembled. *Damn.* He'd put his foot in it, well and truly, and he wasn't sure what to say now. He didn't want to make matters worse.

But already, Ellie was managing a brave smile. 'Thank you, Rolf,' she said. 'I've loved being here. I only wish it could be longer. I would have liked to stay on and be more involved in the Bay's recovery.'

Rolf nodded and held out his hand to shake hers, and wondered why the hell he felt an urge to throw a fatherly arm around her shoulders.

As Ellie watched Rolf Anders hurry off, clearly keen to get on with fixing his ex-wife's roof, she was still trying to absorb his compliment regarding her time with Dave. Had Rolf any idea how incredible the past twenty-four hours had been for her?

She was still feeling embarrassed about her blushing reaction, but luckily, Rolf hadn't made a big deal of it. And the interview had gone well, which, ultimately, was more important.

Ellie couldn't help admiring Dave's dad. Despite his amazing success, he was so very down to earth and humble. And his story of eventually fulfilling the lost dream from his youth was both moving and inspiring.

She'd found herself thinking how nice it must be to have him as a father.

'You're a lucky guy,' she told Dave when she went back into the kitchen. 'Your dad's so cool, so together. I was really impressed.'

'Yeah.' Only the briefest of smiles flickered.

'Is something wrong?' Ellie asked, while running a mental checklist of possibilities. She knew Dave had plenty of food supplies now, thanks to the boat from Cairns, which had also brought fuel to keep the generators going.

'Nothing wrong, exactly.' Then, with a somewhat rueful smile, 'I've just heard from Janet, my kitchenhand. She says the road should be safe to cross by this afternoon, so she's planning to come in to work this evening.'

Of course. Rolf had also told Ellie the road should be clear later today. At the time, she'd been dismayed by this news, but she'd brushed it aside as she'd become absorbed in his story. Now, hearing the same news from Dave, the ramifications of this really hit home and her heart took off like a runaway thief.

The time had come. No more Beacon Bay for her. No more Dave. She had no choice but to turn her back on the best night of her life and pretend it had never happened. Then book the first flight home to Sydney.

Home?

'What about the other roads between here and Cairns?' She tried not to sound too hopeful as she asked this.

'Yeah, I checked. They're all open again.'

Damn. The disappointment in Dave's eyes was not helping her and it certainly didn't help that Ellie was remembering the way they'd woken early this morning and made love again, almost as if they'd known this might be their last chance. And now her unhelpful mind kept flashing heavenly memories.

But her disappointment over leaving wasn't only about the between-the-sheets excitement she would miss. It was the whole package – the man, his café and the community here in this ravaged yet beautiful bayside town.

When tears threatened again, Ellie gave herself a mental shake-down. The last thing Dave needed was her blubbering over what they'd both agreed could only ever be casual. Besides, she'd promised herself she'd stay on top of her emotions this time.

Taking a deep breath, she said, 'This is it, then.' But even as she spoke these words, she found herself wondering if there was any way she could talk her boss into letting her stay on here.

Of course, she could already hear Daphne's response. 'Are you dreaming, girl? Your job is public relations. You deal in celebrities, not bloody small-town news gathering.'

It didn't help that Dave looked as cut up about her departure as she felt. 'Dave, we always knew —'

'Yeah, yeah. Of course. You've gotta do what you've gotta do.'

'And right now, I'd better start checking on flight times.'

'And I've got a mountain of prep to get on with.'

Ellie had only spent a couple of afternoons prepping with Dave, so it made no sense that she should feel nostalgic about performing a few simple tasks like sanitising cutting boards, peeling potatoes, slicing onions, or helping to mix marinades.

Now, instead, she trudged up the stairs to check airlines and ten minutes later, she had a flight booked back to Sydney for that very night.

Ellie was looking quite pale as she came back down the stairs with her packed suitcase and laptop bag and set them on the floor at her feet. Dave tried to tell himself this was because she hadn't bothered with makeup. But he'd seen her without makeup and he knew this paleness was caused by something else.

The same something else that was eating at him.

Hell. He couldn't believe he felt this bad. It didn't make sense.

Ellie was just another girl – and there'd already been a long line of girls in Dave's life. When it came to relationships that lasted, he was crap. He either tired of his girlfriends, or they got tired of waiting for him to commit to something more permanent.

And yet, with Ellie, he'd been aware of an uncanny deeper connection. He knew they'd both felt it. They'd even talked about it in their less guarded moments. And now, when it was time for Ellie to leave, she was way too pale and her eyes were unnaturally shiny, and Dave felt as if he'd swallowed razor blades.

Abandoning the carrots he'd been dicing, he quickly washed and dried his hands. Ellie hitched the strap of her handbag over her shoulder and stretched her lips into a smile that didn't reach her eyes.

Soon they would be separated by thousands of kilometres, and right now they were only a few metres apart, but neither of them tried to step closer. Dave had never felt more helpless.

Ellie spoke first. 'The only sensible thing now is to act like nothing happened, right?'

He probably nodded, but he was too busy thinking that something *had* happened and it was something amazing. So much more than a tumble between the sheets. Something rare and deep.

Of course they'd also known from the outset that this could only ever be a brief hook-up. It was why Ellie had initially made such an effort to keep her distance, and now, the best thing for her was to get out of here fast.

'No talk of missing each other or anything.' Her voice was tight, almost angry.

'Fair enough,' Dave agreed. But this shouldn't be so hard. He'd made an artform of breaking up, and ending this fling shouldn't even qualify as a breakup. But right now, he was pretty sure that his eyes were as damp and glistening as hers.

It was time to concentrate on practicalities. 'I'm not sure if any of the local petrol stations have opened. Do you have enough fuel to get you to the airport?'

She nodded. 'I still have well over half a tank. I've only driven a few kilometres since I've been here.'

'Goodo. And you have your phone? Your charger?'

Now she smiled ever so faintly. 'Yes, Dave.'

He sent a somewhat frantic glance around the kitchen, scanning the benches. 'I don't think you've left anything in here.' Then somewhat desperately, 'Let me help you with your luggage.'

Ellie seemed about to protest, but then relented. 'Thanks. There's just these things.'

Grateful to have something to do, Dave scooped up the suitcase and laptop bag. She turned then, heading for the door and the street, and he followed.

Her shiny green hire car was parked on the other side of the road. They crossed in silence and Ellie pressed the button on her key that opened the boot.

With the luggage stowed and the boot door lowered, there was nothing left but to say goodbye.

Keeping his tone carefully casual, Dave asked, 'You want to stay in touch?'

Ellie lifted her chin to an almost stubborn angle and her eyes glittered. 'Not much point, is there?'

He tried to swallow the hot brick in his throat and the need to haul her close for one last hug was overwhelming. Instead, he kept his hands stuffed in the pockets of his jeans. 'Thanks so much for all of your help, Ellie. You've been amazing.'

'It was fun.' She looked as if she wanted to say more, but then she pressed her lips together tightly, as if she was struggling for control.

Her eyes had an unmissable sheen and Dave almost cried out that she didn't need to go. She should stay and work in the café. Get a job with the local paper. They'd work something out.

Abruptly, she turned to the driver's door, and there was a double-click as she unlocked the car. She had her back to him now and she waggled her fingers over her shoulder in a semblance of a wave.

'Bye, Ellie.' His voice was so choked, he wasn't sure she heard.

She made no response, which gutted him, even though he knew her silence was sensible. Without another word, she opened the door and slipped into the seat behind the wheel.

The car's motor hummed to life, the indicator flicked on and Ellie Bright drove off. Out of the Bay and out of Dave's life.

CHAPTER TWENTY-TWO

The hall attached to Beacon Bay's bowling club was abuzz with happy chatter. A dozen or so local volunteers were gathered around tables piled with fruit that had been delivered by trucks from Cairns, courtesy of generous supermarkets.

Now these good folk, armed with knives and chopping boards, were ready to dice pawpaws, bananas, melons, apples, tomatoes and lychees for the starving cassowaries in their beleaguered forests. Lisa was there, of course, as one of the main organisers, and Heidi had joined her, along with her newly friendly neighbours from across the street – Bert, with grey hair tied back in a braid, and his petite wife, Pamela, dressed in a pretty aqua sarong.

Renata was also there.

Lisa had almost neglected to pass on news of this meeting to Renata, but then she'd relented. After all, Renata *had* told her she'd love to be involved and, true to form, Renata had turned up bang on time, armed with the right equipment, including an apron, all eager smiles and ready to help.

Once again, she was dressed simply in jeans and a T-shirt, but she still managed to add unexpected glamour to any gathering.

Lisa greeted her warmly, or at least, with as much warmth as she could muster. 'Lovely that you could join us here, Renata.'

'Thank you, Lisa. When I told my friend Peggy about this gathering, she had to come too. It's a wonderful project.' Renata nodded to the woman beside her, who was around sixty-ish with curly grey hair. 'You may not have met my neighbour, Peggy. Her house was damaged, so she's staying with me for the time being.'

Lisa smiled politely. 'Nice to meet you, Peggy. I hope you don't have to wait too long before your house is fixed.'

'At least, now the roads are open, things should start to move,' commented Renata.

Lisa nodded. 'I thought you might be in a hurry to get back to Sydney, now that the roads are free.' *Good grief.* As soon as the words were out, she regretted them.

Renata looked momentarily startled, but she recovered quite smoothly. 'No, no, I'm not in any rush.' With another of her gracious smiles, she said, 'I'm hoping to find more ways to help here in the Bay.'

'Lovely.' This time Lisa made her smile as friendly as possible. She didn't enjoy feeling like a villain, and it was pathetic of her to harbour a grudge against this woman. Just the same, she decided it would be safest if she was working at a table as far away from Renata's as possible.

Her first task, however, was to introduce the ranger from Queensland Parks and Wildlife, who'd come to address the assembled volunteers. After he'd thanked everyone for giving up their time, he explained the strategy.

'We have a rather tricky situation while we're waiting for the forests to regrow,' he said. 'Our aim is to supplement the cassowaries' diets, without making them dependent on handouts, but this fruit you're cutting will be very handy. We'll vary the amounts we distribute, as we want to encourage the birds to keep up their normal foraging habits. That's also why we're asking you not to feed them.'

Acknowledging the nods of agreement all round, he went on. 'We'll set up feeding stations with cameras, so we can monitor the birds' behaviour. And some of this fruit will also be dropped to less accessible locations by helicopter.'

'Do you have any idea how long you'll need to feed the birds this way?' The question came from Phoebe Lyons, who was one of the Bay's keenest gossipers and also had a history of power struggles with Lisa on one or two committees.

'It's hard to say,' came the ranger's reply. 'We kept it up for eighteen months after Cyclone Larry.'

This brought a flurry of surprised murmurs.

'But fortunately, Pixie hasn't caused quite so much damage. Oh, and one more thing. We'll be setting up a cassowary hotline and email.' With a smiling nod to Lisa, the ranger said, 'Your committee will give you those details. We want to encourage the community to report sightings and incidents involving orphaned, sick or injured birds.'

After a round of polite applause, everyone set to work, chopping and filling buckets and happily chatting. Most of the chat involved stories of damage to homes, but there was also talk of traumatised or lost pets. Apparently, Bert and Pamela were still looking for their little dog.

'He's a black Staffie and his name's Jock. It's on his collar.' Pamela was close to tears as she recounted her story. 'The cyclone's eye was passing over us and everything was calm, so I let him out into the yard for just a moment. But I hadn't realised the front fence had fallen down and he got away. Then the wind started up again and I guess he was terrified and . . .' A sob broke from her. 'And he probably tried to hide somewhere.'

Of course, there were murmurs of sympathy and promises to keep an eye out.

It was just as they'd almost finished the fruit cutting, and a couple of women had begun heating the big urn in the kitchen and setting out mugs for tea and coffee, that Lisa heard a voice call, 'Renata, have you seen this?'

Phoebe Lyons had a super-wide, almost smirking grin as she held up her phone. 'Someone's put it on Facebook. I'm not sure where they got it from, but it's a photo of you and Rolf Anders.'

Renata's reaction was a somewhat fed-up frown as she glanced at the screen thrust in front of her. 'Oh, yes, I see,' she said. 'That's the night Rolf and I went to dinner at his son's lovely Frangipani Café.'

'The headline's making out you two are a red-hot item.'

'Really? For heaven's sake.' Renata took another frowning look at the phone's screen and then groaned. 'That's the damn press for you. They'll beat up any little thing to grab attention.'

Lisa, having heard this unsettling conversation from two tables away, was trying to carry on unperturbed. But of course, curious heads were swinging in her direction.

Grrrreat. She chose not to look up, but concentrated on chopping the last of a honeydew melon with unnecessarily fierce focus. She knew all too well that no matter what was really going on between Rolf and this woman, the whole Bay would now be convinced they were having a passionate affair.

Which also meant that Lisa would cop another round of looks, stares or smiles that might be amused or pitying or sympathetic – take your pick. And that would go on for weeks.

'I wonder who took the photo?' Phoebe said.

'That was me.'

Heidi's voice. Lisa couldn't hold back her loud gasp. How could her good friend be such a traitor? She stared at her across the table.

Heidi looked so stricken Lisa hastily pulled out her own phone and swiped to the Beacon Bay Facebook page. Sure enough, there were Rolf and Renata, on the footpath outside the café, with the boarded-up window as a backdrop. They weren't touching in any way, but they were certainly smiling and looking ultra pally.

'I took a whole heap of photos that day,' Heidi was saying now, as if somehow this made everything all right. 'Damaged homes and gardens. Grounded and upturned yachts. People in the evacuation shelter. Volunteers cleaning up the soccer fields. I'd been snapping away the whole day and I was doing a quick circuit in the evening when I saw Rolf and Renata. They're our local celebrities, so I thought why not?'

She gave a defensive shrug. 'I sent a big selection of photos off as a package, with a few notes of explanation, but, Renata, I never suggested that you and Rolf were an item. I do apologise. I have no idea how the pic ended up with *that* headline.'

'Daphne, do you know who wrote this?'

Ellie had been back in Sydney for three days. Back to her suburb of endless high-rises. Back in her lonely one-bedroom flat with her dismal view of the neighbouring apartment block's red brick wall and rows of tiny aluminium-framed windows. Back to the daily commute, to getting on with new tasks for her clients, while deliberately avoiding any news about Beacon Bay.

Only problem – one of those clients was Renata Ramsay, who was still in Beacon Bay, and Ellie had just received a text message from her with a rather alarming attachment.

Standing in the doorway to Daphne's office, Ellie held out her phone. 'There's a photo here with a headline that implies Renata's having a blazing affair with Rolf Anders.'

'Are you trying to suggest that's a problem?' Daphne swivelled from her computer. 'She *is* screwing him, isn't she?'

'I have no idea.'

Now Daphne's expression was pitying, as if Ellie was totally clueless. 'The man's living in her house. He's taking her out to dinner.'

'Yes, but Rolf's staying in that house as one of several guests Renata's kindly taken in. The main motel in the Bay was damaged and there was no other available accommodation. He took her out to dinner to thank her for her kindness.'

Daphne's response was a snort followed by an exasperated eye-roll. 'That's so sweet, Ellie. But do you really think that's all there is to their story?'

Instead of answering, Ellie challenged, 'So you did write that headline?'

'Of course I did. Don't be naïve, woman. Look at them.'

As Ellie looked again at the happy faces on her screen, she felt anger rise, filling her chest. 'They're smiling,' she said tightly. 'Big deal.' Then, after an anxious sigh, 'Daphne, you've seen my interviews with both Rolf and Renata. I was so careful not to imply anything about a relationship. Rolf's working on his ex-wife's house. It's a rather tricky situation.'

'Which makes for another great story —' Daphne pointed a finger directly at Ellie. 'A great story that *you* did not make the most of.'

Ellie held up her phone again. 'Well, I've just had a text from Renata and she's not happy.' The poor woman had been inundated with phone calls from her agent, as well as texts and emails from friends and curious colleagues.

'Tell her to suck it up,' snapped Daphne. 'Surely, she's been around long enough to know that any publicity is good publicity.'

Ellie sagged against the doorpost. She couldn't believe her boss was being so crass. The temptation to stomp off down the corridor was huge. She'd never felt so frustrated.

She was so uncomfortably aware of the gaping hole between Daphne's careless claims and the real-life experiences she'd been privileged to witness in Beacon Bay. Everyone she'd met there had been good-hearted in the face of adversity, and yes, maybe even courageous, and all her boss wanted to focus on was a scandal.

Grabbing a fortifying breath, she spoke her mind. 'We're not the gutter press, Daphne. You run a public relations firm. You're a professional dealing with important clients.'

'Are you telling me how to do my job?'

Ahhh . . . Ellie knew she was skating on thin ice here, but she was too angry to be cautious. She held up her phone again. 'I certainly have concerns about this story.'

'But you know damn well that Renata Ramsay's career is on the brink of fading forever. Our job is to grab the public's attention and to hold her in the limelight. And one of the best ways to do that is to create controversy around the message. People love a good gossip. Throw in some debate and you have a winner. Everyone gets involved, giving their two cents worth.'

'But what about the clients you're trashing? Don't they deserve to be consulted first?'

'Oh, for heaven's sake, Ellie, get real.'

In the past, this would have been the signal for Ellie to meekly back down, to accept that her boss knew best, but this morning she was too fired up. She didn't have time to stop and analyse what it was about Beacon Bay that had changed her. She just knew that this was a fight she didn't want to lose.

'If we're talking about getting real,' she said with fresh resolve, 'I *really* think you should contact Renata right now – and try to calm her down. And while you're at it, maybe you should even apologise.'

'Don't be so bloody ridiculous.' Daphne narrowed her eyes, as if she was sizing up her employee and didn't like what she saw.

'If you don't,' Ellie added for good measure, 'I'm pretty sure Renata will be calling her agent and demanding he finds her a new PR company.'

'How dare you.' Daphne's hands clenched and unclenched. 'You know what?'

Ellie gulped. 'You're sacking me?' Far out. Had she really said that out loud?

'Actually, yes,' responded her boss with a sickly smile. 'That's your best suggestion yet. Spot on. Goodbye.'

CHAPTER TWENTY-THREE

'I'm so sorry about that photo.'

When Lisa arrived back at the cottage after a long and busy day, Heidi met her at the front door with a long and anxious face.

Lisa had to ask, 'What's happened now?'

'Nothing new that I'm aware of, thank heavens. But this morning was bad enough. The whole Rolf and Renata flare-up. I can't believe I was so naïve as to send their photo off with the others. I should have known someone might beat it up into a scandal.'

'Oh, Heidi, have you been fretting about this all day?'

'Well, yes, of course I have.' Heidi's eyes widened now, brimming with questions. 'Haven't you?'

'I haven't been dwelling on it.' This was stretching the truth, but Lisa was sure her poor friend had given herself enough grief already. She needed a break.

'I thought you'd be stewing.' Heidi still looked worried.

Lisa managed to smile. 'I guess I've been too busy.'

There was an element of truth in this. Lisa had learned during the divorce that keeping busy was her best way of coping, and so she'd lined up a truckload of distractions today. After the fruit-chopping session, she'd headed straight for the Blunts' plant nursery.

Luckily, everything Melody and Jim had stowed in garages and containers had survived the Pixie ordeal in reasonable condition, and now that Jim had straightened and mended the damaged wire stands, Lisa had spent a happy few hours helping them to set their potted greenery back in place in the nursery.

She'd always found working with plants calming. It was one of the reasons she'd joined the revegetation group. For Lisa it was another version of farming, a connection to the lifestyle built around fields and crops that she'd known throughout her childhood.

She'd always loved the smell and feel of the earth, the pattern of the seasons and the promise that came with each new crop. Working with plants offered a predictable logic she found comforting.

But today, despite seeking out this relaxing diversion, Lisa had still been battling visions of Rolf and Renata's affair splashed all over the internet. Annoyingly, it hadn't helped to tell herself that it was none of her business and not her problem.

Clearly, the sooner that pair were out of the Bay and out of her life, the better.

Still in 'busy' mode, Lisa had gone straight from the nursery to the evacuation centre to check in with the team coordinating the donations of clothes, books and household items dropped off by generous, more fortunate locals. She didn't stay there long, though, as word of the 'scandal' had obviously spread and there'd been too many looks of both the curious and the pitying variety.

Next, she'd called at Dave's café, mainly to make sure that Janet would definitely be turning up to help him, and she'd scored a rather late lunch of coffee and a toasted sandwich, plus the news that one of Rolf's contacts had delivered a handy skip to her house.

Lisa had been planning a Rolf-free day. Under the circumstances, it had surely seemed prudent, but with news of the skip, she'd set off, shoulders braced, to the house.

There, while Rolf continued to work on the roof, she'd cleared up all the mess and rubble in the backyard, tossing timber and plaster and pieces of iron into the skip with immensely satisfying hurls, thumps and crashes.

A good tidy-up always left her feeling better, and she hadn't even mentioned the scandal to Rolf. In fact, she was quite proud of the way she'd managed to remain serene – or at least, a simmering, Lisa-style version of serenity.

Now, determined to hang on to her hard-won Zen, she slipped an arm around Heidi's shoulders and gave her a sympathetic hug. 'I know it's upsetting for you, but you can't take that photo back, and you know what they say about spilt milk.'

Heidi let out a huffing sigh. 'Thanks for being so good about it. I don't enjoy feeling guilty.'

'Heidi, if that's the worst thing you have to feel guilty about, you must be a saint.'

They shared sheepish smiles. Then brightening, Lisa patted the casserole dish she was carrying. 'And in even better news, we don't have to worry about what to cook tonight. Dave's given me this lovely pot of chicken as thanks for helping him out when his kitchenhand was stuck in Tully.'

'Oh, isn't that lovely of him?' Heidi leaned in as Lisa lifted the lid. 'Wow. It smells delicious.'

'Yes. Chicken in a creamy mustard sauce.'

'Yum. Lucky us.' As they went through to the kitchen together, Heidi said, 'I guess I mainly feel bad because this scandal has blown up when Rolf was simply trying to thank Renata.'

'Yes, that seems to be the story.' As Lisa set the pot on the little camping stove, she couldn't help adding, 'But we don't know exactly what he was thanking her for, do we?'

She'd expected a smile in response to this quip, but her friend still looked worried.

THE WIFE'S SECRET   183

Heidi said, 'I guess what's bothering me is – I thought I sensed something in Renata's reaction this morning that made me wonder.'

'How do you mean?'

'I could see she was genuinely upset and annoyed.'

'Yes, but she certainly didn't try to deny a relationship with Rolf.'

'That's true, and yet, I was watching her closely, and I'm pretty sure, if she *was* having it off with him, I would have caught a tiny hint of – I don't know – something like smugness?'

'Perhaps.' Lisa was not enjoying the new slant their conversation had taken. She'd been trying hard not to analyse this situation. How could outsiders ever know the truth? 'Don't forget Renata's a stage performer and no doubt a very good actor.'

'I know, I know. But I really got the very strong sense that there were actually no grounds for scandal.' Bringing a tissue from her pocket, Heidi wiped away a tear. 'That's why I've been so upset.'

'And now it's time to cut yourself some slack, Heidi. And I think we should drop this, don't you? Whatever that pair are up to, it's really none of our business.'

At first Heidi looked surprised and possibly puzzled, but then she nodded, gave a quick salute, followed by a lip-buttoning gesture.

And now there was a wry tilt to the smiles the women shared before Lisa left for the bathroom and another cold shower.

By the end of the day, Rolf was feeling quite upbeat. The fine weather had held and he'd made good progress on the roof repairs. Also, Lisa had called around to deliver him a takeaway coffee from Dave's café, and after complimenting him on the work he'd done, she'd proceeded to tidy the backyard.

Sure, she'd made a hell of a racket. But she'd got on with the job without grumbling over the mess, and it had almost been like the good ol' days. With luck, he might get through this job without World War Three. A guy could only hope.

He wasn't exactly whistling or skipping, but he was certainly in a good mood when he arrived back at Renata's place. The neighbours, Peggy and Roger, were already ensconced in the kitchen, having announced at breakfast that it would be their turn to cook dinner tonight, and Renata was alone to greet him as soon as he came into the house.

'Chicken Rendang,' she said, nodding down the hall to the spicy aromas drifting from the kitchen. Then, in a lowered voice, 'I've told them not to make it too hot.'

Rolf didn't mind a little heat in spicy food, but he smiled. 'Sounds great.'

Renata, however, looked less than happy. 'I suppose you've heard?'

His buoyant mood slipped a tad. 'Heard what?'

'About our scandal?'

Our scandal? Oh, God. What now?

But rather than clarifying, Renata was instantly apologetic. 'Sorry, you poor man. Here you are, after a hard day's work, and I corner you the minute you set foot in the place. Please, come into the lounge and sit down.'

If he was about to hear bad news, Rolf wasn't sure that making himself comfortable would help. He was also conscious that his work overalls were dusty and quite possibly grimy. But Renata would know this and was clearly too distracted to mind.

In gracious hostess mode, she stepped into the lounge room and gestured to an armchair for him. Then, settling herself in the chair opposite, she adjusted a colourful cushion at her back and crossed her elegant legs.

'What's this about a scandal?' Rolf asked as he sat. 'Is someone targeting you?'

'Not just me, I'm afraid. Us.'

'As in you and me?'

She nodded. 'There was a photo taken of us on the night we went to Dave's café. It only shows us standing out on the footpath. It's all quite innocent, but somehow it's ended up in a news gossip column on the internet, along with the very strong suggestion that we're having a raging hot affair. So, of course, it's all over social media now.' Renata thumped the upholstered arm of her chair. 'It's all so bloody annoying.'

Rolf wasn't surprised that she was upset, especially as they both knew the accusations were groundless. But he also wondered if Renata's reactions were complicated by the fact that she'd actually made it quite clear she'd be up for a fling with him. And she'd done so on that very night the photo was taken, after they'd arrived back here from the café.

He knew she'd been disappointed that he'd held back from crossing that line, and it hadn't been an easy choice. Renata was undeniably attractive, but Rolf had already found himself in a thorny situation – back in the Bay, with a tense ex-wife and his son, newly returned and somewhat anxious as he launched his new business. Not to mention the host of locals who knew him and were openly curious about his new lifestyle.

All that on top of the cyclone damage.

The last thing he'd needed was another violent storm in the form of the gossip that would come with an affair.

'So how far has word spread?' he couldn't help asking.

'Oh, it's all over the Bay.'

Great. 'So, Lisa knows?'

'Oh, yes. We were both there at the bowling club, cutting up fruit for cassowaries, when Phoebe Lyons started showing off the story on her phone. Phoebe made a great song and dance about it.'

Interesting. Rolf was extremely surprised that Lisa hadn't mentioned this when she'd called around at the house. The Lisa he'd known around the time of the divorce would have taken massive delight in rubbing his nose in it.

He couldn't help giving her a mental tick of approval.

'I'm sorry this has happened,' he said.

'Yes, it's a damn pain. But heavens, Rolf, you don't need to apologise. If anyone's to blame it's probably *moi*.' Renata pointed to her chest with a well-manicured fingernail, embellished by polish in a lavender tone that matched her silk blouse. 'Seems it was my publicists who blew this all up.'

'Ellie?' Rolf was dismayed by the slug of betrayal he felt. For himself. For Dave. Surely not Ellie? Or had he completely misread the girl?

'No, not Ellie.' Renata's fierce response to this was almost reassuring. 'Her boss, Daphne. Stupid cow.'

The relief he felt now wasn't really warranted. Ellie was back in Sydney and unlikely to see Dave again.

'Do you think we should work on some kind of retraction?' asked Renata.

Rolf wasn't sure it would be worth it. When gossip was unsupported, it usually blew over. 'How do you feel?' he asked.

'Oh, I was angry at first, but I was mainly worried about you.'

'Then stop worrying. It's not worth it.' Especially if he wasn't going to cop grief from Lisa.

Renata smiled now and gave an elaborate, stage-worthy shrug. 'I suppose, if I'm honest, it probably wouldn't hurt my increasingly fragile career to have my name romantically linked with a famous figure like Rolf Anders.'

He smiled. This woman was very adept at dispensing subtle flattery. 'I suppose that's the way the publicist was thinking.'

'Perhaps.'

'Just the same, it's probably time I moved out of here.'

'Oh, no, Rolf, don't feel you have to do that.' Renata now looked quite dismayed.

'No, honestly. I really appreciate your generosity and I've been incredibly grateful for your spare room, but I reckon it'll only take me another day, two at the most, to get the roofing iron back on. And after that I can sleep at the house. It makes sense.'

Renata sighed. 'Now I know why I've never been a fan of common sense.'

CHAPTER TWENTY-FOUR

I've been sacked.

For Ellie, the reality was taking its time to sink in.

Her conversation with Daphne had been like leaping into a whirlpool and her head was still spinning as she walked away from the office.

Her immediate reaction had been one of triumph. She was free. Free to head back to Beacon Bay. But then came the next thought – how reckless was that? A month ago she'd never heard of the place, so why should it be all she could think about now?

And, realistically, what jobs might she apply for in that region? She'd had good results at uni in journalism, marketing and stakeholder engagement. But would the *Cassowary Coast Observer* need another journalist?

Intertwined with these thoughts, of course, was another round of memories of Dave. If she was absolutely, totally honest, none of her work in journalism or PR had been as rewarding or made her feel as bone-deep happy as working in Dave's café. But that was simply a sad fact she'd have to learn to ignore.

Harder to ignore was the painfully clear picture of the last time she'd seen Dave, reflected in the rear-vision mirror of her hire car. A solitary figure standing in the middle of the street outside the café, dark eyes solemn, hands sunk in jeans pockets, not moving as he watched her drive away.

Whenever she thought about that scene, all she wanted was to be with him again, dicing veggies in his café's kitchen, sharing one of his delicious meals, walking with him on a moonlit beach, making him smile, sharing his bed.

But she'd been quite firm when they'd said their goodbyes, and she'd promised herself she wouldn't go through another painful and drawn-out season of grief and regret. It was time to delete those images of Dave. Permanently.

Unfortunately, this wasn't as easy as clicking the rubbish bin symbol on her computer. And now, as Ellie trudged down the street towards Town Hall station, she was conscious that most young women in her situation would have a circle of girlfriends to cheer her up, offering hugs, sympathy and advice along with bucketloads of booze. But Ellie's habit of falling hard for a guy and then focusing all her attention on him had left her neglectful when it came to her female friends.

That was another thing about Dave's café. After only a couple of nights of chatting with clients, she'd sensed a genuine friendliness in the Bay's community.

A southerly buster arrived then, brisk and chilly, picking up litter from the gutter and swirling it around her legs and in her face. The rude interruption brought her back to reality.

What she needed to focus on now was finding a job here in Sydney. Something that would at least cover her rent. If she wasn't careful, she would not only be jobless, but homeless as well.

Jobless, homeless, lonely and loveless.

*

Refreshed from her shower and changed into comfy slacks and a loosely hanging shirt, Lisa found Heidi in a cane chair on the front porch with Juno curled and purring in her lap.

'Our dinner's heating through nicely, but I thought we needed a drink first.' Heidi indicated a wine bottle and glasses on the little table between the two chairs.

'Oh, I like the way you're thinking.' Lowering herself into the cushioned cane chair, Lisa drew in a deep breath and as she released it, she felt any lingering tension in her body let go. Then, from beside her, came the comforting glug of wine being poured.

'Thanks,' she said as Heidi handed her a glass.

By now, the sun had almost set and the sky was flushed with peach and gold behind the ragged silhouette of the sadly damaged trees. At least the street looked tidier. Lisa was relieved that the electricity poles had been straightened and the footpaths cleared of dangling wires.

A couple of large container skips had been delivered and neighbours had been busily filling them. Bert across the road had also mended his broken fence.

'Has there been any news about Pamela and Bert's little dog?' she asked Heidi.

'Not so far. I rang Phil today in case he could help.'

'Phil? Your vet boyfriend in Mission Beach?'

'The vet I've been out with *once*,' Heidi corrected with a somewhat withering glance. 'He and his partners are flat out at the moment.'

'With injured animals?'

'Yes. Mostly stray cats and dogs. I thought Pamela's little Jock might have somehow found his way up there, but Phil hasn't seen him yet. But he said there are plenty of pets being brought in, so he's certainly keeping an eye out for Jock.'

'That's so sad. I'm surprised people didn't bunker down with their animals.'

'I think most people did, but it's been hard with so many fences knocked over. Dogs have been running wild and getting into fights.'

'Goodness. Let's hope they're reunited with their owners soon.'

'Yes. The alternative's pretty grim.'

'Being put down?'

Heidi winced as she nodded and gently stroked Juno's ears.

Gulp. Lisa found herself remembering how she'd taken Rolf to the spot where Tucker lay under the hedge. But emotion-laden memories were dangerous. Today she'd proved that her best way of coping was to remain focused on practical matters.

'Your Phil's a useful contact then.'

'Hmmm. I suppose that's one way of describing him.'

'Sorry,' said Lisa. 'That's me thinking solely in terms of cyclone recovery. I'm sure Phil's also charming and fun and all things sexy.'

'Well, he certainly doesn't have time to be any of those at the moment.'

'I guess not. It'll be some time yet before we get back to normal.'

With that, Juno leapt daintily from Heidi's lap and headed inside. Heidi stood too. 'We should check on that dinner.'

It was at the kitchen table, while they were enjoying their particularly tasty chicken, that Lisa's carefully constructed calmness caved.

Everything was fine at first. They talked about the meal, about Dave and his experiences in restaurants around the world. Heidi shared news from her daughter in Perth, who was apparently very excited about some new guy she was dating.

'She met him online too.'

'It seems to be the way these days.'

'I know. It almost makes me wonder how we ever met people in the past.'

Lisa chuckled.

And then, suddenly, Heidi said, 'If you don't mind my asking, Lisa, how did you and Rolf meet?'

This was so out of the blue Lisa almost choked. Heidi had to know that her history with Rolf was *not* her favourite conversation topic.

Unfortunately, there wasn't much point in refusing to answer. Now that the question had been raised, it would only go on hovering uncomfortably between them.

So, she told Heidi, as concisely as possible, about their meeting on the footpath outside a newsagency in Cairns, with the rain bucketing down and the two of them both caught without umbrellas.

Then, before Heidi could ask for more details, Lisa jumped in with the obvious comeback. 'What about you and Ben? How did you two meet?'

'Oh.' Heidi gave a soft, almost embarrassed little laugh and then a shrug. 'We met in high school.'

Kathunk!

Just like that, Lisa's thoughts unhelpfully flashed straight back to her own high-school days. Gerry Maffucci on the football field, scoring a try with the whole school cheering. Gerry sending her flashing-eyed glances and secret smiles that made her feel as if they were the only two people on the planet. Then, years later, the shameful aftermath . . .

Stop it.

Stop it now.

'Wow,' she said quickly. 'So you guys had that rare high-school romance that actually lasted.'

'We did, yes.' Heidi's happy smile suddenly morphed into a frown. 'What's the matter?'

'Nothing. Why?'

'You look really upset.'

'Well, I'm not.'

'I could have sworn you were remembering something very distressing.'

Lisa shook her head. She certainly didn't want to start down this path.

'Lisa?'

'Honestly, it's nothing.' She might as well throw Heidi a crumb and hope it would be enough. 'Just a guy in high school I'd rather forget.'

'Except you obviously haven't forgotten him.'

Lisa winced. 'I'd still prefer not to talk about him.'

Just her luck, the normally considerate Heidi was shaking her head. 'Sometimes it helps to talk about these things. I won't push, of course, but I promise you can trust me and it might help to get it off your chest.' With a small smile, Heidi added, 'It's better than talking about our husbands, especially given that mine is dead and yours is an ex.'

Grimacing at this, Lisa gave in. 'It was just a silly high-school crush. You know, the old, eat-your-heart-out hero worship from afar.'

'Sounds painful.'

'Oh, yeah.' Reaching for her wine glass, Lisa took a fortifying gulp. 'He was my best friend's brother, which didn't help. And I never even dated him during our schooldays.' And then, she found herself adding, 'But after we finished school, after I moved to Cairns, he – ah – drifted in and out of my life.'

Nervous now, Lisa added quickly, 'I finally got over him, thank heavens. I mean totally over him. And then I was settled with Rolf and the kids. I was happy and my life was sweet.'

Heidi's eyes were huge, like a kid watching a suspense-filled movie. 'Until?'

'What do you mean?' Lisa asked nervously. 'Until what? What are you thinking?'

'I'm not sure, but you've left me hanging. You don't mean that after you married Rolf, you had an affair with this guy?'

'No. No way.'

'Oh. For a minute there you really had me.'

'There was no extramarital affair.' Lisa speared beans with her fork. 'But – okay – I'll admit he did mess with my head. And in the end, I do think that contributed to the divorce.'

Now, it was Heidi who reached for her wine glass as she took in this news, and while she refrained from posing another question, Lisa could read her expression, brimming with curiosity.

'You're waiting for me to fill in the gaps, aren't you?'

'Well – you've left me feeling rather puzzled.'

Lisa suppressed an urge to sigh. 'The problem is, I'm not sure you'll understand, even if I do try to explain. It's kind of ridiculous.'

'I don't mind. You wouldn't be the first out-there friend I've had.'

Lisa couldn't help smiling at this. 'It's just that around the same time that Rolf started wanting to write novels, I happened to see this article in *The Weekend Australian* about a guy from North Queensland who'd made an absolute fortune down on the Gold Coast.'

When Lisa paused for a moment, Heidi jumped in. 'Let me guess. It was this same Gerry fellow.'

'Yeah. Gerry Maffucci. He was selling insurance, of all things. I knew he'd been working for insurance firms pretty much since he left high school, but this story was about how he'd moved south and branched out on his own. And he was raking it in. Making millions. There was a photo of his house in Surfers Paradise. Massive, with all these terraces and walls of glass.'

Heidi was looking quite puzzled now, which was no surprise. 'And you wanted that?'

'No,' Lisa said quickly. 'No, not at all. It wasn't that I wanted to be mega-wealthy like that, or to live in Surfers Paradise. I loved living here and I didn't mind that Rolf's business was much more modest. It was steady and secure and I was happy. But he was talking about giving it all up to be a writer. He was ready to throw it all away. And I saw the story about Gerry and I couldn't bear it. I – I snapped.'

'Wow,' Heidi whispered. 'So, this high-school crush genuinely contributed to your breakup?'

'More or less. In a roundabout way. I told you it made no sense.'

'Did Rolf know?'

'About Gerry Maffucci?' Lisa actually flinched as her face burst into flames. 'God, no. I – I never mentioned him to Rolf.'

Heidi was frowning. And silent. Lisa feared her friend was too shocked to speak, but she could see from her expression that questions were buzzing in her head.

'I don't expect you to understand.' And Heidi certainly wouldn't understand if she'd told her the rest of the Gerry Maffucci story. But she would never go that far.

And now, Heidi was reaching across the table and holding out her hand. And, as Lisa accepted the gesture, the gentle pressure of her friend's hand wrapped around hers said it all. Heidi might not understand, but she wasn't condemning her either.

CHAPTER TWENTY-FIVE

'Hi, Renata, it's Ellie.'

'Oh, Ellie, dear. Hello. How are you?'

'I'm okay.'

Which was barely the truth. Ellie had certainly known better days. This morning, she was sitting on her moth-eaten two-seater in her tiny flat, looking out through a small grimy window to a red brick wall.

The only decorations in her room were family photographs, and her favourite was of her parents on their honeymoon, looking madly in love as they walked hand in hand along a beach. Ellie had no idea where that beach might be, but she had always liked to think that her parents were still together somewhere like that. Endlessly happy.

There was also a photo of her dad and herself when she was a toddler. He was lifting her up in the air and they were both laughing. Again, so happy. Then, her grandmother looking stern, but resplendent in her best navy-blue silk dress, with pearls at her ears and throat and her white hair swept up in an elegant high knot. And finally Ava, Ellie's Scottish cousin, rugged up for winter, complete with boots and a long Shetland scarf, her curly hair escaping from beneath her beanie, with Fergus, her snowy white terrier, at her feet.

Dear God, she missed them all.

But she couldn't tell Renata that she'd rarely felt worse. She needed to get to the point of her phone call. 'I was wondering if you've heard from my boss, Daphne Blackwood?'

'No,' said Renata. 'Not a word.'

This was disappointing, but Ellie wasn't surprised. 'I'm sorry,' she said. 'I tried to get Daphne to retract that story about you and Rolf, or to write another one discounting what she'd implied. At the very least, I thought she should ring you to apologise.'

'That's very good of you, Ellie. But I know what these scandal-mongers are like. And don't worry, I might have been upset when I rang you yesterday, but if I'm honest, having my name linked with Rolf Anders is not the worst thing that's happened to me.'

Ellie let out a little huff of relief. 'Thanks for being so good about it.' She hadn't plucked up courage to ring Rolf, so she asked, 'And – er – how's Mr Anders taking it? I hope he's not too mad.'

'Rolf? Heavens, no. He's hardly worried at all. Water off a drake's back.'

'Really?'

'Yes. He's quite confident it will all blow over and I think he's right. From my perspective, things are already calming down.'

'That's great news. Maybe I'll stop worrying then.'

'Oh, yes, you mustn't worry.'

Ellie sat a little straighter. She may as well tell Renata every-thing. She was bound to find out anyway. 'I should also let you know that I'm no longer with Daphne Blackwood's agency.'

A gasp sounded in her ear. 'Do you mean you've left them?'

'Um, yes.'

'Oh, Ellie. Not because of that story?'

'Not only that.' She wasn't going to confess she'd been sacked. She didn't want Renata to feel responsible or guilty.

But the woman was one step ahead of her. 'You weren't asked to leave, were you?'

No avoiding it now. 'Well, yes, but I brought it on myself. I was so mad at Daphne.'

'Heavens, Ellie. Oh, that's awful. I feel terrible.'

'No, please don't feel bad, Renata. It's in no way your fault. And it's for the best. I'm sure of that. I – I wasn't a good fit.'

A small silence fell then until Renata asked, 'Do you have another job to go to?'

'I'm working on finding one.' Ellie said this with way more confidence than she felt.

'Hmmm.'

'But I won't hold you up any longer. I just wanted to check in with you, to make sure you're okay.'

'That's thoughtful of you, Ellie. Thank you.' There was a hushed, almost shocked timbre in Renata's voice now.

'Bye then, Renata. I've loved working with you and – and all the best.' Ellie hung up quickly before she got too emotional or said anything silly.

'Lisa, look what I've found.'

Lisa was at the Community Hall, sorting through piles of clothing donated by generous locals, when she heard Renata calling to her. Instinctively she stiffened, which was an annoying reaction. She'd been planning to be much warmer towards this woman.

Turning with a smile, she realised that Renata's eyes were extra bright with excitement and she was hurrying forward, holding out a paperback with a rich maroon cover and the author's name in a familiar fancy gold typeface.

Renata was beaming as if she'd unearthed buried treasure. 'One of Rolf's books was in the pile over there.'

'Ah,' said Lisa. 'Yes.'

'I suppose you've read it?'

This was an unfortunate assumption. Lisa couldn't lie and she tried not to mind that she'd been caught out. 'No, I'm afraid I haven't.' A beat later, she asked, 'Have you?'

'Yes, it's just *so* good. Rolf's such a talent.' Stepping closer now, Renata added, 'And let me assure you, there was no double meaning implied in that comment about Rolf's talents.'

'I – I wasn't – I didn't think . . .' Of all the cheek. Lisa struggled to find the response she needed.

Still smiling serenely, Renata lowered her voice and leaned even closer as she said, softly but quite firmly, 'I'm not sleeping with him.'

What did the woman want? A medal? A sympathy card?

Lisa gave what she hoped was a careless toss of her head. 'That's none of my business.'

'Fair enough.' Still relentlessly smiling, Renata placed the book in Lisa's hand. 'But I think you really should read this.'

The fact that the book had been donated for evacuees was a moot point, given that Lisa was currently unable to live in her home. 'I'm not much of a reader – not of fiction, at any rate.'

This brought a frown. 'But you *have* read some of Rolf's stories?'

Lisa couldn't bring herself to answer this. Renata would be appalled if she knew the truth – that Rolf's former wife had refused to read a word of his published novels. It was an unhappy fact she'd never dared to share with anyone.

Fortunately, Renata didn't allow the awkward silence to linger. Possibly, she sensed Lisa's embarrassing position, but for whatever reason, she continued, quietly and smoothly, 'I've read this story as an eBook and I promise you, it's beautiful.'

'Beautiful?' This was an unexpected description. Now it was Lisa who frowned. 'But Rolf writes crime thrillers.'

'True. But his settings are gorgeous and his characters are so well developed and interesting. Trent Amos, the central detective Rolf uses in each of his stories, is explored in great depth.'

'I – I see.'

'Amos's personal life is particularly touching.'

Lisa swallowed. Felt cornered. She didn't dare to look around the hall. There were bound to be other people watching this conversation and even if they couldn't hear the words, they would be taking note of the body language.

'Do yourself a favour and read this, Lisa.' Renata gave the book a somewhat bossy little tap. She was still smiling but there was an unmissable intensity in her eyes. 'Call it a sixth sense, but it almost feels to me as if we were meant to find this here today.'

How could she refuse now? Lisa nodded her thanks, but as she accepted the book, there was no way she could smile. She was too busy fighting a strange urge to cry.

CHAPTER TWENTY-SIX

The Frangipani Café was closed on Mondays, and Dave looked forward to the break after a busy weekend. It gave him the option of a lazy lie-in, which was always welcome, but on this particular morning he knew he wasn't going to relax. He was way too restless.

There was always work to be done, of course. Today, a glazier was arriving midmorning to replace the café's broken front window, which was brilliant news. And there were always orders to be placed for the coming week, ovens to be cleaned, menus to be planned, as well as advance prep to be done.

But first off, Dave needed to get outside, to go for a run on the beach. With luck, being buffeted by a stiff sea breeze as he pounded along on the damp, hard sand might help him to shake off the crappy low mood that had hung over him lately. Ever since Ellie had left.

It made no sense, of course. They'd both agreed to go their separate ways, and moping over a girl was a whole new experience for love-em-and-leave-em Dave Anders. Now it was time to push his way out of this slump.

His best plan, or at least, his *only* plan at this point, was to keep busy – running hard and working hard and trying to make his café a success, despite the odds stacked against him.

Dave was all too aware that cafés and restaurants could be risky businesses at the best of times, and it was going to be so much harder to establish a new eatery in a community struggling after a natural disaster.

He knew his dad was also worried about his chances. But the weird thing was – anything had seemed possible during the few days that Ellie had stayed with him here in the Bay. Something about her pretty smile, her easy companionship, her camaraderie with their customers, her undisguised admiration for his talents – everything about the young woman, if Dave was honest – had given him a fresh injection of confidence and a reason to try harder.

He knew he mustn't lose that momentum simply because she hadn't been able to stay. They'd both known from the outset that she'd be leaving. Even so, the loss of her felt stifling somehow.

Okay, enough of the pity fest.

Swinging out of bed, Dave didn't bother with coffee, making do with a long drink of water before changing into shorts and a singlet and heading for the beach.

Outdoors, the weather was finally beginning to cool down. In another month or so, the steamy summer humidity would give way to balmy sunny days and then there'd be the beautiful tropical winter weather that brought shivering southerners flocking to the north.

Unfortunately, Beacon Bay's landscape would take longer than those couple of months to return to its usual beauty. Currently, ahead of Dave, the headland that formed the northern horizon was dotted with leafless, spiky trunks instead of lush green forest. He had no idea how long it might take before their town's hinterland looked less battered and shattered, but there was nothing he could do about that.

Filling his lungs with a deep gulp of fresh sea air, he started to run, and it wasn't long before his spirits began to lift. He'd known this coastline all his life and he had so many wonderful memories of fun times here with his family.

He and his brothers had spent happy hours, days, nights, even full weeks, fishing and sailing, camping and hiking along this amazing stretch of country. Since those days, Dave had visited incredibly beautiful places in other parts of the world, but this last time when he'd returned from his travels, he'd been gripped by an inescapable sense that this was where he belonged.

Now, the further he jogged along the beach, the calmer and more positive he felt. It wasn't till he'd almost reached the end of the curving line of sand that he recognised the barrel-chested figure standing on the rocky headland and looking out to sea.

'Dad!'

His father turned, grinned and waved. 'Hey there, Dave.' Already, Rolf was making his way from rock to rock and then jumping down to the sand – and doing so rather nimbly for an old codger.

'You been for a run too?' Dave asked him.

His father chuckled. 'Well, for me, it's more of a walk than a run. I've been meaning to come down here for a while now. It's easier since I've moved back to the house.'

'Our house?' Dave asked, surprised. 'Or rather your house – actually, Mum's house.' Annoyed with himself for the awkwardness, he gave a teeth-gritted shake of his head. You'd think he'd be used to their divorce by now.

At least his father didn't seem to mind. 'Yes,' he said. 'The roofing iron's back on, so it makes sense to stay there. The bedroom's fine and I can finish the rest of the job more quickly. And it leaves the room at Renata's place free for Ellie.'

'Ellie?' Dave nearly choked on her name and the sudden racing of his heart had nothing to do with his recent run. 'Not Ellie Bright, the PR girl?'

'Who else? Do we know any other Ellies?' His dad's bushy eyebrows lifted. 'Haven't you heard? She left her job in Sydney, or maybe she lost it. I'm not sure, but she's coming back to the Bay.'

Dave had trouble answering. His emotions were rioting. 'No, I had no idea. She and I – ah – haven't been in touch. We decided there didn't seem much point.' Frantically, he flicked his gaze away from his dad's too-curious eyes and out to the sea and the distant, clear blue skyline.

Ellie was coming back.

But what did this mean? He kept his concentration on the view, watching a flock of seagulls swoop in to land on the shiny, wet sand lapped by the lacy edge of the sea.

'Renata has enlisted Ellie as her personal publicist,' his dad said. 'But on top of that, Renata's so caught up in the Bay's recovery right now, she's keen for Ellie to compile a whole bunch of positive stories about the restoration scene here as well.'

'Right.' Dave swallowed to ease the rawness in his throat. 'Sounds great.' But it also sounded almost too good to be true. Had their local opera star taken on the role of fairy godmother?

Still keeping his gazed fixed on the birds and the backdrop of sea, he asked, 'So, is Ellie here yet?'

'I believe Renata's collecting her later today. She mentioned that Ellie had a few matters to tidy up in Sydney first. To do with her rental, that sort of thing.'

'Yeah, sure. Makes sense.'

His dad was frowning. 'I expected this would be good news for you, Dave.'

'Why would it affect me?'

Now, when Dave finally made eye contact, it was clear his father found him a sausage short of a barbecue.

'What's that look for?'

'I guess I'm just surprised. You and Ellie were getting on so well.'

Dave tried to recall the few times his dad had been at the café when Ellie was also there. The last occasion had been the 'morning after the night before'. Had the vibe between them really been that obvious?

'You didn't say anything about us to Renata, did you?'

'No, son.' His father frowned, as if trying to recall. 'Or, if I did, it would have only been a very casual observation. Honestly, when Renata and Ellie planned this, I wasn't part of the conversation in any way.' Shooting a sharp glance to Dave, 'But it's good news, isn't it?'

'Yeah, sure.' Or, at least, Dave hoped it might be – although he was sure Ellie would be cautious about getting too involved with him again. And if she was staying at Renata's house and working with her, the situation would be totally different.

As Dave walked with his dad to his parked car, his thoughts were once again all over the place. And he was aware of a new kind of weirdness as he jogged back down the beach. He was happy about this news, sure, but kind of nervous too. Ellie's return felt like a way bigger deal than it should be.

He was still trying to think this through, when he arrived back at the café and saw a guy around his dad's age pacing around on the footpath. The fellow was clearly waiting for the café to open, even though there was an obvious 'Closed Mondays' sign on the front door.

Dave was pretty sure this wasn't the glazier. The guy was too early for one thing and his clothes were all wrong, surely?

He looked like a tourist. A stubborn tourist, perhaps?

He had white hair and a closely trimmed beard and was dressed in a bright tropical shirt in flamingo pink and lime green. He'd left several shirt buttons undone to show a gold chain around his neck, as well as curly white chest hair. His shorts were also white – pristine white, as if he'd just walked out of the store where he bought them. And, if possible, his white canvas slip-on shoes were even more immaculate.

'Morning,' Dave said and then, 'Sorry, the café doesn't open on Mondays.'

'Yes, I saw the sign, but that's okay, son.' He had a booming, confident voice that matched his showy looks. 'I was just hoping to have a word with the owner. Dave Anders, is that right?'

'Oh? Okay.' Dave wasn't nervous exactly, but there was a whiff of sham or fraudster about this guy – an aura that he didn't quite trust. 'That's me. I'm Dave.'

This news was met by a beaming smile that showed off unnaturally shiny white teeth. Dave couldn't help thinking – no doubt unfairly – of a crocodile.

Next moment, the grinning guy was holding out his hand and Dave caught the glint of gold from a fat and showy signet ring. 'It's so great to meet you, Davo. I'm an old friend of your mum's. The name's Gerry Maffucci.'

CHAPTER TWENTY-SEVEN

After a very late night that Lisa had spent reading, she was now sleeping in.

When she'd brought Rolf's book back from the Community Hall yesterday, she hadn't mentioned it to Heidi. She'd known it was too much to expect others to understand why she was nervous about reading her former husband's work. But this secrecy had also meant that she wasn't able to start reading until after she'd played three games of Scrabble.

This was Heidi's favourite board game, and Lisa was hopeless, but she felt she owed her friend heaps and she'd given it her best shot. She'd actually won the last game, but she was pretty sure Heidi had somehow engineered that.

So it had been after ten by the time Lisa had turned on the bedside lamp, propped herself up with pillows and set the book in her lap. Then she'd stared nervously at its cover for quite some time.

She knew the barriers between herself and Rolf's stories were entirely of her own making. She was also aware that her mental block about his books would be interpreted by most people as pig-headed stubbornness.

Lisa's problem, or at least part of her problem, was that having made such a song and dance from the moment Rolf had started his first manuscript, keeping her distance from his published work had felt sensible.

A form of self-protection, perhaps? And until now, Lisa had hidden behind the claim that she preferred fact to fiction. She simply didn't understand creative types.

And to a certain extent, this was true. She had no idea how people like Renata or Rolf could be happy making a career out of their voice, or by dreaming up stories, or even, like Heidi, by taking photographs. Their talents were all a mystery to her, their skills as elusive as conjuring tricks.

Her own experience had always been with sensible, practical work. After years spent helping out on her family's farm, she'd moved into jobs in offices – first working for a lawyer in Cairns and then, later, in partnership with Rolf.

Lisa had revelled in being organised and efficient. She was completely in her element when she was looking after the banking, paying bills or posting invoices. She'd actually enjoyed sending out quotes, managing the payroll and making appointments for clients, not to mention keeping a record of expenses and having everything ready for the accountant at tax time.

And then there was filing. *Oh, dear heavens, yes.* More than anything, Lisa had loved filing. The process was so orderly! Everything in alphabetical order? Absolutely. No question.

Later, when computers had replaced so much of that paperwork, Lisa had conscientiously headed off to night classes and learned about spreadsheets and digital calendars and how to generate online purchase orders.

No doubt feminists or artists or other brilliantly creative folk would look down on these tasks as lowly, even mindless. But for Lisa, the office was where her most important work had happened.

It was the kind of useful busyness that she now looked back on with deep nostalgia – although in recent years, she'd tried to make up for the loss of that work by joining committees and community projects.

Nevertheless, she'd accepted Rolf's novel. How could she not, given Renata's insistence? And here it was, waiting to be opened. And read.

It was called *Second Spring*, and on checking the list of titles inside the front cover, she'd learned that it was actually Rolf's second book, following on from *First Snow* and preceding *Third Summer*. The books were seemingly connected to a degree, but according to one of the review quotes, each story could be read as a standalone.

Feeling both nervous and curious, Lisa had turned to Chapter One and, without any further stuffing around, she'd dived in and read the first fifty pages or so.

To her relief, she'd found the story quite enjoyable.

Even so, she was still mystified by the guy she'd once been married to, and whom she'd thought she'd known so well. How had he stitched these sentences together to make such a compelling tale?

Of course, after Renata had made a point of mentioning the main character, Trent Amos, Lisa had paid particular attention to him. In *Second Spring*, Trent had just become a new father. In fact, he'd raced back to Australia from an international mission in Washington, DC, to make it to the maternity ward just in time for the birth.

It was only when Lisa reached the description of the young father's emotions as his baby was born that she realised she was treading on dangerous ground. The writing took the reader right there into the delivery room, and the young man and his emotions were so believable.

Initially scared when the doctor handed over the newborn, while he attended to the mother, Trent Amos had then been overwhelmed by an astonishing rush of love for his tiny son. *But, oh, my God.* Rolf had been reliving his own reactions to their first baby's birth.

Lisa was sure of this. The details of Chris's arrival had been almost exactly the same.

She could remember lying there on the delivery table, helpless, while the obstetrician attended to her nether regions, and watching the awe in Rolf's face as he'd gazed down at the precious pink and white bundle in his arms.

Reading this all these years later, at midnight, she'd had to clench a hand to her mouth to hold back a heart-wrenching sob. She'd known she mustn't wake Heidi, whose room was just nearby, but after that, Lisa had no choice but to continue reading. How could she stop at that moment?

The real whammy, however, had come a chapter or so later.

The story, interspersed with the expected scenes filled with action and crime, had circled back to the young mother. Lara was her name, which Lisa found a tad too close for comfort.

Home from hospital, Lara was coming to grips with her new responsibilities – the endless demands of a tiny newborn, the sleep-deprived nights, the constant feeding and changing, the leaking boobs and the fear that her body might never regain its pre-pregnancy trimness.

During this time, Lara's husband, Trent, had continued with his busy detective work. He had an important case to solve and no paternity leave. His job was too important.

Again, this was similar to Rolf's situation, as leave had also been difficult for him, when he'd been a sole trader and running his own business.

No surprise, in the midst of his drama on the work front, Trent had come home one evening and found Lara tired, hormonal and anxious, with the baby crying, her hair in a messy mop tied up with a rubber band, dishes in the sink and the dinner not yet ready. And she'd looked so woebegone, he'd taken her into his arms for a lovely, comforting hug.

Then the considerate hero had asked, 'What can I do to help?'

And Lara had looked around at their messy kitchen, at their crying baby and their partly prepared meal, and had collapsed, blubbering against her husband's shoulder. 'Just tell me I'm still the prettiest girl on the block.'

Oh.

My.

God.

At this, Lisa had been in absolute danger of waking Heidi. She'd needed to shove a pillow over her face to silence her cries. She couldn't believe this. Rolf had recreated a scene straight from their own real-life experience.

Lisa had cried those very tears.

In the kitchen in their little flat in Cairns, at the end of a particularly difficult day, Rolf had arrived home from work and she'd thrown herself into his arms and he'd asked her that very same question.

'What can I do to help?'

And Lisa had answered with that same absurd 'prettiest girl on the block' response.

It was a detail she'd actually forgotten until this moment, but it all came rushing back to her now. As far as she could remember, they'd both ended up giggling at her ridiculous request, but Rolf had assured her she was the prettiest girl in the whole damn city. He'd been tender and sweet and loving, and she'd been so grateful.

Together, they'd settled baby Chris, and Rolf had finished cooking their dinner. Then, later that night, they'd put little Chris in a baby sling that Rolf had carried and they'd walked, with his arm protectively around her, down to the waterfront in Cairns. There, they'd sat on a bench together, watching the moon rise over Cairns Harbour, spinning dreams about their future as they'd pointed out their favourite stars. The Southern Cross, Orion's Belt, Venus.

Such a simple but lovely way to end her difficult day, and a gentle reminder that a whole world would be waiting for her when those early postnatal weeks were behind them.

Oh, Rolf.

It was breaking Lisa's heart that he still remembered. Everything.

She couldn't help wondering if he'd felt safe to write about this, because he'd known she would never read these pages. Or had he been secretly hoping that she might come across them some day?

Or did her feelings no longer matter to him either way?

Whatever the truth might be, Lisa had known she was in for a sleepless night.

Now, after her reading stint that had gone into the early hours, she was still sound asleep the next morning when the front doorbell rang.

The shrillness yanked her out of her dream about a sailing boat and babies and cut-throat pirates. She felt totally drugged and could only open one squinted eye at best.

The bright daylight filling her bedroom revealed that it was already quite late. Just the same, she didn't want to move.

Keeping perfectly still, she listened for Heidi's movements. Alas, the house remained silent. And then the doorbell sounded again. This time with two impatient rings.

Come on, Heidi, where are you? Please answer it.

Eyes scrunched against the light, Lisa felt for her phone on the bedside table. Blinking, she managed to focus and saw that the time was 9.33am.

Gosh. Had Heidi already left the house?

Lisa wondered if she could just lie there till the bell-ringer gave up and went away. But then it started again, and this time the ringing was followed by rather authoritative knocking. Damn it, she was properly awake now.

Which was when her sleep fog lifted and she realised that this might be some kind of emergency. No one had rung her phone, but did someone in the street need her advice? Her help?

'Coming,' she called, sitting up and swinging her legs over the edge of the bed, before feeling on the floor with her feet for her slippers.

She'd left her summer dressing gown hanging from a hook on the back of the bedroom door, and she grabbed it now, shoved her arms through the sleeves and tied the knot quickly. She might have taken a moment to check her hair in the mirror. She knew it had to be a mess, but if this was an emergency, the state of her hair hardly mattered.

Hurrying down the hallway, she opened the front door. Then frowned. The fellow standing on the doorstep was wearing sunglasses, but he was vaguely familiar. She was sure he wasn't a local, though.

A very flashy bright-orange car was parked out in the street, and the caller was no longer acting as if this was an emergency. In fact, he was dressed like a tourist and he had such a fancypants air about him that Lisa wondered if he was a friend of Renata's.

Someone from the opera? But if so, why would he be knocking on Heidi's door? Goodness, this wasn't Heidi's vet guy, surely?

'Good morning,' Lisa said somewhat primly. 'Are you looking for Heidi?'

'No, no, my dear, I'm actually looking for you.' There was a dramatic pause now, as if he was waiting for her reaction.

She frowned. 'I don't know you, do I?'

'Of course you do, Lisa.' And then he lifted his sunglasses and smiled.

That smile. *Whack.* Lisa knew exactly who it was, but she couldn't quite believe it. Very faintly, because she suddenly felt quite sick, she said, 'Hello, Gerry.'

CHAPTER TWENTY-EIGHT

Despite the regrettably damaged landscape that still looked like a battlefield, Renata enjoyed the drive to Cairns. She'd decided to leave quite early to give herself a whole day in the city before collecting Ellie from the airport.

Today she planned to return this hire car, which she'd initially shared with Rolf until one of his friends had delivered his ute. And she would also check out caryards in the hope of buying her own little run-around. It made sense to have her own wheels now that she'd be spending more time in the north.

To her delight, the hire car's return and the new purchase were achieved by lunchtime with minimal fuss. Paperwork completed, Renata jumped into her neat little silver Mazda and went in search of a good spot for lunch.

The Cairns Pier was always a great option. Cafés with water views abounded, and Renata quickly found a place that suited her, especially as it served seafood chowder, which was pretty much an auto buy for her.

With a lemon, lime and bitters in hand, she sank back into her chair and took in the view of the calm, tropical waters. She watched a catamaran heading out to sea, a tourist boat chugging into berth. Further out, a fishing boat was being circled by seagulls. Consciously she relaxed and thought about the rest of her day.

After lunch, she would enjoy a spot of shopping. She could do with another summery outfit, and she loved the way Cairns dress shops embraced the tropical vibe. Bright florals, floaty tops and colourful sandals were all the go here. Such a pleasant change after the black suits of the south.

With luck, she might also indulge in a little afternoon tea. Goodness, how long had it been since those cream teas of her London days? After that, she would head to the airport.

Renata was looking forward to Ellie's arrival. She'd felt guilty when the girl had lost her job, but that wasn't the only reason she'd hired her.

She was genuinely confident that she and Ellie could work together to achieve good publicity for Beacon Bay and, hopefully, they might be able to attract significant charity donations. Admittedly, Ellie would also help to fill the gap caused by Rolf's departure.

His decision to leave had been an unwelcome surprise. Renata had enjoyed his company immensely and now, as she waited for her meal, she found herself reliving the evening he'd told her his plans to move over to Lisa's place.

She'd been dismayed by the fierceness of her disappointment, and her immediate question had been whether this move was the result of all the gossip circulating about them.

He'd insisted it was simply a practical option. It meant he would get the job done faster. But damn the man – when Rolf had said goodbye the next morning, he'd given her a rather memorable kiss, and then he'd said, 'Pity there were no real grounds for all that gossip.'

'And whose fault was that?' Her response had probably been a shade tart. 'Certainly not mine.'

Rolf's answer had been one of his gentle smiles. 'You know that with Dave and Lisa both still here, I was trying to avoid too much awkwardness.'

'But it's happened anyway.' Watching his thoughtful expression, Renata had added, 'But don't worry, Rolf, I've already told Lisa it's nonsense.'

He'd seemed surprised. 'And she believed you?'

'I think she did. She's not easy to read, though, is she?'

'Ain't that the truth.' His wry smile, as he'd made this final remark, had been tinged with a hint of sadness that left Renata to wonder, yet again, how he really felt about that woman.

Perhaps it was just as well her seafood chowder arrived at that moment. Its deliciousness distracted her from matters she'd already spent far too much time pondering, without arriving at any useful answers.

Lisa couldn't quite believe she was dining in a restaurant in Mission Beach with Gerry Maffucci. From the moment he'd turned up on the doorstep this morning, she'd been in an odd, unhappy daze.

'What on earth are you doing here?' had been her first response, while clutching at Heidi's front-door frame with one hand and at the gaping neck of her dressing gown with the other.

'I've come to see *you*,' Gerry had replied, as if this was the obvious, only possible answer.

Lisa had not been impressed. Apart from the embarrassing fact that she was still in her pyjamas and hadn't washed her face or brushed her hair, seeing Gerry Maffucci in the flesh, after so many years, had felt like some kind of nightmare.

Even so, she'd been on the brink of automatically inviting him inside, as was her normal habit with a visitor, but luckily common sense had prevailed. This visit was not in any way normal.

Gathering as much dignity as she could muster, she'd said instead, 'As you can see, I wasn't expecting visitors.'

'No worries,' Gerry had quipped glibly. 'How about I come back in an hour?'

With her head spinning from this surprise coming on top of her sleepless night, Lisa had found herself helplessly agreeing. And then she'd spent a feverish time showering and dressing and applying makeup, while trying to think what possible reason Gerry might have for turning up out of the blue like this.

It couldn't possibly be like that other time, all those years ago, surely?

After Gerry arrived back, he'd been happy to explain his sudden appearance in the Bay. He had clients in the region whose homes had been damaged. But it seemed he'd also been intrigued by stories in the press about Rolf working to restore Lisa's house – and this had also been when he'd discovered that Lisa was divorced.

'I'm divorced too!' Gerry had announced as if this was the best ever news and some kind of evidence of their stars aligning.

Lisa, however, had been quite dismayed. Okay, so Gerry had made millions, and there'd been a time when the story of his success had impressed the hell out of her. But seeing him now, it was obvious that something else had happened along the way.

It wasn't the white hair or the trendy beard. Such changes were to be expected after all these years. But he was so flashy these days. His jewellery, his teeth, his car, his clothes.

How had she ever found that smile so dangerously captivating? Today it still felt dangerous, but without a glimmer of charm.

When she'd tried to tell Gerry that she had commitments – she was a regular at the Community Centre, after all – he'd quickly intervened.

'Lisa, Lisa, I'm here to donate thousands to your community's restoration project. And you surely have time to come and have lunch with an old friend? I know your son's café isn't open today, but we can head up to Mission Beach. I understand it escaped the cyclone, and I imagine you might prefer a bit of distance from here, so you wouldn't have to worry about gossipers.'

His promise of a generous donation had been the carrot, of course, and Lisa couldn't really see a way of securing the money for her community without also accepting his invitation. So, she'd sent a text to Heidi, letting her know about this new plan.

And here she was, once again wearing Heidi's yellow dress, and sitting at a table with Gerry Maffucci in a spacious dining area with tall potted palms, a diffuser wafting out scents of lemon and ginger, and floor-to-ceiling windows offering magnificent sea views.

Without consulting her, Gerry had already ordered the most expensive champagne on the menu, claiming that this reunion was, after all, a celebration. Then, having checked that Lisa liked seafood, he'd ordered a massively extravagant platter for two.

Possibly because it was a Monday, there were very few other guests in the restaurant. An elderly couple, well dressed, with the conservative, comfortable air of the well to do, and a group of young men no doubt having a business lunch. Lisa and Gerry were served quite promptly, but Lisa felt strangely uncomfortable, sitting there in the middle of a weekday, with a bottle of Dom Pérignon in a silver ice bucket. Soon there was also a three-tiered silver stand, lavishly laden with oysters, prawns, pieces of crab and crispy fish, along with lemon slices, sprigs of dill and a range of dips.

The signet ring on Gerry's little finger glinted as he lifted his champagne flute. 'Here's looking at you, kid.'

She couldn't believe he'd be quite so corny as to borrow one of the most well-known lines from a famous movie like *Casablanca*. He added a somewhat smug grin. 'It's so good to see you again.'

'Cheers,' Lisa managed in response, but she had no chance of matching the confidence in Gerry's smile.

Of course, the wine and food were delicious and under other circumstances, Lisa would probably have been very grateful for such a feast. Today, though, she felt uncomfortable and guilty.

Unfortunately, she knew this guilt wasn't simply the result of indulging in an extravagantly flash meal when so many of the Bay's residents were dealing with significant loss. Her emotional discomfort was irrevocably linked to her history with this man.

CHAPTER TWENTY-NINE

For Renata, the day had been a good one. Not only had she bought a new car, but a new summer kaftan that was a total delight and, to her surprise, a new handbag. A practical shoulder bag in a pretty shade of green, with exactly the right number of compartments for her money purse, her phone, her sunglasses, her passport and travel papers. Not that she was planning to travel any time soon.

Primed with an indulgent afternoon tea of freshly baked scones with jam and cream, she was in the best of moods as she drove into the car park at Cairns airport. She found a reasonably convenient parking spot, retrieved a ticket from the machine and headed for the arrivals hall.

There would be another twenty minutes or so before Ellie's plane was due to land, and like so many others who were waiting, Renata found a seat that offered a view of the arrivals screen and then she took out her phone.

Details of her new car insurance had already been sent via email, which was handy. She also had a message from her agent about a new job offer from Denver, Colorado, for Queen of the Night in

Mozart's *Magic Flute*. It was a role she'd always enjoyed, but she wasn't ready to think about that now.

Earlier in the day, she'd received a text from Ellie, reporting that she was on her way to Sydney airport and super excited. Renata had replied with a thumbs-up and a smiling emoji. Now, as there were no more messages, Renata tapped on her Sudoku app.

She had just successfully completed her second puzzle when the arrivals screen signalled that Ellie's flight had landed. It was on time, which was perfect. She and Ellie should make it back to Beacon Bay before dark. Renata sent a quick text.

Hi Ellie,

I'll be waiting near the baggage carousel.

Rx

Then she stood and gave her shoulders a surreptitious roll as she drew in a deep breath. She'd skipped her usual yoga and vocal exercises today, and her body always seemed to notice the lack. Oh, well, she would make up for it tomorrow.

After her many years of travelling, she knew all too well that it always took ages for passengers to disembark. In Cairns, they often needed to come across the tarmac before entering the terminal, which added to the slowness.

Renata took her time finding a good spot to wait that would give her a view of both the carousel and the incoming passengers.

She checked her phone again. Ellie hadn't responded to her text, but that was okay. She'd probably already stowed her phone in her bag.

Renata amused herself by watching the passengers. There were the usual tourists, many of whom were dressed far too warmly for Cairns, then the reunions of couples and of families, and the serious-faced business folk, complete with laptop bags and phone earbuds.

No sign of Ellie yet. She'd probably been stuck up the back, one of the last to get off.

The baggage carousel started moving, circling with luggage. More and more people grabbed suitcases and headed for the car park. And there was still no sign of Ellie.

Frowning, Renata checked her phone again, but there was no message. She decided she might as well call Ellie. It was probably a waste of time. The girl would pop into her line of sight at any moment.

Her call went straight to voicemail.

Mildly alarmed, Renata hurried back inside the main terminal, scanning the sea of people for a glimpse of Ellie. Surely, at any moment now, she would see her pretty face framed by her golden hair?

When there was still no sign of the girl, she tried to tell herself this was no big deal. She had travelled all over the world so many times, she knew missed flights were a common enough occurrence.

But if Ellie had missed her flight, she would have sent a message, surely? Renata had paid for the flight, but Ellie was a decent young woman. She wouldn't pull a con trick.

Stirrings of panic now sent Renata moving swiftly through the press of people and then almost running to the arrival gate listed for Ellie's flight. There was no one at the gate, but an attendant came out of the tunnel, pushing an elderly woman in a wheelchair.

Renata stepped towards them. The attendant was an attractive woman about her own vintage. 'I'm sorry to bother you, but do you know if all the passengers have come off this plane?'

'Oh, yes, I believe so.' The attendant looked down at the woman in the chair. 'I'm pretty certain you were the last passenger, weren't you, dear?'

The old lady nodded and closed her eyes, as if any kind of movement exhausted her.

'Okay, thank you.' Renata frowned as she looked down the empty tunnel. 'I don't suppose there's anyone else I could ask to see if my friend actually caught the flight, is there?'

'Oh, no, sorry. Not unless you're a law enforcement authority.'

Renata gave a helpless shake of her head.

'The captain doesn't even get to see the passenger manifest,' the attendant added.

'Right, thank you.'

Renata tried to stay calm, but her concern must have shown in her face. As the attendant was about to head off, she turned back. 'You could try the information desk. They might page this person for you.'

'All right, I might do that. Thanks for your help.'

Pushing the wheelchair ahead of her, the woman continued on and Renata pulled out her phone again. She sent another text message to Ellie and then tried calling her. But again, the call went to voicemail.

Now, Renata was truly worried. What on earth could have happened? She didn't fancy the idea of the information desk broadcasting Ellie's name all over the airport, but she was a little desperate and she didn't want to leave without having tried everything she could.

Surely, at any moment, Ellie would bounce into sight, smiling and waving and apologising about a sudden need to hurry to the loo, or something similar.

Fifteen minutes later, however, after several paging calls, Renata had no choice but to leave a final message.

Hi Ellie, I do hope you're OK. Please give me a call or text me. Rx

From the moment Gerry Maffucci had invited Lisa to lunch, she'd known that he was probably going to hit on her. At least she would be prepared for it this time. No way would she allow him to suggest that she owed him any special favours for the lunch, or anything as crass as that. With luck, he wouldn't be quite that sleazy.

Her first impression of him had improved marginally during the meal. At least the conversation was pleasant enough.

Gerry didn't talk too much about his squillions, although he did reveal that he'd actually been through two divorces. Lisa refrained from showing too much curiosity about these, even though she would have liked to know more. She asked instead about his sister, Bianca. She'd lost touch with her old friend. After high school, Bianca had headed south in search of big-smoke excitement, while Lisa had stayed in Cairns.

At first they'd exchanged letters, but these had dwindled to birthday and Christmas cards and then, eventually, these had stopped too.

'Bianca's living in Italy,' Gerry told her.

'Wow!' Lisa could feel her jaw drop. 'That's not what I was expecting to hear.' But then, a moment later, 'Actually, I shouldn't be so surprised. When we were in high school, we used to dream about going to Italy one day, to visit the land of our ancestors.'

'Yep. Well, that's exactly what Bianca did. And while she was there, she fell for a young Italian farmer called Gino.'

'Aww, that's sweet.'

'It was better than sweet. Gino grows grapes, and these days, he has one of Italy's top vineyards. He and Bianca are married and living in an amazing place in Tuscany and they have three children. Two boys and a girl.'

'Wow! That's fantastic. Nice work, Bianca. To go from a cane farm in North Queensland to a vineyard in Tuscany. That's brilliant.'

Lisa was genuinely pleased for her old schoolfriend, but she was also sad that they hadn't kept in touch. For a moment there, she found herself lost in the past, thinking about lost friends. Lost relationships. Lost dreams.

Bianca had followed her dream. And so had Rolf. Meanwhile, ever practical Lisa had kept her vision fixed fair and squarely on the here and now.

But she'd never been one for regrets. She was quite sure that looking back couldn't be helpful, particularly in the company of this man.

She told him about her three sons and all they'd achieved, and he seemed to listen politely. She also talked in a fair bit of detail about the cyclone and the recovery, and again, Gerry mostly paid attention.

By the time they reached the end of their meal, Lisa was pleasantly full and mildly tipsy – she wasn't used to drinking alcohol in the middle of the day. She thanked Gerry for his generosity. He paid for the bill with the flick of an app on his phone, and they went back outside, down the grand front staircase to the palm-fringed car park.

'You don't have to rush back, do you?' Gerry asked this question once they were seated in his car.

Lisa had been about to click her seatbelt in place. Now she frowned and felt a ripple of unease. 'Yes, I should get back to Beacon Bay.'

'I'm sure you work too hard, Lisa. You're a free woman these days and I've booked a nice little villa here. It's right on the seafront. Why don't you come back and relax, have another drink.'

Oh, God. Here it was. She'd known this pressure might come one way or another, but somehow she hadn't expected it to happen when she more or less trapped in Gerry's car. Just showed how clueless she was.

'I'd like to get back to Beacon Bay, please,' she said firmly. 'I – I'm expected.'

Gerry didn't reply, didn't move. For an uncomfortably long stretch of time, he simply sat in the driver's seat, one hand tapping lightly on the wheel as he stared ahead.

What was he waiting for? Did he think she was going to give in? Change her mind?

It was the worst moment for Lisa to look down at her left hand, to see the faint mark where her wedding and engagement rings had sat for so many years. Worse still to recall a shameful day, a day she'd been trying so hard to forget, when she'd been wearing her engagement ring . . .

CHAPTER THIRTY

The engagement ring that Rolf had given Lisa comprised two lovely diamonds in an art deco setting on a narrow, well-worn band. Obviously old-fashioned, but extremely elegant, the ring had originally belonged to Rolf's grandmother.

When his Grandma Ivy heard of her eldest grandson's plans to marry, she'd offered him her precious jewellery, along with the excuse that her arthritic knuckles had become too swollen for wearing rings. And to mark the ring's momentous handover, Rolf's mother had invited Lisa to afternoon tea.

Lisa could still remember every detail of that day, crowded into the small front room of the Anders's modest little cottage. Rolf, his mother, his grandmother and Lisa had sat around a dining table covered with a lace tablecloth, and Rolf's mother had used her best willow-pattern china.

There'd been a blue-and-white teapot, a sugar bowl and milk jug with matching cups, saucers and plates. Mrs Anders had also provided carefully ironed, hand-embroidered napkins, and she'd served iced teacake and lamington fingers that required delicate handling. Meanwhile Rolf's twinkling-eyed grandmother had proudly shown the young couple her photo album filled with faded black-and-white snaps.

Grandma Ivy had been such a very pretty young woman back in the 1920s and she'd looked so happy and very much in love with her tall, handsome fiancé.

'Bill couldn't afford to buy the ring before we were married,' she'd told them. 'So he gave me this ring on my birthday a few years later.'

Lisa had loved the ring immediately. The two matching diamonds made it somehow extra special. She'd liked to think of those sparkling twin gemstones as symbols of herself and Rolf fitting perfectly together.

Many years later, she'd tried to hand that ring back to Rolf. It had been one of the hardest of the many difficult moments during their divorce, but Lisa had never dreamed he might refuse to take it.

'I don't want it,' he'd said, and although he'd been glaring at her, he'd also looked so upset that Lisa had almost thrown her arms around him to comfort him.

She'd tried to insist. 'This ring belongs in *your* family, Rolf.'

And as she'd spoken those words, she'd been hit by an irreversible truth that had pressed like splinters into her heart. She and Rolf were no longer family.

And yet, she still had the ring.

Currently, it was in a box at Heidi's house, in a drawer and buried under T-shirts. After the cyclone, Lisa had toyed with leaving the jewellery box at her damaged house. If anyone had broken in there and stolen it, she'd have a good explanation for why it was no longer in her possession. But of course, she could never allow herself to be so reckless.

But now, with Gerry Maffucci sitting in his car beside her, she was remembering that other time when she'd been wearing the ring and had been totally, thoughtlessly reckless. *Oh, help.*

It had happened decades ago, and yet Lisa was still haunted by the shameful memories. And right now, she was desperate for Gerry to start the damn car and take her back to Beacon Bay.

Why on earth hadn't she thought to bring her own vehicle?

'Thanks very much for the lunch, Gerry.' She'd already thanked him in the restaurant, but she needed to bring this situation to a close. 'I'd really like to get back home now.'

He gave a slow shake of his head. 'No, that's not what you want, Lisa.'

'No?' *Yikes!* 'What do you mean?'

'I mean no, you don't want to hurry away. If you believe that, you're fooling yourself.'

'Don't talk nonsense.'

He stretched out an arm, letting his hand linger on the headrest at the back of her seat. 'You've been working too hard, Lisa. You need to relax.'

'No, I don't. I —'

'And I've missed you.' Gerry flashed her a smile then, the 'come hither' smile that had once sent her skyrocketing.

Now that same smile chilled her to the bone. 'Please, Gerry, take me back to the Bay.'

'Take it easy, kiddo. At least come and see this villa. It's gorgeous, like something out of a movie.'

'No, thank you. I need to get back.'

He gave a shrug. 'But I'm not ready to go back yet.'

'Very well. I'll catch a bus then.' Lisa was about to open her passenger door, when she heard an ominous surround-sound click. *Oh, my God.* Panic flared. 'You haven't locked all the doors?' This wasn't happening, surely? 'You can't lock me in, Gerry.'

She gave her door handle a frantic jiggle. She knew that a front seat passenger should be able to unlock a door, but in that moment she couldn't remember how to. Gripped by an almost suffocating dread, she couldn't think straight. 'Let me out. You can't do this.'

To her horror, Gerry chuckled.

Lisa wanted to hit him, to smack that smirky smile clear off his face, and she was about to yell at him when she heard the clicking sound again.

Instantly, she reached for her door handle and this time it opened. *Thank God.*

'I was only fooling around,' Gerry said, still grinning. 'Stirring you. A bit of fun.'

'Fun?' Was this guy for real? 'I don't happen to share your sense of humour.'

He pulled a face, stretching his mouth downwards at the ends. 'You've changed, Lis.' Only now did he retract his hand from the back of her seat. 'You're way too serious these days.'

This was possibly true, but Lisa wasn't prepared to discuss her faults with this man. 'I guess we've all changed,' she said somewhat primly. 'And as I said, if you want to stay here in your villa, I'm happy to get the bus back to Beacon Bay.'

As Gerry seemed to give this option some thought, Lisa realised she had no idea of bus timetables, but hopefully she'd find some kind of transport heading south.

'Nah,' he said suddenly, giving his steering wheel a thump. 'I'll take you. It's not far.'

With that, he started the engine, revving it rather more than was necessary and took off. He also turned on music – something loud and quite contemporary that Lisa had no chance of recognising. She wondered if he'd kept up with the new trends in the pop music scene, but she wasn't interested enough to ask, and she was grateful that the music meant they didn't need to talk.

When he pulled up at Heidi's place, her friend was on the front porch. Had she been waiting, hoping to catch a glimpse of the infamous Maffucci?

Lisa exited the car quickly. 'Thanks again for the lunch, Gerry.'

She could see him sending a curious glance Heidi's way, but the last thing she wanted was for her friend to go into hostess mode and invite him inside. She closed the passenger door firmly, stepped back and waved to him.

She turned, quickly opened the gate, stepped through and closed it behind her. Then, with all the dignity she could muster, she walked up to the house without looking back. It was only as she heard Gerry take off with another revving roar that she realised she'd forgotten to ask him about his supposedly generous donation plans.

CHAPTER THIRTY-ONE

The joy had completely fallen out of Renata's day. She was both worried and deflated as she drove back to the Bay. She went to her house and stowed her shopping away, but she'd lost all sense of the happy lift these purchases had given her. Popping into the kitchen, she let Peggy and Roger know that she wouldn't need dinner this evening and then promptly drove to the Frangipani Café.

She needed to talk to someone about Ellie, and as the girl had stayed at the café with Dave, he seemed the most likely option.

By the time she pulled up on the seafront, it was almost dark. The air held the last lavender hints of dusk, and noisy parrots were arriving in the trees, no doubt hoping to find enough leafy coverage for the night. Out on the bay, a solitary small boat trekked and a half-moon was lighting a silvery path over the water.

On most similar occasions, Renata would have headed over to the beach to drink in the beauty. This evening she was too worried, and when she saw that the café was closed, her spirits sank even further. Sitting there in her car, wrapped in a cloud of anxious gloom, she wondered if she would ever find out where Ellie was now.

She might have driven off then, if Rolf's vehicle hadn't suddenly appeared. When he pulled up outside the café, Renata let out the breath she'd been holding, and was out of her car quickly and crossing the road.

'Rolf.'

He clicked a key to lock his vehicle, then flashed her a surprised smile. 'Renata, hi.' He shot a pointed glance across the street to her car. 'You have new wheels?'

'Yes. I bought that little Mazda in Cairns this morning.'

'Nice one. Good choice.' He gave a nod back to the café. 'And Dave has a new window.'

'Oh, yes. It looks great, doesn't it? He must be relieved to be getting closer to normal.' She'd been too caught up in her own worries to notice the café's window. Now she got straight to the point. 'Are you visiting Dave?'

'I am, yes. The café's not open to the public tonight, but Dave's invited me to have dinner with him.'

'That's lovely. Look, I don't want to crash your dinner, Rolf, but I'd really like to have a quick word with Dave. I'm worried about Ellie.'

'Oh?' Rolf shot another glance to her car across the street. 'She's not here with you?'

'No. I was expecting her to arrive on a flight from Sydney this afternoon, but she didn't show. And she hasn't answered any of my phone messages.'

Now Rolf was frowning. 'That doesn't sound like Ellie.'

'I'm glad you think so. I was beginning to wonder if I'd completely misread her.'

'I doubt it. Come on, we'll see if Dave knows anything.' About to head across the footpath, Rolf stopped. 'Actually, Dave seemed surprised this morning when I told him Ellie was coming back up here, so he may not be much help.'

Renata couldn't hold back a small sigh. 'Still, it's worth a try.'

'Sure.'

Rolf gave only the lightest knock before the café door opened and a grinning Dave appeared. From behind him wafted the enticing aroma of frying onions. A bowl of colourful salad sat ready on the bench.

'Hi, Dad.' Dave's eyes widened when he saw Renata, but at least his smile held. 'Hi, Renata.'

Rolf wasted no time. 'Renata's concerned about Ellie. She was wondering if you've heard from her today.'

The transformation in Dave was immediate and fierce, as if any worry Renata had felt was now multiplied fivefold.

'I – I'm sorry,' he said. 'I haven't – I mean *we* haven't stayed in touch since Ellie left.' He swallowed somewhat nervously. 'Why? What's happened?'

'I have no idea,' said Renata. 'That's the problem. I was expecting her to arrive on a flight this afternoon. She texted me earlier in the day to say she was on her way to the airport, but since then there's been nothing.'

Dave was pale now. 'That's odd.' Turning, he hurried back to the kitchen and returned, phone in hand, and was already thumbing a text.

Apparently, he had no immediate response, but none of them had expected he would.

Dave slid the phone into his jeans pocket. 'What can we do?' He ploughed an anxious hand through his hair. 'There has to be someone we can ask.'

'I would have tried Ellie's former boss,' said Renata. 'But not much point when they're no longer talking to each other.'

'What about the airline?'

Renata shook her head. 'They can't help. The info desk at Cairns airport had no luck when they paged Ellie, and that was the best they could offer.'

'But there has to be something we can do. Contact the police? The ambulance?'

Rolf spoke now. 'I think that might be jumping the gun, son. I don't suppose you have any family contacts for Ellie?'

'No.' Dave frowned as if he was racking his brains. 'She doesn't have any family here in Australia. Her parents died when she was quite young. Then her grandmother brought her up, but she died a few years back.'

'Hell.' Clearly dismayed, Rolf now lifted a hand over his eyebrows, drawing them together.

Dave gave a cry of utter helplessness. 'So, are you just planning to do nothing, but wait and see?'

The despair in his voice was painful to hear. Renata hadn't realised that his feelings for Ellie ran so deep. 'I'm not sure we have much choice,' she said gently. 'And I'm really sorry I've landed this bad news on you.'

'It's hardly your fault,' said Rolf.

'No, I'm glad you came,' added Dave. 'And you may as well stay. Have something to eat with us.'

'No, no, I never intended —'

'Honestly, I'd prefer it if you stayed. Whatever's happened to Ellie, you're the most likely person to hear from her.' Dave nodded towards the kitchen. 'Come on. I was about to throw on a couple of steaks.'

'Well, thank you.' With a hand flattened against her stomach, Renata said, 'But a small corner of steak will do for me. I've already eaten rather well today.' With a smile, 'But I have to say those onions do smell amazing.'

Dave was reeling as he headed back to the kitchen. He'd already been madly missing Ellie, and since his dad's news this morning that

oming back to the Bay, his emotions had been all over the
it this latest update had totally whacked him for six.

at the hell could have happened? Where was she?

As he set a cast-iron pan on the stove to heat, his imagination
bounced from disastrous possibilities like an accident or a kidnap-
ping to the unhappy thought that Ellie might have pulled a swifty
over Renata somehow – swapped the plane ticket to Cairns for a
flight to Bali, or somewhere else exciting.

But surely the Ellie he'd come to know would never be so deceptive? Their time together *had* been brief, but he'd sensed the essence
of the girl. She was honest and caring and cautious.

The meat sizzled as it hit the hot pan, and Dave found himself
thinking again about Ellie's sad lack of a family. Admittedly, his
own family could annoy the heck out of him at times. While neither
of his clever, super-successful brothers had bothered to ring him
to see how he was coping after the cyclone, at least they'd rung
their mum. And Dave knew he had to accept his own role in their
communication breakdown.

When he'd blithely headed off overseas, he'd rarely bothered to
keep in contact with Chris or Nate. There'd been no fights or nastiness
between them, just a casual laziness. Even so, he knew they were there
if he needed them, and he couldn't imagine his life without them.

What must it be like for Ellie to have no family? No backup?
No safety net?

Hell. What happened at Christmas? On her birthday? Dave
supposed that her sad family situation was a big part of her caution
in casual relationships. She would be hoping for a deeper sense of
connection, a chance of continuity. Some kind of guarantee.

But if she'd lost her job now, on top of everything else, might the
sudden lack of any ties have launched her into 'don't care' territory?

Damn it. A burning smell brought Dave back to the job in
hand. Quickly, he flipped the steaks, relieved to see they weren't too

blackened, and after a minute or two he was slicing the meat and serving it onto a platter, along with glistening piles of caramelised onions.

'Sorry if one side's overdone,' he told his guests. 'I'm afraid I'm a bit distracted.'

The sympathetic response in his dad's eyes plucked a chord deep inside Dave. Yeah, family was important. He felt his throat and chest tighten. His eyes stung. Far out. He was having trouble keeping his shit together.

'Will we eat in the restaurant?' his dad was asking.

'Sure.' The chairs in there were more comfortable than the stools at the bench.

But then, as Dave carried the platter and salad bowl through, he had to make another apology. 'Sheesh, I haven't even set a table.'

'No worries. I can fetch plates and cutlery.' This came from Renata.

'And I'll get glasses,' added his dad.

'Except I haven't thought about wine either.'

'Relax, son. I brought a bottle of red with me.'

Dave hadn't even noticed the bottle sitting on the bench, complete with an impressive label and gold stickers announcing the prizes it had won.

As his dad brought it over to the table, he said, 'I suspect we could all do with a glass of something nice this evening.'

Dave nodded, but now he was reaching for his phone again. He'd been on high alert for any buzzing in his pocket and he was pretty sure there'd been no message, but he had to check.

Nothing there.

Of course.

He'd been foolish to hope.

They settled to the business of eating, interspersed with pleasant but careful conversation. His dad was making satisfying progress on the house. Renata had bought a new car. Dave had some decent bookings for the week ahead. The wine was exceptionally good. There were compliments for the food.

Carefully, no doubt cleverly, his dad asked him questions about Ellie. Dave shared the little he knew about her parents, her grandmother, her travels to the UK.

Both Renata and his dad commented that they'd been impressed by Ellie's interviews. She'd known the right questions to ask, had been prepared to push deeper at times, without being annoying.

Inevitably perhaps, Dave found himself telling them how much she'd seemed to enjoy working here in the kitchen and how the customers had really liked her.

'I certainly had the impression that she was looking forward to coming back here,' said Renata.

Which brought them circling back to the main, worrying question. Where the hell was Ellie now?

In an effort to fill the awkward conversation gap that this caused, Dave asked, 'How about dessert?'

Renata shook her head. 'Thanks, but I couldn't possibly.'

His dad was looking interested, though. And then a phone rang.

CHAPTER THIRTY-TWO

Lisa had never felt so bad. She hadn't been able to talk about Gerry with Heidi, even though she'd known her friend was dead curious and ready to listen.

Lisa had shaken her head, murmured 'Don't ask,' and had gone straight to her room and shut the door.

Once alone, though, all she could manage was to throw herself onto the bed and bury her face in a pillow. She couldn't believe she'd been so stupid. How on earth had she ever thought Gerry Maffucci was worth a minute of her attention? Not just her attention – her girlish lust and her adult envy. How had she never noticed the man was a totally crass and shallow sleaze?

And why in hell's name had it taken her so long to wake up to this?

It was painful to realise after all these years that Gerry had always been this way. A prick right from the start. All that time . . . in high school when his smiles had lured her into foolishly believing he'd invite her to the formal . . . and then again later in Cairns . . .

She couldn't bear to think about that. It was the guilt of that later time that was killing her now.

And to make matters worse, although she'd finally woken up to the truth today, she hadn't even managed to get the promised donation money out of him.

Leopards and spots. Lisa was afraid the old saying applied to her as much as to Gerry.

She was still as hopeless now as she'd been in her teens. Worthless.

Rolf was well rid of her.

Rolf.

Oh, help.

Thinking of him brought noisy tears. Tears of shame. Of remorse.

And clearly, the crying was too much for Heidi. There was knocking on the bedroom door. Then Heidi's voice. 'Lisa. Lisa, darling.'

'Sorry!' Lisa called back, her voice teary and choked. 'I'm okay.'

'But you can't be, you poor thing.'

'I'm just having a moment. Truly. I'll be all right soon.'

'You're sure?'

'Yep.' Drawing a huge breath, Lisa once again willed the tears to stop, but it would only be a temporary reprieve. She knew that. She would take ages to get over this.

'I won't stay in here all night,' she called.

Lisa hadn't turned on any lights, and as Heidi's footsteps slowly retreated, the bedroom was so dark that the mirror's glass was the only thing she could see clearly. Her reflection was ghostly. Ghostly and ghastly. Her face swollen and tear streaked. Her hair a wild tangle.

But as she stared at that hopeless, hapless visage, she knew there was only one possible way she could ever feel better.

Confession. The cleanser of souls.

She hadn't been to church in years and she didn't plan to go now. It wasn't God she needed to talk to, although he was welcome to listen in, if he liked.

Turning on a lamp, Lisa went to the dressing table and opened the middle drawer. She found the jewellery box under the pile of T-shirts and undies.

She picked it up and clutched it tightly to her chest. *Yes*. It had to happen tonight.

In the café, it was Renata's phone that was ringing. She'd left it in her bag hanging over the back of her dining chair, but she quickly retrieved it and managed to answer before the caller hung up.

'Hello.'

Rolf held his breath as he watched her, and he was sure Dave must be doing the same – hoping against hope. He saw the answer in Renata's eyes a split second before she cried out.

'Ellie! Oh, Ellie, it's so good to hear from you.' Then he saw her frown. 'Where did you say you are?' A gasp. 'Oh, my goodness.'

To Dave and Rolf, Renata whispered, wide-eyed, 'Ellie's in hospital. In St Vincent's.'

Rolf was sitting next to Dave. He sensed the jolt of shock that hit his son, and he slipped an arm around his shoulders. They both sat breathlessly still, waiting and watching, trying to read the concern in Renata's face while she listened to her phone.

'Oh, you poor thing,' Renata said at last. 'Yes, I've certainly been worried. No, I'm not in Cairns. I'm back in the Bay now. And yes, yes, I'll tell them.'

Renata listened to Ellie for a little longer, and then she said her goodbyes, disconnected and set her phone on the table. She let out a breath, a sigh. Rolf hoped it was a sigh of relief.

'Is she okay?' This burst from Dave.

Renata nodded. 'Yes, Dave. She's fine. Or at least, she's not in too much pain. But the poor thing. She was on her way to the airport, on a pedestrian crossing, when she was hit by a car.'

'Bloody hell.' This came from Rolf, while bedside him, Dave swore even more fiercely.

'But luckily she doesn't seem to be too badly injured,' Renata added. 'Her back is bruised and the paramedics were worried about a fracture, so they took her straight to the hospital. She's been admitted and they've been doing X-rays and whatever else is needed, and they're waiting for a full radiology report.'

'At least they're being thorough,' said Rolf.

'Yes. There's a holdup, though. Interns waiting for specialist advice, or something. Ellie will be there overnight. Oh, and her phone must have gone flying when she was hit. Into the gutter, perhaps. The paramedics didn't notice it, so she may not get it back. She was using a hospital phone to make that call. Apparently, someone there was very resourceful and tracked down my number via my agent.'

Renata looked a little teary now as she smiled. 'Poor Ellie.' She reached for a paper napkin to dab at her eyes.

Dave had his lips tightly pressed tightly together, as if he was struggling with his emotions too.

'I daresay we'll have to wait till we get more news,' said Renata. And then, as if she was thinking aloud, 'I might need to organise some kind of accommodation for Ellie in Sydney. She might not be able to fly straight away and she's finished up at her apartment, put her things into storage. She could stay at my place, of course. Perhaps I should fly down there.' Taking up her phone again, she said, 'I suppose I should check what flights are available.'

Rolf retrieved the wine bottle now, and he was about to suggest that they could all do with a top-up, when there was a knock at the cafe's door.

A beat later, the door was pushed open and Lisa appeared. Rolf had never seen her looking so pale and tense and strained.

She stood stock still, taking in the scene of the three of them seated around the table with the remnants of their meal, the glasses of wine.

'Oh,' was all she said.

Lisa almost turned and charged straight back out of the cafe.

Coming here had taken so much courage. She'd gone to the house first, hoping to find Rolf alone, but then, when he clearly wasn't there, she'd circled past the café and had seen his parked ute. So she'd bravely headed inside, even though she'd known Dave would be here as well.

But she hadn't expected Renata. How had she missed seeing the bright red hire car? And the three of them looked so – what was the right word? Intimate?

'I'm sorry,' she said. 'I – I . . .' She was struggling to find words again, had no idea how to explain why she was here.

Now Rolf was getting up from the table, and he looked concerned rather than annoyed. 'Hello, Lisa.'

She gave a helpless little nod. 'Hi.'

'Is everything all right?'

'Yes,' she managed, even though she felt anything but all right. And then, because she couldn't just stand there, staring and gaping, like a sideshow clown waiting for a ball to fall into its mouth, she tried again. 'I was hoping to have a bit of a chat with you, Rolf. I went to the house first, then I saw your ute here.'

Good grief. Already, this was way too longwinded. 'No worries,' she said, backing to the door. 'We can talk another time. Sorry to interrupt. I'll leave you to it.'

'No, it's okay.' Rolf took another step towards her. 'Don't go. We've finished dinner.'

'I'm only here as a ring-in,' called Renata. 'I wanted to talk to Dave about Ellie.'

'And we're going to be busy checking flight times now,' chimed in Dave.

Lisa was totally confused. She had no idea why they were talking about Ellie and flight times.

As if realising this, Rolf said, 'We can go back to the house, Lisa. I'll explain about Ellie, and you can tell me whatever it is you wanted to discuss.'

'Are you sure?'

With a chorus of positive responses from all three of them, Lisa realised she might as well depart. 'All right then.' She lifted a hand to wave. 'I'll head over to the house.'

'See you soon,' came Rolf's response as she left.

'Thanks.'

As she started her vehicle, her nerves ramped up more violently than ever. Now she had no choice. Tonight she was finally going to have the conversation.

CHAPTER THIRTY-THREE

When Lisa let herself into the house, her emotions threatened to give way again. The knowledge that Rolf was living here brought back too many memories.

There was still no power. Rolf had a small generator to recharge his power tools, but Lisa had to use her phone's torch, rather than flicking a switch, and the simple act of lighting the stairwell woke echoes of her boys' laughter as they'd chased each other up these stairs.

She reached the living room, turned on the battery-powered lamps Rolf had left, and the space, with all the damaged furniture, carpets and knick-knacks removed, felt huge and empty. So many precious keepsakes she would never see again. The pottery candleholder her grandmother had brought back from Sicily. The gilt-framed photos of Chris and Sophie's wedding. The beautiful painting by an elderly artist in Wongaling Beach.

Now, just two folding camp chairs stood where once there'd been lounges, as sagging and comfortable as old friends, and a wave of sorrow swept through Lisa.

But she mustn't let herself sink into gloom. She needed to concentrate on practical matters, like the great progress Rolf had made on the repairs.

Looking up, she could see that the roof and rafters were almost completely restored. *Well done, Rolf.* And he'd even repaired the skirting board, which hadn't been part of his remit.

The walls and beams would all need repainting, and that meant wrestling with those darned trestles and ladders again. But Lisa had insisted that she would look after that task, so there wasn't much more Rolf needed to do here. Soon he'd be gone.

She looked again to the camp chairs. Rolf must have brought them up from the garage, and she supposed that was where they'd sit to have their talk.

The talk. *Gulp.* She could do with a cuppa. She hadn't had anything to eat or drink since leaving Mission Beach.

She was in the kitchen, and the kettle on the little camp stove was humming to life, when she heard Rolf's vehicle arrive and then his footsteps on the stairs. *Deep breath.*

'Hi,' she called, hoping she didn't look or sound too nervous as he crossed the living room. 'I'm making a cuppa. Would you like one?'

'Yes, please.' Almost immediately, he added, 'But you might have trouble finding clean mugs. I have a habit of letting them pile up in the sink and then forgetting to actually wash them.'

'Yes, I seem to remember.' She managed the briefest of smiles, but she didn't look his way. Nostalgic recollections were unhelpful right now. 'There should be enough extra hot water in the kettle to rinse a couple of mugs,' she said, and as she attended to this, she asked, 'What's this about Ellie and looking for flights?'

'Ellie's been in an accident. Some sort of hit-and-run on a pedestrian crossing.'

'Goodness. The poor girl.'

'Yes, but it doesn't seem too serious, luckily, although she's in hospital until tomorrow at least, and Renata will probably head down there.'

'Renata will?' Lisa set down the mug she'd just dried and frowned at Rolf. 'Why would she do that?'

'She was planning to bring Ellie back here to work for her, as her personal publicist. I guess she feels responsible, especially as Ellie doesn't have any family.'

'Gosh. That's very good of her.' And then, as she jiggled teabags, 'Do you still take your tea black with two sugars?'

'I do. Thank you.'

Lisa turned and lifted the lid on the esky Rolf was using. 'Oh, looks like you don't you have any milk at all.'

Rolf pulled a face, a grimacing apology. 'No, sorry. I guess I wasn't expecting visitors.'

She didn't enjoy black tea, but that was a minor matter compared to the issue she needed to share with him. She managed a gracious smile and added an extra spoonful of sugar to her mug. 'No worries.' Then she switched to the safety of a completely different question. 'Are Renata's neighbours still staying in her house?'

'They are, yes, but hopefully not for too much longer. I've more or less agreed to do some work on their place. It won't be till I've finished here, of course.'

'I wondered if you'd take on other jobs in the Bay. Everyone's talking about how difficult it is to find tradies.'

'Yeah. It's a bit hard to say no.'

'Except that you do have a deadline for your next book, I imagine.'

'I do. It'll be a juggling act. I won't be able to make too many outside commitments.'

The tea was ready. Lisa extracted the bags and handed Rolf a mug. Soon they would run out of small talk.

'So, will we sit in the comfy chairs?' His smile hinted at sarcasm as he pointed to the camp chairs in the empty lounge area.

'Don't have much choice, do we?'

He was still smiling and looking totally relaxed as he eased himself into one of the chairs. 'Have you made a decision about your furniture?'

Lisa nodded. 'I've spoken to the insurance people. It's not really worth trying to get any of it repaired. Seems best to buy new.'

'That should be fun.'

'I suppose it might be.' Now wasn't the time to remember the pleasure they'd had when they'd bought their original furniture together.

As she set her bag on the floor beside her chair, she felt through the soft leather till her fingers found the cube-shaped jewellery box inside. Her heart seemed to take off like a runner from the starting block.

'So,' said Rolf, now that they were both settled and nursing their mugs of tea, 'What would you like to talk about?'

Lisa's heart seemed to stop altogether now. Good heavens, was she strong enough for this?

For her, there was only one way to start. She set the mug on the floor beside her and picked up her bag, unzipped it and took out the jewellery box.

She could see straight away that Rolf recognised the royal blue cube with its gold trim. His smile vanished and he looked as suddenly tense as she felt.

Lisa stood. Her legs were trembling. Her mouth was trembling. As she held out the box, her hand was trembling. 'The last time I tried to give you this, you wouldn't take it, Rolf. But I really need you take it this time.'

'For God's sake, Lisa. What's this about?'

'That's what I'm planning to tell you.'

An uncomfortably long moment passed as she stood there, holding the box, trembling and waiting. She feared Rolf was going to refuse it again, but at last he held out his hand and she placed it in his all too familiar palm.

She couldn't bear to make eye contact. Hurrying back to her chair, she sat, crossed her legs, picked up her mug and took a sip of tea.

Then, with a deep breath, she dived in.

'I don't deserve that ring, Rolf. Some – something happened after we were engaged that I've never been brave enough to tell you.'

In the silence that followed she could hear her heart banging. She stared at the floor, too scared to look up.

'Who was he?' Rolf's voice held a steely note she'd never heard before.

Lisa closed her eyes. Would she get the name out without stammering or sobbing?

There was only one way. She had to spill everything quickly.

'His name's Gerry Maffucci. He lived on a cane farm near ours and I'd pretty much known him all my life. We went to the same school. His sister was my best friend.'

Now that she'd started, she had no choice but to keep going. 'I had a silly crush on him in high school, but we never dated. I thought he was going to take me to the formal, but he didn't. I suppose he was also my first heartbreak.'

Sheesh. Out loud, it sounded so hollow, but Lisa had no desire to embellish this history and she couldn't stop now. 'And then a few years later, he turned up in Cairns with this nonsense story about how I'd always been the one for him, and he couldn't believe I was going to marry someone else. I – I have no idea how I fell for it.'

With her gaze still fixed on the bare floorboards, she said, 'I went to a hotel with him. It was only ever just the once.'

A killing silence fell. She continued to stare at a scratch mark on the floor. She couldn't bear to look up, but out of the corner of her eye, she caught a movement from Rolf as he held up the box.

'And you were wearing this ring while you were having sex with this – this – whoever?'

'Not quite. I – I did take it off.' But it hadn't been until she was in the lift heading up to the hotel room. She could still remember how guilty she'd felt as she'd slipped the ring into her handbag.

'So what happened? Why the hell did you put up with marrying me when you could have had him?'

Put up with you? It hadn't been like that. Could she ever explain this properly? Did she even know how to?

She was surprised she wasn't crying. Her tear ducts were probably too worn out.

'He wasn't serious, of course. I was just another chick to score, and I soon realised I'd made a terrible mistake.'

Taking another hasty mouthful of tea, she chanced an anxious glance in Rolf's direction. She saw the raw emotion in his face and knew she had to get this over and done with. 'I realised that I wasn't in love with him, that I never had been, really. I – I loved you. I wanted to marry you. But I couldn't bring myself to tell you about him. I didn't want to hurt you.'

Until this point, Rolf had made no attempt to open the box, and now he set it down on the floor beside him, as if he was keen to be free of it.

'But the guilt has been eating at me,' Lisa said. 'All these years.'

A heavy sigh broke from him. 'So why wait till now? Why didn't you throw this at me during the divorce? There was plenty of shit flying then, as I remember.'

'I – I guess that's a good question.' But a tough one to answer.

'I suppose you were too busy feeling hard done by,' he said. 'You needed to be the victim in our marriage.'

Ouch. Lisa was tempted to snap back at this dig. But throughout the divorce and its aftermath she'd spent too much time wrapped in anger and righteous indignation. Tonight, she'd come in the hope of peace, not war.

'I – I suppose you're right about that,' she said quietly. 'I didn't mention it because I was protecting myself. I didn't want to give you ammunition.'

After a longish pause Rolf said, 'But that still doesn't explain why you're bringing it up now. I thought we'd both moved on.'

Lisa fiddled with a frayed piece of canvas on the arm of her chair. 'I suppose the timing does seem off, especially as you've been so generous about coming back here and fixing this house for me.'

She drank more of her cooling tea in an attempt to compose herself before she continued. 'Okay. Full disclosure.'

She sat a little straighter, as did Rolf.

'Gerry Maffucci has made loads of money selling insurance, and he turned up here in the Bay this morning, promising big donations for our cyclone recovery projects. He asked me to have lunch with him. And I went, because I wanted that money for the restoration. I knew it was risky, there'd be a catch, and afterwards – no surprise – he expected me to go back to some villa with him.'

Even now, she was cringing at that memory. 'It was incredibly blatant. So crude. There was no way I'd go with him, of course, and I couldn't believe I'd ever been so clueless about him.'

Phew. She'd got it all out and she was still dry-eyed. 'I'm so ashamed of myself, Rolf. I've spent hours in tears since I got back. And – and I just felt I had to confess, even though it's too late and it – it might even be selfish of me to want to offload all this now. Way too late. I'm sorry. I'm such a —'

'Lisa, stop.' Rolf held out a silencing hand. 'I've heard enough.'

Obediently, she stopped and as she did so, her eyes filled with stinging tears. She dashed them away with the back of her hand.

Rolf looked shaken and pale, and she knew it was time to calm down. To back off. She'd thrown her confession at him, whether he'd wanted it or not.

She picked up her mug from the floor and was about to fetch his when she noticed he'd barely touched it. 'Thanks for listening, Rolf. But I'm not asking you for absolution.' She took the mug to the sink. Underneath she found detergent.

Rolf was still in the chair. She squirted a little into the mug, added hot water from the kettle and then she picked up her bag, hitched it over her shoulder.

'I'll say goodnight.' As she crossed the room, she paused by his chair, touched a hand briefly to his shoulder.

Rolf gave a curt nod. 'Goodnight.'

Lisa continued on down the stairs, but she didn't feel as if she'd achieved very much. She supposed there wasn't much point in an apology that came forty years late.

It was only as she reached the bottom that she remembered the other thing she'd been meaning to tell Rolf – news he'd probably much rather hear. For a moment she stood there, wondering if it was too late to bother him now, but it would be good to leave on a more positive note.

Before she lost her nerve, she turned and hurried back up the stairs. Rolf was still in the camp chair, looking uncharacteristically slumped and forlorn. His eyes glistened with a suspicious sheen.

Lisa came to a dismayed halt. Strong, self-controlled Rolf had never looked so lost. The sight of him this way scorched straight to her heart. Her throat was so choked she wasn't sure if she could speak, but she would make everything so much worse if she stood there crying.

'I just wanted to tell you that I read your book *Second Spring*. It's amazing, Rolf. So clever. I really enjoyed it.'

Then, before she turned the evening into an even worse disaster, she gave a quick wave and almost ran back down the stairs. Somehow, she managed to reach the bottom without stumbling or falling.

CHAPTER THIRTY-FOUR

Ellie was not a fan of hospitals. Visiting her gran in her final weeks had been heartbreaking, and Ellie had developed a dread of the spotless corridors, the hushed voices and solemn faces, the trolleys and screens and tubes.

Now, as a patient, however, she was viewing this same scene quite differently. It showed how important perspective could be.

After her traumatising accident, the paramedics and hospital staff had been genuine angels of mercy. So kind, so comforting and efficient.

Finding herself in shock and pain and sprawled on the bitumen, Ellie had been overwhelmed with gratitude for the kind people who'd stopped to comfort her, and then the uniformed men who'd bundled her onto a stretcher and lifted her into the back of an ambulance.

Almost straight away, cooling icepacks had been applied to the bruising on her back, and a friendly middle-aged fellow called Joe had sat with her, all smiles and calming chat, while she'd been whizzed off to hospital.

Sure, there'd been tedious admission forms to fill in, and the hospital still seemed to be a mass of corridors and closed doors and patients lying on trolleys. But for Ellie, there'd been kindness from a cheery guy called Brady who'd pushed her on a trolley down to X-ray. And the radiologist and her assistant had been full of sympathy for Ellie and dismayed that her injuries had been caused by such a callous incident.

A police officer had arrived to question her, but she'd also been kind and sympathetic – and she'd assured Ellie that they should be able to track the culprit, following up on CCTV footage. Then, back in the ward, a nurse called Precious – with shiny black skin, dreadlocks and a smile to match her sweet name – had delivered Ellie more caring words, along with tablets for her pain and advice for the most comfortable positions to lie in.

Ellie had been somewhat depressed and lonely ever since she'd lost her job, which was possibly why she'd been so deeply apprecia-tive of these people's attention.

Anyhow, no point in trying to be too friendly. Ellie would be leaving the hospital soon.

Quite early this morning, a young doctor had come to Ellie's room and told her he was reasonably confident that she didn't have any fractures. She'd only suffered bruising that should heal in a week or two. She would probably be discharged later today, just as soon as they received confirmation via the final radiology report. He couldn't give her a firm time, though, as the specialist involved was particularly busy.

To fill in the boring waiting period, Ellie had showered and changed into clean clothes. After that, she'd decided to sit in a chair, rather than climb back onto the bed. There was only one chair in her room and it was in the corner, opposite the doorway, but she was comfortable seated with icepacks in place and supported by pillows.

She wanted to keep busy, though, or she'd only start wondering about a certain chef and what he might be doing right now – and whether he'd heard the news of her accident. Might he even have tried to phone her?

No, girl, give it a miss.

He couldn't phone her, of course, unless he called the hospital, and that was highly unlikely. The loss of her phone was pretty damned annoying.

Yesterday, when Ellie had headed onto that fateful crossing, she'd been holding the phone in one hand, all ready for the airport check-in process. Then *wham!* She had no idea where it had ended up.

Now she had to worry about the cost of buying a new phone. Worse, there was the nuisance of regathering all her contacts' info. Just the same, Ellie knew she had a lot to be grateful for. Number one being Renata's generosity.

Not only had Renata offered her employment, plus the money for another airfare, she'd also offered her apartment in Newtown for Ellie to use until she felt comfortable enough to make the journey north.

Ellie hoped this would be soon. She was really looking forward to getting back to the Bay. To work, of course. No other reason.

Yeah, right.

This brought her back to thinking about Dave again and it was time to distract herself. There was a pen in her bag, and a kind orderly had brought a newspaper to her room along with the breakfast tray, so she might as well start on a crossword.

It wasn't long before she was happily absorbed. She was trying to work out an answer for *A table of happenings and clear designs (8 letters)* when a male voice spoke her name.

'Ellie.'

The doctor at last. She looked up. Gasped. The person in the doorway was not the doctor.

Oh, my God! Was she dreaming? She couldn't believe it.

'Dave?'

'Hi, Ellie.'

He looked incredibly sexy in faded jeans and a slim-fitting white T-shirt that showed off his impressive chest. He'd tied his hair back into a neat bun and had a backpack hitched over one broad shoulder.

But what was he doing here? How on earth had he found her? So many questions hit her at once.

Dave was still standing just inside the doorway and, given the way they'd parted, Ellie supposed he might be as cautious about this moment as she was.

'How are you?' he asked, his expression full of concern.

It took her a moment or two to recover from the shock, and then she was so ridiculously excited, she needed another moment before she could actually speak. 'I – I'm not too bad, thanks. My back's sore, but it seems I was lucky.'

Dave smiled now. 'That's such great news. We've all been so worried.' This was nice to hear. 'I was sorry to hear what happened about your job.'

'Thanks, Dave.'

'But it's great that Renata snapped you up.'

'Yes, she's amazing.' Ellie had to ask. 'But what are you doing here?'

He gave an amused shrug. 'Three guesses.'

He couldn't have come all this way just to see her, surely? A flood of happiness surged through Ellie, while she simultaneously battled another raft of questions. 'My first guess is that Renata let you know about the accident?'

'Yes, she was actually at the café when you called last night.'

'Okay – so what's happening at the café now? Who's looking after it?'

'Janet's holding the fort, with help from Renata and my mum. I can't stay away for too long, of course.'

Amazing. Sitting right here in this hospital room, Ellie could so easily picture those lovely folk, busy in the Frangipani Café in that pretty little bay at the other end of Australia's long eastern coastline.

Just thinking about the thousands of kilometres that separated Sydney from Beacon Bay, she had to ask, 'How did you get here so quickly?'

'Up at the crack of dawn.' By now, Dave had come further into the room and he set his backpack down beside a tall cupboard. 'Managed to grab a seat on the early flight.'

'Not just to see me?'

His response was another smile, this time accompanied by an eye-roll. 'No, Ellie, to see the Sydney Opera House.' Then his smile turned gorgeous and warm and gentle. 'Of course I wanted to see you. I was so worried.'

Thud. She wanted to give way to the excitement building inside her, but her hard-won habit of caution wouldn't let go. 'But I don't understand. I thought we agreed —'

'Yeah, I know.' Dave had moved to the end of the bed now, less than a metre from her. 'When you left, we agreed that we shouldn't stay in touch.' With another shrug, he said, 'But I'm afraid I chose to break that agreement.'

Ellie stared at him, possibly gaping, unsure how to reply, wanting to understand exactly what this meant.

Now Dave lowered himself onto the edge of the bed. He looked at the chart hooked over the railing, at the crisp sheets that Precious had tucked in so neatly while Ellie had been in the shower. 'I didn't plan to dump a massive explanation on you the minute I arrived.'

'I don't mind.' Truth be told, Ellie was desperate to hear his explanation. 'I'm feeling fine, Dave. Please – keep going.'

His dark brown eyes seemed to shimmer with emotion now. Nervousness? Tenderness? Ellie held her breath.

A knock sounded at the door.

This time, the man in the doorway was almost certainly the doctor. His hair was very short and streaked with grey, and he wore glasses and a neat white shirt, grey suit and a maroon-and-white spotted tie. 'Elinor Bright?' he asked.

'Yes, it's Ellie.' She almost added *sir*.

'Hello, Ellie. I'm Dr Gallagher.'

Dave was already on his feet, and he gave a courteous dip of his head. 'I'll just wait outside.'

'Are you here to take Ellie home?' the doctor asked him.

Dave's eyes widened. 'Well, yes,' he said. 'When she's ready.'

'Very good. No need to leave.' The doctor turned to Ellie with a smile. 'I'm pleased to report that although you have significant bruising, there's no sign of any fractures.'

'Oh, that's great news, doctor. Thank you.'

'So you're free to leave.'

'Yeah, great news,' added Dave.

The doctor nodded to them both. 'A nurse will be here soon to oversee your discharge. Just keep up the regular cold packs for the next twenty-four hours, and after that, heat is the best treatment for those bruised muscles. Heat packs and hot showers and gentle stretches. And the painkillers if you need them.'

'That sounds good. Thank you, doctor.'

With yet another nod and a polite smile, he departed, heading swiftly back down the corridor.

Ellie looked to Dave again. She was relieved her injuries weren't bad. But scant moments ago, before the doctor's good news, Dave had been on the brink of telling her why he'd broken their no-further-contact agreement.

She supposed part of the story might be the fact that she'd already planned to come back to the Bay and, as it was a small town, they were bound to see each other. But would he come all this way to tell her that?

She'd been sure there was more and she longed to hear it.

But Dave was pulling his phone from his jeans pocket. 'I'll just let Renata know the good news,' he said.

He'd barely connected with Renata when Precious appeared.

'You're going home,' she announced to Ellie with a big warm smile.

Dave stepped outside then, and Ellie turned her attention to everything involved with being discharged.

'So what do you think?' Renata was looking almost nervous as she watched Janet and Lisa taste the chocolate cake she'd made that morning in the café's oven.

The three women were in the café, enjoying coffee and Renata's cake, while they planned in more detail how they would tackle running the place in Dave's absence. The broad plan was that Janet would be chef, Renata her kitchenhand, while Lisa looked after all the tab records, the stacking and unstacking of dishwashers, and also helped the high-schoolers with waiting and any other odd jobs required.

Today, Lisa had also discovered that a frangipani tree in her back garden was once again producing new flowers, so she'd picked some to set in little vases on the tables. But Renata had totally trumped her efforts with this chocolate cake.

'It's absolutely amazing,' Janet declared.

Lisa had to agree. 'It's delicious. Is that apricot jam in the middle? I don't think I've ever tasted that combination. And then the lovely, smooth chocolate on top. It's great.'

'Yes, it's apricot jam. I'm so glad you like it.' Renata was beaming now. 'The recipe is from Vienna, where I used to live. I'm not much of a cook, but while I was there I wanted to master something special and I settled on this. The Austrians call it Sachertorte.'

'Well, I'd say you've certainly mastered it,' said Janet. 'It's wonderful.'

'Thank you,' said Renata. 'It was very good of you to let me make it here, where there's not just power, but a proper commercial kitchen.' Then she added more carefully now, 'And as you were more or less supervising, and you've given it your stamp of approval, Janet, I was wondering if we could offer it to customers for dessert.'

'Absolutely!' Janet couldn't have looked more delighted. 'I've been worrying about how I'd manage desserts on top of everything else.'

'I'd be happy to make an extra one,' said Renata. 'The recipe's fun, although I know it's not exactly tropical.'

Janet waved this concern aside. 'No, it's perfect. Anyway, we do still have mango trifle in the fridge. But I'll have to check whether we have your ingredients.'

'That's okay.' Renata winked now. 'I've brought more of everything I need with me.'

'Oh, aren't you an angel?'

Lisa had to agree. She felt rather bad that she'd initially tried to dislike this woman. Renata had no airs and graces, and she was so obviously keen to help any and everyone. 'I know Dave'll be thrilled,' she said.

'I hope so. And you know, Sachertorte is actually rather fitting under the circumstances. It was invented for Prince Metternich when his chef was ill and an apprentice had to step in. The apprentice came up with this cake, and now it's one of Vienna's most famous dishes, along with wiener schnitzel and apple strudel.'

'What a great story,' said Janet.

'It is, isn't it?' Lisa laughed. 'I can see it on the menu. From Vienna to Beacon Bay.'

CHAPTER THIRTY-FIVE

Renata's apartment in Newtown was only ten kilometres from the CBD, and the Uber that Dave organised took them there in next to no time. Ellie wasn't especially familiar with this suburb, as it was well above her pay grade, but she knew its reputation as ultra trendy and popular with young professionals.

She'd certainly heard about the many restaurants and bars in the area, and the Enmore Theatre was famous for its live music. Also, the colourful shops and boutiques on King Street were well known for selling interesting fare such as handmade accessories, retro clothing and rare books.

Renata's two-bedroom apartment wasn't overly flash or large, which made sense, given that she spent so much time travelling, but there were plenty of tall windows that provided views of the pleasant leafy street. French doors opened onto a little patio where pots of bougainvillea and succulents obviously thrived with very little attention.

The living area was comfy and attractive, with honey-toned timber flooring, gorgeous Persian rugs and a beautiful antique dresser displaying an interesting collection of pottery.

'Wow,' Ellie said, as she looked around her, relieved to have made this journey without too much discomfort. 'This feels so homey.'

'It does, doesn't it?' Dave had brought her suitcase and shoulder bag up in the lift, as well as his backpack, and now he set them down on the carpet and joined her in looking about. 'Very nice. Very Renata.'

Ellie took in more details. A small upright piano stood in a corner, and one end of the dining table was crowded with piles of musical scores. Elsewhere, she noted a colourful lamp that might have been Venetian glass, an elegant copper bowl filled with artistic pieces of driftwood, a framed poster of a medieval painting with the words Museo del Prado Madrid printed across the bottom.

No photos, unlike her own flat, where the only decoration had been her few precious family snaps.

'Renata probably collected most of these pieces while she was touring the opera circuit,' she said.

Dave nodded. 'I guess so. I s'pose I should have done more of that, while I was overseas. I always seemed to be too busy.'

Too busy collecting girlfriends? Ellie was glad she kept this unhelpful thought to herself. Her mistrust of guys was a bad habit. And poorly timed, given how incredibly attentive and caring Dave had been. She would hate to hurt him, even though she was still waiting to hear exactly why he'd come to Sydney.

'Now,' he was saying. 'We need to get you comfortable. Would you like to lie down?'

She shook her head. 'Unless I'm sleeping, I'd prefer to sit with a cushion and an icepack or two at my back.'

'So you're not sleepy?'

'No, Dave.'

Quite possibly the tiredness would catch up with her, but for now all she wanted was his explanation. Ellie chose a well-upholstered high-backed lounge chair and Dave hurried to offer her cushions. He also brought her a fresh icepack he'd found in Renata's freezer and a glass of water. 'Or would you like a cup of tea?' he asked.

'No, water's good, thanks.' She would need it to take more medication.

As Dave set the glass on a small table beside her, he said, 'I'll head out soon to buy us a few provisions. Anything in particular you fancy?'

'Heavens, no.' She smiled coyly. 'When it comes to food, I totally trust you, chef.'

'I do a mean curry.' He grinned. 'But pasta carbonara comes to mind. Or mushroom risotto.'

'Any of those would be amazing. I'm getting hungry just thinking about it.'

Dave went back to Renata's kitchen to check out the spices in her pantry, the sauces in the door of her fridge. Then he took out his phone and seemed to be making notes. 'I'll see what's available,' he said.

'Yes, I'm sure you'll have fun checking out the local stores.'

'And there's nothing else you need before I go?'

Are you going to finish telling me exactly why you've abandoned your newly opened café to come here and feed me?

It was a pretty big question, though. Or at least, it seemed that way to Ellie, and Dave was obviously keen to get on with the shopping. 'I'm fine,' she said. 'I have everything I need for the moment. Enjoy King Street.'

While he was away, she went back to finishing the crossword. One particular clue – *Infatuated (7 letters)* – caught her eye. Some of the letters were already in place, and it was easy to see the answer. *Smitten.*

But even as she filled in the blanks, she also knew this word summed her up. She was one smitten kitten. Again.

But was she doomed to crash harder than ever when this idyllic time with Dave ended?

After Rolf's move to the Tablelands, he'd become a reasonably regular visitor to the Burralea pub. Some evenings he'd enjoyed a meal in the big old-fashioned dining room. Or on others he caught up with his electrician mate, Liam Flint. Even though Rolf was concentrating more on his writing than building, the two tradies enjoyed their chats over a peaty dram.

But now that he was back in Beacon Bay, Rolf had avoided the pub. At first, the hotel hadn't actually been open, because of the lack of either power or supplies. Later, while he'd been enjoying Renata's stimulating hospitality, there'd been no real need to head off elsewhere.

Neither of these excuses applied now, but for Rolf, spending any time in a public place was still complicated by the fact that he'd been a local in this small town for so many years, and Lisa still lived here, a pillar of the community. Throw in their divorce and his surprise international-writing success, and his chances of sitting peacefully in the corner of a Beacon Bay bar were pretty much zilch.

This evening, however, twenty-four hours after Lisa's unsettling visit, Rolf had no desire to sit alone in the house while that goddamn conversation circled in his head like a prowling predator. He had to get away.

These weren't issues he wanted to discuss with Renata, or anyone else, for that matter. What he needed was a change of scenery and, hopefully, a clearer head.

He decided Mission Beach was the best option. It offered several places to choose from and it wasn't too far to travel. He'd need to drive back afterwards, but he'd be careful to stay under the limit.

*

Thirty minutes later, a bar on the beachfront beckoned. A timber deck on three sides, shutters pushed back to welcome the balmy, tropical night. Gentle jazz. Unfamiliar faces.

Rolf selected a stool at a broad timber bench and sat with his glass of Laphroaig on the rocks. A gentle breeze brought the scent of frangipani and the soft sounds of small waves washing onto the shore. He opened the notebook he'd brought with him, found the pen in his shirt pocket.

Tonight he wanted to focus his attention on the novel he'd been forced to abandon, to sink back into the world of Trent Amos and his current murder mystery, to reconnect with the main characters.

Rolf started with Jenna. In this novel, she would find herself helping the hero, Trent, to solve a grisly killing. Jenna was Scottish, a widow, living in the Aussie outback and decidedly homesick. She was missing the lochs, the heather-clad hills, the mist. The glens where eagles soared, where deer, wildcats and grouse lived. She was also missing the kindly schoolteacher who'd recognised and acknowledged her intelligence at an early age.

Aha, yes! Already, Rolf was feeling both relaxed and re-energised, grateful that Jenna's emotions were coming through to him, rather like spirits at a seance. He took a sip of his whisky. Damn, it was good. He turned a page in his notebook and began to write.

Jenna's home was still there, even though it was so far away. In her heart —

'Rolf? Rolf Anders?'

Damn it to hell. Rolf wanted to ignore the woman who was calling his name, but already she was coming closer. Somewhere beyond middle aged, she was vaguely familiar. Blonde and well presented in a pale-blue silky top over white slacks.

'It is you, isn't it, Rolf? We've only met briefly. I'm Heidi, Lisa's friend.'

Far out. Just his bloody luck. Rolf dredged up a half-hearted smile. 'Oh, yes, Lisa's staying with you, isn't she? I know she's been very grateful.'

Heidi nodded and smiled. 'I'm just having a night out with a friend from Mission Beach.' She pointed to a table in the far corner of the deck, where a man of her vintage sat with a glass of wine and a bowl that might have held chips or nuts. 'His name's Phil. He has a veterinary clinic in Mission Beach, and since Pixie he's been run off his feet, poor chap. This is the first night he's been able to take a break.'

I know the feeling. Rolf nodded, managed another smile. 'Well, it's good to meet you again, Heidi. I hope you and your friend both enjoy your night.'

'Oh, we will, thanks. But before I leave you, Rolf, I'm going to be a total busybody and let you know that . . .' The woman paused. She seemed nervous suddenly and she looked around, as if gathering courage and then she took a deep breath. 'It's just that – if you ever wanted to give Lisa another —'

'Excuse me,' Rolf interrupted fiercely. 'Please stop right there.'

Deep colour flooded her cheeks.

Too bad if he'd embarrassed her. Rolf had heard enough. 'I don't mean to be rude,' he said, 'but I'm not looking for advice about my relationship with my ex.'

Heidi was nodding now and pressing two fingers to her lips, as if she wished she hadn't spoken.

Almost feeling sorry for her, Rolf said in a kindlier tone, 'Look, I know you and Lisa are good friends and she may have confided in you.'

'No, it's not that,' Heidi said, adding a vigorous shake of her head. 'Lisa hasn't said anything, really. I'm working purely on instinct. And I've just had this really strong sense that she's —'

This time Rolf held out a hand to stop her. He'd been through an extremely difficult twenty-four hours, coming to terms with all that had been said and not said on the previous evening. The conversation had left him with far too many tortuous questions of his own, and he had no desire to add another layer to the emotional tangle that was Lisa-and-Rolf.

'As I said, I appreciate your concern, but I'm not looking for advice.'

'No, of course. I understand.' Heidi had finally got the message. 'My apologies. I'll just say goodnight, Rolf. Enjoy your evening.'

She backed away a few steps now, then turned and almost scurried back to her companion.

Brilliant. This was exactly what he'd been trying to avoid. Rolf downed the rest of his whisky in one long, angry gulp and then went to the bar to fetch another.

CHAPTER THIRTY-SIX

The evening meal Dave produced was a satay peanut stir-fry that might have come straight from a Thai restaurant, except that Ellie had seen him make it from scratch right there in Renata's kitchen.

They ate it at one end of the dining table and, as they did so, they chatted about Beacon Bay. Dave gave her an update on how the cyclone recovery was progressing, and he also shared a quick report from Janet who'd let him know all was well with the café in his absence. At Ellie's request, he told her more about what it had been like growing up in the Bay.

And then she asked, 'So how did the folk up there react, when you decided to come to Sydney?'

'They were great,' Dave said. 'Pretty surprised at first, I guess. I think Renata was expecting that she might come, so she looked mildly gobsmacked. But Dad was all for it.' He shot Ellie an amused smile. 'Did you know he's quite a fan of yours?'

'No, I didn't.'

'Yeah, well, as soon as he gave me the thumbs up, Renata did too. Next minute she was offering to help in the café.'

'She's so generous,' said Ellie.

'Yeah, it's interesting,' said Dave. 'You'd expect her to be a total snob, but instead she gives the impression she really wants to fit in.'

Ellie nodded, but she wasn't surprised. She'd worked with enough celebrities to know that many of them longed for quieter lives and the chance to connect with ordinary folk, out of the limelight.

'That was soooo good,' she said as she cleaned up her plate, making sure she got the very last grains of satay-flavoured rice.

Dave grinned. 'I'll add it to my special-dishes-for-Ellie list.'

'Gosh.'

He lifted an eyebrow. 'Does that bother you?'

'No, it's a lovely thought. I'm flattered. It's just . . .' How could she tell him she was also scared? Scared that she was falling for him too quickly, too deeply, only to be hurt again?

'What is it, Ellie? Is your back uncomfortable? Maybe you should move to the armchair. Or would you like to lie down?'

Her back *had* been starting to ache, but she couldn't sleep yet. She had a question to ask and it was time to stop stalling.

'Perhaps the armchair.' And as soon as she was settled, she said bravely, 'Dave, you do understand that I'll be working for Renata when we go back, and staying at her place, at least at the start?'

'Sure.'

'Okay, that's good, but we still haven't really talked about the real reason you're here. Why you broke our agreement.'

The guy who'd seemed so calm and in control all day suddenly looked less sure of himself. 'Right.' Still standing tall in the middle of the room, he said, 'You – you don't mind that I've come, do you?'

'No.'

He still looked nervous. 'That's a good start, I guess.'

'Actually, I'm *very* pleased to see you.' She pointed to the armchair opposite her. 'But we can't talk while you're standing there. Please, you sit down too.'

He did so, but rather than relaxing, he sat forward, with his hands clasped between his knees. 'Okay. Where were we?'

As if he didn't know. 'You were going to tell me why you decided to break our agreement about no further contact.'

He nodded, his expression serious as he accepted this challenge. 'The thing is, after you left, I learned something about myself.'

Ellie might have panicked, but his dark gaze, as it met hers across the room, was reassuringly gentle. One corner of his mouth lifted in a shy smile.

'Ellie, I realised that the whole *not* staying in touch rule only made sense if I wasn't really interested in you. And, well, that's not how I feel.'

Oh, Dave.

'I understand we haven't known each other very long.'

'No, we haven't.' She'd spent a whole three nights in his flat.

'I tried to tell myself I should do as you requested and just let you go. But the truth is, I am *very* interested in you, Ellie. More interested in you than in any girl I've ever met.'

Ellie liked that he'd chosen the word *interested*. She found it flattering and yet so much safer than a wild declaration of love, and she couldn't help smiling with relief. But as Dave stood and crossed the floor to her now, she also had tears in her eyes.

'I'm just sorry it took an accident to make me come to my senses,' he said, before leaning down to drop a feather-light kiss on her forehead. 'But I hope telling you this hasn't scared you.'

'No,' she told him. 'I'm not scared – and if I'm honest, I should confess to quite a bit of interest too. And I'm especially grateful that you've come and looked after me so beautifully, Dave.'

'My pleasure, ma'am.'

His mock Yankee accent made her smile again, and as she lifted her face up to him now, she said cheekily, 'I suspect I might need another kiss.'

This time he grinned. Then, kneeling in front of her, he held her face in his hands and brushed his lips against hers, tenderly, lovingly . . . and as she began to melt, he deepened the pressure.

So perfect.

It was some time before they broke apart.

He said, 'By the way, the main bedroom is for you. It has a cute little ensuite.'

'Are you sure?' I've been sleeping on my side, so I don't take up much room and —'

'Shush.' He pressed a gentle finger to her lips. 'I'll be just across the hallway if you need me.'

It was hard to trust that nothing would go wrong in the future, but tonight they'd be in separate bedrooms, which was right where they'd started, and Ellie decided that was the perfect place to be.

Rolf was trying to make his second whisky last, although in truth, he was putting even more effort into trying *not* to analyse Lisa's friend's comments.

If you ever wanted to give Lisa another —

He'd cut Heidi off, but the inferences had been hard to miss. The woman clearly believed Rolf should contemplate some kind of reconciliation with his ex.

Seemed she'd been working on intuition after spending time at close quarters with Lisa, and, if he was honest, Rolf hadn't been totally surprised by the conclusion she'd come to. But he'd taken years to readjust after his and Lisa's split, and now, after the previous night's upheaval, he'd come to this bar with the specific aim of *not* thinking about those very possibilities that Heidi had hinted at.

Nevertheless, Rolf couldn't deny the temptation was there. Simmering, refusing to be ignored.

As he sat nursing his glass and staring out past a grove of palm trees to the sea, where a faint moon spilled splashes of silver, he kept seeing Lisa as she'd looked last night. Still slim and pretty in that primrose-yellow dress. No longer a woman ready for battle, but with her face unmasked. So vulnerable.

Trembling all over.

He couldn't remember having ever seen her quite so upset.

When he'd first come back to the Bay, the word *discombobulated* had jumped into his head as the best way to describe Lisa's mood and behaviour. It wasn't a term he would use in his novels. It was too long, too old-fashioned, not generally used by Aussies and too distracting for the reader. Normally, he'd go for something more straightforward – describing a character as thrown, confused or even foxed.

But word choices aside, the reality was that ever since Rolf had been back here, Lisa had mostly seemed upset and frustrated. Even locals had commented that she hadn't been herself. It was as if she'd been totally thrown off course.

He could only assume that his presence was the problem, although Cyclone Pixie deserved a measure of the blame.

Then, last night, Lisa had shared an entirely new layer of tension with him, and the fragility he'd witnessed had cut him deeply. And now, this evening, he'd copped this message from Heidi.

Rolf supposed he should have listened to what the woman had to say. Her motives were almost certainly well meant, but even if he'd been prepared to back down, eat humble pie and speak to her again, he'd left it too late. Heidi and the veterinarian had already headed off.

Which left Rolf to contemplate his options.

As a curlew called its mournful cry into the dark night, he wondered if reconciliation was remotely possible. The risks of even broaching such a step with Lisa were huge.

'Hey! I know who you are, don't I?'

Not another one. Rolf gritted his teeth.

This time the intruder approaching him was male. A guy of about Rolf's own age, with a white goatee and an excessive amount of flashy gold jewellery at his neck, wrist and fingers. He held a fancy cocktail in one hand and wore a smile – no, make that a grin – to match his attention-seeking image.

'It's Rolf Anders, isn't it? I recognised you from the internet photos.'

Great. So he wasn't even a fan. Just a nuisance nosy parker.

Rolf didn't bother smiling, merely gave a curt nod.

'Gotta say you have my sympathy, man.'

Sympathy? This snagged Rolf's attention. 'Excuse me?'

The fellow was grinning again as he shook his head. 'I totally get why you left that woman.'

He was talking about Lisa? Rolf's hackles rose instantly. His fists clenched. 'You should leave now.'

'Hey, mate, don't take it the wrong way. I'm on your side. That Lisa you were married to is a gold-plated bitch. You were well rid of her.'

Rolf would have liked to ignore the jerk, to quaff his drink and depart with all the stiff-backed dignity he could muster. But this guy was talking as if he knew Lisa and curiosity got the better of Rolf. 'Who are you?' he asked coldly.

'The name's Maffucci. Gerry Maffucci.'

Of course. The arsehole who'd caused Lisa so much grief. Rolf supposed he should have guessed. 'Gerry Maffucci,' he said even more coldly. 'You're the man who promised to give a massive donation to the Beacon Bay restoration project.'

Maffucci blinked at this. His mouth opened and shut in a dazed fashion, reminding Rolf of a goldfish.

It wasn't long before he recovered, but he was no longer smiling. 'I might've changed my mind about that.'

I bet you have, you prick. And the decision was made as soon as Lisa knocked you back?

With some reluctance Rolf managed to suppress this response. 'That's a shame,' he said instead. 'The town needs all the help it can get.'

'Nah,' said Maffucci. 'The Bay folk don't need me when they've got that opera-singer bird looking out for them.' He winked at Rolf then. 'But you'd know all about her.'

Once again, Rolf's fists clenched, and his gaze fixed on Maffucci's unnaturally white teeth.

'Yep, as I said,' the smug twerp continued. 'You've made all the right moves, dropping an old duck like Lisa for that other chick.'

Now, Rolf was on his feet. 'I told you before to get lost. I'm telling you again and this time I bloody well mean it.'

'Keep your hair on. Like I said, I'm your friend, Rolf.'

'Like hell you are.' It was hard not to yell at the creep. Rolf was burning with fury, but he didn't want to draw attention, so he kept his voice low and cold as steel. 'I don't need you on my side. You're not worth the time of day.'

At this, Maffucci turned an ugly shade of puce. As he set down his now empty cocktail glass, he seemed to puff up. 'You can't speak to me like that,' he roared.

With no further warning, Maffucci grabbed the nearest stool, gripped its legs and swung it high, ready to smash it down on Rolf's head.

The stool was swooping downwards with fierce momentum, when Rolf threw up his hands and was able to catch it. And, after years of lifting and holding all manner of heavy timbers above his head, he found the strength to stop it in its tracks.

For blistering seconds, Maffucci glared at him, while they both kept a grip on the intended weapon. Maffucci was shaking with anger and bright red in the face, but for Rolf, it was a simple enough matter to wrestle the stool out of the rude jerk's hands. With this accomplished, he stood it neatly back on the floor.

By now the patrons and bartenders had all become their audience and were watching with mouths agape. Ignoring the onlookers, Rolf picked up his notebook and pen, turned abruptly and headed off down the steps and into the night. His only regret was that he'd left a goodly slug of his whisky unfinished in the glass.

CHAPTER THIRTY-SEVEN

Refreshed from a sound night's sleep, Ellie felt so reassuringly comfortable the next morning that she and Dave opted to have breakfast out at one of King Street's popular eateries.

'I reckon I'm also ready to fly,' she told Dave as she tucked into a scrumptious serving of poached pears with granola and yoghurt. 'And you must be anxious to get back to your café.'

'I wouldn't say I'm anxious.'

'Bad word choice. How about keen?'

Dave gave a smiling shrug. 'I'll admit to a certain keenness. I don't like leaving Janet to hold the fort for too long.' He was looking especially gorgeous this morning in his faded jeans, a casual grey sweater and his man bun. 'But only if you're genuinely sure you're okay, Ellie. It's a three-hour flight.'

She assured him that she'd be fine sitting well supported in a padded airline seat, and so he promptly extracted his phone and booked their flights. They would be heading north later this afternoon.

Then, replete after their delicious breakfasts, they found a store that sold phones and Ellie made her selection. Another fifteen minutes later and they were back at Renata's apartment, sitting on her small balcony and enjoying a view of vibrant Japanese maples at their autumn best, while Ellie went through the phone's setting-up process.

It was only then, with this task completed, that she sat back, folded her arms and gave voice to the small concerns that had been niggling her.

'I'm not quite sure how this new job is going to work,' she said. 'I don't totally know what Renata expects. We haven't really had time to discuss it properly.'

'You'll be her personal PR agent, won't you?'

'Yes, and I think she's also really committed to the Bay's restoration project as well.'

'That's a good cause. I imagine you'd be happy to help with it.'

'Yes, you're right. And I'm being silly. Worrying about nothing.'

'Except . . .?' Dave prompted gently.

Ellie let out a small sigh. 'I just hope I haven't been too impulsive. I was kind of at rock bottom when Renata rang. My situation wasn't really desperate, though. I'm sure I would have eventually found a job in Sydney. But then her offer was so enticing. I'd loved being in the Bay. I loved my time with you and I was missing it all so much.'

'Impulsive decisions aren't necessarily wrong,' suggested Dave. 'Sometimes we have to trust our instincts.'

'I guess.'

'It'll be a full-time job, won't it?'

'I believe so.' Ellie flashed him an apologetic smile. 'So I doubt I'll have time to help you in the café.'

'I wasn't expecting that you would.'

'It's going to be quite different, isn't it? For us, I mean.'

With his warm gaze resting on her, Dave smiled. 'But that might not be an entirely bad thing. Not many relationships start with around-the-clock contact.'

'That's true.'

'Although, if I'm honest . . .' Dave walked two fingers across the small wrought-iron tabletop, and when her reached her hand, he tapped it gently. 'I loved having you there day and night.'

'I loved it too.'

His touch sent warmth cascading through Ellie, reminding her of how very much she'd loved everything they'd shared. If she wasn't careful, she'd forget to finish what she'd been planning to tell him.

'While we're being honest,' she said, before she melted completely. 'I can't help feeling nervous about *us* when I go back. But I'm not expecting you to make any promises, Dave. I know that's unrealistic. It's just – I've been through a couple of painful breakups. So I guess . . .' Embarrassed by this admission, she gave a helpless little shrug. 'Once bitten, twice shy? Or in my case, twice bitten, thrice shy?'

Dave had retracted his hand, but now his smile worked its own magic. 'Let's not be too pessimistic before we even start. What about third time lucky?'

This was an uplifting thought, and Ellie wanted to hang on to it, but her life lessons had taught her not to trust anything so random as luck.

Two days after Dave and Ellie arrived back in the north, the power was turned back on in Beacon Bay. The exciting news of its arrival spread fast – via the radio, via text messages from the electricity company, from the council, from friend to friend and, of course, via all forms of social media.

When the big moment actually occurred midmorning, cheers could be heard echoing from street to street, and that evening the welcome appearance of house lights gleaming from so many windows gave the little town an almost festive air.

'I feel like I want to throw a party,' Renata announced as she served up a bolognese pasta for dinner. She might have gone for something a bit showier now that her oven was working again, but she and Ellie had put in a busy day's work, and she'd opted for a very simple version of spag bol. Plenty of spaghetti, mince enhanced by a bottle of Italian sauce she'd found at the supermarket that came complete with roasted garlic, plus a generous heaping of grated parmesan cheese.

'But haven't you already thrown an enormous party?' This question came from Rolf, who was now working on Peggy and Roger's house and had also been invited to dinner.

'That wasn't a proper party. More of a community event. This would be a smaller, more private affair.' Already, Renata was picturing her newfound friends enjoying her deck. The autumn evenings were so pleasant now.

There'd be laughter and happy chatter, strings of lights through the garden, a selection of easy-listening music. She might wear the new kaftan she'd bought in Cairns.

'I suppose you'd want to invite your friends from Sydney who missed out on your birthday?' suggested Peggy.

This was a logical suggestion, but in recent weeks, Renata had developed a new appreciation for people who led average lives that might look boring from the outside but were real and meaningful, nevertheless. This was, actually, a big part of the reason she'd brought Ellie back to the north.

Renata had sensed that the girl had a good nose for stories that other journos chasing big news might overlook. And, after just a couple of days, Ellie had proved her correct.

Already, Ellie had found a wonderful story about a quick-thinking truckie who'd saved a young boy from drowning. She'd also unearthed an absolutely heartwarming snippet about a family whose dog had given birth to a litter of pups right in the middle of the cyclone. The puppies had been a mix of border collie, kelpie and dingo, and the children in the household had gleefully named them Pixie, Windy, Noisy and Storm.

The photo Ellie had taken of the three excited little kids squatting with the new mum and her puppies was just divine.

'No, I won't be inviting the Sydney folk,' Renata said now. 'I want to party with my new friends from here in Beacon Bay. It doesn't have to be enormous or flash. Cheese and biscuits, a few dips, loads of wine. There'd be all of you,' she said, gesturing with a wave of her hand to Rolf, Ellie, Peggy and Roger. 'And I'd like to invite the people I've got to know from the restoration project, plus Lisa and her friend Heidi, of course.'

'And Heidi's veterinarian friend?' Rolf asked.

This was interesting news. Renata knew her eyebrows had lifted. Everyone else looked curious too. 'Does Heidi have a veterinarian friend?'

Rolf nodded. 'A fellow from Mission Beach.'

'Not Phil?' asked Peggy.

'Yes, I'm sure that's the name.'

'Oh, he's a lovely chap. How exciting for Heidi.'

Renata chuckled. 'Then it sounds as if he must definitely be added to the guest list.' With a sympathetic smile for Ellie, she added, 'Sadly, unless we have the party on a Monday evening, Dave and Janet will be busy, but it would be great if they could join us later, when they're finished at the café.'

Roger spoke up now. 'I wouldn't mind going to a party on a Monday night. I reckon it sounds like the perfect way to start the working week.'

Rolf and Peggy were also nodding their approval.

Renata sent another smile across the table to Ellie, who'd been keeping diplomatically quiet. 'I guess that settles it then. I'll check with Dave, of course, but unless you hear otherwise, next Monday will be party night. Mark it in your calendars.'

As she said this, she remembered that by then, she would also need to have made a decision about the job offer in Colorado.

Lisa was at the house. She was dressed in old jeans, a shabby denim shirt and thick gardening gloves, and she was moving pot plants and barbecue furniture from the garage back into the garden when Rolf pulled up in his ute. It wasn't the first time she'd seen him since the night of her confession, and on the other occasions they'd been carefully polite.

There'd been no mention of Gerry, no further discussions of a personal nature. Nevertheless, she'd been aware of an underlying tension that lingered.

'You should have sung out,' Rolf called to her now. 'I've been meaning to ask where you wanted that lot.'

'They're nearly all from the barbecue area,' she told him. 'They were beginning to sulk, stuck here under the house. And you're very welcome to help with that big Rhapis palm. I know it's too much for me.'

'Sure.' After a quick glance around, Rolf frowned. 'You don't have a trolley?'

'I lent it to Melody and Jim. They had so much gear to shift at their nursery and I haven't got it back yet.'

With a quick nod, Rolf set to work, but even with his big strong shoulders, the massive pot was too heavy to shift very far. 'Sorry. Might have to leave that one for the time being.'

'Of course.' She should have realised it would be too much. Rolf might still be muscular, but he was no longer the young Viking she'd married. 'I wouldn't want you to hurt yourself.'

He gave a shrugging smile and turned to a medium-sized pot holding an amazonica. 'I've always loved this guy. Such striking leaves.'

'Yes, it's the same plant we bought back in —' Lisa stopped herself. What was the point?

She hurried back under the house to collect one of the timber outdoor chairs, and Rolf brought out another pot then waited patiently for her to direct its positioning.

With the rest of the plants and three more chairs in place, they carried out the heavy hardwood barbecue table together.

'Thanks,' she said as they set it squarely in line with the brick paving. 'That's about it for now. I'm sure those plants were longing to get back out into fresh air.'

Rolf stood, hands resting on his hips, looking about. 'You've done a great job with this area,' he said. 'I really like this paving.'

'Thanks.'

'Who did it for you?'

Lisa couldn't help a small chuckle. 'I did it. All by myself.'

'Wow!' He looked both impressed and delighted, which was gratifying. 'Good for you. It's amazing.'

'Thanks.'

She realised she should probably leave now. Rolf was still living in this house, while he worked on Renata's neighbours' place, and Heidi had kindly invited Lisa to stay on at the cottage.

'Mind you,' Heidi had said. 'I'm not sure that staying away from that man is the best plan, but if it's what you want, I'm not going to argue.'

It wasn't the first time Heidi had hinted that Lisa and Rolf should consider a reconciliation.

'It's because you're back with your vet,' Lisa had teased her. 'You want everyone else all happily paired up.'

'And why not?' Heidi retorted with a twinkling-eyed, coy smile.

Now, as Lisa was tugging off her gardening gloves, Rolf said, 'I was wondering if you needed any help with transporting your new furniture for the living room. I know most companies deliver, but I have the ute and trailer if you need them.'

'Oh.' Lisa felt quite caught out by his offer. 'Thanks, that's kind of you, but I don't think I'm ready for that. At the moment, I can't even decide what kind of furniture I might want.' She'd tried several times to make plans, but she just didn't seem to be in the right head-space. 'I'm still trying to decide if I should change the colour scheme when I repaint the walls.'

'Fair enough. No rush.'

'I thought I was going to enjoy that next step. It's a great chance to go for a total change, and I should make the most of it, but for some reason, it's – I don't know. I just seem to feel too unsettled to make those decisions.'

Rolf gave a slow, thoughtful nod. 'I'm sure it all takes time.'

'Seems that way. For me, at least.'

Then, as she turned to gather up her bag and car keys, Rolf said, casually, almost as if it was an afterthought, 'I don't suppose you'd be interested in a drink before you leave?'

This was such a surprise, Lisa could only stare at him, momentarily unable to think of an appropriate answer.

A corner of his mouth lifted in a wryly amused smile. 'Saves me drinking on my own.'

Strangely breathless, she had to swallow before she could reply, but then she found that she was smiling too. 'Well, if it stops you from becoming an alcoholic, I should accept your kind offer. We wouldn't want to set a bad example for your sons.'

CHAPTER THIRTY-EIGHT

At this time of day, the back garden was well shaded, and despite the scarcity of foliage, a surprising number of birds chattered in the hedges and trees, where the first tips of green shoots had begun to appear. A pleasant breeze had also found its way across town.

Lisa, surveying her re-established barbecue area, was still glowing from Rolf's unexpected compliment about the paving. But she was also conscious of a nervous flutter, no doubt the result of his surprise invitation. The flutter persisted as she waited for him to return with their drinks.

At least he was back quite soon, bearing glasses, a plate and a cheese knife from upstairs. These he set on the timber table, before extracting a bottle of wine from his vehicle, along with a packet of crackers and a container of blue cheese – a brand that had always been their favourite, back in the day . . .

'This definitely looks too good not to share,' Lisa said. She was trying to sound way more relaxed than she felt, and she focused on remaining calm as she sat with her hands clasped in her lap, watching Rolf as he opened packets and poured wine.

What was it they'd learned about breathing at yoga? *Four seconds in, four seconds out.*

'Here's cheers.' Rolf's expression was warm, but careful, as he lifted his glass.

'Cheers.' Having clinked, Lisa took a sip. 'Oh, yes,' she said. 'Very smooth. I suspect this wine's not from the bargain shelf.'

'Not exactly,' Rolf admitted. 'I may have developed a few expensive tastes.'

'And why shouldn't you, if you can afford it?' She smiled, hoping to send a message that she wasn't nursing grudges about his new affluence.

He shifted the plate towards her. 'Help yourself to the cheese, won't you?'

Lisa cut a slim wedge, set it on a cracker and, as she took a delicious bite, Rolf said, 'I'll be taking the trailer with a load of generators back to the Tablelands shortly. My electrician mate, Liam Flint, sent them down after the cyclone, but I don't want him to have to make another trip.'

With her mouth full, Lisa nodded.

'I was actually wondering if you'd like to come too. To see my place up there.'

Somehow, she managed to swallow without choking. 'Gosh, Rolf. That's out of the blue.'

'You look like you're panicking.'

'I am, a bit.'

Now, his shoulders lifted and then slumped as he released a little huff that might have been a sigh. This was followed by a self-conscious smile. 'I guess I must be nervous too, or I would have taken this more slowly.'

'I – I'm not sure I understand.'

Rolf reached for his glass, perhaps to bolster his courage, took a deep sip, then set it down. 'Okay, I'll try to explain. The thing is,

I've been doing quite a bit of thinking, especially since our – ah – conversation last week.'

'I see.' Lisa tried not to cringe as she remembered that evening. Her shame. Rolf's confused dismay.

'I know these past weeks have been a pretty weird time for both of us. Having me back here, living in your house. The last thing we expected.'

'It's certainly been a challenge.' Lisa was remembering how bitterly she'd resented Rolf's return. At least this wasn't still the case. 'But I do appreciate everything you've done here.'

'And now, I've been thinking about the future.' Rolf shifted his glass, almost as if it was a chess piece. 'Obviously, we're not getting any younger. When we look ahead, the reality is we're facing old age. For both of us, that's the next chapter.'

'Spoken like a true author,' Lisa couldn't help commenting.

They both smiled, their gazes tentatively connecting, and holding.

Lisa saw the flecks of white as well as grey in Rolf's rusty hair and tufty eyebrows, the deep crow's feet edging his eyes, the jawline no longer so defined. She looked down at her wrinkled hands and knew her body showed just as many signs of ageing. They were both fast approaching seventy.

Sometimes this reality was staring her in the face and unavoidable. Other times it was hard to believe. Her mind could play the occasional trick, spinning her momentarily back to her youth with all her dreams ahead of her. But then she would realise how long ago that time had been.

They truly were this age, but how had they got here so quickly?

Rolf said, 'I'd like to have peace in that next chapter.'

Peace. Such a welcome word on so many levels.

'That – that makes good sense, Rolf. I think we'd all like that. The family, I mean. Peace for us and for the boys.'

But what kind of peace did he mean, exactly? Where was this heading?

'I suspect it would help if we had a few more decent conversations.'

Lisa stiffened. 'Please don't tell me you want couples counselling?'

This brought an amused, knowing look. 'I believe many people find counselling very helpful, but no, I'm not about to suggest that for us. However, I do think the biggest destroyers of peace can be the questions left unanswered.'

'What kind of questions?' Lisa asked nervously. What else did Rolf want to know about her? She wasn't quite game to voice this question.

'I don't have specifics.' Rolf toyed with his glass again. 'I just feel that a little more communication, a little more understanding wouldn't hurt.'

If this conversation was an example, Lisa supposed the process shouldn't be too uncomfortable. She nodded.

'Since I've been back here, I've had a certain insight into how your life is these days.' He paused, eyed her cautiously. 'I thought maybe it might be helpful for you to know a little more about mine.'

'By going up to the Tablelands?'

'Well, I'm sure you've earned a break. You've put in a big effort with the cyclone recovery and it wouldn't hurt to spend a little time up there.'

Rolf must know how momentous this suggestion was, given that Lisa had done her best to ignore everything about his life since they'd separated. But now she found it hard to disagree without sounding churlish, and she'd had enough of behaving like a resentful grouch. She realised it had achieved very little.

'Just a couple of days?' she asked.

'Sure.'

'Oh, but I've just remembered it's Dave's birthday the day after tomorrow.'

'You're right.' After only a moment's thought, Rolf said, 'But I doubt he's expecting to celebrate it with us.'

'No, if he has any spare time, he'll want to spend it with Ellie.'

'We can buy him a gift from up on the Tablelands. There's a store that specialises in gourmet rainforest products – Davidson plum jam and roasted macadamia spread, that sort of thing.'

'Um – okay.'

'So you're up for it?'

Lisa nodded.

'That's great.' Rolf cut another wedge of cheese, used the side of the knife to press it onto a cracker, but instead of keeping it for himself, he offered it to her. 'At times it can be good to take a left turn when you usually go right.'

Ellie was really enjoying her new job. Several southern outlets were keen to publish stories that combined Renata Ramsay, the opera star, with a post-Pixie restoration, and collating these tales had been fun. Ellie had loved looking at the post-cyclone scene from Renata's perspective, as an outsider in awe of the way these folk had coped and supported each other.

Beach-dwelling northerners might have a reputation for a laid-back lifestyle, but their stories told of hunkering inside a cupboard during the very worst of the storm, or hiding in the bath under a mattress and listening to the bathroom roof fly away.

There'd been a mini tornado on the edge of the cyclone that had spun just north of Beacon Bay, and an old Queenslander farmhouse had been completely demolished, breaking the hearts of the three generations of one family who'd lived there and loved it. Then there was a pop-up emergency hospital, organised by two of the local GPs and their nurses, as well as the cassowary fruit-cutting team, and all the wonderful donations of clothes and books, household items, kitchen items, bed linen and furniture.

From further afield, a dairy factory on the Atherton Tablelands had sent down a truckload of free milk, butter and yoghurt. And as a side bonus, in the process of gathering these stories, Ellie had also begun to develop a rapport with the local reporters at the ABC and the *Cassowary Coast Observer*. Already, in a short time, they'd enjoyed a few reciprocal tip-offs.

Just today, the local soccer club had approached her, asking for help with applications for funding. Their buildings were covered by insurance, but they needed machinery and equipment for resurfacing the playing fields and mending all the fencing.

Ellie was reasonably familiar with guidelines for submissions – the need for evidence to bolster each claim and the importance of making sure every box was ticked. She was also comfortable with helping to ensure that the executive summary was in easy-to-read plain English.

'You know word's getting to spread that you're good at this caper?' the soccer club's p____ ___ told her. 'You'll probably be flooded with requests for help w___ ____ce and disaster relief claims.'

But Ellie didn't ____ ___r her, there was nothing better than feeling wanted and va__

'Maybe I'm just extra needy,' she admitted to Dave later that night, as they sat on the sandy beach and looked out at an inky black sea and the sky ablaze with stars. 'Is that a thing? To need to be needed?'

'Well, if it's any help, I most definitely need you.'

His arm was around her shoulders and now he pulled her closer for a kiss.

'That helps a great deal,' Ellie murmured.

They'd met on several evenings now, after the café had closed, to share a drink and a chat in the kitchen, or a visit to the beach. When Ellie's back was completely healed, she hoped to join Dave for his morning run.

So far, they hadn't gone to bed together. Partly, this was because Dave was still conscious of Ellie's bruises, but they'd also talked about taking things more slowly this time. Playing it safe?

Perhaps they both wanted to get this right, but Ellie didn't dare to ask this question. She simply kept her fingers firmly crossed.

'Oh, look!' Dave cried, excitedly pointing at the sky. 'A falling star.'

Just in time, Ellie spied it too, a bright little ball shooting in a fast diagonal across the dark sky, a speeding bullet.

'Make a wish,' whispered Dave.

She smiled. 'I already have.' And then she kissed him.

CHAPTER THIRTY-NINE

Almost a decade had passed since the last time Lisa had driven to the Tablelands, but the journey was still very familiar. When the boys were younger, the family had enjoyed several holidays staying in one of the cabins at Lake Tinaroo. The lake provided a beautiful, relaxing setting where the boys could swim in fresh water without fear of stingers or crocodiles, as well as canoeing and fishing to their hearts' content.

Today, travelling beside Rolf in his ute, Lisa was remembering the excitement of those happy times, and the way the boys had always given a cheer when they'd turned left off the highway and headed for the hills.

Fortunately, this area had been far enough north to escape the worst of Pixie's savagery, and the scenery hadn't really changed. The road continued at first through flat farmland with fields of sugar cane, bananas and pawpaws stretching to the distant ranges.

At the tiny town of South Johnstone, a tall sugar mill still dominated the landscape like a sentinel, and from there the road continued gradually upwards, while the mountains appeared to come closer and clearer. Today, Mt Bartle Frere was surprisingly free of the veils of mist and cloud that so often circled its crown. Far higher than the surrounding ranges, it was outlined with razor-sharp clarity against a bright blue sky.

This view disappeared, though, once they began their ascent. Now, as the road wound and climbed, the rainforest crowded close, with the branches of the tallest trees almost meeting overhead.

Behind the ute, the trailer filled with generators rumbled a little, but everything was well strapped down, so there was no bother-some rattling.

'I love watching the way the temperature drops,' Lisa said, keeping an eye on the dashboard gauge.

'Yes,' agreed Rolf. 'It's usually about seven or eight degrees cooler at the top.'

Before the final ascent, they dipped down over the Beatrice River, where white water rushed between sharp, dark rocks and tree ferns grew lush on the banks. Then, climbing again, climbing, climbing, Lisa could finally see the sky and a glimpse of steep grassy hillsides, bare of forest and dotted with cattle.

'I've just remembered the waterfall.' She couldn't help grinning. 'We'll see it soon, won't we?'

Near the top of the range, on the left, the small rocky cliff face and its curtain of water was another landmark their boys had always watched out for with excited anticipation. There'd been occasions when fights had erupted over who'd been the first to spot the spilling water.

And now, with this landmark passed, the view opened up magnificently. They had reached the top and the Tablelands began, stretching and tumbling, green and beautiful.

Lisa wound down the window and drank in the cool, incredibly fresh air, so different from the salty humidity of the coast. In that moment, it almost seemed as if these differences in landscape and atmosphere symbolised the differences between her life and Rolf's since they'd parted.

She wasn't quite sure what to make of that, but she was suddenly nervous again.

What was this trip really about? What did Rolf expect? Were they crazy?

After driving through Millaa Millaa and Malanda and then skirting past the turn-off to Burralea, they reached Rolf's house. Lisa had seen the magazine photos, so she had a fair idea of what to expect, but nothing could really have prepared her for the beauty of his tall timber and glass house set on a tree-studded acreage on the shores of Lake Tinaroo.

'Oh, Rolf.' At first she couldn't move, could only remain strapped in the passenger's seat, gazing through the windscreen with a hand clasped to her chest.

Rolf had always been an expert builder, but with this project, he seemed to have taken his skills to a whole new level.

Turning, Lisa caught the cautious but hopeful look in his eyes, and if he'd been a friend and not her ex, she would have given him a hearty hug of congratulations. 'It's amazing,' she told him instead. 'Just perfect in this setting. Well done, mate.'

'Thanks.' His expression was complicated, but she thought he seemed pleased.

She climbed out of the ute and again felt the fresh, cool air on her face, caught scents that seemed to be a mix of tree trunks and pine needles. 'The boys have been here, haven't they?'

'Chris and Nate have. They loved it.'

'I'm sure they did.'

'Dave's been too busy with the café since he got back.'

Lisa smiled. 'Then I'll enjoy being able to tell him all about it.'

They collected their small items of luggage, and when Rolf opened the front door, Lisa stepped into a beautiful open-plan living area with magnificent red-gum flooring, leather lounges, a natural stone fireplace and huge windows offering views through the trees to the lake.

'Oh, my God, Rolf. This is perfect.' She couldn't believe that some woman hadn't snatched him up already and made this her home. No doubt there'd been several contenders. Actually, Lisa didn't want to think about that.

Rolf showed her to a guest bedroom, tastefully decorated in navy blue and white, with a deep white-curtained window looking out into the trees, and a small but very adequate ensuite.

'This is lovely, thank you,' Lisa told him politely as she deposited her overnight bag on the floor at the foot of the bed. 'It's all very clean. Do you have a housekeeper?'

'Just once a week. A woman called Dodie. She lives in Burralea and gives the whole place a good going over, including washing the sheets, that sort of thing. But she doesn't touch my study, of course.'

'Of course.' Even before he was published, his study had always been sacrosanct, with books and papers strewn all over the place.

They continued to the kitchen, which was just as amazing as everywhere else in the house, with an island bench, a massive stove, a walk-in pantry and more views to the lake.

'I'll put the kettle on,' Rolf said. 'I'm sure we need a cuppa.'

Standing at the sink and looking out, Lisa commented, 'This is a different part of the lake from where we used to stay.'

'Yes, it's well away from the camp sites and tourist spots. That's why I chose it. The inlet here is almost like a secret little cove. There are several other properties, but the trees offer plenty of privacy.' As he reached into a cupboard for mugs, he said, 'Quite a few of the neighbours have boats or canoes, and we visit each other via the water.'

Spying a quaint boatshed down at the water's edge, she said, 'Like in *Swallows and Amazons*?'

'Have you read those Arthur Ransome books?' Rolf was clearly surprised.

'Many years ago, when I was young. In primary school, I suppose. I know I haven't read a lot of fiction, but I did enjoy those. I don't remember much about them, though, except the kids in boats. It was set in the Lakes District, wasn't it?'

'Yes.' Rolf still looked surprised.

Lisa was sure she must have mentioned those books back when they were holidaying on the lake, but perhaps the bitter warfare that came later had wiped such memories. Hopefully, once they sorted out whatever it was they'd come here to discuss, they'd be more relaxed about everything going forward.

Then, perhaps as a kind of peace offering, she found herself saying, 'I've now read three of *your* books too. One paperback and two on Heidi's Kindle.'

'Blow me down.' Behind Rolf, the kettle came to the boil, but he didn't seem to notice.

'They're very good,' Lisa said. 'Great mysteries and plenty of drama, but the characters are interesting too. I can see why they've been so popular.'

'Thanks.' His mouth tilted in a crooked smile. 'In the publishing game, there's always a big chunk of luck, of course.'

'Really?' She thought about the hard work, the hours and hours locked away, hunkered over a keyboard. 'Then it's well-earned luck, I'd say.'

For a moment he stood, staring at her. Then he seemed to remember he was making tea and turned back to the kettle.

Lisa thought she'd caught a shimmer in his eyes. Surely not?

Perched on kitchen stools, Ellie and Renata were enjoying an afternoon coffee break, when Ellie mentioned a certain famous chocolate cake.

'The Sachertorte?' asked Renata.

'Yes, that's the name. I've been hearing so much about it.'

'From Janet, I suppose.'

'Yes, she was raving.'

'That's sweet of her, but I must admit, it is rather yummy. It's my only claim to fame in the kitchen.'

'I was wondering,' Ellie began, but then she faltered.

'Wondering?' Renata prompted.

'No, it's okay.' Her question was far too presumptuous.

'You were wondering if I'd show you how to make it?'

'Well, yes,' Ellie admitted shyly. 'Or at least share the recipe? But I've got a bit of a cheek, haven't I?'

'Nonsense. I'd be happy to share. But if you want to make it for the restaurant, I think you'd need to do that in their kitchen. There are rules about commercial kitchens, if you're selling to the public.'

'Oh, I wasn't thinking of making one to sell. Dave has a few friends coming this evening, after the café closes, for a kind of late-night supper.'

'What a lovely idea.'

'It's his birthday, actually.' Dave's mum had passed this info on to Ellie before she'd headed off to the Tablelands with Rolf – a move that had left the rest of them somewhat agog. Then she'd also heard from Mike Ingram, one of Dave's friends, that a group of them were planning a surprise.

'So it'll be a birthday cake?' Renata beamed. 'How wonderful. That's even better.'

'And I suppose I wanted to show off.' Ellie knew she was overly anxious about making a good impression on Dave's friends.

But Renata was grinning. 'Why not? I've made a career out of showing off.'

'Renata, your singing is hardly showing off. It's a highly special-ised skill you've worked hard to perfect.' Ellie had heard Renata practising out in her studio. All those scales and amazing vocal exercises, the hard work most outsiders overlooked or never even imagined. 'Actually, I'm really hoping you might sing at your party for us.'

Renata pulled a face. 'The good folk of Beacon Bay won't want to hear any of my hifalutin arias.'

'I'm sure we're all desperate to hear you sing.' To Ellie it seemed rather sad that Renata had been so supportive and generous to so many in this community but didn't feel comfortable about sharing the one thing she surely loved more than anything. 'Isn't there a piece that's not too operatic that you still enjoy singing?'

Renata didn't answer at first. Eventually, she said, 'I'll think about it.' Then she got to her feet and went to the pantry. 'Now, let's see. I'm pretty sure I still have all the ingredients for a Sachertorte.'

CHAPTER FORTY

Rolf insisted on taking care of dinner. 'I specialise in very simple barbecues,' he told Lisa. 'A tossed salad, jacket potatoes wrapped in foil and cooked in the coals, and a couple of steaks thrown on the grill.'

'Sounds perfect.' And so very familiar, Lisa thought, remembering the many family barbecues in their past.

His outdoor barbecue was a relatively simple affair made of stone slabs and set at one end of a paved terrace that offered another lovely view of the lake. The paving was made of natural stone – from Herberton, Rolf had told her – and he'd sawn large logs into surprisingly smooth and comfortable seats and had positioned them around a firepit, which now, at dusk, contained a glowing bed of hot coals.

Lisa had donned a light sweater against the evening chill, and Rolf was in a collared, winter-weight shirt, unbuttoned at the neck and not tucked in but hanging loosely. With the sleeves rolled back to just below his elbows, this was his favourite way to dress, and it suited him so well.

Spanish guitar music drifted from a music system, and the first of the sunset splashed streaks of rosy gold across the lake. The setting was quite perfect and under any other circumstances, Lisa might have relaxed and soaked up the beauty. But this evening, even with another of Rolf's very fine reds in hand, she couldn't quite calm the questions circling in her head.

Where was this heading?

What exactly was Rolf expecting?

This afternoon they'd gone into the township of Burralea to shop at the butcher's and the supermarket, and she'd seen friendly locals greeting Rolf with warm smiles. On a couple of occasions, Rolf had introduced her to these friends and he'd simply referred to her as Lisa, without expanding on their relationship, or lack thereof.

This was fair enough. No need to make Mount Everest out of a molehill. They were here to talk, to reach some kind of peaceful understanding. Nothing more.

Yet, strangely, for Lisa, this felt like so much more. Or was that her unreliable imagination?

As Rolf settled their potatoes into the coals, she looked again at the view through the trees. 'You haven't bothered with a garden.'

'No, I don't really have much time for gardening.' Rolf sent a knowing smile in her direction. 'But I suppose you would have gone to town planting up this bank.'

'Probably.' They both were well aware that she wouldn't have been able to resist turning at least some of this land into a garden, and she could easily picture herself planting masses of the bulbs that thrived up here in this more temperate climate. No doubt she'd have rivers of lilies, agapanthus, hippeastrums and irises running down to the water's edge. It would be amazing in springtime.

While she'd indulged in these musings, Rolf had settled on a log opposite her, relaxed with his legs spread comfortably apart. All was quiet – just an occasional soft crackle from the firepit, or the honking calls of magpie geese as they flew in to land on the lake.

'I met your Gerry Maffucci,' he said and, just like that, any possibility of peace was shattered for Lisa.

Instantly, she was seeing Gerry again in his gaudy shirt and jewellery, and she was remembering the pain of the night she'd gone to Rolf with her confession.

She felt sick and couldn't bear to ask for details of how or where Rolf had met Gerry. 'He's awful, isn't he?'

'Gross. A total arsehole.'

Lisa was so busy cringing at all the guilt and shame that had come rushing back, she almost missed what Rolf said next.

'Lisa, I didn't tell you this to make you feel bad. I could see how that guy works. He's a manipulator of the first order. And I'm sure he would have been just as cunning back when you were young.'

'Th – that's very understanding of you, Rolf.'

'I guess you'll be pleased to know I didn't punch him in the teeth, even though I desperately wanted to.'

'So he was that bad?'

'Worse.' They shared the barest of smiles, and then Rolf leaned forward, resting his elbows on his knees. 'Actually, if we're making confessions —'

'Is that what we're doing?' Lisa interrupted nervously.

'Not necessarily, but there's something I never really admitted before, and I probably should have.'

She stiffened. She wasn't sure she was ready to hear what was coming.

'I wasn't unfaithful, in case that's what you're thinking. But I do realise now that I was incredibly stubborn about wanting to give up everything to write.'

'Rolf, we don't need to rake that up again.'

'Just bear with me for a moment.'

She gave a meek nod.

'The thing was, I'd convinced myself that the world owed me that chance to become a writer. As you know, I wasn't able to go to university. After my father died, I had to start work and I got that apprenticeship. But later, once my mum found a job and we were both earning, it was suddenly okay for my brother and sister to head off and get their degrees. Erik was able to spend all those years studying law, no worries. And Annie did accountancy.'

Lisa had known this about Rolf's siblings, but she hadn't realised how deeply their educational opportunities had bothered him. 'You never talked about that.'

'For years I told myself I didn't mind. I suppose there was a certain pride in supporting Mum, in being a breadwinner. Maybe I saw myself as the family's noble hero. It was only later – around the same time that Erik became a judge . . .'

Lisa remembered that time. Rolf had travelled to Brisbane for a family celebration, but Chris and Nate had been in the middle of important high-school exams and she'd stayed at home with them. She hadn't witnessed firsthand all the fuss everyone made over Erik, his mother bursting with pride.

'I suppose I was hit by some kind of delayed midlife crisis,' Rolf admitted. 'I suddenly felt as if I'd been cheated quite badly. I knew I'd done well at school. I knew I had other talents besides wielding a fricking hammer. And I guess the need to prove this just grew too strong.'

Lisa had been an only child, but as the mother of three sons, she had a fair understanding of sibling rivalry. In retrospect, it wasn't difficult to imagine how unfair the situation must have felt for Rolf. 'I suppose on some level I knew that was an issue. But . . .'

Rolf shrugged. 'But we didn't talk.'

'No, we just argued.'

'We certainly did plenty of that.'

She supposed that was when they should have gone to a counsellor. Their lawyer had suggested it, but they'd both resisted the idea.

'I'm sorry,' she said now.

'I'm not asking for an apology, Lisa. I'm the one at fault for not talking this through with you.'

'At the time, I might not have listened.'

Rolf smiled at this. 'Thank you for listening now.'

Renata was at home alone, which was, in recent weeks at least, an unusual situation for her and not a particularly welcome one. Peggy and Roger had left after dinner, heading over to their house armed with tape measures and a notebook, eager to make plans for their bathroom renovation. Equally excited, Ellie had driven off to the Frangipani Café, proudly bearing the excellent Sachertorte she'd made for Dave's birthday.

With the house to herself, Renata was sprawled inelegantly on her lounge, trying to relax but feeling restless. One of Rolf's books lay on the floor beside her, abandoned. She wasn't in the mood for reading, and although the power was back on and she could watch television, that had no appeal either.

She told herself she was pleased that all these people she'd been so eager to help were now very happily occupied elsewhere. Even Lisa and Rolf had taken off together, which was, if nothing else, intriguing.

And yet this evening, left alone, Renata felt quite downhearted and maybe even a little sorry for herself. She had tried hard to be a part of this small coastal town's community, but tonight she wondered if she would ever really fit in here.

People were polite and friendly, but she still felt like an outsider. She almost wished she hadn't announced that she'd throw a party. She was behaving like a diva, wasn't she?

This question brought her thoughts arrowing back to the real source of her angst. She was fifty. Middle aged. On the downward slope and more worried about her singing career's future than she was prepared to admit.

Until now, she'd put on a brave face and had stayed upbeat about the years ahead, but no one here knew how vulnerable she really felt. She'd begun to wonder if she should already be looking at teaching options. Wasn't that the old saying – if you can't do, teach?

She suspected she would probably make a fair fist of training young singers, actually. It would feed into her yearning to be helpful, to give back. But Renata also knew it would feel like stepping down and giving up on everything she'd worked so hard to achieve.

Meanwhile, Brian, her agent, was waiting for her to get back to him about the production of *The Magic Flute* in Colorado. She knew she should be grabbing that Queen of the Night role with both hands, but she'd told Brian she'd give him an answer by the end of the week.

She wasn't quite sure why she was procrastinating. Was it really a resistance to that high-pressure lifestyle, or something more basic like her flagging self-confidence? In the past she'd never been nervous about accepting such a demanding role, but now she worried that it would prove she was no longer up to scratch.

She missed Gerhard. Oh, Lord, how she missed her dear man. For ten years, her level-headed German engineer with a surprising love of classical music had been her life partner. Practical, sympathetic and wonderfully logical, he'd always supported her with sensible advice.

What would you tell me now, Gerhard?

Even as she asked this question, Renata, lying there alone in the silent house, could hear his beautifully deep Germanic-accented voice offering his answer.

Liebling, have faith in yourself. Trust yourself. You're strong. You've found your way over many hurdles. You can do it again.

Ellie was over-the-top with excitement about Dave's birthday celebrations. She'd spent too many of her own anniversaries blowing out candles with only her gran to cheer her efforts, and she looked at any birthday party as a huge deal. The truly exciting element tonight, however, was that this party would be a surprise for Dave.

She'd been really touched that a group of his former school-mates had been keen to do this. She knew Dave was anxious to reconnect with his old friends and their enthusiasm was surely a good sign. Fortunately for Ellie, one of the group, Mike Ingram, worked for the *Cassowary Coast Observer*, and she'd been thrilled when he'd invited her to join them.

The plan was to meet outside the café at 9.45pm. By then, most of the dinner guests would have already left, Dave should be rela-tively free and it wouldn't really matter if a few stragglers witnessed the party or even joined in.

You'll come, won't you? Mike had texted her.

Sure will, she'd replied, *and I'll bring a cake*.

After that, she'd fretted over whether she should make a cake or buy one. But the Sachertorte sounded so interesting, and much to her relief, when she'd made it under Renata's supervision, it had turned out perfectly.

Right now, this precious cargo was sitting on a pottery plate and safely stowed in a solid cane basket on the back seat of Renata's car, which she had kindly lent to Ellie for the evening. Also in the basket were a candle and a box of matches, all ready for the grand surprise entry.

Everything about this venture felt super important to Ellie. She'd even decided to wear her favourite outfit, a white cotton sundress that had narrow straps, a very fitted bodice and a flaring knee-length skirt. With the addition of woven platform sandals and her hair freshly washed and flowing shiny and free, she felt confident and ready for fun.

She soon reached the seafront and once she'd parked, she collected the all-important basket and headed along the footpath.

She could see a group already waiting outside the café. They looked about Dave's age, and the guys were dressed in the same faded jeans and T-shirts that Dave loved to wear. She quickened her pace.

'Ellie!' Mike's voice called to her, and a moment later she was being introduced to the gang. Tony and Grace. Daniel and Chloe. And Angela, Mike's partner. Ellie hoped she would remember their names.

Chloe, with her aqua hair and a tattoo of a seahorse on her neck, should be easy to recall. Angela had curly red hair and orange-framed glasses and a serious expression that was quite transformed when she smiled.

Daniel and Tony were more of a challenge as they both had sun-bleached light-brown hair and were carrying sixpacks, although one of them – perhaps Tony – wore an earring. Grace was the blonde with a bottle of bubbly.

'Oh, you've brought a cake.' Angela was peeking eagerly into the basket. 'It looks amazing.'

'I only brought one candle,' said Ellie, 'But it's a nice fat one, and I thought I'd light it and carry the cake in on the plate.'

'Oh, yes!' enthused Chloe. 'We need a proper surprise grand entry. That'll be perfect.'

The sea breeze blew out Ellie's first attempt to light the candle, but the others huddled around her to create a wall of bodies and the second attempt stayed alight.

'You go ahead and we'll keep close behind you and hopefully the candle will hold,' Mike told her.

'I'll bring the basket,' said Grace.

'And I'll open the door for you,' offered one of the guys, possibly Tony.

'Ready everyone?' This came from Mike. 'Right, let's go.'

CHAPTER FORTY-ONE

As Ellie stepped through the doorway, carrying her birthday surprise, and with the others close behind her, she saw Janet in the kitchen wiping down benches and Dave busily scrubbing at a stove. The restaurant was relatively quiet, although happily chatting diners lingered at two tables.

Janet was the first to look up, sending a frowning glance to the doorway, no doubt worried that these latecomers expected to be fed. But the instant she saw Ellie and the cake, her eyes popped with surprise. She might have also called out, but just in time, she clamped a hand over her mouth.

Ellie couldn't stop grinning as she continued forward. She planned to set the cake on the bench that divided the kitchen from the entry area, where she and Dave had enjoyed their late-night meals together.

Her eyes were on Dave, drinking in the sight of him, his hair tied up and his shoulders and back muscles straining his T-shirt as he concentrated on cleaning the stovetop. Then he must have sensed their presence. He straightened, turned and looked around, and when he saw them, he was rendered even more shocked than Janet.

His dark eyes shimmered with a flood of emotions, as if he was simultaneously surprised and delighted and deeply touched. Ellie felt his reaction land deep inside her and in that same moment, as she reached out to set the cake on the bench, somehow – and she would never be able to work out exactly how – she tripped.

A helpless cry broke from her as the cake slipped and fell, landing on the bench with a sickening splat. The candle flew too and the flame died, while the cake broke into ugly, lumpy pieces.

Left holding an empty plate, Ellie could only stand there, dismayed, while gasps and cries echoed all around her.

Her first impulse was to burst into tears. She couldn't believe she'd ruined such a perfect moment. She didn't want to believe it. But the inescapable evidence was there in front of her on the stainless-steel bench – a skid mark of chocolate icing and scattered chunks of dark cake oozing apricot jam, like a bizarre accident scene.

Ellie felt almost as shattered as she had when she'd found herself lying in a gutter outside the airport. She knew she mustn't cry, though. This was embarrassing enough for Dave without her adding to the drama, so she stood quite still with her eyes closed. It helped not to cry if her eyes weren't open.

'Ellie.'

Dave's voice sounded close and then his arms were around her, pulling her in for a strong and comforting hug.

'Oh, Dave,' she somehow managed without sobbing. 'Happy birthday.' And as she buried her face against the reassuring warmth of his neck, she heard cheers all around them, including from the restaurant.

It was a timely reminder that they had an audience. Ellie straightened, blinked, managed to smile.

'That's one way to make a big impression,' remarked Daniel.

'Oh, I always aim to impress.' She knew it was a weak joke, but under the circumstances, it was the best she could offer. Then more quietly, she added, 'I'm so sorry.'

'No need to be sorry,' said Angela. 'The cake only hit the bench, not the floor.'

'Yeah, I'm sure it's still perfectly edible,' said someone else.

'Course it is.' With two fingers, Dave helped himself to a piece of cake, which he promptly downed and then grinned at them. 'It's totally delicious. Best birthday cake ever.'

Almost immediately, Janet was on the move, collecting small serving plates, knives and forks and setting them on the bench, along with a pile of paper napkins. Mike rescued the candle and reinstated it in the approximate centre of the broken cake, and then Dave produced matches to light it. And everyone, including the two tables of diners, gathered around and began to sing 'Happy birthday to Dave' at the tops of their voices.

The night was getting colder. Lisa and Rolf had finished their meal, but were still sitting outside by the firepit, sharing the last of the wine while they chatted.

The conversation had flowed with an ease that surprised Lisa, but then, she supposed, they did still have quite a bit in common. They certainly enjoyed talking about their boys, sharing snippets from phone conversations and visits with them.

They'd also shared memories – like the summer Chris had grown so tall, so quickly, and he'd piled his enormous breakfast bowl each morning with at least six Weet-Bix. Or that time when they'd been holidaying here at the lake, when Nate, at the tender age of nine, had taken off in a canoe on his own, and then promptly overturned it out in the very middle of the vast and deep water.

'Thank God he was wearing a lifejacket,' Lisa said, remembering.

'You were always so strict about that,' Rolf reminded her. 'And it paid off.'

Dave's recent surprise dash to see Ellie in Sydney also warranted a discussion.

'I don't suppose we should read too much into it, though,' said Rolf.

'No,' Lisa agreed. 'They haven't known each other very long.'

'That's not always a problem, of course.'

As Rolf said this, his gaze met Lisa's and, in the warm glow from the firepit, she could feel the memories of their own first meeting swirling in the air between them like conjurer's smoke.

She switched her attention to the lake. A white mist now lay over its surface, eerie and ghostlike in the faint light cast by a thin slice of moon. She breathed in the cool, clear, incredibly fresh night air.

'It's so different up here,' she said. 'I almost feel as if I've travelled to another country.'

'I know,' Rolf agreed. 'That's one of the things I love about this place.'

Was this a snub? An indication of how keen he'd been to get away from his former life? Wisely, Lisa chose not to pick at that particular bone. 'You've done quite a bit of travelling in recent years,' she said instead.

'I have, yes. Japan, the US, parts of Europe. Mostly for research. And I was keen to check out Sweden to see where my family came from.'

This brought back memories of her friend Bianca and their girl-hood plan to visit Italy together. Instead, Bianca hadn't merely visited Italy, she'd lived there and raised a family with her Italian winemaker.

Again, Lisa didn't mention this. The last thing she wanted was to reopen the Maffucci wound.

Rolf finished his wine, then set the glass aside. 'You've never really wanted to travel.'

'You know I've always been stingy. International travel always felt too extravagant.'

He accepted this with a nod. 'If you could go anywhere, where might you go?'

Her first thought was Italy, but she said instead, 'Oh, I'm sure I'd love Paris.' She gave a casual shrug. 'Or perhaps Prague? I believe it's very beautiful.'

'Yes, I'm sorry I didn't get to Prague. Renata lived in Vienna for many years.'

'Did she? Of course, I remember now. That's where she learned to make her famous chocolate cake. But Vienna's also famous for its classical music, so I guess it would be perfect for her.' Relieved that she could now think about Renata without a hint of a grudge, Lisa asked, 'Have you ever heard her sing?'

'No. She practises in a backyard studio and it's pretty much soundproof. I've caught the odd scale or vocal exercise, but no actual songs.'

'I'd really like to hear her,' Lisa admitted, but then, as the mist began to creep silently up the bank, she shivered.

Rolf was instantly on his feet. 'It's getting too cold to stay outside. Let's go in.'

Lisa brought their empty glasses, Rolf the plates and cutlery. Inside, the house was indeed much warmer, even though the fire in the living room hadn't been lit. In the kitchen, they stacked the dishwasher. Together. Unlike in the past when it had mostly been Lisa's job.

When this was done, they stood facing each other and the world seemed suddenly very quiet. No sounds of traffic. No bird calls. No wind.

'Thanks for a lovely evening.' Lisa spoke politely, as a guest to a host.

Rolf smiled. 'It's been great to talk. Makes a nice change after all those years of silence.'

'I suppose we've been foolish, haven't we? We haven't even exchanged Christmas cards.'

His grey-green eyes sparkled with amusement. 'Very few people send Christmas cards these days.'

'True. They do seem to be going out of fashion.'

'But I'll make a point next Christmas. I'll find the most glittering, festive card out there and post it to you.'

For some ridiculous reason, Lisa wanted to cry. She wouldn't let this happen, but as she stood there fighting a raft of emotions, she found herself saying, on a reckless impulse, 'Rolf, I read that scene in *Second Spring*. You know – when the baby's born.'

He stood very still, gave the briefest nod, and now that she'd started, she had to continue, had to share the memory that had been there like a pain deep within her all evening. 'There's that scene where the young new mother is worn out and she asks her husband – you know – that silly question about the prettiest girl on the block?'

His attempt to smile was lopsided. 'I'm afraid I couldn't help that, Lisa. When I started writing the scene, everything about that time was flooding back to me and it just poured onto the page – and – and I hope you don't mind.'

Her tears were coming now, filling her eyes, blurring her vision. She felt Rolf's hand at her elbow and she didn't flinch, didn't try to move away.

'Lisa,' he said softly, but she couldn't look up, she was too busy trying not to cry.

When she felt the warmth of both his hands on her shoulders, she longed to move closer.

'You were definitely the prettiest girl on the block.' His voice was so gentle. 'Prettiest girl in the whole damn town.'

Oh, Rolf. She couldn't bear to hear these words again, when she was already so lost in the past, in those days when all she'd wanted was to have his arms around her.

And then, it was happening. Rolf was hugging her and she was pressing close to him. And it was no longer a memory. She was feeling the strong wall of his chest and smelling the familiar scent of his aftershave, and her body was stirring in ways that it shouldn't, but she couldn't help it.

Without expectation or warning, she wanted this. Wanted his touch. And even more, his kiss.

Clearly, he wanted this too, and as their lips met she was drowning in sensation and longing. So much longing.

A sensible part of her mind tried to raise a feeble protest. This shouldn't be happening. She should pull away, speak up, but her starved and hungry body had other ideas.

Neither of them spoke. Possibly, they both knew that any words would break the spell. Seemed all they wanted now was to let this mysterious magic take hold, silencing doubts, strengthening desire. Already, Lisa was desperate to feel the amazing, intimate sensations that this man knew how to arouse in her, expertly, tenderly, honestly.

Her room was close by and they moved there together, kissing again when they reached the end of the bed. Their consent was silent and mutual as they both undressed with speedy efficiency.

Perhaps it was helpful that the only light in the room was the faint, mist-shrouded moonlight coming through the gap between the curtains. Lisa was no longer self-conscious or shy. Not when Rolf's kiss and his touch were exactly as she remembered.

All she wanted now was to give and to receive, everything, everything, everything . . .

CHAPTER FORTY-TWO

The party had been fun, the cake perfectly edible, despite its disastrous entry, and Dave was totally chuffed that his friends had not only turned up, but that the surprise had been all their idea.

After sharing the cake and offering Dave many happy returns, Janet and the lingering diners had discreetly departed, leaving the rest of them to enjoy their party. With the café to themselves, the conversation had been jovial. Daniel had proved especially adept at telling jokes, and several times he'd had them in stitches.

There'd been memories shared from schooldays – old friends, old teachers – and gossip exchanged, filling the gaps in Dave's knowledge after the years he'd been away. Stories about who had moved where, what jobs people had now, who had married or had a baby. Sadly someone from their year had died.

Ellie had listened with intense interest. Having allowed too many of her own past friendships to slip through the cracks, she was very conscious of how important these deep and long-term ties could be, so she was especially happy for Dave.

By the time everyone finally departed, it was already past midnight.

'I really like your friends,' Ellie told Dave.

'And they really like you.' He was grinning, looking genuinely happy, as he had all evening.

Casting an eye over the scattered bottles and glasses, she said, 'I should tidy up.'

'No, leave it. This has been the best birthday ever. We don't want to spoil it.' Reaching for her hand, Dave sent her an especially warm, skin-tingling smile. 'Besides, you look far too gorgeous for kitchen work.' With his free hand, he picked up an oversized beach towel that had been draped over a kitchen stool. 'Let's head for the beach.'

Ellie didn't need a second invitation, and their short journey, walking hand in hand over the road and down the track between palm trees to the sand, felt familiar and important, a ritual she hoped might continue long into her future.

Halfway to the water's edge, Dave stopped, spread the towel and they sat. 'Are you sure you're comfortable?' he asked.

'Totally,' Ellie assured him. 'My back's healing really well.'

'That's great.'

The stars and the moon weren't as bright tonight, but there was enough light to see the busy wavelets breaking into delicate foam. The sand was soft beneath them, the air cool and salt-scented.

Dave leaned back on his elbows and looked up at the vast dark sky. 'So, another birthday, another trip around the sun for old Davo.'

'It's amazing to think about that, isn't it?' said Ellie as she stretched out beside him.

'About me getting old?'

'Old-*er*,' she corrected. Then she smiled, dropped a kiss onto his cheek. 'But also, the whole Earth–sun–universe thing.'

'Er . . . I guess.' He sounded puzzled now. 'Actually no, you've lost me. What thing exactly?'

'Oh. Well, this will probably sound pretty random, but some-times I can be in a peaceful place like this – relaxing on the sand, for example, looking out at the sea and the sky. And then, suddenly, I'm conscious that I'm actually sitting on the edge of a giant globe that's spinning in one direction, while it's also circling around the sun on a totally different trajectory. And all of it's part of a bigger galaxy that's part of a massive universe that has existed since time began and goes on forever and ever, and I mean, it's so mind-bending. But it's also very, very real.'

She stopped to take a breath and laughed. 'And I'm not even on drugs.'

'I think I might need them,' said Dave. 'I'm not sure I have the headspace for that line of thinking.'

'I know. Trying to understand the universe is impossible, really. But every so often, I wish those obscene men who keep starting wars would stop for a moment and think about it.'

Reaching for her hand again, Dave laced his fingers with hers. 'I wonder if growing up alone, without parents, has made you feel extra vulnerable.'

'I don't know.' Ellie frowned. She hadn't meant to lead their conversation in such a serious direction. She realised there'd been no mention tonight of Dave's parents, even though word was out about their surprise decision to go away together. But perhaps now wasn't the time to talk about that either.

'Don't worry,' she said. 'I'm not suffering from neuro-existentialism.'

'Now *that's* a very sexy word, even though I have no idea what it means.'

She chuckled. 'I'm not sure I do either, but I read it somewhere. It's something to do with human anxiety caused by neuroscience telling us we're only animals and we have a brain, but no soul. But honestly, I'm not anxious. Most times when I think about how endless and eternal the universe is, it's just like a kind of awe that I want to melt into.'

'Now that's something I totally get.' Dave was grinning now. 'Any time I look at you, I feel a kind of awe I want to melt into.'

And then he was kissing her and they were sinking back onto the beach towel and 'Happy birthday, Dave' were the last words Ellie whispered, before he took her to the moon.

They didn't come back to Earth for quite some time.

Renata woke early, when the world outside was still gently fading from black to pearly grey, but she was, almost instantly, restless. Last night she'd reached a decision and now she felt compelled to act on it.

Slipping out of bed, she pulled on her kimono, picked up a pair of sandals and tiptoed through the house. In the kitchen, she filled a water bottle, then opened the back door extra quietly, so as not to wake the others. On the back step she slid her feet into sandals, then hurried across the dew-drenched lawn to her studio.

She soon located the music she wanted to listen to – a recording she'd made in Berlin when she'd last been on stage as Queen of the Night. The role was a challenge, the character an interesting mix of good and evil, at times cold and calculating, at other times caring and gentle.

But it wasn't so much the acting, but rather Mozart's music that was especially demanding, in particular the famous aria 'Der Hölle Rache', with its repetition of high Cs and several top Fs. At least five years had passed since she'd made this recording, and this morning, she needed the reassurance of listening to it one more time.

Liebling, have faith in yourself. Trust yourself. You're strong. You've found your way over many hurdles. You can do it again.

Slipping headphones on, she pressed play.

She waited till 8am before she rang her agent. By then, Peggy and Roger were up and in the kitchen organising their breakfast, so

Renata, having already finished her coffee and fruit, went back to the studio to make her call.

'Renata. At last. What have you decided about the Denver offer?'

'I'm going to accept,' she said.

'Thank God for that. I was beginning to think you'd gone troppo.'

She almost put Brian in his place, firing a host of reasons why she deeply respected the people in this tropical town, but she feared it would be blithely ignored.

'So I'm guessing you've finally checked your emails?' he asked.

'Not since yesterday morning.' Renata heard his exasperated grunt on the other end of the line. 'Why? Should I check them now?'

'Well, obviously there's no need right this moment. I can tell you the gist of it. I've forwarded you a message from Denver, from the new conductor. He's specifically asking if you're taking on the Queen of the Night role.'

'The orchestra has a new conductor?'

'Yes, Mateo Diaz.'

'Mateo?' Renata was glad she was already sitting down.

'You know him?'

'Yes, of course.' She had first met Mateo during her earliest days in London. At the time, they'd both been students – Mateo, a dreamily handsome, young Spaniard from Bilbao, tall and broad-shouldered, with black curly hair and dark, soulful eyes.

He'd turned all the girls' heads, not to mention their hearts, but to Renata's astonished delight, he'd singled her out. They'd enjoyed the most dizzyingly exciting romance that had lasted at least eighteen months. In the end, though, their budding careers had been more important and their work had taken them in different directions.

Since those heady days, Mateo had conducted many orchestras in the US, including the New York Philharmonic, and he'd married a beautiful Manhattan socialite. Meanwhile, Renata had worked mostly in Europe and Australasia.

'Mateo was asking about me?' she said now, somewhat astonished.

'Absolutely. He seems very keen to work with you and it's an amazing opportunity. You know he's one of the best.'

'Of course.' These days everyone in the opera world knew about Mateo Diaz, and he was especially popular with singers. While many conductors concentrated on the instrumentalists and expected the singers to keep up, Mateo had a reputation for conducting in a way that was sensitive to whatever a singer was doing in that moment.

Working with him would be a very special experience. Renata had heard colleagues speaking about him with something close to reverence. He'd made them feel so supported and secure on stage.

And wasn't that exactly what she needed at this potential tipping point in her career?

Had the gods been listening? Had Gerhard?

'So you'll definitely take that role, won't you?' Brian asked, clearly eager to confirm.

'Well, yes.' She spoke without hesitation. 'I'd be silly not to.'

'Good, I'll send a response, but you should write back to Diaz as well.'

'I will. Thanks, Brian.' Buzzing with excitement now, Renata was checking her email as soon as they disconnected.

And there, on her screen, was the forwarded message.

I believe Renata Ramsay has been offered the role of Queen of the Night in our company's upcoming production of The Magic Flute. *Renata is a very flexible performer, particularly suited to interpreting such a realistic and multifaceted character. I hope we might soon hear news of her acceptance.*

Kind regards,

Mateo Diaz

Renata's heart was light as she typed her reply.

CHAPTER FORTY-THREE

When Lisa woke quite late to find sunlight streaming through the bedroom window, she blinked, trying to remember where she was. And then, in a rush, she remembered. Everything.

She was in Rolf's house. In his spare bedroom. And last night . . .

Oh, my God. It was like waking from a surreal dream and then realising it hadn't been a dream at all. Like diving into a deep pool and then remembering she didn't know how to swim.

Dismayed, she turned to the space in the bed beside her. Rolf was no longer there, but a slight dent in the pillow and the way the bed clothes on that side had been pushed away were evidence that she hadn't been dreaming.

Of course she hadn't been dreaming. The very thing that should never have happened had, most definitely, taken place. Lovemaking at its blissful best. Right here in this bed.

But how ridiculous was that? After everything she and Rolf had been through? After the months of pain leading to the divorce and then their eventual – although admittedly strained – resolution, how the hell could they have been so foolish? So weak and reckless?

It was a question she couldn't answer on her own, and she was remembering now that last night she and Rolf, in a moment of bemused amazement, had shared a whispered agreement to leave any discussion about their midnight madness until morning.

But now morning had arrived and Rolf was gone. Lisa threw back the covers, then realised she was naked. Her clothes from last night were lying in a tangled heap on the floor. Reaching down, she grabbed the sweater as a makeshift shield and hurried to the window.

Below was the lake, its waters shining in the early sunlight. Rolf was standing over near the boatshed at the water's edge, with his arms folded over his solid chest as he looked out, staring, apparently lost in thought.

He was too far away for her to call.

She decided to get dressed. In the bathroom she washed her face, brushed her hair, then went to the kitchen. The kettle was cold, so she brewed up two mugs of tea and carried them outside. For reasons she couldn't quite explain, she was sure it would be easier to have this next, crucial conversation away from the house, in the open air.

The pathway through the trees to the lake was mostly a bare dirt track with occasional stone steps, and she needed to walk carefully so she didn't trip or spill the tea. As she drew closer, though, she couldn't help admiring the attractive little boatshed, clad with timber boards similar to those on the house and, almost certainly, another of Rolf's constructions.

She had almost reached the bottom before he turned and saw her. His expression was serious and her heart began an unhelpful pounding. She felt so uncertain about what might happen next.

'Lisa.' Hurrying forward, Rolf retrieved the mug she held out for him. 'Thank you,' he said politely.

'Good morning, Rolf.'

'It's another beautiful one.'

'It is, yes.' Out on the lake, a raft of black ducks floated close to a clump of reeds. Lisa watched them for a moment or two, then sent a careful glance back in Rolf's direction, but he was drinking his tea and also looking at the water.

She wondered if he was feeling as awkward and baffled as she was. What were they supposed to say?

Behind him, the doors of the boatshed stood open, revealing a timber rowing boat. Oars and coiled ropes hung from a row of hooks on the wall. The outside of the boat's hull was painted green, and the insides were varnished timber with white seats.

She said, 'That's a very neat little craft.'

'Yes, I really enjoyed building it.'

Of course he had built the boat as well the shed that housed it. Lisa supposed she shouldn't be surprised.

'Does it have a name?' From where she was standing she couldn't tell.

'*Svanunge*. It's Swedish for cygnet, or baby swan.'

'That's cute. Were you planning to take it out on the water this morning?'

'Not necessarily, although it's a rather special way to start the day.' After taking another sip from his mug, he said, 'Why don't we sit down while we drink our tea?' He pointed to a garden seat she hadn't noticed before.

'Good idea.' Lisa crossed to it, made herself comfortable – physically comfortable, at any rate – and Rolf joined her. The seat was perfectly positioned to look down the inlet and out to the main body of water.

This view framed by tall trees was quite lovely, but its beauty was lost on Lisa. Now, with Rolf seated beside her, she was too conscious of the previous night's astonishing intimacy – so unexpected and yet so familiar – and so bloody confusing.

What had it been? A giddy moment of madness? An exciting one-night stand? Or the behaviour of a couple who now envisaged a shared future?

'How are you this morning?' Rolf asked her.

She might as well be honest. 'I'd say gobsmacked would be the right word.'

His smile was both fleeting and complicated.

'I certainly wasn't expecting us to . . .' She couldn't finish this sentence. 'Were you?'

'No, not at all.' After only a short pause, Rolf added, 'But for my part, I have no regrets.' Shooting another quick smile to her. 'It was pretty damned amazing.'

Heat flamed in Lisa's cheeks. She hadn't known it was possible to blush at her age. To make matters worse, she was finding it difficult to think straight. She'd found it hard enough to talk to Rolf about Gerry, but trying to try to analyse their own irrational behaviour . . .

Come on, Lisa, deep breath.

What she needed to clarify wasn't so much what had happened last night, or even how it had happened. What was more important now was how Rolf saw their future. How they both saw their future.

Taking a moment to calm herself with more tea, she asked carefully, 'When you invited me up here, I didn't think you were planning for us to get back together. That – that wasn't your plan, was it?'

He shot her a quick sideways glance. 'Would you want to get back together?'

'I asked you first.'

This brought another brief smile. 'Well, no, that certainly wasn't my plan when I invited you here. I just wanted to open some sort of dialogue. A level of understanding.'

'And it was a good plan. I think the conversations we've had so far have been important.'

'I agree. And to be honest, it's been a huge relief. I never enjoyed our silent warfare.'

'I didn't either. Not really.' When Rolf looked surprised, Lisa couldn't help smiling. 'Okay. I know that's probably hard to believe, given the way I carried on. But even when I was so busy hating you, it was really only on one level, if that makes sense.'

'And that level was all about my writing.'

'Plus my need for security.'

'Perhaps if I'd offered you something like a five-year plan —'

'Rolf, we can't go back and try to unpack that time. It's happened. We made big decisions. We're divorced.'

'We are indeed,' he said quietly.

'And just because we got carried away last night . . .'

Out on the water there was a splash that must have frightened the ducks. They took off, lifting into the air with a frantic flapping of wings.

Watching them fly away, their outlines backlit by the bright morning sky, Lisa said, 'It's undeniably lovely here. Just beautiful. But I can't imagine you'd want me back.'

'Would you want to be back with me?'

'That's not the point.'

'Actually, I think it's a very significant part of the point.'

'Okay. Fair enough. So, I guess the thing is . . .' The ducks were mere specks in the sky now, and she found herself marvelling at their freedom. 'Even though it's so beautiful, I'm not sure I would want to live here full-time.'

He nodded at this. 'I'm not sure you would either. You belong in the Bay, Lisa. You're a vital member of the community there and you have so many connections. You'd miss it like hell and you wouldn't want to have to start all over again.'

She was surprised by the sudden relief, as if a weight had been lifted. She said, 'And you wouldn't want to give up the writing.'

'No.'

'Wherever you were, you'd still want to spend most of your days tapping away.'

'Annoying the hell out of you.'

'Oh, I suppose I could always just go outside and garden.' With a shrug, she added, 'But then, if I was here, I'd be the one who was annoying the hell out of you, planting all sorts of things everywhere and anywhere, when you'd rather leave the space in its natural state.'

Rolf didn't respond to this and, as they sat in silence, both staring out at the lake, Lisa realised she was holding her breath.

Eventually, he said, 'So perhaps the status quo is still our best option?'

'I guess it might be.'

'But with improved lines of communication.'

'Yes, I'd like that.'

Even though they'd arrived at this surprising point of mutual agreement, the look they exchanged now was somewhat rueful.

'But last night was so good,' Rolf said next. 'We've still got it, haven't we?'

She gave a shy nod.

'We can be friends, Lisa. Companions even.'

'Friends with benefits?' She couldn't quite believe she'd let this slip. 'That's not mandatory, of course.'

'I certainly wouldn't rule it out.'

Another flush of warmth flooded her cheeks, requiring another deep, calming breath.

'So, are we agreed?' he said. 'We've reached a point where we can settle back into our separate lives for the time being, but we should keep more closely in touch?'

'Yes, I definitely agree with that.' Reaching for his hand, she gave it a gentle squeeze. 'And thank you, Rolf. Thank you for abandoning everything and coming to rescue my house.'

'We can thank Dave for that.'

'Well, yes. But you've been so good about it. I can't believe I was so against the idea at first.'

'Seems we've come a long way.'

Lisa nodded. Now, a cauldron of emotions bubbled inside her and she could feel her mouth twisting as she struggled to tell him the other thing she needed to say. 'Rolf, this is going to sound totally messed up and unbelievable and – and maybe you shouldn't read too much into it. But – but I just wanted to tell you that in spite of everything I've said and done – in – in my own twisted way – I still love you.'

'Oh, Lis.'

The kiss they shared now was gentle and maybe a little shy, but oh so tender.

Afterwards another silence fell until Rolf said, 'So maybe now, looking ahead, if either of us were to get sick, or incapacitated in some way —'

'Oh, yes, that's it!' Lisa was gripped by a burst of happy enthusiasm. She loved nothing better than feeling helpful and needed. With Rolf's writing she'd been useless. 'That's exactly it. If anything was to happen to you, I would gladly come to help you, nurse you, cook meals for you – whatever you needed.'

'And I'd be happy to do the same for you.'

'How brilliant is that? It sounds like we actually have a plan.' She couldn't stop grinning now. 'You know me too well. Nothing makes me happier than a workable plan.'

Slipping an arm around her shoulders, Rolf pulled her closer, dropping another warm kiss on her forehead, and she marvelled that this moment of peace had arrived with no hint of the bitterness and hostility that had shadowed their past.

She let her head remain there, resting against his sturdy shoulder, while she pictured a possible time in the future. Perhaps when they were quite old and frail, and finished with gardening and writing novels and book tours and working on endless committees, they might live companionably together again. It was a concept she could live with, even take comfort from.

As she straightened again, Rolf said, 'So, how's this for a more immediate plan? I take you for a little row out on the lake and then we drive into Burralea for a slap-up brunch?'

For an answer, Lisa jumped to her feet, and, leaving their empty mugs on the garden seat, they headed for the boatshed.

CHAPTER FORTY-FOUR

Ellie found Renata in the kitchen arranging bright orange and pink heliconias in a tall glass vase.

'Aren't these gorgeous?' Renata called to her, as she positioned a long-stemmed blossom just so. 'So vibrant and tropical. It's such a joy that we're getting flowers again.'

'Isn't it just?' Ellie wasn't familiar with many tropical plants and she thought these were very impressive. 'It's exciting to see the green leaves coming back on the trees. Although none of that helps the poor folk who are still waiting for their homes to be repaired.'

Renata nodded, her expression now solemn. 'Peggy and Roger are so grateful that Rolf is fixing their place, but I suppose there's a limit to how many jobs he can take on. I'm sure he'll have to get back to his writing before too much longer.'

'Yes. I don't suppose his publishers will extend his deadline indefinitely.'

'And on that note —'

'Renata, I —'

They had both spoken at once and now both stopped.

'Sorry,' said Ellie. 'I interrupted you.'

'No, you go ahead. What was it you wanted to say?'

'It's just that Mike Ingram from the *Cassowary Coast Observer* contacted me today. He said they have space in their newsroom for another journalist.'

'And they're offering you a job?'

'Yes.'

'And you'll take it?'

'Well, no. I explained that I wasn't really available. I'm working for you.'

'Oh, Ellie.'

To Ellie's surprise, Renata was smiling. 'What's so amusing?'

'It's just that this is actually very fortunate timing. You see, I've accepted a job offer in Denver, Colorado. It's with their opera company, and I've been plucking up the courage to speak to you about it. Of course, if you'd like to come with me, it could be a wonderful opportunity to expand your horizons —'

'Oh, I see.' Ellie knew she should be excited about a chance to travel to the US, and even though she'd only just come back to Beacon Bay, she shouldn't be so worried about leaving Dave again. She tried to smile. 'Would you be away for very long?'

'That's the thing. It's hard to say. Sometimes these offers extend into other opportunities.'

Watching Renata, Ellie felt strangely confused. There was something in the woman's manner that she couldn't quite pinpoint – a kind of hesitation. It prompted her to ask, 'Would you manage okay without me?'

'Well, the Denver company does have its own PR team.'

Right. This made things clearer. 'I see.' Having absorbed this news, Ellie asked, 'So if I read between the lines, might you be hoping to sack me?'

'I would never say I was *hoping* for that, Ellie. I've really appreciated your talents. But, if I can help you by freeing you from your commitments to me, yes, consider yourself sacked.'

'For the second time in a just a few weeks.'

'I hope you don't feel bad. I'll probably regret the decision as much as your former boss does.'

'You've been talking to Daphne?'

'No, but my agent has his ear to the ground and it seems Daphne's now spinning the story that I tricked you into leaving her.'

'Really?' *What a cow.* Keeping this thought to herself, Ellie said more circumspectly, 'How annoying for you.'

Renata shrugged. 'I'm sure we're both well rid of her.' As she fiddled again with the tall stems in her vase, she said, 'If you do take this *Cassowary Coast* job, you should use my car. I won't be needing it. Not for quite some time, at any rate.'

'Gosh, Renata, thank you. You're so generous. I promise I'd look after it.'

'Of course you would. I know that.'

'But I won't stay on in your house,' Ellie added quickly. 'Not that I don't love it here, but I thought I might —'

'Move in with Dave Anders?'

'Yes.'

'That's the best news yet.' Beaming a warm and thoroughly delighted smile, Renata crossed the room and gave Ellie a hug. 'To be honest, Dave is the main reason I was worried about taking you away. I have really good vibes about you and that young man. I believe you're a great match.'

'Thank you.' Ellie's response was an enthusiastic answering hug, squeezing Renata tightly. 'As I don't have a big sister or a mother, I really appreciate hearing that from you.'

'Oh, sweetheart.' They hugged each other again and were both blinking a little when they finally let go. Then Renata said, 'Are you sure you won't be too crowded in Dave's little flat?'

'No. I'll admit it *is* small, but we'll manage. We'll probably turn the second bedroom into a home office. We can have our laptops there, so I can write from home when I need to, and Dave has plans to set up a Facebook page and website for the café. But honestly, I quite like living just above the café. I might even help out there a bit. I really enjoy it.'

Looking around at Renata's beautiful kitchen, Ellie said, 'So, I guess, if Peggy and Roger are also moving out soonish, you'll be able to put this house up for rent while you're away?'

'Or find some deserving family who've lost their home and need a roof over their heads.'

'Of course, I should have guessed you might do that. Renata, you're amazingly generous. We're all going to miss you so much.' Quickly before she became teary, Ellie added, 'But then, this job in Colorado sounds mega exciting.'

Renata nodded. 'I'm starting to get excited. I wasn't sure at first, but I know the new conductor, Mateo Diaz. He's actually an old friend, from back in our student days.'

A new sparkle shone in her eyes as she reported this news, and Ellie couldn't resist asking, 'He wasn't a boyfriend by any chance?'

'Only for about eighteen months or so, many years ago. But yes . . .' Renata looked away, but not before Ellie caught a glimpse of her coy, secretive smile.

Ellie said, 'There's more to this story, isn't there? Come on, spill, Ms Ramsay.'

'Oh, you and your journalist's nose. There's no story really, but Mateo did happen to make contact with me yesterday, and he mentioned in passing that he's no longer married. His divorce was finalised some months back.'

Ellie grinned. 'It was very thoughtful of him to make sure you're up to date.'

'It was, wasn't it?' Turning again, quite possibly to hide another smile, Renata placed the vase on the bench in front of her kitchen window. Then she went to the fridge and extracted a jug of iced tea.

'And now, I really need to concentrate on plans for next Monday's party. I've issued most of the invitations, but come on, little sis, pull up a stool and let's have a cold drink, while we see if there's anyone else I should add.'

In the end, they decided that Renata needed to be quite choosy. She couldn't open up the party to the general community in the same way that she had after Pixie. This time, it was best to restrict her invitations to the people she'd had the most to do with.

With this settled, the next few days seemed to pass in a busy whirr. Ellie rang Mike Ingram to accept his job offer and Renata was on the phone to Brian, double-checking the travel arrangements he'd made for her, as well as packing her suitcases and planning the party. Her initial idea to just have drinks and cheese platters had been somewhat overtaken, as so many of her new friends were keen to contribute dishes.

Lisa and Peggy had volunteered to bring bowls of their favourite salads. Heidi was bringing vegetable kebabs and Roger his specially marinated roast chicken, while Dave had offered a seafood paella. There would even be desserts – Janet's mango trifle and another Sachertorte, courtesy of Ellie, as it had clearly become a new tradition.

Everyone had agreed that Rolf mustn't worry about bringing food, but he'd insisted on contributing wine. Ellie had also prepared a short speech, a vote of thanks, on behalf of everyone.

On Monday evening, the party was planned to begin just as the daylight was giving way to purpling dusk and the lights strung between the trees in Renata's garden offered a glowing welcome.

Lisa arrived early, in plenty of time to help with setting out the two trestle tables and extra folding chairs she'd borrowed from the bowling club, and then she and Renata spread colourful tablecloths.

'It's very good of you to help,' Renata told her.

Lisa waved this aside. 'Ask anyone. I have an annoying habit of needing to be helpful. Now, should we set the chairs in a circle?'

'I think so. The deck's big enough and it's best for conversation, isn't it?'

'Okay. I'm onto it. Also, let me know where you'd like all those plates and cutlery I saw in the kitchen and the baskets with the paper napkins.' Lisa added a chuckle. 'And feel free to tell me if I'm overstepping the mark. I don't want to be too pushy.'

'Don't worry. I'll take all the help I can get.'

As Renata said this, she actually blew a kiss in Lisa's direction, leaving her somewhat agog, but also wincing as she remembered the level of resentment she'd once felt towards this woman.

The party started on a very upbeat note with Heidi bursting across the lawn, bearing her platter of kebabs and followed by her veterinarian friend, while excitedly announcing that her neighbours' dog, missing since the night of the cyclone, had been reunited with his ecstatic owners.

'Can you believe little Jock turned up at Phil's clinic in Mission Beach?' she exclaimed. 'He's very thin, but,' she turned to her companion, 'but you said he'll be fine, didn't you, Phil?' And at his nod, she added, 'Pamela and Bert are over the moon.'

This seemed to be as good a reason as any to start opening bottles and pouring celebratory drinks, and from that point the party continued in the happy way that the best parties do, with plenty of chatter and laughter. The food was, of course, delicious, the drinks of very good quality, the conversations animated and the topics far reaching. Meanwhile, the coloured lights strung between the trees added their own touch of magic.

Rolf, taking all of this in, was conscious that Dave, his youngest and historically most troubled son, had never looked happier. No doubt there were several contributing elements, including the fact that Dave's café was chugging along nicely, and his parents had recently settled on a remarkable peace agreement. But the Ellie factor was huge, Rolf was certain.

The young woman looked especially lovely this evening in a beautiful white sundress, with her copper-gold hair shining, her skin glowing with health, her eyes sparkling with happiness. And to top this off, she managed to move all of her fellow guests by making a deeply touching speech of thanks to Renata.

Ellie spoke about her own personal gratitude for Renata's generosity, as well as Rolf, Peggy and Roger's deep appreciation of her hospitality. Then she went on to outline the surprising number of community activities Renata had been involved with, while never once expecting to be treated like an international superstar.

By the time Ellie had finished, everyone's eyes were shiny, including Renata's, and Rolf was sure his were the same.

'And now,' Ellie announced. 'As if Renata hasn't already been generous enough, she's going to give us lucky folk here tonight one last, extra-special gift.'

'Oh!' squealed Peggy. 'Is she going to sing for us?'

Ellie smiled and nodded. 'She is indeed.'

At this, cheers erupted along with an assortment of excited responses.

'How wonderful!'

'Yes, please!'

'Oh, Renata, at last. I've been dying to hear you sing.'

People had already shifted their chairs to make space for Ellie while she spoke, and now Renata came forward. This evening she looked especially elegant in a long, floaty kaftan of cream silk patterned with dark-green palm leaves.

After she thanked Ellie, giving her a warm hug and a kiss, Rolf wondered if she would ask everyone to move inside for the singing.

She didn't have a sound system out here, or any sort of microphone. But no, this request didn't happen.

'You'll have to bear with me,' she said, looking around at the circle of expectant faces. 'I'll be singing unaccompanied, but don't worry, it's nothing too operatic. I'm pretty sure you all know this song quite well.'

Rolf glanced to Lisa, who was sitting beside him, saw the sheen in her dark eyes as she tried to smile. He slipped an arm around her shoulders, saw that Dave also had his arm around Ellie.

Renata stood quite still, her posture perfect, her head high. Silence fell now. No one moved. They sat transfixed.

Then the singing began. In Italian, Renata's voice rippled into the night. Glorious. Note perfect. Unbelievably beautiful.

'Oh, my goodness,' Lisa whispered as she leaned closer to Rolf. 'She's amazing.'

And, as promised, the song made famous by Andrea Bocelli was one they all knew. But Rolf couldn't help thinking how deeply privileged they were to hear this song now. Surely none of them would ever forget this night – a world-class star sharing her extraordinary talent with a circle of friends in their tiny northern town on the edge of the Coral Sea.

He could feel the air charged with love, with tenderness and also with hope. And then the words changed from Italian to English – 'It's time to say goodbye.'

As the final note faded, the circle of listeners rose in unison to their feet, and there was a long moment of hushed awe before the garden erupted into cheers and applause and cries of 'Bravo!'

'Rolf.' Lisa had been helping with tidying up in Renata's kitchen, but now she hurried outside and found him chatting with Dave. 'Can I have a quick word?'

'Sure.'

'In private?'

'Of course.' He was on his feet and asking Dave to excuse him.

As they walked a little distance away, Lisa could feel her pulse racing at a ridiculous rate. They stopped near a grevillea festooned with lights.

'What is it?' Rolf asked her.

'I was wondering if – if it would be okay if I came back to the house tonight?'

Despite the darkness, she saw his eyes widen. 'Our – sorry, *your* house?'

'Yes. It's just that Heidi has Phil staying with her tonight, and I think they deserve to have her place to themselves.'

'I see. Well, yes, of course.'

'Just the one night.'

Now, Rolf smiled. 'You'd be very welcome.'

'I'll bring my own car.'

'All right.'

'Thanks, Rolf. I'll see you later then.' With this settled and her heart still hammering, she hurried back to the kitchen.

But by now the dishwasher had been stacked and was already busily humming, and the others seemed to have disappeared. Only Ellie was there, conscientiously wiping down a kitchen bench.

'I sent Renata off to bed,' Ellie said. 'She has an early flight to Sydney in the morning.'

'Goodness. So soon? I hadn't realised. How will she get to the airport?'

'I'll take her. She's lending me her car.'

'Right. Okay. And I'll come back and get those trestles and chairs some time tomorrow. And perhaps take down the lights?'

'Dave's looking after the lights.'

Lisa nodded. Seemed everything was taken care of. Standing in the middle of the kitchen, she felt suddenly at a loss. 'I guess I'll say goodnight then.'

'It's been amazing, hasn't it?'

'It has,' Lisa agreed. 'Unforgettable.' She wondered if she should tell Ellie how pleased she was to see Dave so happy, but she was rendered suddenly shy and couldn't quite find the right words. 'Goodnight,' she said instead, then gathered up her handbag and the empty salad bowl and headed outside to her car.

The lights were on when Lisa reached the house.

After locking the car, she continued to the internal stairs and was halfway up these when she remembered that she hadn't brought any nightclothes, not even so much as a toothbrush. Chances were, she was already blushing by the time she reached the top.

The lounge area was much the same as the last time she'd been there, with just the two camp chairs for seating. Rolf was in the kitchen, and a bottle of scotch and two glasses were assembled on the island bench.

'Howdy,' he called when he saw her. 'I was thinking about a nightcap.'

'Sounds good.' Lisa certainly needed something to calm her nerves. She crossed to the kitchen and watched him pour discreet single shots.

It was only when she reached the bench that she saw a familiar jewellery box also sitting on the countertop. She couldn't help a shocked gasp.

'Don't panic,' Rolf said, watching her.

She didn't know what to say, had to press a hand to the thumping in her chest.

'I was talking to Dave tonight,' Rolf said.

Lisa nodded, remembering now that she'd interrupted a rather earnest conversation.

'He told me he wants to ask Ellie to marry him.'

Suddenly, Lisa could breathe again. 'How – how lovely.'

He nodded. 'It is, isn't it?'

'Yes, it really is. Although I'm a bit surprised. I mean, they haven't known each other very long.'

'That's true, but then, Dave did drop everything to race down to Sydney.'

'Yes, of course. He's obviously very keen.'

'And he told me tonight that Ellie has already had her heart quite badly broken more than once and he knows she feels vulnerable. He wants to reassure her, to promise he'll always be there for her.'

'That – that's beautiful.' Lisa allowed herself a moment to feel proud of their son. 'I'm fairly sure Ellie will say yes.'

'I agree.'

She looked again at the box. 'Are you going to offer Dave that engagement ring?'

'I'm certainly considering it. How would you feel?'

She was remembering that long-ago afternoon tea and Rolf's Grandma Ivy, so thrilled to be passing on her precious jewellery to another generation. Then there was the other memory and she felt again a stab of shame, but when she looked up to Rolf, all she saw was forgiveness.

Grateful for this, she said, 'It's a lovely idea, Rolf. I wonder if Dave will be keen?'

'I think he might be. He's also mentioned that Ellie doesn't have any family.'

'Then perhaps it's the perfect way to welcome her into ours.'

This was such an uplifting thought, Lisa found herself happily looking forward to the future, picturing her house with a freshly painted interior and new furniture, and their whole family together for a special celebration. Their three boys would be here with their partners and perhaps there might be a grandchild or two. She would have to start checking catalogues for a new dining table with extension leaves.

Rolf was smiling as he lifted his glass. 'Let's drink to Dave and Ellie.'

'Yes. Let's wish them many years of happiness.'

Instead of retiring to the camp chairs then, Rolf nodded to the balcony. 'It's a beautiful night. Would you like to step outside for a bit?'

'Yes. Great idea.'

He opened the French doors and they went out to the view of the night sky and the shadowy garden. A cool breeze whispered. Autumn had finally arrived in the tropics and the next few months would be perfect. Above them, a slender moon shone.

Looking up to it, Rolf said, 'It makes a big difference with that pine gone. You'll be able to keep an eye on the moon again from here.'

Lisa remembered when he'd first built this house and how they'd loved watching the moon rise. What was that old saying? It's an ill wind that blows no one any good?

Since the cyclonic winds that knocked down the pine, she and Rolf had reached their new understanding and she'd been freed of a guilty burden.

She had so much to be thankful for, so much to look forward to. And now, with their elbows resting on the railing, their shoulders touching, they breathed in the evening air. Relaxed and at peace, once again content to share this beautiful night.

ACKNOWLEDGEMENTS

To begin with, I'd like to thank the two friends I mentioned in the dedication. They're both writer mates who posed questions that helped me arrive at this book.

Firstly, Anne Gracie wrote to me after she'd read *The Summer of Secrets* and wanted to know if I was going to write Rolf Anders's story. It was a question that lingered and niggled over the years that followed, as I'd also liked the way Rolf had presented himself on the page.

He turned up again in *The Happiest Little Town*, but it didn't occur to me that he should have a starring role in a book of his own until last year when I abandoned a story that just wasn't working. It was then that I also remembered Trish Morey's suggestion at a long-ago writing retreat that I should write about a cyclone, especially as I'd experienced several firsthand – and suddenly, in the weird way that muses often work, this story idea came together.

Mind you, when I first started, I didn't know if I was ever going to let Rolf and Lisa get back together and their story path was quite a journey of discovery for me.

I also have other writer mates to thank. Louis Simon, a good friend from the Atherton Tablelands, embodies the surprising combination of clever writing ability along with fab house building skills that inspired Rolf's original appearance. I was also grateful to be able to turn to Louis for post-cyclone building advice while writing this novel.

Laurie Trott, another FNQ writer, and author of *To Kill a Cassowary*, gave me helpful advice about post-cyclone restoration in the Cassowary Coast region. Meanwhile, Helene Young, who's written several books for Hachette and Penguin Australia and is also a former Qantas pilot, answered my question about missing passengers on flights. Where would I be without such helpful friends? I'm grateful to all of them.

I'd also like to thank an incredibly interesting chauffeur, who drove me from Brisbane airport to the Sunshine Coast and who also just happened to be a former highly successful opera singer and happily answered my questions about his life in that world. Serendipity at its sweetest.

As always, however, I doubt any of this would have happened without the support of my very best writer mate, my husband Elliot. Huge thanks again, my dearest man. And big thanks to the team at Penguin Random House and other contributors – publisher Ali Watts, editors Melissa Lane and Nikki Lusk, cover designer Nikki Townsend, publicist Bella Arnott-Hoare, marketer Chi Chi Zhu, proofreader Lauren Carta, and key account manager Adelaide Jensen.

Finally, I'd like to also mention Celine Dion's song 'It's All Coming Back to Me Now'. I heard this on my car radio one afternoon while driving to the gym and it was so powerful and emotional, I had to hunt it down and listen to it again many times as I wrote the final chapters of this story.

Now, I hope you've enjoyed reading about these characters in Beacon Bay as much as I enjoyed creating them.

Warmest wishes,

Barb x

'Barbara Hannay is the queen of feelgood fiction. She wraps you up
in a big warm hug and leaves you with a smile.' *Goodreads*

BARBARA
HANNAY
THE
LIFE
SWAP

'Don't feel you have to stick to the safe path, Tess.
Listen to Luna. She's always been braver than I have.'

Tess is feeling burnt out from her uninspiring job and her busy city lifestyle. Even her personal relationships make her feel as if she's drifting rather than thriving. Having tragically lost her mother a few years earlier, she knows she owes it to herself to make so much more of the precious opportunities life offers.

Her godmother, Luna, who leads a very simple existence in a rustic cottage in the North Queensland rainforest, is also at a crossroads. Keen to expand her jewellery-making business, she needs the new connections that a bustling city offers. When she suggests to Tess that the two of them might swap homes for an extended period, it seems the perfect solution.

**Are they about to discover that taking great
risks can bring even greater rewards?**

**A moving and heartwarming story by the author of
The Garden of Hopes and Dreams and *The Happiest Little Town*.**

BARBARA HANNAY

Happiness has a way of catching up with you,
even when you've given up trying to find it

The Happiest Little Town

Tilly doesn't believe she can ever be happy again
Thirteen-year-old Tilly's world is torn apart when her single
mother dies suddenly and she is sent a million miles from
everything she has ever known to a small country town and
a guardian who's a total stranger.

Kate is sure she will be happy just as soon as she achieves her dream
In the picturesque mountains of Far North Queensland, Kate is
trying to move on from a failed marriage by renovating a van
and making plans for an exciting travel escape. The fresh start
she so desperately craves is within reach when an unexpected
responsibility lands on her doorstep.

**Olivia thinks she's found 'happy enough' until an
accident changes everything**
Ageing former celebrity actress Olivia is used to winning all the
best roles in her local theatre group, but when she's injured
while making a grand stage exit, she is relegated to the wings.
Now she's determined that she won't bow out quietly
and be left alone with the demons of her past.

When these lost souls come together under the roof of the Burralea
Amateur Theatre group, the countdown to opening night has
already begun. Engaging with a cast of colourful characters,
the three generations of women find unlikely friendship –
and more than one welcome surprise.

**From the bestselling author of *The Garden of Hopes
and Dreams* comes a heartwarming and uplifting
story about the joys of new beginnings.**

Powered by Penguin

Looking for more great reads, exclusive content and book giveaways?

Subscribe to our weekly newsletter.

Scan the QR code or visit penguin.com.au/signup